Hot and Sticky BBQ

Passionately Delicious Recipes for the Grill

Ted Reader

ALPHA

Food styling: Chef Ted Reader, Chef Mike McColl
Photography: Per Kristiansen

I dedicate this book to the love of my life, the wonderful Pamela, whose love and support are what give me the inspiration to cook. You are always in my thoughts. Your smile, your beautiful eyes, and of course your strength are my loves.

Let's get sticky.

With all my love,
Your peanut butter bear.

Contents

Introduction

My passion for grilling began when I was young. Memories of my father grilling a 3-inch thick, 4-pound sirloin steak over white-hot coals still make my mouth water. That charcoal grill was old by the time I was born. It was layered with rust but seasoned with intense flavors. Eventually, it melted—or rusted—through, and an air of excitement filled our home at the prospect of getting a new grill. Not! Dad presented us with his new model: a big red wheelbarrow filled with charcoal and topped with an old refrigerator shelf. We were the shame of the neighborhood. All my teenage years were filled with embarrassing but truly delicious wheelbarrow-grilled foods.

I recently took delivery of an authentic tandoori oven from northern India. Simply constructed and made of special clay, it's one of the hottest cooking methods going today. It's the perfect addition to the collection of barbecues and outdoor grills that take up most of my garage and backyard patio. Thankfully, Pamela puts up with my obsession and is always first in line to sample the food I produce from these grills.

Embarrassed as I was by my dad's wheelbarrow grill, it always gave us a delicious meal. I have come to realize that it is not so much the equipment as what you do with it. My collection includes an old faithful charcoal kettle, a combo gas-fired charcoal grill, a number of propane grills, a smoker, that tandoori oven, and an open Brazilian fire pit. Tender, juicy steaks; succulent golden chicken breasts; smoky Atlantic salmon—they're just as good off that wheelbarrow as out of my tandoori oven.

It's all about grillin' and lovin' it. Like good loving, good grilling requires creativity and imagination. My friends joke that I have so many barbecues that if I arranged them like a drum kit I could hold nightly performances. They make light of my trademark showmanship, but they don't realize that to me, barbecuing is not just cooking—it's performance art. Like any artist, I take my inspiration from many sources—people I meet, restaurants I enjoy, things I read, places I visit, and so on. Once inspiration hits me, the performance is on!

This book reflects more than 25 years of cooking—the early years spent barbecuing salmon on the ski hill in Whistler, British Columbia; grilling steaks at the Olde School in Brantford, Ontario; feeding thousands a baseball-themed menu at the SkyDome Hotel in Toronto; then when I was a chef for President's Choice, traveling to grill competitions, developing grill-themed retail products, and working on the *Dave Nichol Cookbook* and the *President's Choice Barbecue Cookbook*.

My love for the grill really unfurled itself when I became the barbecue guy on *Cottage Country Television*. Planked salmon, hay-wrapped steak, foot-high burgers—now I could be crazy *and* grill.

In my current phase, I'm a television chef, a food consultant, and a writer, and I'm constantly traveling. When I was in India, I enjoyed an outstanding meal of traditional tandoori food, which prompted me to buy that tandoori oven. In Brazil, I experienced the white-hot open pit fire grilling of the Gauchos and promptly came home to build one in my backyard (as long as they're invited, the neighbors are all for it). Recalling these culinary adventures and the many more fascinating encounters I've enjoyed over the years got me thinking about a book that would share this delicious knowledge. *Hot and Sticky BBQ* is a culmination of all I've been lucky enough to see, touch, and feel. These juicy tidbits that have ignited my passion for grilling and flown it to new heights are now yours to share.

I'll take you into a world of new flavors as you try recipes that might seem at times a little bizarre but will always be fun to cook and even more fun to eat. I believe that when you grill, there are really no rules. Experimenting with a variety of flavors will only make you a better griller. I have tried to put together a collection of recipes that everyone can use. We will go from simple to advanced, from easily found ingredients to ingredients that will finally pull you into that Asian supermarket you've always meant to visit. It should feel like an adventure every time.

Sometimes the best part of a meal is the beginning. A hot bowl of soup, whether it is Charred Corn Chowder or the Denver Hamburger Soup I picked up from a flight attendant in Colorado, warms the soul and fills the belly. I love to dunk a piece of grilled bread into a hot bowl of soup.

Salads have been an integral part of my repertoire since my *Cottage Country* days because they are the perfect side dish for any grilled entrée. From Firecracker Coleslaw to Roquefort Grilled Potato Salad with Smoked Garlic Dressing, we got it all.

First impressions are always important, and appetizers are the introduction to a perfect meal. My Jumbo Shrimp Parfait is a spectacular presentation with tons of shrimp and lots of big flavors. From the simple Kielbasa with Apricot Mustard Glaze to Cinnamon-Skewered Lamb Kebobs with Coconut Chili Chutney, the road to impressive beginnings lies before you. I say go for it!

Scrumptious sides are the dishes that enhance and complete your main course. A grilled steak is not complete without a baked potato, and in my case it's overstuffed with all kinds of goodies and baked a second time. Baby back ribs need some of my Cheesiest Baked Macaroni and Cheese. Grilled Chicken just has to have some mashed sweet potatoes with marshmallow butter. My personal favorite is sautéed mushrooms and onions tossed with crumbled blue cheese—no need for a recipe, just lots of mushrooms, onions, and blue cheese. Sides are often forgotten or neglected, but to me they are the most important part of the meal because they frame my performance at the grill.

I love a great sandwich, and I actually believe that sandwiches are their own food group. Begin with the best bread you can make or afford. Roasted Garlic and Rosemary Baguette makes a great grilled steak sandwich. A soft onion roll is a perfect base for grilled chicken or vegetables. Next comes the main ingredient, whether it's steak, planked salmon, pulled pork, or hamburger. Finally, the condiments and garnish— roasted chipotle mayonnaise, grilled vegetables, hot and spicy mustard, and fresh lettuce. Flavor is what it's all about, and the more flavor, the tastier the sandwich.

The "Lip-Smacking Tenderloins" chapter is the real meat of the book. Great-flavored cuts of beef, lamb, pork, game, *et al* are the essence of grilling. I include a guide to cuts of steaks. Steak is probably one of the easiest foods to grill, and my Hand Touch Method to test for doneness makes it even easier. I recall once waking up in the middle of the night after dreaming of the steak that I had eaten that night at the Chicago Chop House. It was a 24-ounce bone-in rib eye seasoned with Cajun spices and grilled to medium rare. It melted in my mouth like butter. I love a great steak so much, I actually wake up salivating.

Chicken is one of the most popular meats to grill, and Devil's Brewed Roast Chicken is the kicker. A whole chicken is seasoned and then the rump end is set over an open can of beer, allowing the chicken to stand up. Slowly grill-roasted, the bird steams from the beer on the inside and gets crispy on the outside. It's dramatic and delicious and a great way to flex your cooking muscles.

I've even included drinks and desserts. Lydia's Banana Boats are perfect for kids of any age. Slow-roasted pineapple is to die for over vanilla ice cream. Smoked Chocolate and Crème Fraîche Ice Cream stretches the limits to the breaking point, but don't knock it until you try it. For the more traditional, there's Strawberry and Rhubarb Crisp grill-baked in a cast-iron pan. Oh, but don't forget to try the Chocolate Banana Rum Milkshakes guaranteed to cure what ails you.

Throughout the book I use a unique method of calculating grill time. I call it the Beerometer, and it equates grill time with volume of beer consumed. In other words, if a recipe takes 5 to 15 minutes to grill, for most guys and gals that would be the same time it takes to consume 1 beer. Here's a handy reference:

Time	Beerometer
5 to 15 minutes	1 beer
15 to 30 minutes	2 beers
30 to 45 minutes	3 beers
45 to 60 minutes	4 beers

You get the drift.

Given some of the taste combinations I've devised for this book, you'll agree that I'm pushing the barbecue envelope to the limit. But why not? When grilling, the goal is to have as much fun as possible and turn each meal into your own personalized work of art. So get out there and perform.

Now I'm gonna go set up my tandoori oven and maybe a red wheelbarrow, too. Hmmm … I feel another book coming on.

Cheers,
Teddy

Acknowledgments

I cook with my heart and soul. My passion arrives not just from within but from all those whom I have had the pleasure to encounter. If I were to acknowledge all, my list would be as long as one of my grocery shopping lists. Because space is limited, I want to thank the following:

My family, whose love and encouragement know no boundaries, and especially my mother, Astrida, and father, Alex, whose support has been without question. Thank you.

Chef Mike McColl: Thanks for all your support in creating new and exciting recipes. You rock.

The crew of King of the Q Television, Inc.

Jessica Reader: Thanks for all your help.

Plumrose USA, Rupari Foodservice, UNI Foods: Steven Mintz, one of my biggest supporters. Thanks for all the support.

Celtrade Canada, Ron McAvan: Thanks for the daily chat and being a great guy.

Jack Daniel's: Mmmmm delicious.

Napoleon Barbecue: The best gas grills anywhere.

Weber Bullet Smoker: Tasty treats come out of this Weber.

Heritage Salmon: Because Atlantic salmon from Heritage doesn't get any better.

Nicole de Montbrun of Penguin Books (Canada): Thank you for believing in me and providing me with the opportunity to be creative and a little crazy.

Renee Wilmeth at Alpha Books: Thanks for believing in my recipes.

Chef Luther Miller: A crazy Canuck chef with a passion for flavor and a lot of beer.

Chef Olaf Mertens: You can cook, baby!

Chef Dale McCarthy, Chef Daddio: You are the stern chef, a man of detail and precision. Thank you for all your help in providing food for the many.

Per Kristiansen Photography: You make it look so beautiful and delicious.

Shaun Oakey: The editor who made my recipes sing.

Thanks a lot.

Cauldrons from the Hearth

Denver Hamburger Soup

On a recent flight to Denver, I had the pleasure of chatting with a flight attendant named Sherry. She gave me the recipe for this hearty, warming soup. Thanks, Sherry—it's not only original but also delicious.

½ cup butter
1 large onion, diced
4 cloves garlic, minced
2 stalks celery, diced
2 carrots, diced
2 large potatoes, peeled and diced
½ cup all-purpose flour
10 cups beef stock or broth
2 lbs. regular ground beef or turkey
1 TB. dried oregano
1 tsp. ground cumin
1 tsp. chili powder

1 tsp. salt
1 tsp. ground black pepper
¼ cup vegetable oil
1 TB. Worcestershire sauce
1 tsp. hot sauce
Salt and pepper to taste

GARNISHES
2 cups shredded cheddar cheese
½ cup bacon bits
½ cup sour cream
2 green onions, finely chopped

In a large soup pot, melt butter over medium-high heat. Add onion, garlic, celery, carrots, and potatoes; sauté until onions are transparent, 4 to 5 minutes.

Stir in flour; cook, stirring constantly, for 2 minutes. Add beef stock in stages, stirring until fully incorporated. Bring to a boil, reduce heat and simmer for 30 minutes, stirring frequently to prevent sticking.

Meanwhile, in a large bowl, mix ground beef, oregano, cumin, chili powder, salt, and pepper.

Heat oil in a large frying pan over medium-high heat. Sauté beef until fully cooked. Using a slotted spoon, transfer ground beef to soup. Season with Worcestershire sauce, hot sauce, salt, and pepper. Simmer for another 15 minutes.

Serve in warmed soup crocks garnished with cheddar cheese, bacon bits, sour cream, and green onions. Serve with lightly buttered toasted hamburger buns.

SERVES 8 TO 10

Wendy's Chipotle Venison Chili with Southern Jalapeño Cornbread

My good friend Wendy is a fabulous chef who used to have a catering company called Babette's Feast. Once, while I was her chef for a year, we made a huge pot of Wendy's amazing Chipotle Venison Chili. Her client was ecstatic with this hot pot of warmth.

---

3 lbs. venison shoulder, cut into 1-inch cubes

1 (7 oz.) can chipotle chilies in adobo sauce, puréed

8 cloves garlic, minced

1 TB. salt

2 tsp. black pepper

2 tsp. ground coriander

2 tsp. ground cumin

2 tsp. paprika

½ cup all-purpose flour

½ cup vegetable oil

1 large Spanish onion, diced

8 slices thick-cut bacon, cut crosswise into ½-inch strips

2 poblano peppers, seeded and diced

2 red bell peppers, diced

1 bottle honey brown lager

2 (14 oz.) cans diced tomatoes

2 cups sweet corn kernels (about 4 ears)

2 TB. chopped fresh cilantro

3 green onions, finely chopped

1 lime, juiced

Salt and pepper to taste

Sour cream, for garnish

Shredded Monterey Jack cheese, for garnish

In a large bowl, season venison with half the chipotle chili purée, garlic, salt, black pepper, coriander, cumin, and paprika. Mix well. Marinate, covered and refrigerated, for 24 hours.

Sprinkle flour over venison and toss to coat. In a large soup pot over medium-high heat, heat oil. Working in batches if necessary, brown venison with onions until liquid has evaporated and onions are brown, 10 to 15 minutes. Using a slotted spoon, transfer venison and onions to a bowl.

Continued ...

In the same pot, sauté bacon until crispy. Drain off excess oil. Return venison and onions to the pot. Add remaining chipotle chili purée, poblano peppers, red peppers, beer, and tomatoes with their juice. Bring slowly to a boil over medium heat, stirring occasionally. Reduce heat to low and cook chili, uncovered and stirring occasionally, for one hour or until venison is extremely tender. Stir in corn, cilantro, green onions, and lime juice. Cook until corn is tender, about 15 minutes. Season with salt and pepper.

Ladle chili into mugs or crocks and garnish with dollops of sour cream and Monterey Jack cheese. Serve with Southern Jalapeño Cornbread (recipe follows).

SERVES 8 TO 10

Southern Jalapeño Cornbread

2 cups sifted all-purpose flour	2 to 3 jalapeño peppers, seeded and finely chopped
1 cup sugar	2 cups milk
2 TB. baking powder	2 eggs, beaten
1 tsp. salt	2 TB. melted butter
1 cup yellow cornmeal	

Preheat oven to 400°F. Grease a shallow 13×9-inch baking pan.

In a large bowl, sift together flour, sugar, baking powder, and salt. Stir in cornmeal and jalapeño.

Stir in milk and beaten egg. Add melted butter and stir until just mixed.

Turn into baking pan. Bake until golden brown and a toothpick inserted in the center comes out clean, about 20 minutes. Cut into squares and serve hot with butter.

SERVES 8 TO 10

Creamy Smoked Garlic and Cheddar Chowder

Roasted garlic is one of the hottest culinary trends. It has even been used in ice cream (a little different, but it sure beats smoked salmon ice cream). For this chowder, I like to use smoked garlic. It has the same sweetness as roasted but with the added dimension of hickory smoke. If you don't have time to smoke the garlic, substitute roasted garlic.

3 heads smoked garlic (about 24 cloves) (page 200)	4 cups vegetable or chicken stock
4 slices bacon, diced	2 cups heavy cream
1 large onion, diced	1 TB. chopped fresh thyme
1 stalk celery, diced	1 TB. Worcestershire sauce
2 large Yukon Gold potatoes, peeled and diced	Salt and pepper to taste
¼ cup all-purpose flour	2 cups shredded white cheddar cheese
	2 TB. chopped fresh chives, for garnish

Peel smoked garlic cloves and finely chop all garlic. Set aside.

In a large soup pot over medium heat, cook bacon until just crispy. Using a slotted spoon, remove bacon and set aside. Add onion, celery, and potatoes to the pot and sauté until onions are soft, 4 to 5 minutes. Sprinkle in flour, stirring constantly. Whisk in stock, one ladle at a time, until fully incorporated. Bring to a boil, stirring.

Reduce heat to low. Add cream, smoked garlic, thyme, and Worcestershire sauce. Cover and simmer, stirring occasionally, until potatoes are tender, 15 to 20 minutes.

Season to taste with salt and pepper. Stir in cheddar cheese and reserved bacon. Serve garnished with chives.

SERVES 8 TO 10

Smoked Ham and Squash Chowder

This recipe, for convenience, uses store-bought ham. But if you have the time—and a smoker—there is nothing more rewarding than tending your smoker, sucking back a few cold pops, then creating some wonderful meals from a tasty smoked ham.

---

3 TB. butter

1 large onion, diced

3 cloves garlic, minced

1 jalapeño pepper, seeded and finely chopped

4 cups diced butternut squash

1 TB. Bone Dust BBQ Spice (page 203)

¼ cup all-purpose flour

6 cups chicken stock

3 cups diced smoked ham

1 cup heavy cream

¼ cup maple syrup

2 TB. chopped fresh sage

Salt and pepper to taste

2 cups shredded Monterey Jack cheese

In a large soup pot, melt butter over medium heat. Add onion, garlic, and jalapeño pepper; cook, stirring frequently, until onion is tender, 3 to 4 minutes.

Add squash; cook, stirring frequently, for another 3 to 4 minutes. Add Bone Dust BBQ Spice and flour, stirring until mixed, about 1 minute.

Add chicken stock, stirring until fully incorporated. Bring to a boil, reduce heat, and simmer, uncovered and stirring occasionally, until squash is soft and soup is thickened, about 45 minutes. If necessary, add a little more stock to thin soup.

Stir in ham, cream, maple syrup, and sage. Return to a boil, stirring, and cook for 10 minutes. Season with salt and pepper.

Serve topped with Monterey Jack cheese.

SERVES 8 TO 10

Grilled Chicken, Shrimp, and Sausage Gumbo

Visiting New Orleans is a favorite pastime of mine, not only because of all the great food, partying, and music there, but also because it is truly a culinary mecca. Some of the greatest American chefs have come from New Orleans: Paul Prudhomme, the father of Cajun cuisine; John Folse; and of course, Emeril Lagasse.

The key to a great gumbo is the roux. Roux is equal parts cooked butter or oil and flour. To make a true gumbo, you must first have the patience to prepare a mahogany roux. This requires a bit of time, but all great things take time, and this gumbo just happens to be one of the great culinary creations. A gumbo can consist of virtually anything you want. My favorite is this combination of grilled chicken, andouille sausage, and jumbo shrimp.

---

4 (6 oz.) boneless, skinless chicken breasts

1 lb. extra-large shrimp (16 to 20), peeled and deveined

¼ cup Bone Dust BBQ Spice (page 203)

¾ cup vegetable oil (divided use)

½ lb. andouille or other smoked pork sausage

½ cup all-purpose flour

4 cloves garlic, minced

1 jalapeño pepper, finely chopped

1 large onion, diced

2 stalks celery, diced

12 cups chicken stock

1 large green bell pepper, diced

3 green onions, finely chopped

2 cups sliced okra

Louisiana hot sauce

Salt and pepper to taste

Cooked white rice

¼ cup chopped fresh parsley, for garnish

Preheat grill to medium-high.

Coat chicken and shrimp with Bone Dust BBQ Spice and ¼ cup oil. Grill chicken until fully cooked, 5 to 6 minutes per side; set aside to cool. Grill shrimp until just cooked and opaque, 2 to 3 minutes per side; set aside to cool. Grill sausage until lightly charred and heated through, 4 to 5 minutes per side; set aside to cool.

Continued . . .

Slice chicken into 1-inch cubes. Cut each shrimp in half lengthwise. Slice sausage into ¼-inch-thick rounds. Set aside chicken, shrimp, and sausage.

In a large soup pot, heat remaining ½ cup vegetable oil over medium-high heat. Add flour; cook, stirring constantly with a wooden spoon, until roux is golden brown, 2 to 3 minutes, being careful not to burn roux; if necessary, reduce the heat to medium. If black specks appear in roux, discard it and start over.

Add garlic, jalapeño pepper, onion, and celery. Cook, stirring, until tender, 3 to 5 minutes.

Whisk in stock, one ladle at a time, until fully incorporated. Bring to a boil, stirring. Reduce heat to low. Add green pepper, green onions, and okra. Cover and cook for 20 minutes, stirring occasionally.

Fold in grilled chicken, shrimp, and sausage. Return to a boil. Season to taste with Louisiana hot sauce, salt, and pepper.

Place a large spoonful cooked white rice in each soup bowl and ladle gumbo over rice. Garnish with parsley.

SERVES 8 TO 10

Szechwan Hot and Sour Soup

I have to say that one of my favorite soups is hot and sour, a soup that combines the spice of the Orient with the sour of vinegar. This one will make your mouth pucker and sing.

¼ cup vegetable oil

1 tsp. sesame oil

2 TB. chopped fresh ginger

4 cloves garlic, chopped

3 jalapeño peppers, finely chopped

1 onion, thinly sliced

1 red bell pepper, thinly sliced

1 yellow bell pepper, thinly sliced

1 large carrot, julienned

1 cup bamboo shoots, julienned

1 cup sliced shiitake mushrooms

8 cups chicken stock

¼ cup soy sauce

¼ cup rice wine vinegar

¼ cup Thai sweet chili sauce

1 cup thinly sliced Grilled Butterflied Pork Tenderloin with Wasabi Teriyaki Glazing Sauce (page 316)

1 cup cubed firm tofu

3 green onions, thinly sliced diagonally

Salt and pepper to taste

In a large soup pot, heat vegetable and sesame oils over medium-high heat. Add ginger, garlic, jalapeño peppers, and onion; sauté until onion is tender, about 4 minutes.

Add red pepper, yellow pepper, carrot, bamboo shoots, and shiitake mushrooms. Sauté for another 4 minutes. Add chicken stock. Bring soup to a rolling boil.

Stir in soy sauce, vinegar, and chili sauce. Adjust these seasonings if necessary to give you the proper balance of hot and sour.

Before serving, add pork, tofu, and green onions; heat through. Season to taste with salt and pepper.

SERVES 8

Magic Mushroom Soup

Mushrooms are truly magical—some are even hallucinogenic, but that's a whole other story. Here's a rich and creamy soup made with a variety of flavorful mushrooms. Finish this soup with a drizzle of truffle oil for added richness.

---

4 TB. butter	1 cup sliced oyster mushrooms
4 cloves garlic, minced	2 TB. chopped fresh thyme
1 large onion, diced	¼ cup all-purpose flour
2 stalks celery, diced	4 cups chicken stock
2 cups sliced shiitake mushrooms	1 cup heavy cream
1 cup sliced white mushrooms	Salt and pepper to taste
1 cup sliced brown cremini mushrooms	2 cups shredded white cheddar cheese

---

In a large soup pot, melt butter over medium-high heat. Sauté garlic, onion, and celery until tender, about 4 minutes. Add sliced shiitake, white, brown cremini, and oyster mushrooms and thyme; sauté until mushrooms are tender and almost all the mushroom liquid has evaporated, 8 to 10 minutes.

Reduce heat to medium. Stir in flour. While stirring, slowly add chicken stock until fully incorporated. Bring soup to a boil, reduce heat, and simmer for 30 minutes, stirring occasionally.

Add cream and return to a boil; season to taste with salt and pepper.

Ladle soup into warm bowls, and garnish each bowl with ¼ cup shredded cheddar cheese.

SERVES 8

Cream of Cauliflower Soup with Smoked Chicken Cakes

The summer harvest brings about beautiful heads of gleaming white cauliflower. Cream of cauliflower soup is one of my favorites. I recall Chef Chris Klugman serving a to-die-for cream of cauliflower soup with veal brains at Bistro 990 in Toronto. I only hope my version is as tasty as his.

---

3 cloves garlic, minced	8 cups chicken stock
1 large onion, diced	1 TB. fresh thyme
1 head cauliflower, cut into 2-inch pieces	Salt and pepper to taste
2 green apples, peeled and chopped	1 cup heavy cream
2 cups diced and peeled Yukon Gold potatoes	Sprigs of fresh thyme, for garnish

---

Place garlic, onion, cauliflower, apples, and potatoes in a large soup pot. Add chicken stock, thyme, salt, and pepper.

Bring to a boil over medium-high heat. Reduce heat to low and simmer, uncovered and stirring occasionally, until potatoes and cauliflower are tender, 30 to 40 minutes.

Meanwhile, make Smoked Chicken Cakes (recipe follows).

Purée soup in batches in a blender. Return soup to pot and stir in cream. Reheat gently. Adjust seasoning with salt and pepper.

To serve, place one smoked chicken cake in the center of each of eight large soup plates. Pour ¾ cup soup around each cake. Garnish with sprigs of fresh thyme.

Continued ...

Smoked Chicken Cakes

1 red onion, sliced

4 cups shredded smoked chicken

2 cups coarsely ground whole-wheat cracker crumbs

2 cups shredded Monterey Jack cheese

1 cup chopped green onions

½ cup diced red bell pepper

½ cup diced green bell pepper

½ cup gourmet BBQ sauce

¼ cup Bone Dust BBQ Spice (page 203)

2 TB. honey

Hot sauce to taste

Salt and black pepper to taste

Preheat oven to 375°F. Lightly grease a baking sheet.

In a large bowl, combine red onion, chicken, cracker crumbs, cheese, green onions, red pepper, green pepper, BBQ sauce, Bone Dust BBQ Spice, honey, hot sauce, salt, and black pepper. Form into eight cakes. An ice-cream scoop makes this job a little easier.

Place chicken cakes on baking sheet and bake until heated through, 10 to 12 minutes.

SERVES 8

Grilled Summer Vegetable Soup

The first year in our new home, Pamela and I decided to plant a vegetable garden. This is a recipe we created using some of our backyard produce.

¼ cup + 2 TB. olive oil

¼ cup apple cider vinegar

1 large onion, quartered

1 large leek, cut in half lengthwise and washed of all grit

1 zucchini, cut in half lengthwise

1 large bulb fennel, cut in half lengthwise

2 red bell peppers, cut in half lengthwise

8 plum tomatoes

2 ears corn, shucked

Salt and pepper to taste

4 cloves garlic, minced

1 very small habanero pepper, seeded and finely chopped

2 stalks celery, sliced

2 large Yukon Gold potatoes, peeled and diced

8 cups vegetable or chicken stock

1 lb. green or scarlet runner beans, cut into 1-inch pieces

1 TB. chopped fresh thyme

1 TB. chopped fresh basil

Preheat grill to medium-high.

In a large bowl, whisk together ¼ cup olive oil and vinegar. Add onion, leek, zucchini, fennel, red peppers, tomatoes, corn, salt, and pepper. Toss together well.

Grill vegetables, turning occasionally, until lightly charred and just tender, 10 to 15 minutes. Remove from heat and let cool. Slice all grilled vegetables into 1-inch pieces and set aside.

In a large soup pot, heat remaining 2 tablespoons olive oil over medium heat. Add garlic, habanero pepper, and celery; sauté until tender, 3 to 4 minutes. Add potatoes and stock. Bring to a boil, reduce heat to low, and simmer for 10 minutes.

Add sliced grilled vegetables, green beans, thyme, and basil. Cook, stirring occasionally, until potatoes are tender, about 15 minutes. Season to taste with salt and pepper. Serve with grilled crusty bread.

SERVES 8 TO 10

Beata's Chilled Sour Dill Pickle Soup

One day my love came home from work with a jar of soup. Her assistant, Beata, had made her family's Sour Pickle Soup. Although a little wary at first, we gave it a try. Beata had said to serve it either hot or cold, so we tried both. My favorite is the chilled version, but Pamela prefers the hot. Use really good pickles for this recipe. Homemade are best, but a really good kosher dill works just as well.

2 TB. olive oil
1 clove garlic, minced
1 small onion, diced
1 carrot, diced
2 large Yukon Gold potatoes, diced
½ cup long-grain rice
6 cups chicken stock
2 tsp. Worcestershire sauce
1 sprig fresh dill
8 sour dill pickles (store-bought) or Spicy
    Garlic Dill Pickles (page 175), grated

1 cup heavy cream
Pinch cayenne pepper
Salt and black pepper to taste

GARNISHES
1 cup sour cream
1 TB. chopped fresh dill
1 tsp. lemon juice
1 sour dill pickle, thinly sliced

In a large soup pot, heat oil over medium-high heat. Add garlic, onion, and carrot; sauté until tender, about 3 minutes. Add potatoes and rice; cook, stirring, for 1 minute. Add stock, Worcestershire sauce, and dill sprig. Bring to a boil, reduce heat, and simmer, uncovered, until rice and potatoes are fully cooked, 20 to 30 minutes.

Add grated pickles and cream. Return to a boil and simmer until pickles are tender, about 15 minutes. Season with cayenne, salt, and black pepper. Let cool completely. Refrigerate until needed.

Just before serving, whisk together sour cream, dill, and lemon juice. Season with salt and pepper.

To serve, ladle soup into chilled bowls and garnish with a dollop dill sour cream and three thin slices of dill pickle.

SERVES 8

Chilled Avocado and Lobster Soup with Habanero Peppers

This soup will refresh you on the hottest of summer days.

---

2 live lobsters (each about 1½ lbs.)

¼ cup olive oil

2 cloves garlic, minced

1 small habanero pepper, seeded and finely chopped

1 red onion, diced

6 cups chicken or lobster stock

3 avocados

1 large ripe mango, peeled and diced

2 green onions, chopped

¼ cup fresh lime juice

1 TB. chopped fresh cilantro

Salt and pepper to taste

Pinch cayenne pepper

Sour cream and fresh cilantro sprigs, for garnish

Steam live lobsters over boiling water for 6 to 8 minutes per pound. Remove from steamer and let cool. (If you do not have a steamer large enough to hold lobsters, boil them in a large pot of salted water for 6 to 8 minutes per pound.)

Crack lobster shells and remove all meat. (Use the shells to prepare lobster stock, if you wish.) Cut meat into ¼-inch cubes. Cover and refrigerate.

In a medium saucepan, heat oil over medium-high heat. Sauté garlic, habanero, and red onion until tender, 2 to 3 minutes. Add chicken stock; bring to a rolling boil. Remove from heat and let cool completely.

Peel and dice avocados. Sprinkle with a little lime juice to prevent avocado from turning brown.

In a large bowl, combine avocado, mango, green onions, lime juice, and cilantro. Fold in lobster meat and season to taste with salt and black pepper. Pour in chilled chicken stock mixture and gently stir until fully mixed. Add cayenne; adjust seasoning if necessary. Cover and refrigerate for up to 4 hours.

To serve, ladle soup into chilled bowls or mugs and garnish with a dollop sour cream and a sprig fresh cilantro.

SERVES 6

Bloody Caesar Gazpacho Soup with Quahogs and Horseradish Honey

In Canada, we are partial to a drink called a Bloody Caesar, made with vodka and Clamato juice, a blend of tomato and calm juices. I like the drink so much I figured why not concoct a soup for the summer?

1 red onion, diced

1 stalk celery, sliced

½ seedless cucumber, peeled and chopped

2 cloves garlic, chopped

1 jalapeño pepper, seeded and diced

1 red bell pepper, roasted, seeded, peeled, and diced

2 cups ripe cherry tomatoes

2 cups tomato juice (divided use)

½ cup olive oil

1 TB. chopped fresh dill

1 TB. chopped fresh basil

1 cup clam juice

1 tsp. celery salt

Salt and pepper to taste

Hot sauce to taste

GARNISHES

24 quahogs or other large-shell clam, shucked

¼ cup Horseradish Honey (recipe follows)

½ cup vodka

1 cup diced, seedless cucumber

1 cup diced red onion

2 TB. chopped fresh dill

½ cup freshly grated horseradish

In a blender or food processor, purée red onion, celery, cucumber, garlic, jalapeño, red pepper, and cherry tomatoes. Add half the tomato juice, olive oil, dill, and basil. Purée until smooth.

Transfer gazpacho to a large bowl. Whisk in remaining tomato juice, clam juice, and celery salt. Season to taste with salt, pepper, and hot sauce. Place three shucked quahogs in each bowl and drizzle with Horseradish Honey. Garnish as desired.

SERVES 8

Conttnued . . .

Horseradish Honey

½ cup clover honey
1 TB. freshly grated horseradish

2 sprigs fresh thyme

In a small saucepan, heat honey over medium-high heat, stirring occasionally, for 15 minutes. Add horseradish and thyme sprigs; heat, stirring, for 5 more minutes. Remove from heat and pour into a sterilized canning jar. Let cool for 24 hours for flavors to meld.

Corn Chowder with Truly the Very Best Atlantic Lobster Cakes

From the cold waters off the coast of Maine comes the succulent North Atlantic lobster. Tender, rich lobster meat makes this chowder a winner. Don't skimp on the lobster!

3 TB. butter

1 large onion, diced

3 cloves garlic, finely chopped

2 cups Yukon Gold potatoes cut in ½-inch cubes

1 TB. Bone Dust BBQ Spice (page 203)

4 to 6 cups chicken, vegetable, or lobster stock

4 cups fresh peaches and cream corn kernels (from about 6 ears of corn)

2 TB. chopped fresh thyme

¾ cup whipping cream

Salt and pepper to taste

Sprigs fresh dill, for garnish

Tip

To give the chowder a great charred flavor, grill the cobs of corn for 5 to 8 minutes, turning, until slightly charred and golden brown. Then use a sharp knife to cut the grilled kernels from the cob.

In a large soup pot, melt butter over medium heat. Add onion and garlic; cook for 3 to 4 minutes or until tender.

Add potatoes; cook for another 3 to 4 minutes.

Add Bone Dust BBQ Spice and stock. Bring to a boil, reduce heat, and simmer, uncovered and stirring occasionally, for 45 minutes or until potatoes are soft and soup is thickened. If necessary, add a little more stock to thin soup.

While soup is simmering, make lobster cakes (recipe follows).

Add corn and thyme to soup; continue to simmer for 15 minutes.

Whip cream until it's just thickened and fold into hot soup. Adjust seasoning with salt and pepper.

To serve, place 1 lobster cake in the center of each of 8 large soup plates. Pour ¾ cup corn chowder around each cake. Garnish with sprigs of fresh dill.

Continued ...

Truly the Very Best Atlantic Lobster Cakes

You can also use fresh crabmeat or even shredded whitefish like cod or haddock in this recipe. These cakes are also wonderful on their own served with a little remoulade sauce or spicy mayonnaise.

½ cup mayonnaise

1 egg

2 green onions, thinly sliced

1 TB. chopped fresh cilantro

1 TB. chopped fresh dill

1 TB. lemon juice

1 tsp. Bay Seasoning (page 205)

1 tsp. chopped garlic

½ tsp. ground cumin

½ tsp. curry powder

1½ lbs. cooked Atlantic lobster meat

Salt, pepper, and Louisiana hot sauce

1½ cups coarsely ground whole-wheat cracker crumbs

Preheat oven to 375°F.

In a large bowl, whisk together mayonnaise, egg, green onions, cilantro, dill, lemon juice, Bay Seasoning, garlic, cumin, and curry powder.

Gently fold in cooked lobster meat. Season to taste with salt, pepper, and Louisiana hot sauce.

Add cracker crumbs and gently mix until everything binds together loosely.

Form into 8 small cakes. You can use an ice-cream scoop to make this a little easier.

Place lobster cakes on a lightly greased baking sheet and bake for 10 to 12 minutes or until heated through.

SERVES 8

Helluva Halloween Pumpkin Soup

I love Halloween, and nothing is more in season than the pumpkin. Linus believed in the Great Pumpkin, and I believe that if Linus had had this soup, he would have seen the Great Pumpkin for sure.

3 lbs. fresh pumpkin flesh cut into 2-inch chunks
¼ cup olive oil
1 tsp. cinnamon
1 tsp. cayenne pepper
2 tsp. salt
3 TB. butter
4 cloves garlic, chopped
1 large yellow onion, chopped

2 jalapeño peppers, seeded and finely chopped
8 cups chicken stock
1 TB. chopped fresh sage
1 cup whipping cream
Salt and freshly ground black pepper
½ cup orange blossom honey
½ cup sour cream
8 (5 inch) cinnamon sticks

Preheat oven to 375°F.

In a roasting pan, toss together pumpkin chunks, oil, cinnamon, cayenne pepper, and salt. Roast for 45 to 60 minutes or until pumpkin is lightly roasted and tender. Set aside.

In a large soup pot, melt butter over medium-high heat. Sauté garlic, onion, and jalapeño peppers for 3 to 5 minutes, stirring occasionally, until translucent and tender.

Add roasted pumpkin and chicken stock. Bring to a rolling boil, reduce heat to medium-low, and simmer, uncovered and stirring occasionally, for 20 to 30 minutes or until tender. Using a hand blender or food processor, purée soup until smooth.

Add sage and cream. Return soup to a boil, and season to taste with salt and pepper.

Serve immediately garnished with a drizzling of orange blossom honey, a dollop sour cream, and a cinnamon swizzle stick.

SERVES 8

Roasted French Onion Soup with Maple Syrup and Gruyère and Cheddar Cheeses

One of the most popular soups is French onion soup, a rich soup created with slowly caramelized onions, red wine, and beef broth and garnished with a crisp crouton topped with melted Gruyère cheese.

---

6 large sweet onions, sliced

12 cloves garlic, finely chopped

1 tsp. ground cumin

1 tsp. chili powder

¼ cup + 2 TB. olive oil

Salt and pepper

½ cup whisky

¼ cup maple syrup

2 TB. chopped fresh herbs (any combination of parsley, sage, rosemary, thyme, or savory)

2 bay leaves

1 tsp. cracked black peppercorns

8 cups beef broth

16 slices French bread

1 cup shredded Gruyère cheese

1 cup shredded Vermont white cheddar cheese

Preheat oven to 375°F.

In a roasting pan mix together onions, garlic, cumin, chili powder, and ¼ cup olive oil. Season to taste with salt and pepper. Roast onion mixture, stirring occasionally, for 45 to 60 minutes or until slightly charred and tender.

In a large soup pot heat the remaining 2 tablespoons olive oil over medium-high heat. Add roasted onion mixture and sauté for 10 minutes, stirring constantly.

Deglaze onions with whisky. Stand back as you add whisky, as it may flambé. Stir to scrape up any brown bits. Add maple syrup, fresh herbs, bay leaves, peppercorns, beef broth, and salt to taste. Bring to a rolling boil, reduce heat to medium-low, and simmer, stirring occasionally, for 30 minutes. Adjust seasoning with salt and pepper. Discard bay leaves.

Preheat broiler. On a baking sheet, lightly toast bread slices on both sides to make croutons.

Ladle soup into eight ovenproof crocks. Top each with 2 croutons and ¼ cup Gruyère and cheddar cheeses. Broil for 3 to 5 minutes or until cheese melts and bubbles. Serve immediately.

SERVES 8

Half-Baked Potato Soup

For this hearty winter soup, I use large Yukon Gold potatoes and bake them until they are half baked—tender on the outside but still hard in the center.

6 large Yukon Gold potatoes
2 TB. coarse kosher salt
¼ cup butter
1 large yellow onion, finely diced
4 cloves garlic, minced
2 stalks celery, finely diced
1 leek, including pale green part, thinly sliced
8 cups chicken stock
1 cup whipping cream
1 TB. chopped fresh thyme
Salt and freshly ground black pepper

GARNISHES

1 cup sour cream
1 cup crumbled crisp bacon
½ cup shredded yellow cheddar cheese
½ cup shredded Gruyère cheese
4 green onions, thinly sliced
½ small red onion, diced
1 (200 g) pkg. Hickory Sticks Smoked Flavor potato matchsticks

Preheat oven to 425°F.

Wash and scrub potatoes. Season wet potatoes with coarse kosher salt; roast for 45 minutes or until still a little firm in the center. Let cool for 30 minutes. Cut potatoes into 1-inch chunks.

In a large soup pot, melt butter over medium-high heat. Sauté onion, garlic, celery, and leek for 4 to 5 minutes, stirring occasionally, or until translucent and tender.

Add potatoes and chicken stock. Bring to a rolling boil, reduce heat to medium-low and simmer, stirring occasionally to prevent sticking, for 30 to 40 minutes or until thick. Purée soup in a blender or food processor.

Return soup to heat. Add cream and thyme; simmer for 10 minutes more. Season to taste with salt and pepper.

To serve, ladle soup into 8 large soup bowls. Garnish with a large dollop sour cream, a generous sprinkle of bacon bits, shredded cheddar and Gruyère cheese, green onions, red onion, and Hickory Sticks.

SERVES 8

Cedar-Planked Salmon Chowder

If one was to say that I had a signature dish, it would be cedar-planked salmon. I have planked salmon as well as hundreds of other foods. I love salmon and believe that the only way to perfectly cook it every time is to plank it.

This recipe is a variation on the classic recipe from my *Sticks and Stones Cookbook: The Art of Grilling on Plank, Vine and Stone.*

Cedar-Planked Salmon

6 Atlantic salmon fillets (each 6 oz.), skinned
¼ cup Salmon Seasoning (page 204)
Sea salt
1 lemon, halved

Special equipment: 1 untreated cedar plank (at least 12 × 12 inches and ½- to ¾-inch thick), soaked in water overnight

Preheat grill to high.

Season salmon fillets with Salmon Seasoning.

Sprinkle plank with sea salt. Place plank on the grill and close the lid. Let the plank heat for 3 to 5 minutes or until it starts to crackle.

Place salmon fillets on the plank. Close the lid and bake for 12 to 15 minutes or until fish flakes easily with a fork. Periodically check the plank; if it is burning, spray it with water.

Squeeze lemon over salmon.

Carefully remove the plank from the grill and transfer salmon to a cutting board. Let salmon cool before adding to chowder.

Continued . . .

Salmon Chowder

4 slices bacon, diced

3 cloves garlic, minced

1 yellow onion, diced

2 stalks celery, diced

3 TB. all-purpose flour

3 cups fish stock

4 Yukon Gold potatoes, peeled and diced

2 cups half-and-half cream

1 TB. chopped fresh dill

1 tsp. lemon zest

Planked salmon (recipe precedes)

Salt and freshly ground black pepper

In a large saucepan over medium-high heat cook bacon until crisp. Remove with a slotted spoon and set aside. Add garlic, onion, and celery to bacon drippings and sauté for 2 to 3 minutes or until tender. Add flour and stir until absorbed.

Add fish stock a little at a time, stirring after each addition until smooth.

Add potatoes. Bring to a boil, reduce heat to medium-low and simmer for 20 minutes, stirring occasionally, or until potatoes are tender.

Stir in cream, dill, and lemon zest. Return to a slow boil.

Cut cooled planked salmon into ½-inch chunks. Gently stir salmon and reserved bacon bits into chowder. Season to taste with salt and pepper.

Serve immediately.

SERVES 8

Grilled Ranch Chicken Soup with Chili Dumplings

Here's a hearty soup that is great for warming the soul. Loaded with chicken and topped with tender chili-spiced dumplings, it's a meal in a bowl!

8 boneless skinless chicken breasts (each 6 oz.)

2 TB. Bone Dust BBQ Spice (page 203)

2 TB. vegetable oil

1 lime, juiced

Salt to taste

2 TB. butter

4 cloves garlic, minced

1 onion, diced

1 leek, diced

2 stalks celery, diced

2 carrots, peeled and diced

2 parsnips, peeled and diced

2 TB. chopped fresh herbs (parsley, sage, and thyme)

8 cups chicken stock

CHILI DUMPLINGS

2½ cups all-purpose flour

2 tsp. baking powder

1 tsp. chili powder

1 tsp. salt

1 TB. dried parsley

¼ tsp. black pepper

¼ cup vegetable oil

½ to 1 cup buttermilk

In a bowl, mix together chicken breasts, Bone Dust BBQ spice, oil, and lime juice. Marinate, covered and refrigerated, for 4 hours.

Preheat grill to high.

Remove chicken from marinade and season with salt. Grill for 5 to 6 minutes per side or until fully cooked and lightly charred. Cut into 1-inch chunks and set aside.

In a large soup pot, melt butter over medium-high heat. Add garlic, onion, and leek; sauté for 3 to 4 minutes or until translucent and tender. Add celery, carrots, and parsnips; sauté for 4 minutes. Add herbs and chicken stock. Bring to a boil, reduce heat to medium-low, and simmer, uncovered and stirring occasionally, for 30 minutes.

Meanwhile, prepare dumplings. Sift flour, baking powder, chili powder, and salt into a large bowl. Stir in parsley and black pepper. Make a well in the center and add oil and ½ cup buttermilk. Stir together to make a soft dough, adding more buttermilk if necessary.

Add chicken to soup and return to a simmer. Drop 16 spoonfuls dumpling batter on top of the simmering soup. Continue to simmer, uncovered, for 8 to 10 minutes or until dumplings are puffed and cooked through.

Serve immediately.

SERVES 8

Sexy Salads

Chunky Blue Cheese Dressing

My all-time favorite dressing is blue cheese. A steakhouse staple, it goes best with iceberg lettuce, but try it drizzled on grilled steaks or chicken. Use Danish blue or French Roquefort.

1 cup mayonnaise	2 tsp. Worcestershire sauce
1 cup sour cream	½ tsp. salt
¼ cup cold water	2 green onions, finely chopped
2 TB. lemon juice	Freshly ground black pepper
1 cup crumbled blue cheese	

In a large bowl, whisk together mayonnaise, sour cream, water, and lemon juice.

Stir in blue cheese, Worcestershire sauce, salt, and green onions. Season to taste with pepper.

Transfer to a sealed container and refrigerate until needed. Will keep up to one week.

MAKES ABOUT 3 CUPS

Creamy French Parmesan Dressing

There is a steakhouse in Bentonville, Arkansas, called Fred's. This is my version of their killer Creamy French Parmesan.

---

1 cup grated Parmesan cheese	2 cloves garlic, minced
1 cup mayonnaise	1 TB. chopped fresh thyme
1 cup sour cream	2 tsp. Worcestershire sauce
¼ cup cold water	1 tsp. paprika
¼ cup white wine vinegar	¼ tsp. cayenne pepper
2 TB. Dijon mustard	Salt and freshly ground black pepper

In a medium bowl whisk together Parmesan cheese, mayonnaise, sour cream, water, vinegar, and mustard. Stir in garlic, thyme, Worcestershire sauce, paprika, and cayenne. Season to taste with salt and pepper. Transfer to a sealed container and refrigerate until needed. Will keep up to one week.

MAKES ABOUT 3 ½ CUPS

Astrida's Lemon Vinaigrette

My mom is a great cook. She makes some wonderful dishes, but I love her lemon vinaigrette the best, next to her roast chicken, beet borscht, and peanut butter balls.

½ cup lemon juice
2 TB. white vinegar
1 TB. chopped fresh parsley
1 TB. chopped fresh dill
1 TB. sugar

2 tsp. mustard powder
2 cloves garlic, minced
1 cup vegetable oil
Salt and freshly ground black pepper

In a small bowl, whisk together lemon juice, vinegar, parsley, dill, sugar, mustard powder, and garlic.

While whisking, slowly add vegetable oil in a steady stream.

Season to taste with salt and pepper.

Transfer to a sealed container and refrigerate until needed. Will keep up to one week.

MAKES ABOUT 1½ CUPS

Russian Dressing

I love the sweet and sour flavors of Russian dressing. Kraft makes a great Russian dressing, which I like to use in various BBQ sauce recipes. But here's my own for outstanding salads.

½ cup honey

½ cup ketchup

¼ cup white vinegar

1 TB. lemon juice

2 tsp. paprika

1 tsp. mustard powder

1 tsp. celery salt

½ tsp. cayenne pepper

1 cup vegetable oil

Salt and pepper

In a medium bowl whisk together honey, ketchup, vinegar, lemon juice, paprika, mustard powder, celery salt, cayenne, and vegetable oil. Season to taste with salt and pepper.

Transfer to a sealed container and refrigerate until needed. Will keep up to one week.

MAKES ABOUT 2½ CUPS

Green Goddess Ranch Dressing

You do not often see this classic dressing on menus or in the supermarket these days. I think Green Goddess was one of the first ranch-type dressings.

1 cup mayonnaise

1 cup sour cream

½ cup buttermilk

¼ cup white vinegar

2 TB. Dijon mustard

1 TB. lemon juice

2 anchovy fillets, minced

1 bunch green onions, finely chopped

2 cloves garlic, minced

¼ cup chopped fresh parsley

2 TB. chopped capers

1 TB. chopped fresh dill

1 TB. chopped fresh thyme

1 tsp. coarsely ground black pepper

1 tsp. Worcestershire sauce

¼ tsp. cayenne pepper

Salt

In a medium bowl, whisk together mayonnaise, sour cream, buttermilk, vinegar, mustard, and lemon juice until smooth.

Add anchovies, green onions, garlic, parsley, capers, dill, thyme, black pepper, Worcestershire sauce, and cayenne. Season to taste with salt.

Transfer to a sealed container and refrigerate until needed. Will keep up to one week.

MAKES ABOUT 3 CUPS

Maple Onion Balsamic Vinaigrette

The key to this dressing is the roasting of the onion prior to making the dressing. It brings out the natural sweetness of the onion.

1 large sweet onion, sliced	½ cup balsamic vinegar
3 cloves garlic, halved	¼ cup maple syrup
2 TB. + 1 cup olive oil	2 TB. chopped fresh basil
Salt and pepper	2 TB. Dijon mustard

Preheat oven to 425°F.

In a small baking dish, toss onion and garlic with 2 tablespoons olive oil. Season to taste with salt and pepper. Roast onions for 30 to 45 minutes or until lightly charred and tender.

In a food processor purée, onion mixture. Add balsamic vinegar, maple syrup, basil, and mustard. Turn processor on and add remaining 1 cup olive oil in a slow, steady stream until dressing is emulsified.

Season to taste with salt and pepper.

Transfer to a sealed container and refrigerate until needed. Will keep up to one week.

MAKES ABOUT 2 CUPS

Spicy Grilled Jalapeño Dressing

Try this salad dressing on grilled vegetables and as a marinade for chicken or fish.

---

6 large jalapeño peppers
4 shallots, peeled
¼ cup lime juice
1 TB. chopped fresh cilantro
1 tsp. Bone Dust BBQ Spice (page 203)

1 tsp. chopped garlic
½ to 1 tsp. sugar
½ cup vegetable oil
Salt and freshly ground black pepper

Preheat grill to medium-high.

Place jalapeño peppers and shallots on a grill screen and grill, turning occasionally, until nicely charred. Let cool. Peel and seed jalapeño peppers.

In a food processor, purée jalapeño peppers and shallots until smooth. Add lime juice, cilantro, Bone Dust BBQ Spice, garlic, and sugar. Turn on processor and slowly pour in vegetable oil until dressing is emulsified. Season to taste with salt and pepper.

Transfer to a sealed container and refrigerate until needed. Will keep up to one week.

MAKES ABOUT 1 ½ CUPS

Thousand Islands Dressing

Try this dressing as a dip for fresh vegetables as well as drizzled on crisp iceberg lettuce.

1½ cups mayonnaise

½ cup ketchup

2 TB. lemon juice

1 TB. white vinegar

3 green onions, chopped

1 small red onion, finely diced

3 anchovies, minced

2 cloves garlic, minced

2 TB. chopped gherkins

2 TB. finely chopped capers

1 TB. chopped fresh parsley

1 tsp. mustard powder

1 tsp. dried dill

1 tsp. black pepper

Salt

In a bowl, whisk together mayonnaise, ketchup, lemon juice, and vinegar. Stir in green onions, red onion, anchovies, garlic, gherkins, capers, parsley, mustard powder, dill, and black pepper. Season to taste with salt.

Transfer to a sealed container and refrigerate until needed. Will keep up to one week.

MAKES ABOUT 3 CUPS

Roasted Garlic Caesar Dressing

Caesar salad is one of the most popular salads on restaurant menus. Roasting the garlic takes away the sharpness of raw garlic and adds a natural sweetness to the dressing. This dressing is also good as a marinade for grilled chicken.

12 large cloves garlic, peeled
1½ cups olive oil
6 anchovies, minced
¼ cup Dijon mustard
1 lemon, juiced (about ¼ cup)

2 TB. red wine vinegar
1 TB. Worcestershire sauce
¼ tsp. hot sauce
½ cup grated Parmesan cheese
Salt and pepper

Tip

For a twist, add bacon bits to the dressing and serve as a dip or sauce.

Preheat oven to 325°F.

Place garlic cloves in an ovenproof dish. Cover with olive oil and roast for 30 to 40 minutes or until garlic is golden brown and tender. Let cool.

Remove cloves from oil, reserving oil, and in a medium bowl mash until smooth.

Stir in anchovies and mustard. While stirring add lemon juice, vinegar, Worcestershire sauce, and hot sauce. Continue stirring and add reserved roasted garlic oil in a slow, steady stream.

Stir in Parmesan cheese and season to taste with salt and pepper.

Transfer to a sealed container and refrigerate until needed. Use this dressing on crisp romaine leaves garnished with extra cheese, croutons, and crispy bacon bits.

MAKES ABOUT 2½ CUPS

Warm Bacon Mustard Dressing

Not all dressings need to be served cold. This one is meant to be served warm. Prepare it ahead and store in the refrigerator for up to two weeks. Warm it in the microwave for 30 to 45 seconds, then enjoy drizzled over fresh spinach or crisp greens.

---

8 slices smoked bacon	2 TB. chopped fresh parsley
3 cloves garlic, minced	1 TB. chopped fresh sage
½ cup cider vinegar	1½ cups olive oil
¼ cup Dijon mustard	Hot sauce
¼ cup grainy mustard	Salt and pepper
¼ cup honey	

In a large skillet, fry bacon over medium heat until crisp. Drain on paper towels and let cool. Coarsely chop bacon and set aside.

In a bowl, whisk together garlic, vinegar, Dijon mustard, grainy mustard, honey, parsley, and sage. While stirring, add olive oil in a steady stream until incorporated. Stir in reserved bacon. Season to taste with hot sauce, salt, and pepper.

Transfer to a sealed container and refrigerate until needed. Will keep up to two weeks. Reheat before using.

MAKES ABOUT 3 CUPS

Rice Noodle Salad with Spicy Sesame Soy Vinaigrette

The key to this spicy salad is the chili-seasoned soy sauce. The vinaigrette can double as a marinade for beef, chicken, or shrimp. Look for sambal oelek in Asian markets.

1 lb. rice vermicelli noodles
6 cups warm water
4 green onions, thinly sliced
1 red onion, sliced
1 carrot, peeled and julienned
1 green bell pepper, thinly sliced
2 cups bean sprouts
2 cups snow peas, trimmed and cut into thin strips
½ cup crushed peanuts, for garnish

SPICY SESAME SOY VINAIGRETTE
2 green onions, finely chopped
2 cloves garlic, minced
½ cup rice wine vinegar
¼ cup mirin (sweet rice wine)
¼ cup chili soy sauce
¼ cup honey
2 TB. toasted sesame seeds
2 TB. sambal oelek
1 TB. minced fresh ginger
1 TB. sesame oil
1 tsp. pepper
¾ cup vegetable oil
Salt

Place rice noodles in a bowl, and cover with warm water. Let stand for 30 to 45 minutes, until noodles are softened. Drain and rinse under cold water. Drain again and set aside.

Prepare vinaigrette: In a medium bowl, whisk together green onions, garlic, rice wine vinegar, mirin, soy sauce, honey, sesame seeds, sambal oelek, ginger, sesame oil, and pepper. Slowly whisk in vegetable oil in a steady stream and whisk until incorporated. Season to taste with salt.

In a large bowl, combine noodles, green onions, red onion, carrot, green pepper, bean sprouts, and snow peas. Pour over ½ cup vinaigrette, and toss to mix. Season to taste with pepper. Serve garnished with crushed peanuts.

SERVES 6 TO 8

Tropical Coleslaw

Good dark rum is what adds the punch to this salad. While on the set of *King of the Q*, my co-host thought I was nuts when I added rum to this dressing. But no combination is ridiculous—just different.

---

4 green onions, thinly sliced

2 carrots, shredded

1 small green cabbage, thinly sliced

1 ripe mango, peeled and diced

1 red onion, sliced

2 cups diced fresh pineapple

2 TB. chopped fresh cilantro

2 shallots, finely chopped

¼ cup white vinegar

¼ cup pineapple juice

2 TB. Dijon mustard

2 TB. dark rum

1 TB. sugar

2 tsp. toasted cumin seeds

½ cup vegetable oil

Pinch cayenne pepper

Salt and pepper

In a large bowl, combine green onions, carrots, cabbage, mango, red onion, pineapple, and cilantro.

In a small bowl, whisk together shallots, vinegar, pineapple juice, mustard, rum, sugar, and cumin seeds. While whisking, add oil in a steady stream, whisking until incorporated. Season to taste with cayenne, salt, and pepper.

Add dressing to cabbage mixture and toss to fully mix. Season to taste with salt and pepper. Cover and refrigerate for 1 hour.

SERVES 6 TO 8

Barley and Corn Salad

 Barley is not just for soup. It is wonderful as a warm side dish to grilled chicken, lamb, or beef— and in this salad!

4 cups water
1 tsp. salt
1½ cups quick-cooking barley
4 ears corn, shucked
1 large red onion, thinly sliced
4 green onions, thinly sliced
1 cup peas

⅓ cup vegetable oil
¼ cup white wine vinegar
2 TB. chopped fresh mixed herbs
1 TB. chopped fresh garlic
2 tsp. Bone Dust BBQ Spice (page 203)
Salt and pepper

In a medium saucepan, bring water and salt to a rolling boil. Add barley. Cook until tender, 20 to 30 minutes. Drain and cool.

Meanwhile, preheat grill to high.

Grill ears of corn and red onion slices until slightly charred and tender, turning frequently. Remove from grill and let cool. Cut corn kernels from the cob and dice onion.

In a large bowl, combine barley, corn, red onion, green onions, peas, oil, vinegar, herbs, garlic, and Bone Dust BBQ Spice. Mix thoroughly. Season to taste with salt and pepper.

Chill before serving.

SERVES 8

Cucumber and Radish Salad with Yogurt Dressing

My grandmother used to prepare this salad for me on hot summer days at the cottage. She would go to a local farmer and pick his best produce as well as ask him for his unpasteurized homemade yogurt. It was a delicious salad.

1 bunch radishes, thinly sliced	¼ cup chopped fresh dill
6 green onions, thinly sliced	1½ cups yogurt
1 red onion, sliced	2 TB. lemon juice
1 large seedless cucumber, peeled and thinly sliced	Salt and freshly ground black pepper

In a bowl, combine radishes, green onions, red onion, cucumber, and dill. Stir in yogurt and lemon juice; season to taste with salt and pepper.

Chill before serving.

SERVES 6

Turkish Wedding Rice Salad

Turkish Wedding Rice is a hot dish that is thought to bring good luck to newlyweds. It is also thought to be an aphrodisiac. Any food that stimulates the heart and loins is a must! My version is in the form of a salad, cooling for the summer.

1½ cups long-grain rice

3 cups water

1 tsp. salt

3 boneless, skinless chicken breasts
   (each 6 oz.)

2 TB. Bone Dust BBQ Spice (page 203)

3 green onions, diced

1 onion, diced

1 red bell pepper, diced

½ cup toasted pine nuts

½ cup currants or raisins

¼ cup dried cranberries

¼ cup chopped fresh parsley

1 TB. chopped fresh oregano

2 tsp. cinnamon

Salt and pepper

In a medium saucepan, bring rice, water and salt to a boil. Remove from heat, cover, and let stand for 1 hour or until rice is tender. Transfer rice to a cookie sheet and spread out evenly. Let cool completely.

Preheat grill to medium-high.

Rub chicken breasts with Bone Dust BBQ Spice, pressing spices into meat. Grill chicken until fully cooked, about 5 minutes per side. Remove from grill and let cool.

Dice chicken and put it in a large bowl. Add rice, green onions, onion, red pepper, pine nuts, currants, cranberries, parsley, oregano, and cinnamon. Season to taste with salt and pepper.

Chill before serving.

SERVES 8

Antipasto Olive Salad

This chunky salad is wonderful on its own or as a filling for a great sandwich. If you want a little extra heat, add diced jalapeño or pickled peperoncini. This salad also is great with the addition of spicy salami.

2 zucchini	2 cups black olives, pitted and sliced
Olive oil	2 cups marinated artichokes, drained and quartered
Salt and pepper to taste	2 cups diced mozzarella cheese
1 red onion, diced	1 cup gherkin pickles, drained and cut in half lengthwise
1 red bell pepper, diced	¼ cup capers, drained
1 yellow bell pepper, diced	¼ cup red wine vinegar
3 cloves garlic, minced	¼ cup olive oil
2 cups pimento-stuffed green olives, sliced	1 TB. chopped fresh oregano

Preheat grill to medium-high.

Cut zucchini lengthwise into ½-inch-thick slices. Brush slices with olive oil and season with salt and pepper. Grill zucchini until lightly charred and tender, 4 to 5 minutes per side. Remove from grill and let cool. Cut into ½-inch cubes.

In a large bowl, combine zucchini, onion, red pepper, yellow pepper, garlic, green olives, black olives, artichokes, mozzarella, gherkins, capers, vinegar, olive oil, and oregano. Season to taste with salt and pepper. Mix thoroughly.

SERVES 6 TO 8

Multi-Bean Salad with Bacon and Warm Honey Mustard Dressing

Multi-bean salads are delicious. This combination of fresh green and yellow wax beans with firm dried beans is a real treat. If you don't have time to cook dried beans, use canned ones. Rinse them under cold water and drain them well.

½ cup dried red kidney beans

½ cup dried white navy beans

½ cup dried chick peas

½ cup dried black-eyed peas

1 lb. green beans, trimmed

1 lb. yellow wax beans, trimmed

1 onion, sliced

1 red bell pepper, sliced

12 slices bacon, fried crisp and diced

2 TB. chopped fresh parsley

3 cloves garlic, minced

½ cup olive oil

¼ cup old-fashioned grainy mustard

¼ cup honey

¼ cup cider vinegar

Hot sauce

Salt and pepper

Place kidney beans, navy beans, chick peas, and black-eyed peas in a large saucepan and cover with cold water. Let stand for 24 hours. Drain beans and rinse under cold running water. Return beans to saucepan and cover with cold water. Bring to a boil, reduce heat, and simmer, uncovered and stirring occasionally, until tender, 45 minutes to 1 hour. Drain and rinse under cold running water until cool. Drain again.

Meanwhile, blanch green and yellow wax beans in a pot of boiling salted water for 2 minutes. Drain and cool under cold running water. Drain again.

In a large bowl, combine cooked dried beans, blanched beans, onion, red pepper, bacon, and parsley.

In a small saucepan, combine garlic, olive oil, mustard, honey, and vinegar. Season to taste with hot sauce, salt, and pepper. Pour hot dressing over bean salad, toss well and serve immediately.

SERVES 8 TO 10

Roquefort Grilled Potato Salad with Creamy Smoked Garlic Dressing

Blue cheese and grilled potatoes are a perfect mix. Serve this salad hot off the grill so the cheese melts and the salad gets sticky. Serve with grilled steaks or tasty burgers.

2 lbs. mini new potatoes	2 stalks celery, thinly sliced
Salt and pepper to taste	2 green apples, cut into ½-inch cubes
¼ cup olive oil	1 green bell pepper, diced
1 large red onion, sliced	1½ cups crumbled Roquefort cheese
4 green onions, sliced	1 cup Creamy Smoked Garlic Dressing (recipe follows)

Cut potatoes in half and place in a large saucepan. Cover with cold water and bring to a boil over high heat. Add salt. Reduce heat to low and simmer potatoes for 15 minutes or until just tender. Drain and let cool.

Preheat grill to medium-high.

Toss potatoes with olive oil, salt, and pepper. Place in a grill basket. Grill potatoes for 6 to 8 minutes per side or until lightly grilled and charred. Carefully transfer potatoes to a large bowl. Add red onion, green onions, celery, apples, green pepper, Roquefort, and Creamy Smoked Garlic Dressing. Season to taste with salt and pepper. Mix thoroughly and serve immediately.

SERVES 6 TO 8

Continued . . .

Creamy Smoked Garlic Dressing

Lots of smoked garlic makes this a great dressing for potato and pasta salads. You can never have enough garlic in a dressing.

1 head smoked garlic (8 to 12 cloves) (page 200) or roasted garlic (page 201)
1 cup mayonnaise
1 cup sour cream
½ cup grated Parmesan cheese
¼ cup chopped fresh parsley

¼ cup apple cider vinegar
2 TB. Dijon mustard
1 TB. lemon juice
1 TB. Worcestershire sauce
Salt and pepper to taste

Peel garlic cloves and mash until smooth.

In a large bowl, whisk together garlic, mayonnaise, sour cream, Parmesan, parsley, vinegar, mustard, lemon juice, Worcestershire sauce, salt, and pepper.

Transfer to a sealed container and refrigerate until needed. Will keep up to 1 week.

MAKES ABOUT 3 CUPS

Grilled Vegetable Salad with Maple Balsamic Vinaigrette and Goat Cheese

You can grill virtually any kind of vegetable. To grill root vegetables, first blanch in boiling water until tender. For softer vegetables (peppers, eggplant, zucchini), season with oil, vinegar, salt, and pepper and grill until lightly charred. Mushrooms are my favorite grilled vegetable, and the grill adds a big boost of flavor to any mushroom.

1 large sweet onion, sliced
2 zucchini, thinly sliced
8 large mushrooms, quartered
2 red bell peppers, sliced
1 bunch asparagus, cut into 2-inch pieces
1 TB. Bone Dust BBQ Spice (page 203)
2 TB. olive oil
½ cup crumbled goat cheese
1 TB. chopped fresh thyme
Salt and pepper

MAPLE BALSAMIC VINAIGRETTE
¼ cup balsamic vinegar
3 TB. maple syrup
2 TB. Dijon mustard
1 TB. chopped fresh thyme
½ cup olive oil
Salt and pepper

In a large bowl, toss together onion, zucchini, mushrooms, bell peppers, and asparagus. Season with Bone Dust BBQ Spice and olive oil. Toss again to coat. Place vegetables in a grill basket.

Preheat grill to medium-high.

Meanwhile, prepare dressing: In a small bowl, whisk together balsamic vinegar, maple syrup, mustard, and thyme. Whisk in olive oil in a slow, steady stream until dressing is emulsified. Season to taste with salt and pepper.

Grill vegetables until lightly charred and tender, 8 to 10 minutes per side.

Transfer vegetables to a large bowl. Toss with vinaigrette, goat cheese, and thyme. Season to taste with salt and pepper.

SERVES 8

Tip

For ease in grilling, use a grill basket.

Three-Tomato, Peach, and Mozzarella Salad

My chef friend Christine Chamberlain calls this dish the ultimate summer salad. It's extremely refreshing and easy to make. Use as many varieties of tomatoes as you can find.

---

2 large vine-ripened red tomatoes	8 balls fresh mozzarella cheese, quartered
2 large vine-ripened yellow tomatoes	¼ cup fresh basil leaves, thinly sliced
2 large vine-ripened orange tomatoes	¼ cup olive oil
3 ripe peaches, peeled and cut into wedges	3 TB. balsamic vinegar
1 sweet onion, thinly sliced	Salt and freshly ground black pepper
3 green onions, thinly sliced	Fresh basil leaves, for garnish

---

Core tomatoes and slice each tomato into eight wedges. Place tomatoes in a large bowl and add peaches, sweet onion, green onions, mozzarella cheese, and sliced basil.

Drizzle with olive oil and balsamic vinegar. Season to taste with salt and pepper.

Arrange salad on a serving platter and garnish with basil leaves. Serve immediately.

SERVES 6 TO 8

Lentil and Crab Salad

I first had this salad in Jamaica while filming *King of the Q*. It was loaded with fresh crab and green lentils. My version adds some bite with jalapeños and Dijon. Serve with grilled shrimp or salmon.

2 (14 oz.) cans cooked green lentils, drained and rinsed

1 cup fresh lump crabmeat

1 red onion, sliced

1 leek, cut in half lengthwise and cleaned well

1 yellow bell pepper, diced

4 green onions, thinly sliced

1 large green jalapeño pepper, seeded and diced

4 cloves garlic, minced

¼ cup Dijon mustard

¼ cup olive oil

2 TB. chopped fresh parsley

2 TB. lemon juice

2 TB. white wine vinegar

Salt and pepper

In a large bowl, combine lentils, crabmeat, red onion, leek, yellow pepper, green onions, jalapeño, and garlic.

In a small bowl, whisk together mustard, oil, parsley, lemon juice, and vinegar. Pour over lentil mixture, season to taste with salt and pepper, and mix thoroughly. Cover and refrigerate for 1 hour.

SERVES 6 TO 8

Steamed Mussel Salad with Lemon Horseradish

Eaten hot or cold, fresh mussels are tasty little treats. Here, the mussels' sweet and salty flavor takes on the flavors of the marinade. Try this recipe with clams, too.

3 to 5 lbs. fresh mussels
¼ cup olive oil
4 shallots, sliced
4 cloves garlic, minced
1 jalapeño pepper, seeded and diced
¼ cup white wine
1 onion, sliced
1 leek, cut in half lengthwise, cleaned well
   and thinly sliced

1 red bell pepper, thinly sliced
¼ cup freshly grated horseradish
2 TB. chopped fresh parsley
2 TB. grainy mustard
2 TB. lemon juice
1 TB. chopped fresh thyme
Salt and pepper to taste

Clean and beard mussels. Set aside.

In a large pot, heat oil over high heat. Add shallots, garlic, and jalapeño; sauté for 2 to 3 minutes or until tender. Stir in mussels and white wine. Cover and let mussels steam for 5 to 6 minutes or until the shells have opened. Transfer mussels and broth to a large bowl. Discard any mussels that did not open.

Add onion, leek, red pepper, horseradish, parsley, mustard, lemon juice, thyme, salt, and pepper. Mix thoroughly. Let cool, then cover and refrigerate for at least 2 hours.

To serve, pour mussel salad onto a serving platter and dig in.

SERVES 4 TO 6

Shrimp and Avocado Pineapple Boats

Large, ripe, golden pineapples give this salad a burst of sweetness. If you wish, grill slices of pineapple and glaze with a mixture of rum and maple syrup. The char flavors of the grill complement the pineapple beautifully.

2 ripe pineapples	Salt and pepper
1 red onion, diced	1 lb. (20 to 30) large shrimp, peeled and deveined
2 stalks celery, diced	2 TB. Bay Seasoning (page 205)
2 avocados, peeled and diced	2 tsp. curry powder
3 green onions, chopped	1 tsp. ground cumin
1 cup mayonnaise	¼ cup lemon juice
2 TB. lemon juice	¼ cup olive oil
1 TB. chopped fresh dill	

Cut pineapples in half from top to bottom. Scoop out pineapple from each half to make a boat with walls about ½ inch thick. Dice pineapple.

In a bowl, combine 2 cups diced pineapple, red onion, celery, avocados, green onions, mayonnaise, lemon juice, and dill. Season to taste with salt and pepper. Set aside.

Preheat grill to medium-high.

In a bowl, toss together shrimp, Bay Seasoning, curry powder, cumin, lemon juice, and olive oil.

Grill seasoned shrimp, basting with any remaining olive oil mixture, until just cooked through, 2 to 3 minutes per side. Toss shrimp with pineapple mixture.

Spoon salad into four pineapple boats. Serve immediately.

SERVES 4 AS A MAIN COURSE, 8 SHARING A STARTER

Shrimp and Pasta Salad

Here's a refreshing summer pasta salad bursting with flavor. The more shrimp you add, the better this one gets.

---

1 lb. fusilli
1 lb. baby cold water shrimp, thawed and
    deveined
2 cups cherry tomatoes, halved
2 shallots, finely diced
3 green onions, sliced
2 cups sugar snap peas, blanched and cooled
½ cup toasted walnut halves
Salt and freshly ground black pepper to taste

DRESSING
1 bunch flat-leaf parsley, chopped
½ cup toasted walnut halves
2 TB. chopped garlic
1 tsp. grated lemon zest
½ cup olive oil
¼ cup lemon juice

Cook pasta in a pot of boiling salted water until just tender. Drain pasta and spread it out on a cookie sheet lined with wax paper; let cool.

In a large bowl, combine pasta, shrimp, tomatoes, shallots, green onions, snap peas, and walnuts. Salt and pepper to taste.

To make the dressing, place parsley, walnuts, garlic, and lemon zest in a food processor. Pulse until well blended and nuts are ground. Add olive oil and lemon juice. Pulse until fully mixed.

Pour dressing over pasta mixture. Mix thoroughly and season to taste with salt and pepper. Chill before serving.

SERVES 8

Cabbage, Smoked Ham, and Cheddar Salad with Roasted Red Pepper Vinaigrette

Use a really good-quality smoked ham for this salad. When I have the time I like to smoke my own hams over corncobs or cracked pecans, which add a sweet nutty flavor to the ham.

1 small Savoy cabbage, thinly sliced
1 red onion, thinly sliced
4 green onions, thinly sliced
1 red bell pepper, thinly sliced
12 oz. smoked ham, cut into strips
2 cups diced medium cheddar cheese
1 TB. chopped fresh sage

ROASTED RED PEPPER VINAIGRETTE
2 red bell peppers, roasted, peeled, and seeded
2 cloves garlic, minced
2 TB. Dijon mustard
¼ cup red wine vinegar
1 TB. crushed red chilies
3 TB. olive oil
Salt and pepper

In a large bowl, combine cabbage, red onion, green onions, red pepper, ham, cheese, and sage. Set aside.

To make vinaigrette, in a food processor, purée roasted red peppers and garlic. Add mustard, vinegar, and crushed chilies. With the motor running, slowly add olive oil in a steady stream until dressing is emulsified. Season to taste with salt and pepper.

Pour dressing over salad. Adjust seasoning. Chill for 1 hour before serving.

SERVES 8

Grilled Chicken Salad with Fire-Roasted Tomato Jalapeño Vinaigrette

Tender chicken and ripe avocado is a refreshing blend. If you want to make this salad ahead, don't add the croutons until just before serving.

4 (6 oz.) boneless, skinless chicken breasts
2 TB. Bone Dust BBQ Spice (page 203)
Vegetable oil
1 sweet onion, cut into 1-inch chunks
2 red bell peppers, cut into 1-inch chunks
1 avocado, peeled and diced
4 green onions, sliced
2 cups croutons (homemade or store-bought)

FIRE-ROASTED TOMATO JALAPEÑO VINAIGRETTE
6 plum tomatoes
4 jalapeño peppers
1 small onion, cut into wedges
¼ cup olive oil
3 TB. red wine vinegar
3 TB. water
1 TB. chopped fresh oregano
2 cloves garlic, minced
Salt and pepper

Preheat grill to medium-high.

Season chicken with Bone Dust BBQ Spice, pressing spices into meat. Brush with oil. Grill for 5 to 6 minutes per side or until fully cooked and lightly charred. Remove from grill and let cool.

Make vinaigrette: Grill-roast tomatoes, jalapeño peppers, and onion for 10 to 15 minutes, turning occasionally, until charred and tender. (Be careful when turning tomatoes, as they will be soft.) Remove from grill and let cool. Peel tomatoes. Peel and seed jalapeño peppers.

In a food processor, pulse tomatoes, jalapeño peppers, onion, oil, vinegar, water, oregano, and garlic. Season to taste with salt and pepper. Set aside.

Cut chicken into 1-inch chunks and put in a large bowl. Add sweet onion, red peppers, avocado, green onions, and croutons. Add dressing and season to taste with salt and pepper. Toss well. Let stand for 15 minutes before serving.

SERVES 6 TO 8

Steakhouse Tomato and Sweet Onion Salad with BBQ Dressing

One of my favorite menu items when eating in some of America's greatest steakhouses is a beefsteak tomato and onion salad. I especially like it when the salad is garnished with crumbled French or Danish blue cheese. It is a really easy recipe. All you need is wonderful fresh beefsteak tomatoes and sweet onions—and of course the awesome dressing.

4 large beefsteak tomatoes
2 large sweet onions (Vidalia, Texas Sweet,
    or Maui)
Freshly ground black pepper
1 TB. chopped fresh basil
Crumbled blue cheese

BBQ DRESSING
1 (28 oz.) can plum tomatoes, seeded and
    drained

2 anchovy fillets
1 cup gourmet BBQ sauce
3 TB. grated horseradish (jarred will do)
2 TB. cider vinegar
1 TB. chopped fresh basil
1 TB. chopped garlic
2 tsp. Bone Dust BBQ Spice (page 203)
Salt and pepper to taste
½ cup olive oil

Slice tomatoes into ½-inch-thick rounds. Slice onions into ¼-inch-thick rounds. On a large platter, alternate slices of tomato and onion. Season with pepper to taste.

To make dressing, place tomatoes, anchovies, BBQ sauce, horseradish, vinegar, bail, garlic Bone Dust BBQ Spice, salt, and pepper in a food processor. Pulse until smooth. Turn on the processor and slowly add olive oil until dressing is emulsified.

Spoon dressing over tomato and onion slices. Garnish with chopped basil and crumbled blue cheese.

SERVES 8

Red Beet Salad with Honey Orange Vinaigrette

For a little change to this salad, try roasting the beets instead of boiling them. It brings out their natural sweetness.

---

5 beets, cooked, cooled, and peeled

1 onion, thinly sliced

1 orange, peeled and cut in segments

1 TB. chopped fresh thyme

1 tsp. coarsely ground black pepper

¼ cup orange juice

3 TB. olive oil

1 TB. orange blossom honey

Salt

Tip

In season look for golden white beets. Great sweet flavor with a different look!

Slice beets in half lengthwise, then thinly slice crosswise.

In a medium bowl, thoroughly combine beets, onion, orange segments, thyme, and pepper.

In a small bowl, whisk together orange juice, olive oil, and honey. Pour over beet mixture and mix thoroughly. Season to taste with salt.

Chill and serve.

SERVES 8

Grilled New Potato and Cheddar Salad

Buy the smallest red and white new potatoes you can find. This way you might not have to cut the potatoes for the salad. Using a grill basket for the potatoes will make grilling them a lot easier.

1 lb. mini red new potatoes	1 TB. chopped fresh parsley
1 lb. mini white new potatoes	1 to 2 tsp. Bone Dust BBQ Spice (page 203)
1 small red onion, diced	½ cup mayonnaise
1 cup shredded yellow cheddar cheese	2 TB. red wine vinegar
1 TB. chopped garlic	1 TB. Dijon mustard
1 TB. chopped fresh rosemary	Salt and pepper

In a large pot of salted water, boil potatoes for 15 to 20 minutes or until just tender. Drain and cool.

Preheat grill to medium-high.

If necessary, cut potatoes into halves or quarters to make bite-size pieces. Place in a grilling basket and grill for 15 minutes or until lightly charred and tender, turning the basket twice. Transfer potatoes to a large bowl.

Add onion, cheese, garlic, rosemary, parsley, and Bone Dust BBQ Spice. Mix well.

In a small bowl, whisk together mayonnaise, vinegar, and mustard. Pour over potato mixture. Season to taste with salt and pepper and mix thoroughly.

Chill and serve.

SERVES 8

Grilled Spicy Potato Salad with Tart Apples

The tartness of the apples cools the heat of the habanero chili pepper. Wear rubber gloves when seeding the habanero peppers—they're *hot!*

6 Yukon Gold potatoes
1 sweet onion, sliced ½-inch thick
1 red bell pepper, sliced ½-inch thick
1 poblano pepper, sliced ½-inch thick
2 TB. vegetable oil
2 tsp. Bone Dust BBQ Spice (page 203)
2 Granny Smith apples
1 TB. lemon juice

DRESSING
1 to 2 (if you dare) habanero peppers, seeded
2 TB. lemon juice
2 TB. white vinegar
1 TB. chopped garlic
1 TB. chopped fresh cilantro
1 tsp. sugar
⅓ cup vegetable oil
Salt and pepper

Cook potatoes in a pot of boiling salted water for 20 minutes or until just tender. Drain and let cool. Cut potatoes into ½-inch-thick slices.

In a bowl, gently toss together potatoes, onion, red pepper, poblano pepper, vegetable oil, and Bone Dust BBQ Spice. Place vegetables in a grill basket.

Cut apples into 1-inch cubes and toss with lemon juice to keep apples from turning brown. Set aside.

Preheat grill to high.

While the grill is heating, make dressing. In a food processor purée until smooth habanero peppers, lemon juice, vinegar, garlic, cilantro, and sugar. Slowly add oil until dressing is emulsified. Season to taste with salt and pepper.

Grill vegetables, turning occasionally, for 10 to 15 minutes or until slightly charred. Transfer to a large bowl.

Drain apples and add to vegetables. Pour over dressing, season to taste, and mix thoroughly.

SERVES 8

Green Mango Salad

While in Chicago, it is a must to eat at Arun's, Chicago's best Thai restaurant. This salad is delightfully spicy.

1 green mango, peeled and pitted
1 red bell pepper, cut into thin strips
1 green bell pepper, cut into thin strips
1 red onion, thinly sliced
1 TB. chopped fresh cilantro

DRESSING
¼ cup Sweet Thai Chili Sauce
3 TB. rice vinegar
2 TB. vegetable oil
1 TB. finely chopped garlic
2 tsp. sugar
1 tsp. finely chopped fresh ginger
Salt and pepper

Cut mango into batons about ½-inch thick and 3 inches long. Place in a large bowl. Add red pepper, green pepper, red onion, and cilantro.

In a small bowl, whisk together Sweet Thai Chili Sauce, rice vinegar, vegetable oil, garlic, sugar, and ginger.

Pour dressing over mango mixture and season to taste with salt and pepper. Toss well.

Chill and serve.

SERVES 6

Tip

A green mango is an unripe mango. It has a sour flavor—which is why this salad has a sweet dressing.

Grilled Zucchini Salad with Roasted Tomato Vinaigrette

Be careful not to overgrill the zucchini or it will turn mushy and brown.

VINAIGRETTE
6 plum tomatoes
3 TB. roasted garlic olive oil
2 TB. balsamic vinegar
1 TB. chopped garlic
1 TB. chopped fresh oregano
Salt and pepper

4 zucchini, sliced diagonally ½-inch thick
1 large sweet onion, sliced
2 TB. balsamic vinegar
2 TB. roasted garlic olive oil
¼ cup chopped fresh basil
2 TB. grated Parmesan cheese

Preheat grill to medium-high.

Place tomatoes on the grill. Reduce heat to medium and roast tomatoes, turning occasionally, for 10 to 15 minutes or until charred and tender. Be careful when turning tomatoes, as they will be soft. Do not turn off the grill.

Let cool. Remove and discard skin.

Place tomatoes in a food processor. Add oil, vinegar, garlic, and oregano. Pulse until smooth. Season to taste with salt and pepper. Set vinaigrette aside.

In a large bowl, toss together zucchini and onion. Add balsamic vinegar, oil, and salt and pepper to taste. Mix thoroughly. Place zucchini mixture in a grill basket.

Grill for 10 to 15 minutes or until zucchini and onions are tender and slightly charred.

Transfer vegetables to a large bowl. Add vinaigrette, toss well and season to taste. Garnish with basil and Parmesan cheese.

SERVES 8

Grilled Bread Salad with Gorgonzola

If you can't find creamy Gorgonzola blue cheese use Cambazola or Roquefort or Maytag Blue.

---

1 loaf crusty Italian white bread
4 TB. balsamic vinegar (divided use)
3 TB. + ¼ cup roasted garlic olive oil
Salt and pepper
1 red onion, diced

1 roasted red bell pepper, diced
1 roasted yellow bell pepper, diced
1 bunch arugula, washed and patted dry
1 cup crumbled Gorgonzola
2 TB. chopped fresh basil

Slice bread in half lengthwise.

Mix together 2 tablespoons vinegar and 3 tablespoons oil. Season to taste with salt and pepper. Brush liberally onto the cut sides of the bread. Let marinate for 15 minutes.

In a large bowl, toss together red onion, red pepper, yellow pepper, arugula, Gorgonzola, and basil. Set aside.

Preheat grill to medium-high.

Grill bread, turning once, until lightly browned all over and crisp. Cut bread into 1-inch cubes and add to salad.

Add remaining ¼ cup oil and 2 tablespoons vinegar. Season with salt and pepper and toss thoroughly.

Serve immediately.

SERVES 8

Spicy Grilled Vegetable Salad with Smoked Chipotle Dressing

 Chipotle chilies are smoked jalapeño peppers. You can find them dried or wet in cans. If you're using dried chipotle chilies, soak them in warm water for 1 to 2 hours beforehand.

1 large red onion, sliced

2 zucchini, thinly sliced

8 large mushrooms, quartered

1 red bell pepper, sliced

1 yellow bell pepper, sliced

1 orange bell pepper, sliced

1 bunch asparagus cut into 2-inch pieces

2 TB. olive oil

1 TB. Bone Dust BBQ Spice (page 203)

1 TB. chopped fresh cilantro

Salt and pepper

DRESSING

½ (7 oz.) can chipotle chilies, puréed

¾ cup olive oil

½ cup cider vinegar

¼ cup honey

2 TB. chopped fresh cilantro

1 tsp. ground cumin

1 tsp. salt

2 limes, juiced

In a large bowl, toss all vegetables together. Season with oil and Bone Dust BBQ Spice. Toss. Place in a grill basket. Preheat grill to medium-high.

To make dressing, in a food processor combine chipotle chilies, oil, vinegar, honey, cilantro, cumin, salt, and lime juice. Blend until smooth.

Grill vegetables for 8 to 10 minutes per side until lightly charred and tender.

Transfer vegetables a large bowl. Toss with dressing and fresh cilantro. Season to taste with salt and pepper. Serve immediately.

SERVES 8

Cucumber and Horseradish Salad

Finely grated fresh horseradish is best in this salad. If you substitute prepared horseradish, make sure to drain it first.

---

1 English cucumber
1 red onion, thinly sliced
½ cup grated fresh horseradish
3 TB. olive oil

2 TB. chopped fresh mint
2 TB. lemon juice
1 tsp. ground cumin
Salt and pepper

Cut cucumber in half lengthwise. Thinly slice cucumber halves.

In a large bowl, toss together cucumber, onion, horseradish, oil, mint, lemon juice, and cumin. Season to taste with salt and pepper.

Chill and serve.

SERVES 6 TO 8

Grilled Leek and Shrimp Salad

Make sure you wash the leeks really well to get all the grit and sand out of them.

VINAIGRETTE

⅓ cup olive oil

¼ cup rice wine vinegar

2 TB. chopped fresh cilantro

1 TB. chopped fresh ginger

1 TB. Dijon mustard

2 green onions, finely chopped

Salt and pepper

4 large leeks, cut in half lengthwise

1 large red onion, sliced

1 red bell pepper, cubed

1 yellow bell pepper, cubed

1 lb. large shrimp, peeled and deveined

2 TB. olive oil

2 TB. rice wine vinegar

1 tsp. ground cumin

1 tsp. crushed chilies

Preheat grill to high.

To make vinaigrette, whisk together oil, vinegar, cilantro, ginger, mustard, green onions, and salt and pepper to taste. Set aside.

Cut leeks into 2-inch chunks and place in a large bowl. Add red onion, red and yellow peppers, shrimp, olive oil, vinegar, cumin, crushed chilies, and salt and pepper to taste. Gently toss to mix thoroughly. Place mixture in a grill basket.

Grill vegetables and shrimp for 4 to 5 minutes per side or until tender and slightly charred.

Carefully arrange vegetables and shrimp on a serving platter. Pour vinaigrette over top and serve.

SERVES 6 TO 8

Shrimp and Pasta Salad

Baby shrimp are plentiful in this recipe, but you can also grill jumbo shrimp for a different taste and texture.

1 lb. fusilli	**DRESSING**
1 lb. cold cooked baby shrimp	1 bunch Italian parsley, chopped
1 pint cherry tomatoes, stemmed and halved	2 TB. chopped garlic
1 shallot, finely diced	1 tsp. lemon zest
1 cup toasted walnut halves (divided use)	½ cup olive oil
	¼ cup lemon juice
	Salt and freshly ground black pepper

Cook pasta in a pot of boiling salted water until just tender. Drain pasta and spread evenly on a cookie sheet lined with wax paper to cool. Spread out pasta evenly to it cools and doesn't all stick together.

In a large bowl, place cooled pasta, shrimp, cherry tomatoes, shallots, and half the toasted walnuts.

To make dressing: Place parsley, remaining walnuts, garlic, and lemon zest in a food processor. Pulse until well blended and nuts are ground. Add olive oil and lemon juice. Pulse until fully mixed.

Pour dressing over pasta-shrimp mixture. Mix thoroughly and season to taste with salt and pepper.

Chill and serve.

SERVES 8

Sesame Shrimp and Snap Pea Salad

This is a very simple salad recipe. I like to use the best-quality sesame oil and rice vinegar that I can find. A perfect side dish for grilled tuna or salmon.

---

1 lb. (21 to 30 per lb.) jumbo shrimp, peeled
   and deveined
2 TB. salt
6 cups water
1 lemon, sliced
1 lb. sugar snap peas
1 cup sliced radishes

3 TB. rice wine vinegar
2 TB. chopped fresh cilantro
2 TB. dark Asian sesame oil
1 TB. black sesame seeds
1 TB. toasted white sesame seeds
Sea salt

Toss shrimp with salt. Let stand for 15 minutes, then rinse under cold running water.

Bring 6 cups water to a rolling boil. Add sliced lemon and shrimp; cook for 3 to 4 minutes or until shrimp are opaque and just cooked through. Drain and rinse under cold running water until shrimp are cool. Drain again.

Discard any sugar snap peas that are not perfect. Remove stem end and string from each pod.

In a bowl, toss together shrimp, sugar snap peas, radishes, vinegar, cilantro, sesame oil, and black and white sesame seeds.

Season to taste with sea salt and serve.

SERVES 6 TO 8

Grilled Portobello Mushroom Salad

Hearty, meaty-textured Portobello mushrooms are one of my favorite vegetables—or fungi—to grill. They're as good as a steak.

8 large Portobello mushrooms, stems removed
1 tsp. salt
4 cups hot water
½ cup honey
½ cup hoisin sauce
¼ cup soy sauce
¼ cup rice vinegar

1 TB. coarsely ground black pepper
1 TB. chopped fresh cilantro
1 TB. sesame seeds
1 TB. grainy mustard
1 tsp. dark Asian sesame oil
Salt
3 bunches arugula
½ cup crumbled goat cheese

Brush mushroom caps with a damp cloth to remove any dirt. Place mushrooms in a large bowl. Dissolve salt in hot water and pour over mushrooms, submerging mushroom caps so gills fill with water. Cover with plastic wrap and let mushrooms steep for 15 minutes.

Meanwhile, in a bowl, whisk together honey, hoisin sauce, soy sauce, vinegar, pepper, cilantro, sesame seeds, mustard, and sesame oil. Season to taste with salt.

Drain mushroom caps and pat dry with paper towels. Place mushroom caps gill side up in a glass dish. Pour honey-hoisin marinade over mushroom caps and let marinate for 2 hours.

Preheat grill to medium-high.

Remove mushroom caps from marinade, reserving marinade for basting. Place mushrooms gill side up on grill. Grill for 4 to 5 minutes per side, basting frequently with reserved marinade.

Remove mushrooms from grill and let stand for 3 minutes to slightly cool and set. Thinly slice mushrooms and serve each cap over a bed of arugula. Garnish with crumbled goat cheese.

Tip

Soak the mushrooms in warm water for 15 minutes so the mushrooms won't dry out when grilling and will remain tender.

SERVES 8

Marinated Mushroom Salad with Curried Raspberry Vinaigrette

Pouring a warm dressing over the mushrooms tenderizes them.

---

1 lb. button mushrooms, cleaned and quartered if large

½ lb. oyster mushrooms, cleaned and torn

½ lb. cremini mushrooms, cleaned and quartered if large

½ lb. shiitake mushrooms, cleaned and thinly sliced

1 large red onion, diced

1 bunch green onions, thinly sliced

2 red bell peppers, thinly sliced

1 TB. chopped fresh rosemary

4 cloves garlic, chopped

½ cup vegetable oil

¼ cup raspberry vinegar

1 TB. sugar

1 tsp. curry powder

Salt and pepper

In a large bowl, combine mushrooms, red onion, green onions, red peppers, rosemary, and garlic.

In a small saucepan, mix oil, raspberry vinegar, sugar, and curry powder. Slowly heat dressing, stirring, but do not let it boil.

Pour hot dressing over mushroom mixture and toss gently. Season to taste with salt and pepper.

Cover and let mushrooms marinate for 4 hours until tender. Adjust seasoning, gently mix, and serve.

SERVES 6 TO 8

Singapore Noodle Salad

You can find Singapore noodles in Asian markets and specialty food stores. Look for a yellow spaghettilike (but wider) egg noodle. (You can also find great BBQ pork tenderloin and roast pork in Asian markets.)

1 lb. Singapore noodles
½ lb. barbecued pork, shredded
1 red onion, thinly sliced
6 green onions, thinly sliced
1 green bell pepper, thinly sliced
1 red bell pepper, thinly sliced
2 oranges, peeled and cut in segments
¼ cup vegetable oil

¼ cup orange juice
2 TB. soy sauce
1 TB. chopped fresh cilantro
1 tsp. curry powder
1 tsp. sesame oil
1 tsp. Asian hot sauce
Salt and pepper to taste

Cook noodles according to package instructions. Drain, cool under cold running water, and drain again.

In a large bowl, combine noodles, pork, red onion, green onions, green and red peppers, orange segments, vegetable oil, orange juice, soy sauce, cilantro, curry powder, sesame oil, hot sauce, salt, and pepper. Toss well and serve.

SERVES 6 TO 8

Ruby Red Cabbage Slaw

Don't make this salad too far in advance or it will lose its brilliant color and crisp texture.

---

1 small red cabbage, thinly sliced	1 red onion, thinly sliced
½ cup vegetable oil	4 green onions, thinly sliced
¼ cup cider vinegar	2 Granny Smith apples, thinly sliced
1 TB. mustard seeds	1 TB. chopped fresh parsley
1 TB. brown sugar	1 TB. chopped fresh thyme
1 tsp. mustard powder	1 tsp. toasted caraway seeds
Salt and pepper	

In a large bowl, mix together cabbage, oil, vinegar, mustard seeds, brown sugar, mustard powder, and salt and pepper to taste. Mix thoroughly. Cover and let marinate for 2 hours or until cabbage is tender.

Add red onion, green onions, apples, parsley, thyme, and caraway seeds. Toss well, adjust seasoning, and serve.

SERVES 8

Memphis-Style Creamy Coleslaw

I have spent a fair amount of time in Memphis, the mecca of ribs in the South. Nothing goes better with ribs or BBQ than a creamy coleslaw. It is almost traditional.

½ green cabbage, very finely sliced
2 large carrots, grated
1 onion, finely chopped
3 green onions, chopped
2 TB. sugar
1 TB. white vinegar

½ tsp. salt
½ cup mayonnaise
2 tsp. mustard powder
1 tsp. black pepper
¼ tsp. cayenne pepper

In a large bowl, combine cabbage, carrots, onion, green onions, sugar, vinegar, and salt. Let marinate for 1 to 2 hours, tossing occasionally.

Mix in mayonnaise, mustard powder, black pepper, and cayenne.

Refrigerate until ready to serve.

SERVES 8

Firecracker Coleslaw

A rainbow of colors makes this coleslaw festive and the Spicy Grilled Jalapeño Dressing gives it a bang.

---

1 small white cabbage, thinly sliced

2 carrots, grated

1 red onion, sliced

1 large red bell pepper, julienned

1 large green bell pepper, julienned

1 large yellow bell pepper, julienned

1 large orange bell pepper, julienned

1 bunch green onions, thinly sliced

¼ cup chopped fresh cilantro

1 cup Spicy Grilled Jalapeño Dressing (page 34)

Hot sauce

Salt and pepper

In a large bowl, combine cabbage, carrots, onion, bell peppers, green onions, and cilantro.

Place jalapeño dressing in a microwave-safe container and heat in a microwave on high for 30 to 45 seconds. Pour warm dressing over cabbage mixture. Season to taste with hot sauce, salt, and pepper.

Mix thoroughly, chill, and serve.

SERVES 8

Cheesy Macaroni Salad

This is a great picnic or cottage party salad. What truly makes it is the variety of cheeses. I like to use strong-flavored cheeses. Look for the double elbow macaroni known as gemelli. The noodles are larger than regular macaroni and make the presentation of the salad much nicer.

1 lb. double elbow macaroni (gemelli)	1 red onion, thinly sliced
2 TB. olive oil	1 carrot, peeled and grated
1 cup mayonnaise	½ cup shredded medium or old yellow cheddar cheese
½ cup sour cream	½ cup shredded old white cheddar cheese
2 TB. white wine vinegar	½ cup shredded Emmenthal cheese
2 TB. lemon juice	¼ cup grated Parmesan cheese
1 tsp. paprika	¼ cup chopped fresh parsley
1 tsp. ground cumin	1 TB. chopped fresh dill
1 tsp. black pepper	Salt and pepper
1 bunch green onions, thinly sliced	

Cook pasta in a pot of boiling salted water until al dente (just tender). Drain, toss with olive oil, and let cool.

In a large bowl, whisk together mayonnaise, sour cream, vinegar, lemon juice, paprika, cumin, and black pepper. Add pasta, green onions, red onion, carrot, all four cheeses, parsley, and dill. Mix well. Season to taste with salt and pepper.

Cover and refrigerate for 1 to 2 hours before serving.

SERVES 8

Luxurious Appetizers

Ultimate BBQ Dip for Chips

Buy chips, make dip, dunk chips, and eat. Repeat, repeat, repeat …

1 cup softened cream cheese	2 shallots, diced
¾ cup sour cream	2 green onions, chopped
¼ to ½ cup hickory smoke–flavored BBQ sauce	1 TB. Bone Dust BBQ Spice (page 203)
	1 tsp. Worcestershire sauce
1 TB. maple syrup	Your favorite chips and crudités

In a food processor, blend cream cheese, sour cream, BBQ sauce, and maple syrup until smooth. Add shallots, green onions, Bone Dust BBQ Spice, and Worcestershire sauce. Pulse until fully mixed. Transfer to a serving bowl and chill. Serve with chips and vegetables.

MAKES ABOUT 2½ CUPS

Grilled Eggplant Antipasto Bundles

This is an easy hors d'oeuvre that you can prepare in advance so you, too, can enjoy the party.

1 large firm eggplant	¼ cup chopped oil-packed sun-dried tomatoes
¼ cup + 1 TB. balsamic vinegar	2 TB. chopped flat-leaf parsley
¼ cup olive oil	1 TB. chopped fresh basil
1 TB. Bone Dust BBQ Spice (page 203)	Salt and pepper to taste
2 green onions, chopped	2 to 3 large vine-ripened tomatoes
1 shallot, finely chopped	Fresh basil leaves and freshly grated Parmesan cheese,
¾ cup goat cheese	for garnish

Cut ½ inch off the top and bottom of eggplant. Stand eggplant upright and cut it into eight ¼-inch-thick slices. Rinse eggplant slices under cold water. Place eggplant slices in a bowl and add ¼ cup balsamic vinegar, olive oil, and Bone Dust BBQ Spice. Toss gently to coat evenly. Let marinate for 15 minutes.

Meanwhile, preheat grill to medium-high.

Remove eggplant from marinade (reserving any remaining marinade). Grill eggplant slices until cooked through and lightly charred, 4 to 5 minutes per side. Remove from grill, brush with reserved marinade, and let cool.

Preheat oven to 325°F.

In a small bowl, combine green onions, shallot, goat cheese, sun-dried tomatoes, parsley, basil, remaining 1 table-spoon balsamic vinegar, salt, and pepper. Spread 1 heaping tablespoon goat cheese mixture evenly over each egg-plant slice. Roll up eggplant tightly from the thin end. Secure with a toothpick if necessary.

Arrange eggplant bundles on a baking sheet. Bake bundles just until cheese starts to melt, 5 to 10 minutes.

To serve, slice each tomato into eight ½-inch-thick slices. Arrange tomatoes on plates or a platter. Drizzle tomatoes with olive oil and balsamic vinegar. Top each with a warmed eggplant bundle. Garnish with basil leaves and Parmesan cheese.

SERVES 4 TO 8

Portobello Mushrooms Stuffed with BBQ Pulled Pork

These stuffed mushrooms can be a perfect appetizer or even a main course.

---

8 large Portobello mushroom caps

MARINADE
4 cloves garlic, minced
1½ cups vegetable oil
1½ cups apple cider vinegar
1 cup maple syrup
1 cup gourmet BBQ sauce
2 TB. Herb Mustard Rub (page 208)

STUFFING
1 red onion, lightly grilled and sliced
4 green onions, sliced
1 red bell pepper, diced
1 green bell pepper, diced
4 cups shredded cheese (cheddar and Monterey Jack)
2 cups pulled Redneck Riviera Smoked Boston Butt (page 318)
½ cup gourmet BBQ sauce
¼ cup maple syrup
2 TB. Herb Mustard Rub (page 208)

Soak mushroom caps in hot water for 15 minutes. Drain on paper towels.

Make marinade: In a large bowl, whisk together garlic, oil, vinegar, maple syrup, BBQ sauce, and Herb Mustard Rub. Add mushroom caps, turning to coat well. Let marinate for 1 hour.

Preheat grill to medium-high.

Grill mushrooms gill side up, turning once, until lightly charred and tender, 4 to 5 minutes per side. Let cool. Reduce grill temperature to medium.

Make stuffing: In a medium bowl, stir together red onion, green onions, red pepper, green pepper, cheese, pulled pork, BBQ sauce, maple syrup, and Herb Mustard Rub. Using a ½-cup ice cream scoop, top each mushroom cap with 1 scoop stuffing.

Return mushrooms to the hot grill. Close the lid and bake until stuffing is hot, 10 to 12 minutes.

SERVES 8

Grilled Prosciutto-Wrapped Figs Stuffed with Gorgonzola and Walnuts

Use only fresh figs for this starter. Dried figs will overcook on the grill and be tough.

---

8 large ripe Black Mission or green figs
½ cup crumbled Gorgonzola cheese, softened
¼ cup walnut pieces
2 TB. honey

1 TB. balsamic vinegar
2 tsp. chopped fresh rosemary
Salt and freshly ground black pepper
8 slices prosciutto

Preheat grill to medium-high.

Cut off figs stems and cut figs three-quarters the way down through the center. Do not cut all the way through.

In a small bowl, combine Gorgonzola, walnuts, honey, balsamic vinegar, and rosemary. Season to taste with salt and pepper. Divide cheese mixture into eight equal portions. Stuff each fig with cheese mixture, pressing lightly to fill fig cavity. Carefully wrap each fig with one slice prosciutto.

Place figs on the grill with cheese filling facing upward. Grill for 3 to 4 minutes to crisp prosciutto. Carefully move figs to a cool part of the grill. Close the lid and bake figs until cheese is melting and prosciutto is crispy, about 5 minutes.

Serve figs with baby greens and drizzled with balsamic vinegar.

SERVES 4 TO 8

Grill-Roasted Sweet Pepper and Goat Cheese Bruschetta

This is a favorite around the backyard grill. It's easy to prepare and is a perfect starter to any party. This dish is also great with grilled mushrooms, eggplant, or peaches.

1 red bell pepper	2 TB. balsamic vinegar
1 yellow bell pepper	1 TB. chopped fresh oregano
1 orange bell pepper	1 TB. lemon juice
1 green bell pepper	Salt and pepper to taste
1 small red onion, quartered	8 (¾-inch-thick) slices rustic Italian bread
3 cloves garlic, minced	1 cup soft creamy goat cheese
¼ cup olive oil	

Preheat grill to medium-high.

Grill-roast peppers and onion, turning occasionally, until peppers are charred black and blistered and onion is lightly charred and tender, 10 to 15 minutes.

Transfer hot peppers to a large bowl and cover with plastic wrap. Let stand for 10 minutes. Peel and seed peppers and pat dry with paper towels. Cut peppers into ½-inch-thick slices. Return to bowl. Thinly slice onion and add to peppers. Add garlic, oil, vinegar, oregano, lemon juice, salt, and pepper. Toss well.

Grill bread slices for 1 to 2 minutes per side or until crisp. Spread each slice with 1 heaping tablespoon goat cheese. Sprinkle with black pepper. Top with roasted pepper mixture. Drizzle with extra olive oil and balsamic vinegar.

SERVES 8

Cedar-Planked Brie with Oyster Mushroom and Roasted Garlic Crust

I have a similar recipe in my cookbook *Sticks and Stones: The Art of Grilling on Plank, Vine and Stone.* For your next party, plank a few wheels of Brie and watch your guests go crazy. This is a showstopper and one of my personal favorites.

3 TB. olive oil

2 shallots, diced

3 cups sliced oyster mushrooms

Salt and pepper

2 small (each 125 g) Brie wheels

1 head roasted garlic (page 201)

2 green onions, finely chopped

2 TB. chopped fresh thyme

2 TB. apple cider vinegar

2 TB. olive oil

2 tsp. coarsely ground black pepper

Special equipment: 1 untreated cedar plank (at least 6 × 12 inches and ½ inch thick), soaked in water for 2 hours

Heat oil in a large frying pan over medium-high heat. Cook shallots and mushrooms, stirring occasionally, until mushrooms are tender, 5 to 6 minutes. Season with salt and pepper to taste. Let cool.

Preheat the grill to high.

Cut the top rind off the Brie.

In a bowl, mash roasted garlic with a fork. Stir in sautéed mushrooms, green onions, thyme, vinegar, oil, pepper, and salt to taste. Spread mushroom mixture evenly over Brie wheels.

Place the plank on the grill and close the lid. Let the plank heat until it starts to crackle, 5 to 7 minutes. (If the wood catches fire, use a spray bottle of water to put out the flames.) Carefully open the lid (it will be smoky) and place cheese on the plank. Close the lid and bake cheese until it begins to melt and bubble, 8 to 10 minutes.

Remove planked cheese from the grill. Serve with fresh baguettes and plenty of napkins. This is truly oooeey-gooeey good.

SERVES 8

Grilled Shrimp with Mango Chutney

Use jumbo shrimp for this recipe. Larger shrimp tend to be a little more forgiving on the grill and will not overcook too quickly.

MANGO CHUTNEY

2 ripe mangos, peeled and diced
2 small red chilies, finely chopped
½ cup sugar
½ cup water
2 TB. chopped fresh ginger
2 TB. lemon juice
1 tsp. black pepper
1 tsp. cinnamon
¼ tsp. nutmeg
Salt to taste

MARINADE AND BASTE

4 cloves garlic, minced
¼ cup vegetable oil
¼ cup Grand Marnier
¼ cup mango juice or orange juice
1 TB. chopped fresh thyme
1 TB. Bay Seasoning (page 205)
2 tsp. curry powder
1 tsp. crushed red chilies

24 jumbo shrimp (1½ to 2 lbs.), peeled and deveined

To make chutney, in a medium saucepan over medium-high heat, combine mangos, chilies, sugar, water, ginger, lemon juice, black pepper, cinnamon, nutmeg, and salt. Bring to a boil, reduce heat to medium-low, and simmer, stirring occasionally, until chutney is thick, about 15 minutes. Let cool.

To make marinade, in a small bowl, whisk together garlic, oil, Grand Marnier, mango juice, thyme, Bay Seasoning, curry powder, and crushed chilies. Add shrimp, stirring to coat. Marinate for 20 minutes.

Meanwhile, soak 24 bamboo skewers in water for 20 minutes. Preheat grill to medium-high.

Skewer one shrimp onto the end of each bamboo skewer. Reserve marinade for basting. Grill shrimp, basting with reserved marinade, until opaque and just firm to the touch, 3 to 4 minutes per side. Serve immediately with mango chutney for dipping.

SERVES 8

Jamaica Roadside Shrimp Boil

While traveling around Jamaica, I grabbed every opportunity to devour tasty bags of peppery roadside shrimp. Even though these shrimp aren't fresh out of the fishing nets, here's my delicious version. Buy live shrimp if you can find them. They have the most flavor, and it's a lot of fun to eat them whole. Pull the head from the body and suck the head for all its salty goodness, then peel the body and eat the meat.

1 onion, sliced	4 cups water
1 Scotch bonnet pepper, sliced	¼ cup Bone Dust BBQ Spice (page 203)
4 cloves garlic, chopped	2 TB. salt
2 sprigs fresh thyme	2 lbs. jumbo shrimp, unpeeled
2 bottles beer	

In a large soup pot over high heat, bring onion, Scotch bonnet pepper, garlic, thyme, beer, water, Bone Dust BBQ Spice, and salt to a rolling boil.

Add shrimp and boil until shrimp are just cooked through and firm to the touch, 8 to 10 minutes.

Drain shrimp and serve immediately with lemon wedges and plenty of napkins.

SERVES 4 TO 6

Smoked Scallops with Prosciutto, Pistachios, and Three-Citrus Salsa

Scallops smoked in a conventional smoker have a firm but tender texture and golden brown color. If you do not have a smoker, grill the scallops until just cooked through, 2 to 3 minutes per side. Let cool and then follow the remaining instructions.

24 jumbo sea scallops (about 2 lbs.)
3 TB. Bay Seasoning (page 205)
Hickory or peach smoking chips
16 thin slices prosciutto, torn in half lengthwise
½ cup coarsely crushed pistachios
Arugula

THREE-CITRUS SALSA
1 lemon
2 limes
1 seedless orange
½ small red onion, diced
1 jalapeño pepper, seeded and finely diced
1 red bell pepper, diced

1 green onion, finely chopped
1 TB. chopped fresh mint
1 TB. honey
1 TB. lemon juice
1 TB. olive oil
1 tsp. chopped fresh ginger
Salt and pepper to taste

Tip

Buy large, firm scallops and ask for the freshest available. Make sure they have not been packed in heavy brine.

Prepare your smoker according to manufacturer's instructions to a temperature of 175°F.

Rub scallops with Bay Seasoning, pressing seasoning into meat. Arrange scallops on the top rack of the smoker. Close lid and smoke scallops for 1½ to 2 hours, replenishing smoking chips, coals, and water as required. Scallops are done when they are firm to the touch and a uniform pearly white color inside. Remove scallops from smoker and let cool.

To make salsa, cut the top and bottom off the lemon, limes, and orange. Stand each fruit on one end and cut away the peel and pith from top to bottom. Working over a bowl to catch the juices, cut alongside each membrane to remove fruit segments. Squeeze any liquid from the membranes over the fruit. Add red onion, jalapeños, red pepper, green onion, mint, honey, lemon juice, oil, ginger, salt, and pepper. Stir well.

To serve, slice each scallop into three rounds. Fan three scallops in the center of each plate to form a circle. Fill the center of scallop ring with 2 tablespoons salsa. Top with a few ribbons of prosciutto and garnish with crushed pistachios. Arrange some arugula alongside and drizzle arugula with olive oil.

SERVES 8

Champagne Oyster Shooters with Mango Salsa

During a taping of one my *King of the Q* episodes, one of my guests proposed to his girlfriend. He dropped to one knee and popped the big question: Do you like oysters? Because if you don't we can't get married. She said yes, and I prepared them their engagement shooters on the beaches of Jamaica.

Okay, it didn't happen exactly like that, but it was on camera, she said yes, and they had oysters before the question popping.

MANGO SALSA
1 shallot, finely chopped
1 green onion, finely chopped
1 cup diced peeled mango
1 TB. chopped fresh cilantro
1 TB. olive oil

1 TB. lime juice
1 tsp. habanero hot sauce
Salt and pepper to taste

8 large fresh oysters, ice cold
Chilled champagne

Prepare mango salsa by combining shallot, green onion, mango, cilantro, oil, lime juice, hot sauce, salt, and pepper. Shuck oysters and place one oyster in each of eight shot glasses. Top each oyster with 1 tablespoon mango salsa. Fill each glass to the brim with champagne. Shoot 'em back. Ask for more and keep on loving.

SERVES 2 TO 4

Grilled Chesapeake Bay Crab Cakes with Bacon Ranch Dipping Sauce

The best crab cakes come from the Captain's Gallery restaurant in the crab capital of America, Crisfield, Maryland. These cakes are best if made with fresh crab meat from the Chesapeake Bay, but you can substitute snow or Dungeness crab.

---

1 medium egg
2 green onions, thinly sliced
½ cup mayonnaise
1 TB. chopped fresh dill
1 TB. lemon juice
1 tsp. finely chopped garlic

1 tsp. Bay Seasoning (page 205)
1½ lbs. cooked fresh Chesapeake Bay blue crabmeat
Salt and pepper
Hot sauce
2 cups coarse cracker crumbs

Preheat gill to medium. Spray a grill topper with nonstick cooking spray.

In a large bowl, whisk together egg, green onion, mayonnaise, dill, lemon juice, garlic, and Bay Seasoning. Gently fold in crabmeat. Season to taste with salt, pepper, and hot sauce.

Add cracker crumbs and mix gently until mixture binds together loosely. Form into eight cakes. (An ice-cream scoop makes this job a little easier.)

Place lobster cakes on grill topper and grill, without turning, until crisp on the outside and heated through, 12 to 15 minutes. If you want, you can baste them with melted butter. I would.

Serve with Bacon Ranch Dipping Sauce (recipe follows).

SERVES 8

Bacon Ranch Dipping Sauce

4 slices bacon, diced and cooked crisp

1 shallot, diced

2 green onions, finely chopped

1 cup sour cream

1 cup ranch dressing

1 cup mayonnaise

¼ cup grated Parmesan cheese

1 TB. chopped fresh herbs (parsley, dill, and thyme)

1 TB. Worcestershire sauce

2 tsp. cracked black pepper

Hot sauce and salt to taste

In a bowl, whisk together all ingredients.

MAKES ABOUT 4 CUPS

Smoked Chicken Wings

Doing your own smoking is quite rewarding and not as difficult as you may think. It does take a little extra patience, but the results are delicious. For this recipe I like to use whole chicken wings, tips attached. Serve these babies with lots of ice-cold beer.

5 lbs. jumbo whole chicken wings
1 cup Bone Dust BBQ Spice (page 203)
Hickory smoking chips
½ cup gourmet BBQ sauce

¼ cup Sriacha chili sauce
¼ cup melted butter
2 TB. lemon juice

Tip

You can find Sriacha chili sauce in Asian food stores.

Season chicken wings with Bone BBQ Dust Spice, rubbing spices into meat. Set aside.

Prepare your smoker according to manufacturer's instructions, with about 12 coals. Bring smoker to 200°F. Adjust vents to maintain this temperature.

Place chicken wings on smoker racks, place lid on smoker, and add soaked hickory smoking chips. Smoke wings until fully cooked and firm to the touch, 2½ to 3 hours, adding coals, wood chips, and water as necessary.

While wings are smoking, prepare sauce. In a small saucepan over medium heat, whisk together BBQ sauce, chili sauce, butter, and lemon juice. Bring to a low boil and simmer for 5 minutes. Set aside. Just before wings are done, reheat sauce.

Remove wings from smoker and toss in hot BBQ sauce. Consume immediately.

SERVES 6 TO 8

Sticky Honey Garlic Ginger Chicken Wings

What goes with chicken wings best? Ice-cold frosty beer. With these sticky wings I recommend honey brown lager for the guzzling. Also have lots of wet naps and napkins on hand.

3 lbs. jumbo chicken wings (about 36)	2 TB. finely chopped fresh garlic
¼ cup Indonesian Cinnamon Rub (page 209)	2 TB. lemon juice
2 TB. vegetable oil	2 tsp. sesame oil
½ cup honey	Salt and pepper to taste
¼ cup soy sauce	2 green onions, chopped
2 TB. finely chopped fresh ginger	1 TB. toasted sesame seeds

Trim wing tips from chicken wings and save for another use. Cut wing in half at the joint. Place wing pieces in a large bowl and toss with Indonesian Cinnamon Rub and vegetable oil. Marinate, covered and refrigerated, for 24 hours.

To make sauce, in a large bowl, combine honey, soy sauce, ginger, garlic, lemon juice, sesame oil, salt, and pepper. Set aside.

Preheat grill to medium.

Place chicken wings in a grill basket. Grill wings, turning every 5 or 6 minutes, until fully cooked, golden brown and crisp, 10 to 12 minutes per side.

Remove wings from grill basket and add to sauce. Add green onions and sesame seeds. Toss well and serve immediately.

SERVES 4

Kama Sutra Cinnamon-Skewered Chicken Thighs

This is one of my favorite grilling recipes. The combination of cinnamon and chicken makes for an exotic appetizer worthy of any Kama Sutra lover.

6 boneless, skin-on chicken thighs
2 TB. Indonesian Cinnamon Rub (page 209)
12 thin cinnamon sticks, at least 6 inches long
6 cloves garlic, chopped

½ cup honey
¼ cup melted butter
2 TB. curry paste
1 TB. finely chopped fresh ginger

Tip

I find my cinnamon sticks for skewering at bulk spice shops and in the bulk section of grocery stores. Prepackaged or jarred cinnamon sticks are usually not long enough.

Preheat grill to medium-high.

Rub chicken thighs with Indonesian Cinnamon Rub, pressing spices into meat. Cut chicken thighs in half lengthwise. Skewer each half onto the end of a cinnamon stick.

In a small bowl, whisk together garlic, honey, butter, curry paste, and ginger.

Grill chicken thighs, basting generously with sauce, until chicken is fully cooked, 4 to 6 minutes per side.

SERVES 6

Grilled BBQ Chicken Quesadillas

Lots of cheese and lots of chicken produces lots of ooey-gooey goodness. Be careful not to burn the tortillas on the grill.

3 (each 6 oz.) boneless, skinless chicken breasts

2 TB. Bone Dust BBQ Spice (page 203)

1 cup hickory smoke–flavored BBQ sauce (divided use)

2 ears corn on the cob, boiled

3 cloves garlic, minced

1 small red onion, diced

1 jalapeño pepper, seeded and finely diced

1 yellow bell pepper, diced

1 TB. chopped fresh cilantro

Salt and pepper

8 (7 inch) flour tortillas

2 cups shredded Monterey Jack cheese

1 cup shredded cheddar cheese

Oil

Preheat grill to medium-high.

Rub chicken breasts with Bone Dust BBQ Spice, pressing spices into meat. Grill chicken, basting with ½ cup BBQ sauce, until fully cooked, 5 to 6 minutes per side. Let cool. Thinly slice across the grain. Set aside.

Working over a large bowl, slice corn kernels from cobs. Add garlic, onion, jalapeño, yellow pepper, cilantro, salt, pepper, and ¼ cup BBQ sauce.

Brush four tortillas with remaining ¼ cup BBQ sauce, leaving a ½-inch border around the edge. Mix cheeses together. Sprinkle half cheese over each tortilla. Spread 2 tablespoons corn mixture evenly over cheese. Top with chicken, then remaining corn salsa and cheese. Moisten edges of tortillas with water and top with the remaining tortillas, pressing down firmly on the edges to seal.

Preheat grill to medium.

Brush each tortilla with oil. Grill tortillas, turning once, until lightly charred and crisp and cheese is melted, 2 to 4 minutes per side.

Let cool for 5 minutes. Cut into wedges and serve with Ultimate BBQ Dip (page 76).

SERVES 8

Lamb Chops with Dijon Goat Cheese Dunk

Use small, tender lamb. Use racks that tend to have smaller loins, which makes these chops a perfect size for bite-size hors d'oeuvres. This Dijon Goat Cheese Dunk is also good for dunking your favorite body parts.

2 frenched lamb racks (5 to 7 ribs each)
¼ cup Old Montreal Steak Spice (page 202)
¼ cup olive oil
¼ cup balsamic vinegar
2 cloves garlic, minced
½ cup softened goat cheese
¼ cup softened cream cheese

¼ cup maple syrup
¼ cup Dijon mustard
2 TB. lemon juice
1 TB. chopped fresh rosemary
1 TB. prepared horseradish
Salt and pepper to taste

Cut between rib bones to make chops about ¾ inch thick. Rub chops with Old Montreal Steak Spice, pressing spices into meat. Place chops in a glass dish large enough to hold them in one layer, and drizzle with olive oil and balsamic vinegar. Turn to coat. Let marinate for 30 minutes.

Meanwhile, in a small bowl, stir together garlic, goat cheese, cream cheese, maple syrup, mustard, lemon juice, rosemary, horseradish, salt, and pepper. Transfer to a serving bowl.

Preheat grill to medium-high.

Grill lamb chops for 3 to 5 minutes per side for medium doneness. Transfer to a serving platter.

To enjoy, dunk chops into Dijon Goat Cheese Dunk.

SERVES 4 TO 6

Peach and Pork Satays

When grilling satays, place the meat over the heat near the edge of the grill, leaving the exposed bamboo skewer hanging off the edge of the grill. This will allow you to turn the skewers easily without burning your fingertips.

---

2 lbs. pork tenderloin, trimmed
4 cloves garlic, minced
½ cup Southern Comfort
½ cup peach or orange juice
2 TB. Bone Dust BBQ Spice (page 203)
2 TB. vegetable oil
1 TB. chopped fresh oregano
1 TB. crushed red chilies

2 ripe peaches, each cut into 8 wedges
Cracked black pepper
8 slices bacon, partially cooked

SOUTHERN DIPPING SAUCE
¼ cup Southern Comfort
1 cup gourmet BBQ sauce
Dash or two hot sauce

Soak 16 bamboo skewers in water for 30 minutes. (Or use metal skewers.)

Slice each tenderloin crosswise into eight 1- to 2-inch chunks (each about 2 ounces). Press firmly on each slice to slightly flatten.

In a glass dish large enough to hold pork in one layer, whisk together garlic, Southern Comfort, peach juice, Bone Dust BBQ Spice, oil, oregano, and chilies. Add pork, turning to coat. Marinate, covered and refrigerated, for 2 hours.

Preheat grill to medium-high.

Season peach wedges with cracked black pepper. Cut each piece of bacon in half and wrap one half around each peach wedge. Skewer one peach piece onto each skewer.

Remove pork from marinade (reserving marinade) and skewer one piece of pork onto each skewer, keeping it tight against peach.

To make dipping sauce, in a small bowl, whisk together Southern Comfort BBQ sauce and hot sauce.

Grill satays, basting with sauce, until pork is just cooked through and bacon is crisp, 3 to 4 minutes per side. Serve with dipping sauce.

MAKES 16 SATAYS

Grill-Roasted Kielbasa with Apricot Mustard Glaze

My friend Duane in Chicago introduced me to this treat. I was a little skeptical at first, but it turns out to be a perfect party pleaser.

APRICOT MUSTARD GLAZE
½ **cup apricot jam**
¼ **cup honey**
¼ **cup prepared mustard**
2 **TB. water**

1 **TB. chopped fresh parsley**
Salt and pepper

1-lb. piece Polish kielbasa (8 to 12 inches)

To make glaze, in a medium saucepan over medium-high heat, whisk together apricot jam, honey, mustard, water, and parsley until smooth. Remove from heat. Season to taste with salt and pepper.

Preheat grill to medium-high.

Grill kielbasa until lightly charred and just starting to crisp, 3 to 4 minutes per side. Transfer to a cutting board.

Slice kielbasa every ¼ inch about ¾ the way through. This is to allow the center of the kielbasa to get hot. Place kielbasa on the upper level of the grill or to the side for indirect cooking.

Baste kielbasa with apricot glaze, making sure glaze gets in between the slices. Close lid and cook, basting occasionally, until the kielbasa is heated through, crispy and heavily glazed, 15 to 20 minutes.

Slice into rounds and serve.

SERVES 4 TO 6

Chicken Yakitori with Green Onion and Maple Hoisin Glaze

In 1989, I began work at the newly opened SkyDome Hotel in Toronto. With thousands of meals being served daily out of 14 kitchens, I quickly learned a great deal about cooking for big numbers. In the SkyDome Windows Restaurant, a chef named Torichi made hundreds of delectable chicken, beef, shrimp, and pork satays for every event. Here is my version of Torichi's little skewers.

---

4 (each 6 oz.) boneless skinless chicken
   breasts
¼ cup rice wine vinegar
2 TB. soy sauce
1 TB. sesame oil
1 TB. chopped fresh ginger
1 TB. chopped garlic
1 tsp. curry powder
1 tsp. ground black pepper

MAPLE HOISIN GLAZE
¼ cup maple syrup
¼ cup hoisin sauce
¼ cup orange juice
1 TB. chopped fresh cilantro
4 green onions, thinly sliced
2 tsp. sesame seeds
Salt and pepper

Soak 24 (8-inch) bamboo skewers in warm water for 1 hour.

Slice each chicken breast lengthwise into 6 thin strips, about 1 ounce each. Carefully thread one chicken strip onto one end of each skewer.

In a glass dish large enough to hold chicken skewers, whisk together vinegar, soy sauce, sesame oil, ginger, garlic, curry powder, and pepper. Add chicken, turning to coat. Marinate chicken, covered and refrigerated, for 4 hours.

Preheat grill to medium-high.

To make glaze, in a bowl, whisk together maple syrup, hoisin sauce, orange juice, cilantro, green onions, and sesame seeds. Season to taste with salt and pepper.

Remove chicken skewers from marinade, discarding marinade. Grill skewers, basting with maple hoisin glaze, for 2 to 3 minutes per side or until chicken is fully cooked. Serve with leftover glaze as a dip.

MAKES 24 SKEWERS

Grilled Spicy Buffalo Wings with Blue Cheese Dressing

When I was a college student, we often spent Friday and Saturday nights in Buffalo nightclubs, eating crispy fried wings and guzzling cold beer.

3 lbs. jumbo chicken wings (about 36)	½ cup Hell's Fire Chili Paste (page 206)
½ cup Durkee Hot Sauce or Franks Redhot Hot Sauce	¼ cup lemon juice
	Salt to taste

Trim wing tips from wings and cut through the joint to separate the winglet from the drummette. Place wing pieces in a large bowl, and toss with hot sauce, Hell's Fire Chili Paste, and lemon juice. Season with salt.

Cover, refrigerate, and marinate for 24 hours.

Preheat grill to medium.

Remove chicken wings from marinade and place in a grill basket.

Grill wings for 10 to 12 minutes per side, turning every 5 to 6 minutes, or until fully cooked, golden brown and crisp.

Carefully remove from grill basket and serve with Chunky Blue Cheese Dressing (page 28).

SERVES 4

Margarita Wings

Wings and beer are a great combination, but I especially like the way tequila and wings work together. Besides, a few shots of tequila always make cooking a little easier—and tastier.

3 lbs. (about 36) jumbo chicken wings
3 TB. lemon pepper
3 TB. vegetable oil

MARGARITA WING SAUCE
1 cup honey
¾ cup prepared mustard
½ cup lime juice
¼ cup gold tequila
3 TB. chopped fresh cilantro
2 TB. hot sauce

Preheat grill to medium.

Trim wing tips from wings and cut through the joint to separate the winglet from the drummette. Place wing pieces in a large bowl, and toss with lemon pepper and vegetable oil.

To make margarita wing sauce: In a large bowl, whisk together honey, mustard, lime juice, tequila, cilantro, and hot sauce. Set aside.

Place seasoned chicken wings in a grill basket.

Grill wings for 10 to 12 minutes per side, turning every 5 to 6 minutes, or until fully cooked, golden brown, and crisp.

Carefully remove wings from grill basket and add to margarita wing sauce. Toss well and serve.

SERVES 4

Infiniti Dip

You have probably heard of seven-layer dip and nine-layer dip. Well, here's one called Infiniti Dip. I developed this recipe for the crew of Patrick Racing. It started out as seven layers and just kept on growing. The deeper the dish you use, the more layers you can create. It's a little over the top, but so am I.

   You will need to do a little bit of basic preparation before you start assembling the layered dip. You could buy premade salsa and guacamole, but I prefer to make my own.

Guacamole

2 avocados, peeled and seeded	2 cloves garlic, minced
3 TB. lemon juice	3 green onions, finely chopped
1 TB. chopped fresh cilantro	Hot sauce, salt, and black pepper
½ small red onion, diced	

In a bowl, mash avocados with a fork. Stir in lemon juice, cilantro, onion, garlic, and green onions. Season to taste with hot sauce, salt, and pepper. Cover and refrigerate.

MAKES ABOUT 2 CUPS

Fire-Roasted Four-Pepper Salsa

2 red bell peppers, halved and seeded	2 to 3 smoked chipotle chilies in adobo sauce, puréed
1 yellow bell pepper, halved and seeded	1 TB. chopped garlic
1 green bell pepper, halved and seeded	1 TB. chopped fresh cilantro
1 red onion, peeled and quartered	1 TB. lime juice
2 TB. olive oil	Salt and coarsely ground black pepper to taste

Preheat grill to high.

On a lightly greased grill, roast red, yellow, and green peppers and red onion until charred all over and tender. Peel any loose skin from peppers. Dice peppers and onion; place in a large bowl.

Add olive oil, puréed chipotle chilies, garlic, cilantro, lime juice, salt, and pepper. Mix thoroughly, cover, and refrigerate at least 1 hour.

MAKES 2 TO 3 CUPS

Salsa Verde

Also known as Green Salsa, this salsa is made from roasted poblano chili peppers and tomatillos. The tomatillo is a fruit that looks like a small green tomato. If you can't find tomatillos, substitute green tomatoes.

---

6 tomatillos, chopped

2 poblano peppers, roasted, peeled, seeded and diced

2 jalapeño peppers, seeded and finely chopped

1 small yellow onion, finely diced

4 cloves garlic, minced

4 green onions, finely chopped

¼ cup chopped fresh cilantro

2 TB. white vinegar

2 TB. olive oil

Pinch ground cumin

Salt and pepper

In a bowl, mix tomatillos, poblano, and jalapeño peppers, onion, garlic, green onions, cilantro, vinegar, and olive oil. Season to taste with cumin, salt, and pepper.

MAKES ABOUT 2 CUPS

Continued...

Other needs:

8 plum tomatoes, finely chopped	2 cups shredded yellow cheddar cheese
1 red onion, diced	2 cups shredded Monterey Jack cheese
1 bunch green onions, finely chopped	2 (16 oz.) jars Chili Con Queso Cheese Sauce
1 jar (12 oz.) pickled sliced jalapeño peppers	2 cups shredded spicy Pepper Jack cheese
1 cup sliced pitted black olives	1 (500 ml) tub sour cream
1 cup bacon bits	2 cups shredded mozzarella cheese
¼ cup chopped fresh cilantro	1 cup Hickory Sticks Smoked Flavor potato matchsticks
1 (19 oz.) can refried beans	

Prepare Guacamole, Fire-Roasted Four-Pepper Salsa, and Salsa Verde.

In a bowl, mix tomatoes, red onion, green onions, pickled jalapeños, olives, bacon bits, and cilantro. Set aside.

To assemble Infiniti Dip, spread even layers of the ingredients in a 6-inch-deep glass casserole dish in the following order:

Layer 1: all the refried beans

Layer 2: half the Fire-Roasted Four-Pepper Salsa

Layer 3: 1 cup cheddar cheese

Layer 4: half the Guacamole

Layer 5: 1 cup Monterey Jack cheese

Layer 6: 1 jar Chili Con Queso Cheese Sauce

Layer 7: half the Salsa Verde

Layer 8: 1 cup spicy Pepper Jack cheese

Layer 9: half the sour cream

Layer 10: 1 cup mozzarella cheese

Layer 11: rest of the Fire-Roasted Four-Pepper Salsa

Layer 12: 1 cup cheddar cheese

Layer 13: rest of the Guacamole

Layer 14: 1 cup Monterey Jack cheese

Layer 15: the second jar Chili Con Queso Cheese Sauce

Layer 16: rest of the Salsa Verde

Layer 17: 1 cup spicy Pepper Jack cheese

Layer 18: half the sour cream

Layer 19: 1 cup mozzarella cheese

Layers 20 through 26: all the tomato/green onion/olive mixture

Cover with plastic wrap and refrigerate for 2 hours to allow the dip to set.

To serve, garnish the top of the dip with Layer 27, Hickory Sticks. Serve with tortilla chips.

SERVES 8 TO 12

Cinnamon-Skewered Lamb Kebabs with Coconut Chili Chutney

While on a recent trip to India I came across a coconut chutney that was superb, a blend of freshly grated coconut and hot chili peppers. It's a great accompaniment to lamb or chicken.

---

16 (5 inch) cinnamon sticks
2 lbs. boneless leg of lamb
¼ cup vegetable oil
¼ cup rice vinegar
2 TB. curry powder
1 TB. chopped fresh cilantro

1 TB. minced ginger
1 tsp. salt
½ tsp. ground cinnamon
4 cloves garlic, minced
1 red chili pepper, minced

Soak cinnamon sticks in warm water for 1 hour.

Trim lamb of any excess fat. Cut lamb into ½-inch cubes.

Skewer about 2 ounces (2 cubes) lamb onto one end of each cinnamon stick.

In a glass dish large enough to hold kebabs, whisk together oil, vinegar, curry powder, cilantro, ginger, salt, ground cinnamon, garlic, and chili pepper. Add lamb skewers, turning to coat. Cover and refrigerate for 2 hours to marinate.

Preheat grill to medium-high.

Remove lamb kebabs from marinade, discarding marinade. Grill for 3 to 4 minutes per side for medium.

Serve immediately with Coconut Chili Chutney (recipe follows).

SERVES 8

Tip

Save your empty coconut shells and use as wood chips on your grill. They add great flavor.

Continued . . .

Coconut Chili Chutney

1 coconut

2 TB. vegetable oil

2 green finger chili peppers, sliced

1 red finger chili pepper, sliced

1 onion, sliced

3 cloves garlic, minced

¼ cup rice wine vinegar

¼ cup water

1 TB. sugar

½ tsp. nutmeg

Salt and pepper

Hammer an ice pick or screwdriver into the black dots at the end of the coconut; drain and reserve water. Tap coconut with the hammer to break it into pieces.

Use a vegetable peeler to remove the skin from the coconut meat. Shave coconut in a food processor. Set aside.

Heat oil in a medium saucepan over high heat. Add chilies, onion, and garlic; sauté, stirring, for 3 to 4 minutes or until tender.

Add shaved coconut; sauté for another 3 to 4 minutes.

Add reserved coconut water, vinegar, water, sugar, and nutmeg. Bring to a boil, reduce heat to medium-low, and simmer, stirring occasionally, for 10 minutes. Season to taste with salt and pepper.

Remove from heat and transfer to a bowl. Cool completely, then cover and refrigerate until needed.

MAKES ABOUT 1½ CUPS

Turkish Shish Kebabs with Pomegranate Glaze

 Pomegranate molasses, used in the glaze, can be found in specialty food stores and in Middle Eastern markets.

1 lb. ground lamb
2 TB. minced fresh ginger
2 TB. chopped fresh cilantro
2 TB. Worcestershire sauce
1 tsp. black pepper
1 tsp. curry powder
1 tsp. cayenne pepper
½ tsp. ground cumin
½ tsp. ground coriander
1 small onion, finely chopped
4 cloves garlic, minced
Salt

POMEGRANATE GLAZE
½ cup pomegranate molasses
½ cup red currant jelly
¼ cup dry sherry
1 TB. chopped fresh mint
1 TB. olive oil
4 cloves garlic, minced
Salt and pepper

Soak eight (10- to 12-inch) bamboo skewers in hot water for 1 hour. (Or use metal skewers.)

Preheat grill to medium-high.

In a bowl, combine lamb, ginger, cilantro, Worcestershire sauce, black pepper, curry powder, cayenne, cumin, coriander, onion, and garlic. Season to taste with salt.

Divide into eight equal-size portions. Moisten your hands with cold water and knead each portion to ensure that each is fully mixed with spices. Mould each portion around each skewer, shaping it into a uniform sausage about 6 inches long.

To make pomegranate glaze, combine molasses, red currant jelly, sherry, mint, oil, and garlic. Season to taste with salt and pepper.

Grill kebabs for 8 to 10 minutes, turning every couple minutes and basting with pomegranate glaze, until golden brown but still juicy and pink inside.

Serve with remaining glaze.

MAKES 8 KEBABS

Lobster-Stuffed Devilled Eggs

What can I say except it's devilishly good.

---

12 extra-large eggs	1 tsp. Bone Dust BBQ Spice (page 203)
½ cup mayonnaise	Dash hot sauce
1 TB. chopped fresh dill	½ lb. lobster meat (fresh or frozen)
1 TB. Dijon mustard	Salt and pepper
1 TB. lemon juice	Sprigs of fresh dill

Place eggs in a large pot and cover with cold water. Bring to a boil over high heat. Cover the pan and remove from the heat. Let stand 15 minutes.

Drain eggs and run under cold water for 15 minutes.

Peel eggs, being careful not to break whites.

Using a sharp knife cut eggs in half lengthwise.

With a small spoon, carefully remove yolk and place in a bowl.

Arrange whites on a cookie sheet lined with paper towel.

Mash yolks. The best way to do this is to press them through a fine sieve. If you do not have one, just mash them with a fork.

Mix in mayonnaise, dill, mustard, lemon juice, Bone Dust BBQ Spice, and hot sauce.

Pick through lobster meat to make sure there are no bits of shell. Break lobster meat into very small pieces and add to egg mixture. Gently mix eggs and lobster together to make a sticky mass. Season to taste with salt and pepper.

Spoon lobster mixture into each egg white. Pile it high, as these are killer eggs.

Garnish with sprigs of dill.

MAKES 24 YUMMY EGGS

Grilled Oysters Stuffed with Snow Crab and Bacon in a Mango BBQ Sauce

I served this recipe at the Taste of CART event at the Mid Ohio Race Course in August 2000. It was one of three recipes that helped me win the CART Best Chef Competition.

½ lb. snow crabmeat, thawed and drained

6 slices bacon, cooked crisp and diced

2 cloves garlic, minced

1 small onion, finely chopped

1 TB. chopped fresh dill

1 TB. lemon juice

Dash hot sauce

Salt and pepper

16 oysters

1 mango, peeled and pitted

½ cup BBQ sauce

Preheat grill to medium-high.

In a bowl, mix together crabmeat, bacon, garlic, onion, dill, and lemon juice. Season to taste with hot sauce, salt, and pepper.

Using an oyster knife, shuck oysters over a bowl. Strain liquid into crab mixture.

Remove oysters from their shells and set aside. Place 1 heaping tablespoon crab mixture in each of 16 half shells. Top each with an oyster.

In a food processor purée mango until smooth. Add BBQ sauce and blend until incorporated.

Place stuffed oysters on a grill screen. Top each oyster with 1 tablespoons mango sauce. Place on the grill, close the lid, and cook for 10 to 12 minutes or until mango sauce and stuffing are hot.

Carefully remove from the grill and serve.

SERVES 4

Russian Oyster Shooters

Sometimes, a little liquor helps the oysters slide down.

---

4 oysters, shucked
5 oz. ice-cold Russian vodka
4 tsp. freshly grated horseradish

Hot sauce
1 lemon
Cracked black pepper

Place one oyster in each of four shot glasses. Pour 1¼ ounce vodka over each oyster.

Top each oyster with 1 teaspoon horseradish and a dash of hot sauce.

Squeeze a little lemon juice over each oyster and season with pepper.

Shoot it and enjoy.

SERVES 4

Never Lose Clams Casino

I love clams, whether raw on the half shell or steamed, but what I like most is baked clams. My version of the classic Clams Casino uses lots of cheese and smoky bacon. When buying clams (a.k.a. quahogs), choose large hard-shell Atlantic clams such as cherrystone, littleneck, or topneck.

---

12 large cherrystone or littleneck clams	Salt and pepper
4 slices bacon, diced	½ cup grated Parmesan cheese
2 cloves garlic, minced	½ cup shredded mozzarella cheese
¼ cup finely chopped onion	¼ cup shredded Swiss cheese
½ red bell pepper, finely chopped	¼ cup dry bread crumbs
½ cup tomato sauce	Coarse salt
1 TB. chopped fresh parsley	

Using an oyster knife, shuck clams and set aside in the refrigerator for later.

In a frying pan over medium-high heat, cook bacon for 3 to 5 minutes or until just crisp. Drain off all but 2 tablespoons bacon fat.

Add garlic, onion, and red pepper; sauté for 3 to 5 minutes or until tender. Stir in tomato sauce and parsley; quickly bring to a boil. Remove from heat and season to taste with salt and pepper. Let cool slightly.

In a bowl, mix together Parmesan cheese, mozzarella cheese, Swiss cheese, and bread crumbs.

Preheat oven to 425°F.

Spread a layer of coarse salt on a baking sheet. Put clams back in the shells and arrange them evenly on the baking sheet.

Place 1 tablespoon bacon-onion mixture on top of each clam, and top each clam with cheese-and-bread-crumb mixture.

Bake clams for 8 to 10 minutes or until cheese is melted and golden brown.

Let rest for 3 minutes before serving.

SERVES 6

Mustard Leaf Steam-Grilled Mussels with Dijon Cream Sauce

If you can't find mustard leaves, use pine needles, seaweed, or collard greens.

---

2 bunches large mustard greens

2 lbs. blue mussels, bearded and rinsed

2 TB. sea salt

2 TB. mustard seeds

2 TB. chopped fresh thyme

2 TB. butter

2 large shallots, sliced

4 cloves garlic, minced

¼ cup dry sherry

¼ cup Dijon mustard

1 TB. grainy mustard

1 cup whipping cream

Salt and freshly ground black pepper to taste

Wash mustard greens to remove any dirt, then soak leaves in cold water for 15 minutes.

In a large bowl, toss mussels with salt, mustard seeds, and thyme. Set aside.

In a small saucepan over medium-high heat, melt butter. Sauté shallots and garlic for 3 minutes or until translucent. Add sherry, Dijon mustard, and grainy mustard; bring to a boil. Add cream and return to a boil. Reduce heat to medium-low and simmer for 5 minutes or until sauce evenly coats the back of a wooden spoon. Remove from heat, season with salt and pepper, and keep warm.

Preheat grill to high.

Working quickly, lay half leaves on the grill. Add seasoned mussels and cover with remaining mustard leaves. Close the lid and let mussels steam-grill for 10 to 12 minutes or until the they open.

Carefully remove and discard the top mustard leaves. Transfer mussels to a large bowl (discard any that have not opened). Add Dijon cream sauce, toss, and serve with a fresh baguette.

SERVES 4

Rosemary-Skewered Salmon Satays with Honey Tangerine Glaze

When buying rosemary for this recipe look for long, large branches with stems thick enough to be able to support the weight of the salmon.

---

8 (6 inch) thick rosemary branches
1½ lbs. thick Atlantic salmon fillets, skinned
3 TB. Licorice Rub (page 212)
3 TB. olive oil

HONEY TANGERINE GLAZE
¼ cup honey

¼ cup orange marmalade
¼ cup Cointreau or Grand Marnier
¼ cup tangerine or orange juice
1 TB. chopped fresh mint
½ tsp. cayenne pepper
Salt and pepper

Soak rosemary branches in warm water for 1 hour.

Cut salmon into 24 1½-inch cubes; place in a bowl. Add Licorice Rub and olive oil; toss well.

Thread three cubes salmon onto each rosemary branch and place in a glass dish to marinate for 20 minutes.

Meanwhile, prepare glaze by combining honey, marmalade, Cointreau, tangerine juice, mint, and cayenne in a small saucepan. Over low heat, stir constantly until thoroughly mixed and smooth. Remove from heat and season to taste with salt and pepper.

Preheat grill to medium-high.

Grill salmon skewers for 2 to 3 minutes per side, basting with honey tangerine glaze. Serve immediately with remaining glaze for dipping.

SERVES 4

Shrimp Parfait with Lucifer Cocktail Sauce

Shrimp cocktail has to be one of my favorite dishes. The best I've ever had comes from St. Elmo Steakhouse in Indianapolis. Their shrimp cocktail is known for its serious kick of fresh horseradish—sinus burner for sure.

My only complaint about restaurant shrimp cocktails is that there is never enough shrimp. My own recipe solves that problem. It's not cheap, but it is certainly delicious.

LUCIFER COCKTAIL SAUCE	**2 TB. lemon juice**
½ cup freshly grated horseradish	**1 TB. white vinegar**
½ cup ketchup	**2 tsp. hot sauce**
½ cup chili sauce	**Salt and pepper to taste**

In a small bowl, stir together horseradish, ketchup, chili sauce, lemon juice, vinegar, hot sauce, salt, and pepper. Refrigerate until ready to serve.

MAKES ABOUT 2 CUPS

Crab Salad

---

1 lb. crabmeat	**1 TB. lemon juice**
½ small red onion, diced	**1 TB. grainy mustard**
¼ cup mayonnaise	**Dash hot sauce**
1 TB. chopped fresh dill	**Salt and pepper to taste**

In a bowl, stir together crabmeat, onion, mayonnaise, dill, lemon juice, mustard, hot sauce, salt, and pepper. Refrigerate until needed.

MAKES ABOUT 2 CUPS

Shrimp Halves

6 cups water	8 peppercorns
¼ cup lemon juice	2 tsp. salt
2 sprigs fresh dill	2 lbs. large shrimp (21 to 30 per lb.), peeled and deveined

In a large saucepan bring water to a boil. Add lemon juice, dill, peppercorns, and salt; return to a boil.

Add shrimp; cook for 3 to 4 minutes or until shrimp are opaque and just cooked through. Drain and rinse under cold water until cool. Drain again.

With a sharp knife, slice each shrimp in half lengthwise.

Cover and refrigerate until needed.

Grilled Tiger Shrimp

20 jumbo tiger shrimp, peeled and deveined, tails left on	3 TB. olive oil
3 TB. Bay Seasoning (page 205)	1 lime, juiced
	Special equipment: 4 semi-circular metal skewers

In a bowl, toss shrimp with Bay Seasoning, olive oil, and lime juice. Marinate for 30 minutes.

Thread five shrimp onto each skewer. Cover and refrigerate until needed.

Continued ...

The Parfait

Fire-Roasted Four-Pepper Salsa (page 98)   4 sprigs fresh dill

Guacamole (page 98)   4 lemon wedges

Place 1 large spoonful crab salad into each of four large parfait or milkshake glasses.

Onto this, spoon a little Fire-Roasted Four-Pepper Salsa. Top with a dollop guacamole.

Layer 6 to 8 shrimp halves in each glass and top with a dollop cocktail sauce.

Repeat this layering until you reach the top of the glass, ending with a layer of shrimp halves. Refrigerate for 1 hour.

Preheat grill to medium-high.

Grill skewered jumbo shrimp for 2 to 3 minutes per side or until opaque and just cooked through.

Garnish each parfait with a dill sprig and lemon wedge. Balance a skewer of shrimp on top of each parfait.

Serve immediately.

SERVES 4

Bacon-Wrapped Scallops with Maple Chili Glaze

Atlantic scallops are a real treat, especially those from the cold waters of the Bay of Fundy. My mom and dad had their honeymoon in Digby, Nova Scotia, Canada's most famous scallop town. On one of my excursions I had some delicious bacon-wrapped scallops glazed with maple syrup. Here's my version.

---

8 slices thick bacon

16 fresh jumbo scallops, trimmed of muscle

1 TB. Bone Dust BBQ Spice (page 203)

¼ cup maple syrup

¼ cup orange juice

1 TB. chopped fresh dill

1 TB. sambal chili paste

1 TB. olive oil

2 green onions, finely chopped

Salt and pepper to taste

Soak 16 (6-inch) bamboo skewers in hot water for 30 minutes.

Fry bacon until it is just starting to get crispy, about halfway done. Drain on paper towels and cut each slice in half.

Drain scallops well and pat dry with paper towels.

Sprinkle scallops with Bone Dust BBQ Spice. Wrap each scallop with a half slice bacon.

Skewer one scallop (running the skewer through bacon and scallop) onto one end of each skewer. Set aside.

In a bowl, whisk together maple syrup, orange juice, dill, sambal chili paste, oil, green onions, salt, and pepper.

Preheat grill to medium-high.

Place scallops on a grill screen and grill for 3 to 4 minutes per side, basting liberally with maple chili basting sauce, or until bacon is crisp and scallops are just done. Be careful not to overcook.

Serve with remaining basting sauce.

MAKES 16 SKEWERS

Tandoori Jumbo Prawns

We were sailing in the backwaters of the Indian Ocean outside Cochin, India. It was dark, and I was wet from a tropical rainstorm. The clouds parted as we docked on the shore of the canal. The open grill with spurting hot coals fired back up. Dinner was moments away. Red snapper fillets, grouper steaks, and the largest prawns I had ever seen, marinated in tandoori spices and waiting to be grilled. The host chef invited me to join his staff on the grill to prepare this seafood feast. I jumped at the opportunity. Here is the recipe.

¾ cup lemon juice
¼ cup chopped fresh ginger
1 TB. red chili powder
1 tsp. salt
8 cloves garlic, minced
24 jumbo prawns (5 to 6 per lb.), peeled and
   deveined, tails left on
½ cup melted butter

TANDOORI SAUCE
¾ cup plain yogurt
¼ cup whipping cream
2 TB. chopped fresh ginger
1 tsp. turmeric
1 tsp. red chili powder
1 tsp. ground white pepper
1 tsp. garam masala
8 cloves garlic, minced

In a large, shallow dish whisk together lemon juice, ginger, chili powder, salt, and garlic. Add prawns, turning to coat well, and marinate for 20 minutes.

Meanwhile, make tandoori sauce. In a large bowl, stir together well yogurt, cream, ginger, turmeric, chili powder, pepper, garam masala, and garlic.

Remove prawns from marinade, discarding marinade, and add to tandoori sauce. Gently stir to completely coat prawns. Marinate, covered and refrigerated, for 1 hour.

Preheat grill to medium-high.

Thread four prawns onto each of six metal skewers.

Grill prawns for 3 to 4 minutes per side, basting with melted butter.

Serve immediately.

SERVES 6

Octoberfest Pig's Tails

The Kitchener-Waterloo area hosts the largest Octoberfest celebration outside Germany. Pig's tails are a specialty of the area, with the largest consumption during Octoberfest. Allow yourself a lot of time to prepare these, as well as a lot of warm wet towels to clean your hands with—this is the stickiest recipe in the book!

---

3 lbs. fully trimmed and cleaned pig's tails (about 12)
3 bottles beer
6 whole cloves
8 peppercorns
2 bay leaves
Salt to taste

SWEET-AND-SPICY SAUCE
½ cup brown sugar
½ cup ketchup
¼ cup water
2 TB. Worcestershire sauce
Salt and pepper

Place pig's tails in a large stockpot. Pour in beer and add enough water to cover tails. Add cloves, peppercorns, bay leaves, and salt.

Bring to a rolling boil, reduce heat to medium-low, and simmer, uncovered, for 2 hours.

Preheat oven to 375°F.

Remove pig's tails from the pot and set on a lightly greased baking sheet. Discard cooking liquid. Season tails with salt and roast for 45 minutes, checking periodically that they are not burning.

Meanwhile, make sweet-and-spicy sauce. In a small bowl, whisk together brown sugar, ketchup, water, and Worcestershire sauce. Season to taste with salt and pepper.

After 45 minutes, baste pig's tails with sauce. Roast for another 15 minutes to caramelize. Remove from oven, baste again with sauce, and serve immediately with wet cloths.

SERVES 6

Grilled Portobello Mushrooms Stuffed with Smoked Chicken and Oka Cheese

Three of my favorite ingredients brought together in one simple recipe. For the chicken, try my Devil's Brewed Roast Chicken (page 357).

8 large Portobello mushrooms
4 cups hot water
¼ cup olive oil
¼ cup + 1 TB. cider vinegar
Salt and freshly ground black pepper to taste
1 small yellow onion, finely diced
2 cups shredded smoked chicken

1½ cups shredded Oka cheese
½ cup softened cream cheese
¼ cup BBQ sauce
1 TB. chopped fresh sage
½ cup dry bread crumbs
½ cup grated Parmesan cheese

Brush any dirt off mushrooms and cut off and discard stems. Put mushroom caps in a large bowl, and cover with hot water; let stand for 15 minutes to allow mushrooms to soften. Drain and pat dry on paper towels.

In the same bowl, mix together olive oil, ¼ cup cider vinegar, salt, and pepper. Add mushroom caps, turning to coat well, and let marinate while you make the stuffing.

In a bowl, stir together onion, smoked chicken, Oka cheese, cream cheese, BBQ sauce, sage, and remaining 1 tablespoon vinegar. Season to taste with salt and pepper. Divide mixture into eight equal portions and flatten to the size of the mushroom caps.

In a small bowl, combine bread crumbs and Parmesan cheese. Set aside.

Preheat grill to medium-high. Spray a grill screen with nonstick cooking spray. Place on the grill and preheat for 5 minutes.

Grill mushrooms gill side down for 4 to 5 minutes or until slightly charred and just tender.

Turn mushrooms over and place stuffing mixture on each cap. Top with a liberal dusting of bread crumb mixture. Close the lid and cook for 7 to 8 more minutes or until cheese is hot and bubbling and bread crumbs are golden brown.

Serve with mixed greens dressed with Astrida's Lemon Vinaigrette (page 30).

SERVES 8

Grape Leaf-Wrapped Camembert with Bacon and Roasted Onion Topping

When the wrapped Camembert is slowly grilled, the cheese takes on a sweet nutty aroma from the grape leaves.

1 large onion, thinly sliced	1 TB. chopped fresh thyme
2 TB. olive oil	Salt and cracked black pepper
1 tsp. salt	Dash cider vinegar
½ tsp. ground cumin	1 small (125 g) wheel Camembert
½ tsp. chili powder	4 large grape leaves
8 slices smoked bacon	Spiced olive oil for basting

Preheat oven to 400°F.

In an ovenproof dish toss together onion, oil, salt, cumin, and chili powder. Roast, stirring two or three times, for 30 to 40 minutes or until onions are lightly charred and tender. Let cool.

Meanwhile, fry bacon until crisp. Drain on paper towels and let cool. Crumble bacon.

Chop roasted onions and mix with bacon and thyme. Season to taste with salt, pepper, and a dash cider vinegar.

Using a butter knife, scrape the white mould off the top of the Camembert. Season with cracked black pepper.

Lay grape leaves in a circle, overlapping slightly. Pat the top of the leaves dry with paper towels.

Place Camembert in the center of the leaves. Top with onion mixture, and spread it evenly. Wrap leaves over Camembert and press firmly to seal. If necessary, brush the edge of the leaves with olive oil to help form a seal.

Preheat the grill to medium-low.

Place wrapped Camembert on the grill onion-topping side up and grill for 8 to 12 minutes or until cheese is soft. Press gently with a butter knife to check.

Remove from grill to a serving plate. Let cool for 2 minutes, then carefully unwrap leaves from cheese. Spread or spoon warm cheese over baguette slices.

SERVES 4

Burgers and Sandwiches

The Burger Is Better with Butter

I love a great hamburger. For years I searched in vain for the ultimate burger. But during that time, I did stumble across information on the original burger. These were fried—often in butter—and the buns were brushed with butter, then griddled. I decided to take this classic one step further: put the butter *in* the burger!

I made this burger once on my TV show *Cottage Country*. Piled with all the works, it must have been a foot high!

---

3 lbs. regular ground beef
4 TB. butter, softened
1 onion, finely chopped
3 cloves garlic, minced
1 TB. chopped fresh parsley
1 TB. Worcestershire sauce

1 TB. Dijon mustard
Pinch cayenne pepper
Salt and freshly ground black pepper
6 or 12 burger buns
½ cup melted butter (for brushing buns)

Preheat grill to medium-high.

In a large bowl, mix together beef, butter, onion, garlic, parsley, Worcestershire sauce, and Dijon mustard. Season to taste with cayenne pepper, salt, and black pepper.

Form into 12 4-ounce patties as uniform in size as possible. A flatter burger will cook more evenly and faster than a ball-like burger.

Grill burgers for 4 to 5 minutes per side for medium-well.

Brush burger buns with melted butter and grill cut side down until crisp and golden brown.

Serve with your favorite burger garnishes. I like the works, and my list of the works is obscene.

SERVES 6 OR 12

The Ultimate Burger Garnish List

Any of these items can be used on beef, chicken, turkey, or fish burgers. Remember, there are no rules when building a better burger. Just use your imagination and have fun. Build a different burger with every grilling adventure.

Ketchup

Mustard (prepared, Dijon, Pommery, honey mustard, or spicy)

Relish (green, zucchini, tomato, or corn)

Pickles (sour dills, bread and butter, kosher, or Spicy Garlic Dills, page 175)

Onions (red, white, yellow; sweet or tart; raw, fried, or grilled)

Salsa

Cheese (aged cheddar, Swiss, Brie, Cambozola, mozzarella, blue, jalapeño Jack, Muenster, processed, Camembert, goat cheese, or provolone)

Peameal bacon

Bacon

Italian sausage patty

Bratwurst sausage

Fried egg

Pickled egg

Grilled Portobello mushrooms

Lettuce (green leaf, red leaf, iceberg, or romaine)

Tomato (red, yellow, or green as long they are fresh and full of flavor)

Peanut butter

Grilled vegetables (peppers, mushrooms, onions, zucchini, eggplant, and asparagus)

Blue cheese dressing

Ranch dressing

Caesar dressing

Sauerkraut

BBQ sauce

Mayonnaise

Steak sauce

Jalapeño peppers (fresh or pickled)

Pickled banana peppers

Sautéed mushrooms

Chili

Nacho cheese sauce

Avocado

Hot sauce

Oyster sauce

Grilled bologna

Grilled shrimp

Deep-fried breaded onion rings

Deep-fried breaded oysters

Deep-fried breaded clams

BBQ pulled pork (page 324)

Pickled beets

Hummus

Tzatziki

French onion dip

Anchovies

And the very best burger topping: The Stuff (page 122)

The Stuff

Many fast-food chains offer their own special toppings. McDonald's has its special sauce, In-N-Out Burger in California has its Thousand Island–style dressing, and in my town of Toronto, Lick's has its Guk. I've created what I call The Stuff. It is all your burger needs instead of ketchup, mustard, or relish.

1 (7 oz.) can chipotle chilies in adobo sauce
1¼ cups sour cream
½ cup cream cheese, softened
¼ cup mayonnaise
½ cup shredded aged cheddar cheese

1 lime, juiced
3 green onions, finely chopped
½ tsp. salt
¼ tsp. coarsely ground black pepper

Tip

Chipotle chilies in adobo can be found in many supermarkets or Mexican grocery stores. They add spice and a smoky flavor.

In a food processor, purée chipotle chilies and adobo until smooth. Set aside 2 tablespoons and refrigerate or freeze the remainder for use in other recipes.

In the food processor, blend until smooth 2 tablespoons chipotle purée, sour cream, cream cheese, and mayonnaise.

Add cheddar, lime juice, green onions, salt, and pepper. Pulse to just blend.

Adjust seasoning if necessary. Refrigerate for 1 hour before using.

MAKES 2¹/₂ CUPS

The Original Ham-Burger

I decided that it was time to put some "ham" back in the hamburger. This all-pork burger uses diced smoked ham in with the ground pork, offering great texture and more flavor. A truly chin-dripping sandwich!

2 lbs. regular ground pork
1 lb. (¼-inch-thick) slices Black Forest ham or back bacon, diced
1 onion, finely chopped
4 cloves garlic, minced
¼ cup Dijon mustard
2 TB. chopped fresh parsley
2 tsp. black pepper
2 tsp. crushed red chilies

1 tsp. ground dried sage
Pinch cayenne pepper
Salt to taste
6 or 12 burger buns
½ cup melted butter

GARNISHES
From the list, baby! Check the list! (page 121)

Preheat grill to medium-high.

In a large bowl, combine ground pork, ham, onion, garlic, mustard, parsley, black pepper, crushed chilies, sage, cayenne pepper, and salt.

Form into 12 equal-size patties. (A flatter burger will cook more evenly and faster than a ball-like burger.)

Grill burgers for 4 to 5 minutes per side for medium-well.

Brush burger buns with melted butter and grill cut side down until crisp and golden brown.

I recommend garnishing these HAM-burgers with Swiss cheese, fresh tomatoes, lettuce, spicy mustard, and grilled back bacon, eh?

SERVES 6 OR 12

Pamela's Three-Meat Burgers

 My dearest Pamela makes some incredibly tasty burgers. She likes to make them really thin and cook them quickly so they are crispy on the outside and just done on the inside.

1 lb. regular ground beef	1 small egg
1 lb. ground veal	1 TB. chopped fresh parsley
1 lb. ground pork	2 tsp. Worcestershire sauce
3 cloves garlic, minced	Salt and pepper to taste
1 small onion, finely chopped	6 or 12 large burger buns
2 green onions, finely chopped	½ cup melted butter

Preheat grill to medium-high.

In a large bowl, combine beef, veal, pork, garlic, onion, green onions, egg, parsley, Worcestershire sauce, salt, and pepper.

Form into 12 equal-size patties. (A flatter burger will cook more evenly and faster than a ball-like burger.)

Grill burgers for 2 to 3 minutes per side for medium-well.

Brush burger buns with melted butter and grill cut side down until crisp and golden brown.

Serve with your favorite burger garnishes. I like to stack these burgers and add layers of cheese and grilled onions and mushrooms.

SERVES 6 OR 12

Christine's Bistro Burger Stuffed with Smoked Gruyère and Topped with Mashed Potatoes and Caramelized Red Onion Gravy

Beef, cheese, mashed potatoes, and gravy all on one plate—it doesn't get much better than this. Christine is a decadent chef with a passion for great-tasting burgers. This is her favorite recipe.

---

3 lbs. ground sirloin
2 cloves garlic, minced
1 small red onion, finely chopped
3 TB. BBQ sauce
1 TB. chopped fresh thyme
Salt and pepper to taste

1 lb. shredded smoked Gruyère cheese
8 sourdough burger buns
½ cup melted butter
Goat Cheese Mashed Potatoes (page 177)
Caramelized Red Onion Gravy (recipe follows)

In a large bowl, combine sirloin, garlic, onion, BBQ sauce, thyme, salt, and pepper.

Form into 16 equal-size patties. (A flatter burger will cook more evenly and faster than a ball-like burger.)

Pressing firmly between your hands, shape Gruyère cheese into eight pucks a little smaller than the diameter of the patties.

Place a puck of cheese on eight of the patties, cover with the remaining patties, and press the edges together to seal in cheese. Cover and refrigerate for 1 hour to allow meat to set.

Preheat grill to medium-high.

Grill burgers for 4 to 5 minutes per side for medium-well.

Brush burger buns with melted butter and grill cut side down until crisp and golden brown.

Place a stuffed burger on the bottom of each toasted bun. Top with a scoop of Goat Cheese Mashed Potatoes. Ladle Caramelized Red Onion Gravy over potatoes and burger. Top with top half of bun.

Eat with a knife and fork.

SERVES 8

Continued . . .

Caramelized Red Onion Gravy

¼ cup butter
3 red onions, sliced
4 cloves garlic, minced
¼ cup all-purpose flour
1 TB. chopped fresh thyme

1½ cups beef stock
½ cup red wine
½ cup steak sauce
Salt and pepper

In a medium saucepan, melt butter over medium heat. Cook onions and garlic, stirring occasionally, until onions are tender and golden brown, 15 to 20 minutes.

Stir in flour and thyme. Cook, stirring constantly, for 4 to 5 minutes, being careful not to burn flour.

Add beef stock ½ cup at a time, stirring constantly until smooth and thickened. Stir in red wine and steak sauce. Reduce heat to low and simmer for 15 minutes, stirring occasionally.

Season to taste with salt and pepper. Keep warm until needed.

MAKES ABOUT 2½ CUPS

Portobello Mushroom Lamb Burgers

Portobello mushrooms are meaty and have a full-bodied flavor that blends perfectly with lamb. If you are not a fan of lamb, use ground sirloin instead.

---

4 large Portobello mushroom caps, cleaned	2 TB. chopped fresh rosemary
¼ cup olive oil	1 TB. Worcestershire sauce
¼ cup balsamic vinegar	2 tsp. black pepper
Salt and pepper to taste	2 tsp. curry powder
3 lbs. ground lamb	1 tsp. ground cumin
6 cloves garlic, minced	½ cup goat cheese
1 onion, diced	12 pocket-style pita breads
½ cup golden raisins	1 bunch arugula
¼ cup grainy mustard	Hummus, tzatziki, or mayonnaise, for garnish

---

In a large bowl, combine Portobello mushroom caps, oil, vinegar, salt, and pepper. Marinate for 2 to 4 hours.

Preheat grill to medium-high.

Remove mushroom caps from marinade and discard marinade. Grill mushroom caps until tender, 5 to 6 minutes per side. Let cool. Cut each mushroom cap in half and thinly slice each half crosswise.

In the bowl, combine lamb, garlic, onion, raisins, mustard, rosemary, Worcestershire sauce, pepper, curry powder, cumin, and salt to taste. Fold in mushrooms.

Form into 12 equal-size patties. (A flatter burger will cook more evenly and faster than a ball-like burger.)

Grill burgers for 4 to 5 minutes per side for medium-well.

Top each burger with goat cheese and close lid for 1 minute or until cheese is soft.

Warm pita breads on grill. Cut 1 inch off one side of each pita and gently separate each side to form a pocket. Fill pocket with lamb burger and arugula and garnish with humus, tzatziki, or mayonnaise.

SERVES 6 OR 12

Sassy BBQ Chicken Burgers

These burgers are not too hot and spicy, but if you want them that way, use a spicy BBQ sauce. Try this burger with ground turkey, too.

2 lbs. ground chicken

3 boneless, skinless chicken breasts (about 1 lb.), diced

1 small red onion, finely chopped

2 cloves garlic, minced

1 jalapeño pepper, finely chopped

1¼ cups gourmet BBQ sauce (divided use)

¼ cup coarse fresh bread crumbs

1 TB. Bone Dust BBQ Spice (page 203)

Vegetable oil

6 or 12 potato bread hamburger buns

Whatever garnish you desire

Combine ground chicken, diced chicken, onion, garlic, jalapeño, ¼ cup BBQ sauce, bread crumbs, and Bone Dust BBQ Spice.

Form into 12 equal-size patties. (A flatter burger will cook more evenly and faster than a ball-like burger.) Cover with plastic wrap and refrigerate for 2 hours to allow burgers to set.

Preheat grill to medium-high.

Brush burgers with oil. Grill burgers, brushing each side with remaining 1 cup BBQ sauce, until juices run clear and burger is well done, 4 to 5 minutes per side.

Grill buns cut side down until toasted.

Serve burgers on buns. I like these loaded with pickled hot peppers, processed cheese, and bacon.

SERVES 6 TO 12

Screech Salmon Burgers

A little Newfoundland Screech rum will make anything taste delicious. Make sure to save a few shots of Screech for the chef.

---

2 lbs. skinless Atlantic salmon fillets
1 egg white
2 large shallots, finely chopped
2 green onions, finely chopped
2 TB. lemon juice
2 TB. Screech
1 TB. chopped fresh dill
1 TB. hot prepared horseradish
1 tsp. Bone Dust BBQ Spice (page 203)

Vegetable oil
4 to 8 egg buns or bagels

GARNISHES
Thinly sliced red onion
Softened cream cheese
Capers
Mom's Tartar Sauce (recipe follows)

Cut salmon into 1-inch pieces. Place salmon in a food processor and pulse until coarsely chopped and salmon begins binding together. Transfer to a bowl.

Add egg white, shallots, green onions, lemon juice, Screech, dill, horseradish, and Bone Dust BBQ Spice. Combine well.

Form into eight equal-size patties. (A flatter burger will cook more evenly and faster than a ball-like burger.) Cover with plastic wrap and refrigerate for 2 hours to allow burgers to set.

Preheat grill to medium-high.

Brush burgers with vegetable oil. Grill burgers for 4 to 5 minutes per side for medium-well. Grill buns until toasted.

Serve burgers on buns garnished with red onion, cream cheese, capers, and a healthy dollop tartar sauce.

SERVES 4 TO 8

Tip

Salmon burgers are delicate, so using a grill topper will make turning these burgers a lot easier.

Continued . . .

Mom's Tartar Sauce

Got to love your mom!

1½ cups mayonnaise
½ cup zucchini relish

1 TB. lemon juice
Salt and pepper

In a bowl, whisk together mayonnaise, relish, and lemon juice. Season to taste with salt and pepper. Cover and refrigerate. Sauce keeps, refrigerated, for up to 2 weeks.

MAKES APPROXIMATELY 2 CUPS

Grilled Vegetable Burgers

Over the last year or so I have had numerous requests for low-fat or vegetarian recipes. This is a new avenue for me, but I think you will enjoy this tasty veggie burger.

2 TB. olive oil

4 cloves garlic, minced

1 red onion, diced

8 shiitake mushrooms, thinly sliced

1 red bell pepper, diced

1 jalapeño pepper, finely chopped

1 cup corn kernels (thawed if frozen)

1 cup green peas (thawed if frozen)

1¼ cups tomato sauce (divided use)

1 (14 oz.) can chick peas, drained, rinsed and mashed

¼ cup grated Parmesan cheese

¼ cup pine nuts, coarsely chopped

1 TB. chopped fresh basil

1 TB. balsamic vinegar

¼ to ½ cup fresh bread crumbs

Cayenne pepper

Salt and pepper

8 balls bocconcini cheese, each cut into 4 or 5 slices

8 hamburger buns

Sliced vine-ripened tomatoes and alfalfa sprouts, for garnish

Heat oil in a large nonstick frying pan over medium heat. Sauté garlic, onion, and mushrooms until tender, 3 to 5 minutes. Stir in red pepper, jalapeño, corn, and green peas; cook until hot, 3 to 5 more minutes. Remove from heat and let cool.

Stir in ¼ cup tomato sauce, chick peas, Parmesan, pine nuts, basil, vinegar, and enough bread crumbs to bind mixture firmly. Season with cayenne, salt, and pepper.

Form into eight equal-size patties. Cover and refrigerate for 2 hours to set.

Preheat grill to medium. Spray a grill topper with nonstick cooking spray.

Spray burgers with nonstick cooking spray. Grill burgers on topper until golden brown and heated through, 4 to 5 minutes per side.

Top with remaining 1 cup tomato sauce and slices of bocconcini. Close lid and cook burgers for 1 minute or until cheese has melted.

Lightly toast buns. Serve burgers on buns with tomatoes and alfalfa sprouts.

SERVES 8

Grilled Tuna and Vegetable Pan Bagnat

My version of this classic French sandwich is made with all the vegetables and the tuna being grilled first. Use a grilling basket to make grilling the vegetables a lot easier. This is one big sandwich—and it's perfect for a picnic. It's big, baby! Big!

---

1 red onion, sliced

1 zucchini, halved and sliced crosswise

1 red bell pepper, cut into wedges

1 yellow bell pepper, cut into wedges

1 green bell pepper, cut into wedges

8 jumbo white mushrooms, sliced ¼ inch thick

1 bunch asparagus, trimmed

½ cup olive oil (divided use)

½ cup red wine vinegar (divided use)

Salt and pepper

2 tuna steaks (each about 6 oz. and 1 inch thick)

3 cloves garlic, minced

4 anchovy fillets, minced

¼ cup chopped fresh basil

2 TB. Dijon mustard

½ cup sliced black olives

¼ cup drained capers

1 (18-inch-long) baguette

2 vine-ripened tomatoes, thinly sliced

2 cups mixed baby greens

Preheat grill to medium-high.

In a large bowl, combine onion, zucchini, bell peppers, mushrooms, asparagus, ¼ cup olive oil, and ¼ cup vinegar; toss well. Season to taste with salt and pepper.

Place vegetables in a grill basket and grill until slightly charred and tender, 5 to 6 minutes per side. Transfer vegetables to a bowl and let cool.

Meanwhile, season tuna steaks with salt, pepper and a little olive oil. Grill for 2 to 3 minutes per side for medium-rare. Let cool.

In a bowl, whisk together remaining ¼ cup olive oil and vinegar, garlic, anchovies, basil, and mustard. Season dressing to taste with salt and pepper.

Drain grilled vegetables. Add olives, capers, and dressing. Toss gently.

Cut tuna steaks into ¼-inch-thick slices.

Cut baguette in half lengthwise. Arrange grilled vegetable mixture evenly over the bottom half the baguette. Top with layers of tuna, tomatoes, and salad greens. Top with the top half the baguette. Wrap tightly in plastic wrap, and refrigerate for 1 hour for flavors to blend.

Unwrap sandwich and, using a sharp serrated knife, slice into four or eight pieces. Serve immediately or wrap pieces individually for a picnic.

SERVES 4

Grilled Chicken Caesar Wrap

I love Caesar salad, and as a grilling freak, I even like to grill the romaine lettuce and smoke the garlic and bacon. For a quicker sandwich, use store-bought Caesar dressing instead of the marinade recipe here.

3 (6 oz.) boneless, skinless chicken breasts	1 TB. cracked black pepper
1 TB. Bone Dust BBQ Spice (page 203)	1 tsp. hot sauce
4 cloves garlic, minced	1 tsp. Worcestershire sauce
4 anchovy fillets, minced	Salt to taste
½ cup olive oil	12 slices bacon
¼ cup grated Parmesan cheese	6 (10 inch) flour tortillas
¼ cup red wine vinegar	2 cups shredded mozzarella cheese
2 TB. Dijon mustard	½ head romaine lettuce, leaves cut into ½-inch-thick chiffonade
2 TB. lemon juice	Red onion, thinly sliced
1 TB. chopped fresh thyme	½ cup store-bought creamy Caesar dressing

Rub chicken with Bone Dust BBQ Spice, pressing seasoning into meat. Place chicken between two sheets of plastic wrap and lightly pound with the smooth side of a meat mallet until ½ inch thick.

To prepare Caesar marinade, in a bowl, whisk together garlic, anchovies, oil, Parmesan, vinegar, mustard, lemon juice, thyme, pepper, hot sauce, Worcestershire sauce, and salt. Set aside ¼ cup marinade.

Lay chicken flat in a glass dish large enough to hold it in one layer. Pour over remaining ¾ cup marinade, turning chicken to coat. Marinate, covered and refrigerated, for 4 hours.

Meanwhile, cook bacon until crisp. Drain on paper towels. Crumble bacon and keep warm.

Preheat grill to medium-high.

Grill chicken, basting with reserved marinade, until fully cooked and golden brown, 4 to 5 minutes per side. Remove chicken from the grill and thinly slice crosswise.

Warm tortillas on the grill until soft and lightly charred. Place half a sliced chicken breast down the center of each tortilla. Top each with ⅓ cup shredded cheese, a little lettuce, bacon, and a few onion rings. Drizzle with store-bought Caesar dressing. Fold the bottom of tortilla up about 3 inches and roll up tortilla from one side to form a wrap. Repeat with remaining tortillas and serve immediately.

SERVES 6

Grilled Philly Cheese Steak Sandwiches

While at the state fair in Syracuse, New York, I came across a booth called The World of Cheese Steak, a tribute to the great Philly cheese steak, with more than 12 versions of different cheese steak sandwiches. Make sure you have beer for this feat of a sandwich!

4 (4 oz.) cube steaks

4 cloves garlic, minced

¼ cup soy sauce

2 TB. brown sugar

2 TB. Worcestershire sauce

1 TB. cracked black pepper

1 large red onion, sliced

4 jumbo white mushrooms, thickly sliced

1 green bell pepper, cut into ¼-inch slices

1 red bell pepper, cut into ¼-inch slices

1 poblano pepper, seeded and thinly sliced

2 TB. olive oil

1 tsp. ground fennel

½ tsp. cayenne pepper

Salt and pepper to taste

4 slices provolone cheese

4 slices mozzarella cheese

4 slices Swiss cheese

4 (6 inch) hoagie buns, halved crosswise

2 TB. melted butter

4 tsp. mayonnaise

BBQ sauce

Tip

Cube steak is an inexpensive cut of beef that has been tenderized.

In a glass dish large enough to hold steaks in one layer, whisk together garlic, soy sauce, brown sugar, Worcestershire sauce, and black pepper. Add steaks, turning to coat. Marinate, covered and refrigerated, for 4 hours.

Meanwhile, in a large bowl, toss together onion, mushrooms, green pepper, red pepper, poblano pepper, oil, fennel, cayenne pepper, salt, and pepper.

Once meat has marinated, preheat grill to high.

Grill vegetables in a grill basket until lightly charred and tender, 8 to 12 minutes per side. Transfer to a bowl and adjust seasoning.

Grill steak for 2 to 3 minutes per side for medium doneness. Top steaks with vegetable mixture. Top with slices of provolone, mozzarella, and Swiss cheese. Close the lid and cook for 1 to 2 minutes or until cheese melts.

Brush buns with melted butter and grill until golden brown and crisp. Top each bun with a cheese steak, drizzle with mayonnaise, and add top of bun.

Serve immediately with a side of BBQ sauce.

MAKES 4 SANDWICHES

Grilled Bologna Steak Sandwiches

A must-have at Rich Stadium in Buffalo while watching the Bills. Ask the deli server in your grocery store to slice the bologna in rounds ¼ to ½ inch thick. It makes for a much better sandwich than using thin sliced bologna.

4 (4 oz.) slices bologna	4 slices mozzarella cheese
2 TB. honey mustard	4 large kaiser or onion buns
Freshly ground black pepper	½ cup tomato relish
4 slices Havarti cheese	4 leaves green leaf lettuce

Preheat grill to medium-high.

Grill bologna until bologna is lightly charred and hot, 3 to 4 minutes per side. Brush top with honey mustard and season with black pepper. Top each with a slice of Havarti cheese and mozzarella cheese. Close the lid and cook until cheese melts.

Toast buns. Spread tomato relish on the bottom half of each bun. Top with grilled bologna, add lettuce, and top with the top half of bun.

Serve immediately with extra tomato relish.

MAKES 4 SANDWICHES

Grilled Halibut Fishwich

Halibut is a most delicious fish: rich with flavor, tender, and delicious. When I'm in the mood for deep-fried halibut, I usually go to my local fish and chips restaurant. But when I'm in the mood for something lighter, I make this grilled sandwich.

---

4 (4 oz.) fresh skinless halibut fillets

2 TB. Bay Seasoning (page 205)

2 TB. vegetable oil

4 cloves garlic, minced

¼ cup lemon juice

¼ cup Dijon mustard

2 TB. chopped fresh thyme

Salt and pepper to taste

¼ cup melted butter

8 slices sourdough bread

4 leaves green leaf lettuce

2 cups Tropical Coleslaw (page 39)

Ted's Tartar Sauce (recipe follows)

Season halibut with Bay Seasoning, pressing seasoning into flesh. Brush halibut with oil.

In a glass dish large enough to hold halibut in one layer, whisk together garlic, lemon juice, mustard, thyme, salt, and pepper. Add halibut, turning to coat, and marinate, covered, for 30 minutes.

Preheat grill to medium-high.

Grill halibut, basting with melted butter, until just cooked through and lightly charred, 3 to 4 minutes per side.

Grill bread until slightly crisp. Butter bread. Top four slices of bread with halibut. Top with leaf lettuce and coleslaw. Top with remaining slices of bread.

Serve immediately with my tartar sauce. (I like my mom's on page 130, but mine just works better for this sandwich.)

MAKES 4 SANDWICHES

Ted's Tartar Sauce

1 dill pickle, finely chopped
1 small shallot, diced
1 green onion, chopped
1 cup mayonnaise

2 TB. chopped capers
1 TB. lemon juice
Cayenne pepper
Salt and pepper

In a bowl, stir together pickle, shallot, green onion, mayonnaise, capers, and lemon juice. Season to taste with cayenne, salt, and pepper.

MAKES ABOUT 1 CUP

Aunt Corlis's Bread and Butter Pickles

My aunt Corlis makes the best pickles and relishes—awesome garnishes for burgers, hot dogs, and sandwiches.

---

12 seedless cucumbers	1 tsp. dill seed
6 onions, sliced	1 tsp. mustard seeds
¼ cup salt	1 tsp. celery seeds
1½ cups brown sugar	2 cups cider vinegar
2 tsp. turmeric	

Cut cucumbers into ¼-inch slices. In a large bowl, toss cucumbers and onions with salt. Cover with ice water and let soak for 4 hours.

Drain cucumbers and onions and rinse with cold water. Let drain for 10 minutes.

In a large saucepan combine brown sugar, turmeric, dill seed, mustard seeds, celery seeds, and cider vinegar. Bring to a boil.

Add cucumbers and onions; heat for 5 minutes. Do not boil. Transfer to sterilized canning jars and seal at once.

MAKES ABOUT 4 QUARTS

Sweet Corn Relish

Sweet corn relish—made with fresh sweet peaches and cream corn—is one of my favorite garnishes for a hot dog or hamburger. To get the fresh kernels, hold a shucked ear upright in a bowl and with a sharp knife slice the kernels from the cob.

½ cup corn flour

¼ cup mustard powder

1½ TB. turmeric

4 cups cider vinegar (divided use)

6 cups peaches and cream corn kernels cut from the cob (about 12 ears)

1½ cups chopped green cabbage

4 red or sweet onions, diced

1 large red bell pepper, diced

1 large green bell pepper, diced

2 cups sugar

2 TB. salt

1 TB. mustard seeds

1 TB. celery seeds

1 TB. dried thyme

In a small bowl, blend corn flour, mustard powder, and turmeric with a little cider vinegar to form a smooth paste.

In a large pot combine turmeric paste, peaches and corn, cabbage, onions, bell peppers, vinegar, sugar, salt, mustard seeds, celery seeds, and thyme. Bring to a boil. Reduce heat to medium-low and simmer, uncovered, for 45 minutes, stirring occasionally to prevent sticking.

Transfer to sterilized canning jars and seal at once.

MAKES ABOUT 4 QUARTS

Grilled Back Bacon on a Bun with Maple Beer BBQ Sauce

Also known as peameal bacon, back bacon is a salt-cured pork loin that is crusted with cornmeal. It can be purchased thinly sliced or in whole pieces. I prefer to buy a whole piece and slice it ½-inch thick. The presliced back bacon is too easy to overcook on the grill.

1½ lbs. whole back or peameal bacon
   (about 12 inches long)
4 kaiser rolls, sliced
4 slices cheddar cheese
Thinly sliced red onion

MAPLE BEER BBQ SAUCE
1 bottle beer
1 cup BBQ sauce
½ cup maple syrup
½ cup grainy mustard
3 cloves garlic, minced
2 tsp. chopped fresh thyme
1 tsp. coarsely ground black pepper
¼ tsp. salt

Brush bacon to remove cornmeal crust. Slice bacon into 24 slices, each ½-inch thick.

To prepare sauce, in a saucepan bring beer to a boil. Reduce heat and simmer until beer has reduced by half. Add BBQ sauce, maple syrup, mustard, garlic, thyme, pepper, and salt. Return to a boil and simmer for 10 minutes, stirring occasionally. Remove from heat.

Meanwhile, preheat grill to medium-high.

Grill bacon for 2 to 3 minutes per side, basting liberally with beer BBQ sauce, until cooked through and tender.

Toast buns lightly. Places six slices of grilled bacon on the bottom half of each bun. Top with extra basting sauce, cheddar cheese, and onion slices, and finish with top half of bun.

MAKES 4 SANDWICHES

Tap House Grilled Cheese

This recipe is dedicated to the folks at the Tap House in Cleveland, Ohio—a bar that gives new meaning to the grilled cheese sandwich. This is my version of their great sandwich.

¼ cup butter

8 thick slices Texas white bread

8 thick slices processed cheese

4 thin slices red onion

4 slices Monterey Jack cheese

16 slices fried bacon

4 slices Swiss cheese

4 slices beefsteak tomato

Salt and pepper to taste

Preheat grill to medium.

Butter one side of each slice of bread. Place four slices of bread butter side down.

Lay one slice processed cheese in the center of the bread. Top with red onion, Jack cheese, bacon, Swiss cheese, tomato, and another slice of processed cheese. Top with a slice of bread butter side up. Repeat for remaining sandwiches.

Grill sandwiches for 3 to 4 minutes per side, turning frequently to prevent burning, until bread is golden brown and crisp and cheese is melted.

Slice on the diagonal, season with salt and pepper, and serve with ketchup.

MAKES 4 SANDWICHES

Grilled Honey Mustard Glazed Salmon Sandwich

While living in Banff, Alberta, I worked for Sunshine Ski Resort. During spring skiing season, a favorite lunchtime sandwich was grilled salmon on a crusty roll. My version of that sandwich incorporates sweet honey and honey mustard.

---

4 (4 oz.) Atlantic salmon fillets, skinned

2 TB. Salmon Seasoning (page 205)

2 TB. vegetable oil

¼ cup grainy mustard

¼ cup honey

2 TB. chopped fresh dill

1 TB. lemon juice

4 cloves garlic, minced

Salt and pepper

8 slices pumpernickel rye bread

4 TB. butter

2 cups Cucumber and Horseradish Salad (page 63)

4 TB. Green Goddess Ranch Dressing (page 32)

4 leaves green leaf lettuce

Preheat grill to medium-high.

Season salmon fillets with Salmon Seasoning, rubbing spice into flesh. Brush salmon with oil.

Combine mustard, honey, dill, lemon juice, and garlic. Season to taste with salt and pepper.

Grill salmon for 3 to 4 minutes per side, basting with honey mustard glaze, until salmon is medium done and lightly charred.

Grill rye bread until slightly crisp, and butter slices. Top four slices of bread with salmon. Top each with ½ cup Cucumber and Horseradish Salad and drizzle with Green Goddess Ranch Dressing. Garnish with leaf lettuce and finish with a second slice of bread.

Serve immediately.

MAKES 4 SANDWICHES

My Cheese Steak Sandwich

Here's a melt-in-your-mouth sandwich for you. Using the most tender cut of beef, it's loaded with sautéed onions and mushrooms and topped with Brie. Have lots of napkins on hand, for it's sure juicy.

---

4 (6 oz.) beef tenderloin filets	1 TB. chopped fresh thyme
2 TB. Old Montreal Steak Spice (page 202)	1 TB. Dijon mustard
2 TB. butter	Salt and pepper to taste
6 cloves garlic, minced	8 slices Brie
1 onion, diced	4 slices baguette (each about 4 inches long)
2 cups sliced brown mushrooms	1 bunch arugula

Season beef with Old Montreal Steak Spice, rubbing spice into meat. Cover and set aside.

In a frying pan over medium-high heat, melt butter. Sauté garlic and onion for 2 to 3 minutes or until tender. Add mushrooms; sauté for 10 to 15 minutes, stirring occasionally, until liquid has evaporated and mushrooms are tender. Remove from heat and add thyme, mustard, salt, and pepper. Mix well. Set aside and keep warm.

Meanwhile, preheat grill to medium-high.

Grill steaks for 2 to 3 minutes per side for medium-rare.

Top each steak with one-fourth the mushroom mixture and two slices Brie. Close the lid and grill until cheese starts to melt.

Lightly toast each slice of baguette. Top with arugula and then cheese steak.

MAKES 4 SANDWICHES

Ballpark Chili Cheese Dogs

Some may say that the hot dog is what makes this sandwich, but I feel it's the bun and the condiments. Whether it's ketchup, mustard, relish, onion, sauerkraut, hot peppers, or cheese, condiments are the key to making the dog taste good. I personally think that chili and cheese make the dog best. The messier it is, the better it is.

---

2 lbs. regular ground beef
2 tsp. ground cumin
2 tsp. chili powder
1 tsp. black pepper
½ tsp. salt
1 large onion, diced
4 cloves garlic, minced
2 (19 oz.) cans red kidney beans, rinsed and drained

2 (14 oz.) cans diced tomatoes
3 poblano chili peppers, seeded and diced
2 TB. chopped fresh cilantro
8 hot dogs
8 soft sesame egg hot dog rolls
2 cups shredded cheddar cheese

Season beef with cumin, chili powder, pepper, and salt. In a frying pan over medium heat, brown with onions and garlic until liquid has evaporated and onions are brown, about 7 to 10 minutes. Stir in red kidney beans, tomatoes, and chilies. Simmer, uncovered, over medium heat for 1 hour, stirring occasionally to prevent scorching. Stir in cilantro.

Preheat grill to medium-high.

Grill hot dogs according to package instructions. Lightly toast hot dog rolls. Place a hot dog in each roll. Pour a generous amount of chili over each hot dog. Top with cheddar cheese.

Serve with plenty of napkins and, if desired, a side dish of extra chili.

SERVES 8

Grilled Turkey Steak Clubhouse with Praline Bacon

The key to this recipe is the praline-glazed bacon. It's a mix of brown sugar and ground pecans. A little sweet blends well with the turkey.

---

4 (5 oz.) boneless turkey steaks

2 TB. Malabar Pepper Rub (page 200)

¼ cup cider vinegar

2 TB. vegetable oil

¼ cup brown sugar

¼ cup ground pecans

2 TB. water

1 tsp. Worcestershire sauce

½ tsp. vanilla

½ tsp. coarsely ground black pepper

12 slices thick bacon

1 large beefsteak tomato

8 slices multi-grain bread

Mayonnaise

4 leaves green leaf lettuce

1 small red onion, thinly sliced

4 slices Swiss cheese

Rub turkey steaks with Malabar Pepper Rub, pressing seasoning into flesh.

In a glass dish large enough to hold turkey steaks, whisk together vinegar and oil. Add turkey steaks, turning to coat. Marinate, covered and refrigerated, for 2 hours.

In a small saucepan over medium heat, combine brown sugar, pecans, water, Worcestershire sauce, vanilla, and black pepper. Bring to a boil, reduce heat and simmer, stirring occasionally, for 5 minutes or until syrup is thick. Set aside.

In a large frying pan, fry bacon until it is just crisp. Add brown sugar syrup. Turn bacon to coat; remove from heat and keep warm.

Preheat grill to medium-high.

Grill turkey steaks for 4 to 5 minutes per side or until fully cooked and lightly charred.

Cut eight thin slices from tomato. Toast bread slices. Spread one slice of toast with mayonnaise. Add lettuce, two tomato slices, and red onion. Slice turkey steak against the grain and lay over onions. Add three slices praline bacon, and top with one slice Swiss cheese and a second slice toast. Repeat for remaining sandwiches.

MAKES 4 SANDWICHES

Grilled Lemon Chicken with Herbed Goat Cheese Spread and Roasted Red Peppers

This great summer picnic sandwich can be served hot or cold.

4 (6 oz.) boneless skinless chicken breasts
¼ cup Herb Mustard Rub (page 208)
¼ cup lemon juice
2 TB. olive oil
2 large red bell peppers, roasted, peeled, seeded, and sliced

HERBED GOAT CHEESE SPREAD
1 (200 g) log soft creamy goat cheese
¼ cup lemon juice

3 green onions, chopped
2 TB. olive oil
2 TB. chopped fresh basil
2 TB. chopped fresh parsley
1 TB. chopped fresh mint
1 tsp. cracked black pepper
Salt to taste
1 loaf sourdough black olive baguette
1 bunch arugula

Season chicken with Herb Mustard Rub. In a glass dish large enough to hold chicken, whisk together lemon juice and olive oil. Add chicken, turning to coat. Marinate, covered and refrigerated, for 4 hours.

Meanwhile, prepare Herbed Goat Cheese Spread by combining goat cheese, lemon juice, green onions, olive oil, basil, parsley, mint, pepper, and salt. Cover and refrigerate until needed.

Preheat grill to medium-high.

Slice baguette diagonally into eight 1-inch-thick slices. Brush one side of each slice with olive oil.

Grill chicken breasts for 5 to 6 minutes per side or until fully cooked and golden brown. Remove from grill and thinly slice against the grain.

Lightly grill bread slices, olive oil side down.

Place arugula leaves on four slices of bread. Top each with a chicken breast. Top with roasted red peppers. Spread goat cheese on remaining four slices of bread and top sandwiches.

Serve immediately.

SERVES 4

Grilled Muffuletta Sandwich

This recipe is offered in celebration of the 40 or 50 muffuletta sandwiches I have eaten at Central Grocery in New Orleans. Serve this grilled version with an ice-cold beer.

---

3 (6 oz.) boneless skinless chicken breasts

1½ TB. Bone Dust BBQ Spice (page 203)

3 cloves garlic, minced

2 TB. olive oil

2 TB. red wine vinegar

8 slices pancetta

1 loaf round Italian bread

6 leaves green leaf lettuce

2 tomatoes, thinly sliced

½ small seedless cucumber, thinly sliced diagonally

8 slices prosciutto

8 slices spicy capocollo

8 slices provolone cheese

OLIVE SALAD

1½ cups sliced pimento-stuffed green olives

1 small red onion, diced

1 stalk celery, finely diced

1 green bell pepper, diced

1 red bell pepper, diced

4 green onions, chopped

3 cloves garlic, minced

¼ cup grated Parmesan cheese

¼ cup olive oil

2 TB. red wine vinegar

1 TB. chopped flat-leaf parsley

1 TB. chopped fresh basil

1 TB. Dijon mustard

1 tsp. crushed chilies

Salt and pepper to taste

Rub chicken breasts with Bone Dust BBQ Spice. In a glass dish large enough to hold chicken, whisk together garlic, olive oil, and vinegar. Add chicken, turning to coat. Cover and refrigerate for 4 to 6 hours.

To make salad, in a bowl, combine olives, onion, celery, green and red peppers, green onions, garlic, Parmesan cheese, olive oil, vinegar, parsley, basil, mustard, crushed chilies, salt, and pepper. Mix well, cover, and refrigerate. (Salad can be made a few hours in advance.)

Preheat grill to medium-high.

Continued ...

Grill chicken for 5 to 6 minutes per side or until cooked through. Let cool. Grill pancetta for 1 to 2 minutes per side or until crisp. Drain on paper towels. Thinly slice cooled chicken.

Slice the top off the loaf of bread. (Don't eat the top—you will need it for the lid.) Scoop out the middle to make a bread bowl, leaving a wall about ½-inch thick. Spoon in half the olive salad. Top with lettuce, tomatoes, and cucumbers. Add chicken, pancetta, prosciutto, capocollo, and provolone cheese. Top with remaining olive salad. Cover with bread lid, wrap tightly in plastic wrap, and refrigerate for 1 hour.

Cut loaf into six or eight wedges and serve with a green salad and ice-cold beer. (Try a Dixie—that's what I drink with my Central Grocery muffuletta.)

SERVES 1, 2, 3, OR 4

Seaside Grilled Shrimp Fajitas with Mango Salsa

There is a little restaurant in Seaside, California, called Turtle Bay. Over the past few years, I have had the pleasure of eating a few meals there. It is just what a chef needs after a full day of cooking on the race circuit at Laguna Seca. This is my version of this tasty dish.

16 jumbo shrimp, peeled and deveined
2 TB. Herb Mustard Rub (page 208)
2 TB. olive oil
4 (10 inch) flour tortillas

1 cup Black Bean Paste (recipe follows)
1 cup Mango Salsa (recipe follows)
2 cups Firecracker Coleslaw (page 72)

Soak four bamboo skewers in hot water for 30 minutes. (Or use metal skewers.)

In a bowl, combine shrimp, Herb Mustard Rub, and olive oil. Toss to evenly coat shrimp. Thread four shrimp onto each skewer. Marinate, covered and refrigerated, for 20 minutes.

Preheat grill to high.

Grill shrimp for 2 to 3 minutes per side or until opaque in color and shrimp are tender and just done. Keep warm on grill.

Warm tortillas on the hot grill for 30 seconds per side.

Spread 1 tortilla with ¼ cup black bean paste. Top with one skewer of shrimp, removing the skewer. Top with 1 or 2 tablespoons mango salsa and finish with ½ cup coleslaw.

Fold the bottom quarter of tortilla up to the center. Starting from the side, roll tortilla into a cylinder. Repeat with remaining tortillas.

Serve with extra salsa, guacamole (page 98), and sour cream.

SERVES 4

Tip

Use the leftover black bean paste and mango salsa as a dip for potato chips or tortilla chips.

Continued . . .

Black Bean Paste

1½ cups cooked black beans, rinsed and
    drained if canned
1 TB. lemon juice
1 tsp. Bone Dust BBQ Spice (page 203)
1 TB. chopped fresh cilantro

2 jalapeño peppers, chopped
3 green onions, chopped
1 clove garlic, minced
½ cup frozen sweet corn kernels, thawed
Salt and pepper to taste

In a food processor, blend until smooth black beans, lemon juice, and Bone Dust BBQ Spice.

Add cilantro, jalapeño peppers, green onions, and garlic. Pulse to blend.

Transfer bean mixture to a mixing bowl. Add corn, salt, and pepper. Mix thoroughly. Refrigerate at least 1 hour before using.

MAKES 2 CUPS

Mango Salsa

1 ripe mango, peeled, seeded, and diced
1 small red onion, diced
2 green onions, chopped
1 clove garlic, minced
1 lime, juiced

1 TB. chopped fresh cilantro
1 TB. olive oil
Dash hot sauce
Salt and pepper

In a bowl, combine mango, red onion, green onions, garlic, lime juice, cilantro, and olive oil. Season to taste with hot sauce, salt, and pepper.

MAKES ABOUT 2 CUPS

Grilled Pizza

Quick BBQ Pizza Dough

This simple recipe for pizza dough requires no proofing time. Perfect for when you're in a hurry.

---

1 cup all-purpose flour
1 cup corn flour
¼ cup grated Parmesan cheese (divided use)
1 TB. Bone Dust BBQ Spice (page 203)
1 TB. chopped fresh cilantro
2½ tsp. baking powder

¼ cup butter, diced
½ to ⅔ cup milk
Olive oil
Salt and pepper, to taste
Special equipment: 1 perforated pizza pan

In a bowl, stir together all-purpose flour, corn flour, 2 tablespoons Parmesan cheese, BBQ spice, cilantro, and baking powder. Add butter; rub in with fingertips until mixture resembles coarse bread crumbs.

Stir in enough milk to form a dough. Turn out onto a lightly floured surface and knead for 2 to 3 minutes or until dough is smooth. (If not using dough immediately, wrap in plastic wrap and refrigerate until needed.)

Roll out the dough to a 10-inch circle. Transfer to a perforated pizza pan.

To parbake the pizza crust:

Preheat oven to 425°F.

Brush pizza dough with olive oil. Sprinkle with remaining 2 tablespoons Parmesan cheese, salt, and pepper.

Bake for 6 to 8 minutes or until the dough is partially cooked and lightly colored.

Use immediately in the following recipes or with your favorite sauce and toppings.

MAKES DOUGH FOR 1 (10 INCH) PIZZA

BBQ Pulled Pork Pizza

While on a trip to northwest Arkansas, I had the pleasure of eating some tender, juicy pulled pork at Penguin BBQ in Fayetteville. There was so much on my plate that I took the remainder over to a buddy's place. That evening we made an outstanding pizza with the leftover pork.

¾ cup hickory smoke-flavored BBQ sauce (divided use)

1 Quick BBQ Pizza Dough (page 152), parbaked

1½ cups shredded mozzarella cheese

1½ cups shredded cheddar cheese

2 cups pulled Redneck Riviera Smoked Boston Butt (page 318)

1 small sweet onion, sliced

1 cup sliced mushrooms

½ cup hot banana pepper rings

Preheat grill to medium.

Spread ½ cup BBQ sauce evenly over pizza crust, leaving a ½-inch border around the edge.

Combine mozzarella and cheddar cheeses. Sprinkle evenly over pizza.

Toss pulled pork with remaining ¼ cup BBQ sauce. Spread pork, onion, mushrooms, and hot peppers over cheese.

Grill pizza with the lid closed until cheese melts and toppings are hot, 8 to 10 minutes. Check periodically that crust isn't burning. If crust darkens too quickly, reduce heat to low.

Remove pizza from grill and cut into 6 slices.

SERVES 2 TO 3

Grilled Pizza with Three Cheeses, Roasted Garlic, and Bacon

Three of my favorite toppings—cheese, garlic, and bacon—make a delicious pizza. Double the toppings for pure decadence.

¼ cup olive oil from roasted garlic (page 201)
1 Quick BBQ Pizza Dough (page 152), parbaked
Salt and freshly ground black pepper
12 cloves roasted garlic (page 201)
½ cup soft creamy goat cheese
1½ cups shredded mozzarella cheese

1 cup shredded Monterey Jack cheese
1 small sweet onion, sliced
1 red bell pepper, roasted, peeled, seeded, and cut into ¼-inch strips
8 slices bacon, partially cooked and cut into ½-inch pieces
1 TB. chopped fresh rosemary

Preheat grill to medium.

Brush olive oil evenly over pizza crust, leaving a ½-inch border around the edge. Season to taste with salt and pepper.

Mash roasted garlic. Mix together garlic and goat cheese. Spread evenly over pizza crust. Combine mozzarella and Jack cheeses. Spread evenly over pizza. Top with onion, red pepper, and bacon. Season with salt and pepper.

Grill pizza with the lid closed until cheese melts and toppings are hot, 8 to 10 minutes. Check periodically that crust isn't burning. If crust darkens too quickly, reduce heat to low.

Remove pizza from grill, sprinkle with rosemary, and cut into 6 slices.

SERVES 2 TO 3

BBQ Chicken Pizza with Artichokes and Four Cheeses

Pizza is the most popular finger food after potato chips and French fries. A summer barbecue wouldn't be complete without a great pizza.

¼ to ½ cup **BBQ sauce**
1 **Quick BBQ Pizza Dough (page 152),** parbaked
1 cup shredded **Swiss cheese**
1 cup shredded **mozzarella cheese**
1 cup shredded **Monterey Jack cheese**

1 (6 oz.) jar marinated **artichoke hearts,** drained
2 cups shredded **grilled chicken**
1 small **red onion,** sliced
½ cup crumbled **goat cheese**
1 TB. chopped fresh **cilantro**

Preheat grill to medium.

Spread BBQ sauce evenly over pizza crust, leaving a ½-inch border around the edge.

Combine the Swiss, mozzarella, and Monterey Jack cheeses. Sprinkle evenly over the pizza.

Quarter artichoke hearts and pat dry with paper towels. Arrange artichoke hearts, chicken, and red onion on top of cheese. Sprinkle with goat cheese. Transfer to a perforated pizza pan.

Grill pizza, with the lid closed, for 5 to 7 minutes or until cheese melts and the toppings are hot. Check periodically to see that crust is not burning. If crust darkens too quickly, reduce heat to low and continue to grill.

Remove pizza from grill, sprinkle with cilantro, and cut into six slices.

SERVES 2 TO 3

Tip

For the chicken, try my Devil's Brewed Roast Chicken (page 357).

Shrimp and Brie Pizza with Almond Pesto

The beauty of pizza is that you can put anything you want on top. Here, the richness of the Brie blends well with shrimp. If you are not a fan of shrimp, try crab, lobster, or even smoked salmon. A delicious twist on a classic.

⅓ cup Almond Pesto (recipe follows)
1 Quick BBQ Pizza Dough (page 152), parbaked
1 lb. jumbo shrimp, peeled and deveined
1 TB. Bay Seasoning (page 205)

1 TB. olive oil
1 small (125 g) wheel Brie
1 small sweet onion (Vidalia, Texas Sweet, or Maui), sliced
¼ cup grated Parmesan cheese

Preheat grill to medium.

Spread Almond Pesto evenly over pizza crust, leaving a ½-inch border at the edge.

Pat shrimp dry with paper towels. Slice each shrimp in half lengthwise. In a bowl, toss shrimp with Bay Seasoning and olive oil. Lay shrimp evenly over sauce.

Using a sharp knife, cut white rind from Brie. Cut Brie into ¼-inch-thick slices and then into 1-inch squares. Lay Brie on top of shrimp. Sprinkle with onion slices and Parmesan cheese. Transfer to a perforated pizza pan.

Grill pizza, with the lid closed, for 5 to 7 minutes or until cheese melts and toppings are hot. Check periodically that the crust is not burning. If the crust darkens too quickly, reduce heat to low and continue to grill.

Remove pizza from grill and cut into six slices.

SERVES 2 TO 3

Almond Pesto

1 large bunch fresh basil

½ cup chopped flat-leaf parsley

½ cup toasted slivered almonds

¼ cup grated Parmesan cheese

6 cloves garlic, chopped

2 TB. chopped fresh dill

2 TB. hot water

1 TB. lemon juice

1 tsp. black pepper

½ tsp. salt

⅔ cup olive oil

Wash basil and remove leaves; pat dry. In a food processor combine basil, parsley, almonds, Parmesan cheese, garlic, dill, water, lemon juice, pepper, and salt. Blend until finely chopped. With the motor running, add oil in a steady stream until fully incorporated. If the mixture is too thick, add a little more hot water to give you a better spreading consistency.

MAKES 1½ CUPS

Breakfast

BBQ Breakfast Pepper Baked Eggs

Want to grill your eggs? Use bell pepper halves to hold the eggs. This is an easy breakfast recipe that is delicious.

4 large red or yellow bell peppers	2 tsp. Bone Dust BBQ Spice (page 203)
1 large red onion	1 TB. chopped fresh thyme
8 large shiitake mushrooms	8 large eggs
2 TB. olive oil	1 cup shredded cheddar cheese

Preheat grill to medium-high.

Cut bell peppers in half through the stem. Carefully remove the seeds and ribs. Set peppers aside.

Slice onion into rounds. Toss onions with mushrooms, oil, and Bone Dust BBQ Spice.

Grill onions and mushrooms in a grill basket until slightly charred and tender, about 10 minutes.

Dice onions and mushrooms. Place in a bowl and toss with thyme.

Grill peppers, turning twice, until they just start to get soft, about 5 minutes.

Transfer peppers, cut side up, to a grill topper. Place 2 tablespoons mushroom mixture in each pepper. Crack an egg into each pepper. Grill peppers with the lid closed for 5 minutes. Top eggs with cheddar cheese. Close lid and bake for 3 more minutes or until cheese melts.

Serve with grilled peameal bacon steaks, grilled toast, and a breakfast shake.

SERVES 8

Cast-Iron Breakfast Strata

This wonderful breakfast egg pudding can be prepared the night before and baked on the grill in the morning. You can also add cooked bacon when you add the cheese.

---

4 TB. vegetable oil (divided use)
1 large onion, thinly sliced
2 cups sliced mushrooms
2 TB. chopped fresh herbs
Salt and pepper to taste

8 day-old croissants
2 cups shredded aged white cheddar cheese
12 large eggs
1½ cups heavy cream

In a large frying pan, heat 2 tablespoons oil over high heat. Sauté onion until tender and slightly caramelized, 5 to 7 minutes. Add mushrooms; cook, stirring frequently, until mushrooms are tender and all oil has evaporated. Stir in herbs, salt, and pepper. Let cool.

Tear croissants into 2-inch cubes. In a large bowl, combine croissants, mushroom mixture, and cheddar cheese. Gently mix and season to taste with salt and pepper.

Brush a large, deep, cast-iron pan with the remaining 2 tablespoons oil. Transfer croissant mixture to the cast-iron pan.

In another bowl, whisk together eggs and cream. Season to taste with salt and pepper. Pour mixture over croissants, filling to the edge of the pan. (Depending on the size of your pan, you might need to add an extra egg and a little more cream.) Gently push all mixture down into egg mixture. Cover with plastic wrap and refrigerate overnight.

Preheat grill to medium-high.

Remove plastic wrap from strata and cover loosely with foil. Place on the grill, close the lid, and bake for 45 minutes. Remove the foil, close the lid, and cook for another 15 minutes or until the top has puffed and browned. A wooden skewer inserted in the middle should come out clean and dry.

Carefully remove from grill and let sit for 10 minutes before serving.

SERVES 6 TO 8

Mucked-Up Eggs

My dad used to make this breakfast for me as a kid. The definition of a mucked-up egg is two soft-boiled eggs spooned over diced buttered toast and then mucked up with a spoon. Here's my updated version of this classic family recipe.

---

3 TB. butter

1 small onion, diced

2 cups halved button mushrooms

2 green onions, chopped

1 TB. chopped fresh parsley

1 TB. honey mustard

8 slices bacon, cut in ½-inch pieces

Salt, black pepper, and cayenne pepper to taste

6 thick slices white bread

8 large eggs

Hot sauce

Tip

This is the perfect cure for any hangover

Melt butter in a large frying pan over medium-high heat. Cook onion and mushrooms, stirring occasionally, until golden brown, 10 to 12 minutes. Transfer to a bowl and toss with green onions, parsley, and honey mustard.

In the same pan, fry bacon until crisp. Add to mushroom mixture and season with salt, black pepper, and cayenne pepper. Remove from heat and keep warm.

Toast bread. Butter bread and cut into ½-inch cubes. Toss with mushroom mixture.

Soft-boil eggs for 3 minutes.

Spoon equal amounts mushroom mixture into four wide-mouthed beer glasses.

Carefully peel eggs and spoon 1 egg into each glass. Season to taste with salt, pepper, and hot sauce and stir until mucked up.

SERVES 4

Breakfast Grilled Steak and Eggs

Here's a lumberjack breakfast treat for those days when you wake up screaming hungry. If it's a weekend, have a beer with this hearty breakfast. While I was working as a chef for a hunting and fishing lodge in northern Ontario, there was a fishing guide named Mountain, and his daily breakfast would include the following: 1 (8 oz.) steak, 1 lb. bacon, 12 slices toast, 8 eggs, 4 cups coffee, 2 beers, and 1 shot Jack Daniel's.

---

4 (8 oz.) beef tenderloin steaks

¼ cup + 1 TB. Hell's Fire Chili Paste (page 206)

2 TB. butter

1 large Spanish onion, sliced

1 large red bell pepper, thinly sliced

2 cups sliced shiitake mushrooms

1 tsp. chopped fresh sage

Salt and pepper

1 lb. breakfast sausages

4 extra-large eggs

Rub steaks with ¼ cup Hell's Fire Chili Paste. Marinate, covered and refrigerated, for at least 2 hours or overnight.

Melt butter in a large frying pan over medium-high heat. Sauté onion, red pepper, and mushrooms until golden brown and tender, 8 to 10 minutes. Stir in the remaining 1 tablespoon Chili Paste, sage, and salt and pepper to taste. Remove from heat and keep warm.

Preheat grill to medium.

Grill sausages until fully cooked and crispy, 8 to 10 minutes. Set aside sausages, loosely covered with foil.

Grill steaks for 3 to 5 minutes per side for medium-rare. Set aside steaks, loosely covered with foil.

On the grill side burner (or on the stove), fry eggs in a little butter or oil.

Put steaks on plates and top each steak with mushroom mixture. Top with sausages and top with a fried egg.

Serve with a cold beer.

SERVES 4

The Muffin for Breakfast and Lunch

Fruit-flavored muffins are pretty good, but personally I believe that muffins should be loaded with bacon, cheese, and other good stuff. Try these savory muffins on for size! They're awesome served with poached eggs or a steak.

8 slices thick-cut bacon, diced	½ cup melted butter
4½ cups all-purpose flour	2 green onions, finely chopped
4 tsp. baking powder	1 cup ¼-inch cubes cheddar cheese
1½ tsp. salt	1 cup ¼-inch cubes Swiss cheese
2 large eggs	1 TB. chopped fresh parsley
2 cups whole milk	Pinch cayenne pepper

Tip

For a bizarre twist, use a Cajun injector filled with warmed Cheez Whiz and inject the cheese into the center of the muffin.

Fry bacon until crisp; set aside to drain on paper towels. Set aside 1 tablespoon bacon fat.

Preheat oven to 425°F. Grease a muffin pan.

In a large bowl, sift together flour, baking powder, and salt.

In a separate bowl, beat together eggs, milk, butter and reserved bacon fat. Pour into the flour mixture; stir quickly to mix completely. Gently fold in bacon, green onions, cheddar cheese, Swiss cheese, parsley, and cayenne.

Spoon into muffin tins, filling to the top. Bake until golden brown and cheese is bubbling, 18 to 25 minutes.

MAKES 12 REALLY BIG MUFFINS

Scrumptious Sides

Grilled Asparagus with Raspberries and Asiago

Tender, sweet asparagus is perfect for the grill. Place the spears across the grill bars to keep them from falling through the grates.

---

2 bunches asparagus, trimmed
2 TB. olive oil
2 TB. raspberry-flavored vinegar
Salt and pepper to taste

1 TB. chopped fresh thyme
½ pint fresh raspberries
¼ cup shredded Asiago cheese

Preheat grill to high.

In a large bowl, gently toss asparagus with oil, vinegar, salt, and pepper.

Place asparagus across the grill and cook, turning carefully, until tender and crisp, 3 to 5 minutes.

Return asparagus to the bowl. Add thyme; drizzle with extra raspberry vinegar and olive oil. Season to taste with salt and pepper. Toss well.

Arrange asparagus on a platter and garnish with fresh raspberries and Asiago cheese.

SERVES 8

Down-Home Collard Greens

My first experience with collard greens came while on a culinary expedition to New Orleans. Famed Chef Leah Chase, owner and operator of Dooky Chase Restaurant, prepared this dish for me along with some of the best fried chicken I've ever had. This is my version of her collard greens.

1 bunch collard greens (1 to 1½ lbs.)	¼ cup chicken stock
2 TB. kosher salt	2 TB. corn syrup
2 TB. vegetable oil	2 TB. cider vinegar
1 onion, diced	2 TB. butter
6 cloves garlic, minced	Salt and pepper
2 jalapeño peppers, seeded and diced	

Cut stems off collard greens and discard. Stack leaves on top of each other. Roll leaves from the side to form a cigar shape. Thinly slice collard cigar into a chiffonade.

Wash sliced collards in cold water; drain well. Transfer leaves to a bowl and toss well with kosher salt. Let stand for 15 minutes. Rinse under cold water and drain well. (Use a salad spinner to remove as much moisture as possible.)

In a large, deep skillet over medium-high heat, heat vegetable oil. Sauté onion, garlic, and jalapeño until tender, 3 to 5 minutes. Add collard greens and chicken stock. Bring to a boil, reduce heat, and simmer greens for 10 minutes, boiling off excess moisture. Stir in corn syrup, vinegar, and butter. Season to taste with salt and pepper.

Serve immediately with your favorite ribs and chicken.

SERVES 4 TO 6

Tip

Be sure to wash the greens well to remove grit and sand.

Marinated Corn on the Cob

One of my clients asked me to develop some new menu items for Lee Roy Selmon's, a restaurant in Tampa, Florida. In one of our "ideation" sessions we got to discussing corn on the cob, and it was said that a restaurant in Nashville served a marinated corn on the cob. Well, into the kitchen we went, and out came this recipe. It is a perfect dish for any picnic or party.

---

12 ears peaches and cream corn, unhusked
¼ cup olive oil
1 cup Bay Seasoning (page 205)

MARINADE
1 small onion, diced
2 cloves garlic, minced

1 cup gourmet BBQ sauce
1 cup water
½ cup olive oil
½ cup apple cider vinegar
3 TB. Bay Seasoning (page 205)
2 TB. lemon juice

Pull the husk away from the ear without removing it, and remove the silk. Twist the husk at the base—don't remove it; it makes a handy handle. Rub corn with olive oil and Bay Seasoning. Place on a steamer rack over boiling water and steam corn until just done, about 8 minutes.

Make marinade: In a glass dish large enough to hold corn, whisk together onion, garlic, BBQ sauce, water, oil, vinegar, Bay Seasoning, and lemon juice.

Lay corn in marinade, turning to coat, with the husks over the edge of the dish. Marinade should completely cover corn. Marinate at room temperature for 2 to 4 hours.

Serve at room temperature.

SERVES 6 TO 12

Grilled Eggplant

This is a great side dish, but you can also coarsely chop the eggplant and mix it with a little seasoning and olive oil. Spread on grilled rustic Italian bread slices for eggplant bruschetta.

---

1 large eggplant	1 TB. chopped fresh rosemary
2 TB. salt	1 tsp. crushed red chilies
4 cloves garlic, minced	1 tsp. ground cumin
½ cup olive oil	Salt and pepper to taste
½ cup red wine vinegar	

Cut eggplant into ½-inch-thick rounds. In a large bowl, toss eggplant with salt. Let stand for 30 minutes to extract the bitterness from eggplant. Rinse under cold water and drain well.

In the bowl, whisk together garlic, oil, vinegar, rosemary, chilies, cumin, salt, and pepper. Add eggplant, turning to coat well. Let marinate for 2 hours.

Preheat grill to medium-high.

Remove eggplant from marinade (reserving marinade for basting). Grill eggplant, basting liberally with reserved marinade, until slightly charred and tender, 5 to 7 minutes per side.

SERVES 6

Grilled Oyster Mushroom and Gorgonzola Polenta

Polenta is perfect for the grill. You could eat it hot out of the pot, but I like to allow it to set and then cut it into squares, triangles, circles, or diamonds. Brush the polenta cakes lightly with oil and grill. Be careful not to overcook the polenta, or it will become hard and taste like sawdust.

---

2 cups chicken stock
1 cup milk
3 TB. butter
½ tsp. salt
1¼ cups cornmeal
Grilled Oyster Mushrooms (recipe follows)
2 shallots, chopped

3 green onions, diced
¾ cup crumbled Gorgonzola
½ cup Parmesan cheese
1 TB. chopped fresh oregano
Salt and pepper to taste
Olive oil

Lightly grease a cookie sheet.

In a large saucepan over medium-high heat, bring chicken stock, milk, and butter to a gentle boil. Stir in salt. While stirring, pour in cornmeal in a steady stream. Reduce heat to medium-low and stir every couple minutes for 15 to 20 minutes, until mixture is soft and pulls away cleanly from the sides of the pot.

Remove from heat and stir in grilled mushrooms, shallots, green onions, Gorgonzola, Parmesan cheese, oregano, salt, and pepper.

Pour mixture onto the cookie sheet and spread to a thickness of 1½ inches. Cover with plastic wrap and let cool.

Cut polenta into 3-inch squares or triangles or use cookie cutters to make various shapes.

Preheat grill to medium-high.

Brush polenta pieces with olive oil and grill until lightly charred and crisp on the outside, 4 to 6 minutes per side.

Serve warm with grilled lamb, shrimp, or chicken.

SERVES 8 TO 10

Grilled Oyster Mushrooms

8 large oyster mushrooms (about ½ lb.)
4 cloves garlic, chopped
¼ cup olive oil

¼ cup balsamic vinegar
1 TB. chopped fresh oregano
Salt and pepper to taste

In a bowl, soak mushrooms in warm water to cover for 5 minutes. (The mushrooms will absorb moisture so that during the grilling, they do not burn and dry out.)

Drain mushrooms and combine with garlic, oil, vinegar, oregano, salt, and pepper. Let marinate for 30 minutes.

Preheat grill to medium-high.

Remove mushrooms from marinade (reserving marinade for basting) and grill, basting frequently with the reserved marinade, until tender and slightly charred, 3 to 5 minutes per side.

Let cool slightly. Tear or slice mushrooms into strips.

Grilled Portobello Mushroom Fries

Thick wedges of giant Portobello mushrooms make an incredible fry. Or top your burger with them.

---

8 very large (5 to 6 inches across) Portobello
    mushroom caps
8 cloves garlic, minced
1 cup hickory smoke–flavored BBQ sauce
½ cup vegetable oil

½ cup balsamic vinegar
¼ cup honey
2 TB. Bone Dust BBQ Spice (page 203)
2 TB. chopped fresh rosemary
Coarse salt and cracked black pepper to taste

In a large bowl, soak mushrooms in hot water to cover for 15 minutes. Drain on paper towels.

In the bowl, whisk together garlic, BBQ sauce, oil, vinegar, honey, Bone Dust BBQ Spice, rosemary, salt, and pepper. Slice each mushroom into 1½-inch-wide sticks. Add to marinade and stir to coat well. Let marinate for 15 minutes.

Preheat grill to medium-high.

Grill mushrooms until tender and lightly charred, 2 to 3 minutes per side. Season with coarse salt and serve immediately.

SERVES 4 TO 6

Foil-Baked Stuffed Red Onions

I love onions—baked, fried, raw, sautéed, in soup—you name the onion dish and I will eat it. I had my most memorable onion while passing through Vidalia, Georgia, one May. I stopped at a roadside stand and bought a few (hundred) sweet Vidalia onions. I peeled one, sliced it, and seasoned it with salt. That was it. Tangy, sweet, and delicious.

---

4 medium-large red onions, peeled
8 slices bacon, diced and cooked almost crisp
4 cloves garlic, minced
2 green onions, finely chopped
½ cup shredded Oka cheese
¼ cup chopped walnuts

2 TB. cider vinegar
1 TB. chopped fresh parsley
Pinch cayenne pepper
Salt and pepper to taste
Olive oil

Preheat grill to high.

Cut a ½-inch-thick slice from the top of each onion and, using a melon-ball cutter, scoop out the center, leaving a shell of about 3 or 4 onion layers.

In a bowl, combine bacon, garlic, green onions, Oka, walnuts, vinegar, parsley, cayenne, salt, and pepper.

Cut four sheets of foil about 12 inches square. Brush one side of each sheet with oil. Place an onion shell on each sheet. Stuff each onion with cheese mixture, carefully pressing the stuffing firmly into place.

Wrap each onion tightly in the foil. Grill, turning occasionally, until onions are tender, 40 to 50 minutes. Remove from grill and carefully unwrap onions.

Cut each onion in half. Serve with T-bone or porterhouse steaks.

SERVES 4 TO 8

Drunken Peppers

If you like hot peppers on your pizza or as a side to your favorite sandwich, this recipe should make your day hot and spicy.

---

2 lbs. banana peppers	1 TB. black peppercorns
1 lb. jalapeño peppers	4 cups white vinegar
1 lb. red finger chili peppers	2 cups water
1 large red onion	1 cup vodka
2 TB. mustard seeds	½ cup sugar
1 TB. dill seeds	½ cup kosher salt

Wash a 4-quart crock or other sealable nonplastic container. Dry thoroughly.

Cut hot peppers and onion into ½-inch-thick slices. Place peppers, onion, mustard seeds, dill seeds, and peppercorns in the crock.

In a large saucepan, bring vinegar, water, vodka, sugar, and salt to a rolling boil. Remove from heat and let cool for 5 minutes.

Pour over pepper mixture and stir thoroughly.

Let cool completely. Cover and refrigerate for at least 5 days to allow peppers to pickle.

Serve with your favorite sandwiches and burgers. Peppers will keep, refrigerated, for 8 weeks.

MAKES A SMALL KEG OF HOT PEPPERS

Spicy Garlic Dill Pickles

When I worked at Rhodes restaurant in Toronto back in the mid-1980s, we used to prepare our own crunchy, slightly spicy dill pickles. This is my version of these tasty pickles.

5 lbs. pickling cucumbers (about 5 inches long)	⅔ cup kosher salt
3 banana peppers	⅔ cup sugar
4 jalapeño peppers	3 TB. mustard seeds
1 large Spanish onion	2 TB. black peppercorns
16 cloves garlic, minced	1 TB. coriander seeds
½ cup chopped fresh dill	1 TB. dill seeds
5 cups white vinegar	1 TB. crushed red chilies
2½ cups water	3 bay leaves

Wash a 5-quart crock or other sealable nonplastic container. Dry thoroughly.

Cut cucumbers lengthwise into 4 or 6 wedges, depending on thickness. Slice banana and jalapeño peppers into thin rings, seeds and all. Cut onion into ½-inch-thick slices. Place cucumbers, peppers, onion, garlic, and dill in the crock.

In a large saucepan, bring vinegar, water, salt, sugar, mustard seeds, peppercorns, coriander seeds, dill seeds, chilies, and bay leaves to a rolling boil. Remove from heat and let cool for 5 minutes.

Pour over cucumber mixture and stir thoroughly.

Let cool completely. Cover and refrigerate for at least 5 days to allow cucumbers to pickle.

Serve with your favorite sandwiches and burgers. Pickles will keep, refrigerated, for 8 weeks.

MAKES A SMALL BARREL OF PICKLES

Overstuffed Twice-Baked Potatoes

Twice-baked potatoes, loaded with three cheeses, bacon or ham, and green onions, are a creamy and delicious accompaniment to any steak. Try different cheeses, as well as grilled chicken or BBQ pulled pork in place of the ham.

---

4 large (10 to 12 oz.) baking potatoes, scrubbed

8 cloves roasted garlic (page 201), mashed

1 roasted red pepper, peeled, seeded, and diced

3 green onions, chopped

1 cup diced smoked ham

½ cup crumbled creamy goat cheese

½ cup shredded smoked Gruyère cheese

½ cup shredded mozzarella cheese

2 TB. butter

2 tsp. Bone Dust BBQ Spice (page 203)

Salt and pepper to taste

Preheat oven to 400°F.

Bake potatoes on the oven rack until tender, about 1½ hours. Let cool slightly. Do not turn off oven.

Cut potatoes in half lengthwise. Carefully scoop out flesh and place in a large bowl, reserving skins on a baking sheet. Mash flesh and add roasted garlic, red pepper, green onions, ham, goat cheese, Gruyère, mozzarella, butter, Bone Dust BBQ Spice, salt, and pepper. Mix thoroughly.

Spoon potato mixture into potato skins, pressing firmly to stuff them really well.

Return potatoes to oven and bake until heated through, 10 to 15 minutes. Serve immediately.

SERVES 8

Goat Cheese Mashed Potatoes with Pulled Pork Gravy

Potatoes can't get any better than this. Rich and creamy mashed potatoes flavored with goat cheese and topped with a BBQ pulled pork gravy. A meal in a bowl.

---

2 lbs. Yukon Gold potatoes, peeled
3 TB. butter
½ cup heavy cream
¼ cup soft creamy goat cheese
¼ cup finely chopped fresh thyme
Salt and pepper to taste

PULLED PORK GRAVY
2 TB. butter
1 small red onion, sliced
4 cloves garlic, minced
2 cups oyster mushrooms, sliced
2 cups pulled Redneck Riviera Smoked Boston Butt (page 318)
½ cup beef stock
1 cup gourmet BBQ sauce
2 TB. malt vinegar
Pinch cayenne pepper

In a large pot of boiling salted water, cook potatoes until tender, 15 to 20 minutes. Drain well and return pot to low heat for 1 minute to dry potatoes.

While potatoes are cooking, prepare gravy. Melt 2 tablespoons butter in a large frying pan over medium-high heat. Cook onion, garlic, and mushrooms, stirring occasionally, until onions are golden brown and mushrooms tender, 8 to 10 minutes. Season to taste with salt and pepper.

Stir in pulled pork and heat, stirring, for 5 minutes. Whisk together beef stock and BBQ sauce; stir into pork mixture. Stir in vinegar, cayenne, and salt and pepper to taste. Remove from heat.

Mash potatoes. Beat in 3 tablespoons butter, cream, goat cheese, thyme, salt, and pepper.

Spoon mashed potatoes onto 6 plates. With the spoon, make a crater in the center of potatoes. Fill with gravy and serve immediately.

SERVES 6

Mashed Sweet Potatoes with Marshmallow Butter

Marshmallows and butter. Heaven can wait—pass the sweet potatoes.

---

2 lbs. sweet potatoes
½ cup heavy cream
¼ cup finely chopped fresh sage
¼ cup maple syrup
3 TB. butter
Salt and pepper

MARSHMALLOW BUTTER
1 cup mini white marshmallows
½ cup chopped toasted pecans
¼ cup butter
2 TB. orange juice
Pinch cayenne pepper

Peel sweet potatoes and cut into 3-inch chunks. In a large pot of boiling salted water, boil sweet potatoes until tender, 15 to 20 minutes. Drain well and return pot to low heat for 1 minute to dry potatoes.

While sweet potatoes are boiling, prepare marshmallow butter. In a microwave-safe dish, combine marshmallows, pecans, butter, orange juice, and cayenne pepper. Microwave on High for 1 to 2 minutes until marshmallows have softened and butter is melted. Stir mixture together.

Mash sweet potatoes. Beat in cream, sage, maple syrup, and butter. Season to taste with salt and pepper.

Spoon mashed sweet potatoes onto serving plates. With the spoon, make a crater in the center of potatoes. Spoon 2 tablespoons marshmallow butter into each crater and serve immediately.

SERVES 6 TO 8

Stuffed Tomatoes

 Big vine-ripened tomatoes are perfect for stuffing. My Pamela grew some tomato monsters one summer. One even weighed in at 2 pounds, 2 ounces!

---

4 ripe field tomatoes
½ cup chopped fresh herbs (basil, oregano, parsley)
½ cup grated Parmesan cheese

1 TB. finely chopped garlic
1 TB. olive oil
Salt and pepper to taste

Preheat grill to medium.

Cut tomatoes in half crosswise. Carefully remove and discard seeds.

In a bowl, combine herbs, Parmesan, garlic, oil, salt, and pepper. Fill tomatoes with cheese mixture.

Grill tomatoes until tender and cheese is starting to melt, 8 to 10 minutes.

MAKES 8 STUFFED TOMATOES

Cherry's Spot Rice and Peas

On the highway from Ocho Rios to Kingston in Jamaica, in an area called Faith's Pen, there is a row of about 35 roadside food stands that serve everything from jerk chicken, steamed fish, and festival (a funky fried dough) to curried goat and jerk pork. My friend Barrington was quite fond of Cherry's Spot and suggested we film a segment there. Well, Cherry's makes one hell of a great rice and peas, and this is my take on the recipe.

¼ cup vegetable oil

1 onion, diced

4 cloves garlic, minced

1 TB. finely chopped fresh ginger

1 green Scotch bonnet pepper, thinly sliced

4 green onions, chopped

1 bay leaf

2 cups long-grain rice

1 TB. chopped fresh thyme

4 to 5 cups chicken stock or water

½ cup coconut milk

2 cups cooked kidney beans

Salt and pepper

In a large saucepan, heat oil over medium heat. Sauté onion, garlic, and ginger until onion is tender, 3 to 4 minutes. Add Scotch bonnet pepper, green onions, bay leaf, rice, and thyme; cook, stirring, for 2 minutes. Stir in chicken stock and coconut milk. Cover and bring to a boil. Stir in beans, cover, and reduce heat to low. Simmer for 15 to 20 minutes, stirring gently once, until rice is cooked. Season to taste with salt and pepper.

Discard bay leaf and serve immediately.

SERVES 8 TO 10

Bacon and Cheddar Flapjacks

These delicious pancakes can be served at breakfast drizzled with maple syrup or as an appetizer garnished with BBQ pulled pork. This is in honor of my friend Kevin Hearn, of the Barenaked Ladies.

1 cup all-purpose flour
¼ cup corn flour
1 tsp. baking soda
½ tsp. salt
1 large egg
1 cup whole milk
2 green onions, minced

1 clove garlic, minced
4 slices bacon, cooked and chopped
1 cup shredded cheddar cheese
1 tsp. Bone Dust BBQ Spice (page 203)
Pepper to taste
4 TB. butter (divided use)

In a bowl, mix together all-purpose flour, corn flour, baking soda, and salt. In a small bowl, whisk together egg and milk. Slowly whisk milk mixture into dry mixture until fully incorporated and there are no lumps. Let rest at room temperature for 2 hours.

Fold into batter green onions, garlic, bacon, cheese, Bone Dust BBQ Spice, and pepper.

Melt 1 tablespoon butter in a large nonstick frying pan over medium-high heat. Pour ¼ cup batter into the pan for each pancake, making three pancakes at a time. Cook until the surface bubbles. Turn pancakes and cook for 1 to 2 minutes or until golden brown. Repeat until all batter is used up.

MAKES 12 PANCAKES

The Cheesiest Baked Macaroni and Cheese

If you are watching what you eat, stay away from this recipe. It's a killer!

---

1 lb. macaroni

3 TB. butter

1 small onion, diced

¼ cup all-purpose flour

2½ cups milk

1 cup heavy cream

1 cup Velveeta cheese

1 cup shredded white cheddar cheese

2 cups shredded yellow cheddar cheese

1 tsp. paprika

1 tsp. dry mustard

½ tsp. black pepper

Salt to taste

1 cup frozen peas

2 cups crumbled potato chips

Preheat oven to 350°F. Grease a 2- to 3-quart casserole dish.

In a large pot of boiling salted water, cook macaroni until it is barely tender. Drain and let cool.

In a large saucepan over medium-low heat, melt butter. Sauté onion until transparent and tender, 2 to 3 minutes. Stir in flour until incorporated. Slowly pour in milk and cream, stirring constantly until the mixture is smooth. Cook, stirring frequently, until sauce is thickened, 10 to 15 minutes.

Whisk in Velveeta and cheddar cheeses until smooth. Remove from heat and stir in paprika, mustard, pepper, and salt.

Combine cooked pasta and peas in the casserole dish; stir. Pour in warm cheese sauce and mix thoroughly.

Bake until bubbling, 20 to 30 minutes. Sprinkle with crumbled potato chips and bake for another 10 minutes.

Let rest for 10 minutes before serving.

SERVES 8

Jumbo Stuffed Mushrooms

 Buy the largest white mushrooms you can find, with firm white caps. The larger the mushroom, the deeper the cavity to fill with some tasty goodness.

---

8 very large field mushrooms
½ cup fresh bread crumbs
½ cup shredded provolone cheese
¼ cup grated Parmesan cheese
2 TB. water

1 TB. chopped fresh basil
2 tsp. chopped garlic
6 slices double smoked bacon, diced and fried crisp
Salt and pepper to taste

Preheat grill to medium.

Remove stems from mushrooms and clean caps. Pat dry.

In a bowl, stir together bread crumbs, provolone cheese, Parmesan, water, basil, garlic, bacon, salt, and pepper.

Fill mushroom caps with cheese mixture, gently pressing mixture into caps.

Place mushroom caps on the grill. Close the lid and bake for 10 to 15 minutes or until mushrooms are tender, stuffing is golden brown, and cheese is melted.

SERVES 8

The Best Sautéed Mushrooms

Nothing beats a great grilled steak. But as important as the steak is, the side dishes are just as important. They key to these mushrooms is a hot frying pan to sear the mushrooms on the outside, keeping them juicy on the inside.

¼ cup vegetable oil

1 lb. large white mushrooms, quartered

3 cloves garlic, minced

2 tsp. Bone Dust BBQ Spice (page 203)

Salt

Heat a large frying pan over high heat for 5 minutes. Add oil and heat until it starts to smoke.

Add mushrooms; sauté for 4 to 5 minutes, stirring occasionally, until golden brown and crisp. Add garlic; sauté for 1 minute.

Add Bone Dust BBQ Spice and season to taste with lots of salt.

Serve immediately with your favorite grilled steak.

SERVES 4

Foil-Roasted Shallots, Corn, and Shiitake Mushrooms

Wrapping vegetables in foil bundles allows them to steam, staying tender and flavorful.

16 shallots, peeled and halved

4 ears corn, cut into 1-inch rounds

12 shiitake mushrooms, stems removed, quartered

4 cloves garlic, thinly sliced

2 TB. cider vinegar

2 TB. melted butter

1 TB. chopped fresh thyme

Salt and pepper to taste

Preheat grill to medium-high.

In a bowl, toss together shallots, corn, mushrooms, garlic, thyme, vinegar, butter, salt, and pepper.

Place mixture in the center of an 8×12-inch sheet of foil. Fold to seal.

Place on the grill, close the lid, and roast for 20 to 30 minutes or until hot and tender.

Serve with Roberto Moreno's Lime Veal Chop (page 308), if desired.

SERVES 8

Foil-Steamed Asparagus with Blue Cheese

I like to use thinner asparagus, which cooks quickly and is tender.

2 lbs. asparagus	3 TB. butter
4 shallots, finely chopped	2 TB. lemon juice
1 TB. pink peppercorns	Salt to taste
1 TB. chopped fresh thyme	1 cup crumbled blue cheese

Preheat grill to high.

Lay two 12-inch-square sheets of foil on top of each other. Pile asparagus in the center of the foil. Sprinkle with shallots, pink peppercorns, and thyme. Dollop with butter and drizzle with lemon juice. Fold over and seal the foil.

Place the bundle on the grill, close the lid, and bake asparagus for 12 to 15 minutes or until it is tender and hot.

Carefully remove the bundle from the grill and open the package. The steam will be hot. Transfer asparagus to a serving platter. Season with salt and garnish with crumbled blue cheese.

SERVES 6 TO 8

Creamed Spinach

I've tried many versions of creamed spinach, but none match my mother's recipe.

1 lb. fresh spinach	¼ cup cream cheese
3 TB. butter	¼ tsp. nutmeg
1 shallot, diced	Pinch cinnamon
2 cloves garlic, minced	1 TB. chopped fresh parsley
1 cup whipping cream	Salt and pepper to taste

Remove woody stems from spinach. Wash spinach well in cold water. Drain and pat dry with paper towels. Roughly chop spinach.

In a frying pan, melt butter over medium heat. Sauté shallot and garlic for 2 to 3 minutes or until translucent and tender. Add spinach; sauté for 5 minutes or until spinach is wilted and water has evaporated from the pan.

Add cream and cream cheese, stirring until smooth. Bring to a boil and reduce liquid, stirring frequently, until sauce is thick. Season with nutmeg, cinnamon, parsley, salt, and pepper.

Serve immediately.

SERVES 4

Grilled Parsnips and Carrots with Vanilla Maple Syrup

Before grilling root vegetables, it's best to blanch them in boiling salted water until they are just tender.

---

1 vanilla bean
¼ cup maple syrup
3 large carrots, peeled
6 parsnips, peeled
2 sweet onions, peeled and cut into 8 wedges
2 TB. olive oil

2 TB. balsamic vinegar
1 TB. Bone Dust BBQ Spice (page 203)
3 green onions, finely chopped
1 TB. chopped fresh thyme
Salt and pepper

Slice vanilla bean in half lengthwise, and scrape seeds into a small saucepan. Add vanilla bean and maple syrup. Heat over medium heat for 5 minutes. Let cool for 1 to 2 hours to allow the flavors to combine. Discard vanilla bean.

Preheat grill to medium-high.

Cut carrots and parsnips into 3-inch lengths. Cut any thick chunks in half lengthwise.

Blanch carrots and parsnips in boiling salted water for 3 to 5 minutes or until just tender. Drain and let cool slightly.

In a bowl, toss together carrots, parsnips, onions, olive oil, balsamic vinegar, and Bone Dust BBQ Spice. Place mixture in a grill basket and grill for 5 to 6 minutes per side or until lightly charred and tender.

Carefully remove vegetables from the basket and in a clean bowl toss with green onions, thyme, and vanilla maple syrup. Season to taste with salt and pepper.

Serve immediately.

SERVES 4 TO 6

Southern Corn and Cheddar Pudding

Canned creamed corn is the secret to making this pudding rich and creamy.

5 eggs	½ tsp. baking powder
1 cup milk	½ tsp. salt
1½ cups whipping cream	¼ tsp. black pepper
⅓ cup all-purpose flour	3 dashes hot sauce
1 (14 oz.) can creamed corn	2 cups canned or thawed frozen corn kernels
1 TB. sugar	1½ cups shredded cheddar cheese

Preheat oven to 375°F. Butter a 9×9×3-inch baking dish.

Whisk eggs in a large bowl. Add milk, cream, flour, creamed corn, sugar, baking powder, salt, pepper, and hot sauce. Stir until combined. Fold in corn kernels and cheddar cheese. Pour into the baking dish.

Bake 45 to 50 minutes or until the top is golden brown and a knife inserted in pudding comes out clean.

SERVES 8

Bourbon Baked Beans

A barbecue just isn't a barbecue without a crock full of baked beans. I like a little whiskey in my recipe, but you can leave it out if you wish.

1 lb. thick sliced bacon, cut in ½-inch pieces

3 onions, diced

8 cloves garlic, minced

4 (14 oz.) cans baked beans (your favorite brand)

1 cup ketchup

½ cup molasses, honey, or maple syrup

½ cup prepared mustard

¼ cup malt vinegar

2 TB. mustard powder

2 TB. Worcestershire sauce

1 TB. chopped fresh thyme

1 tsp. black pepper

1 tsp. hot sauce

Salt

½ cup bourbon

In a large saucepan, fry bacon until just crisp. Drain bacon on paper towels. Drain all but 3 tablespoons bacon fat. Add onions and garlic; sauté for 4 to 5 minutes or until soft.

Add baked beans, ketchup, molasses, prepared mustard, vinegar, mustard powder, Worcestershire sauce, thyme, pepper, hot sauce, and crispy bacon.

Over medium-low heat, heat beans for 20 to 30 minutes, stirring occasionally, until hot. Season to taste with salt, stir in bourbon, and serve.

SERVES 8 TO 10

Grilled Fingerling Potatoes and French Shallots

These crispy grilled potatoes make a great accompaniment to any steak or chicken dish.

---

1 lb. fingerling potatoes	2 TB. lemon juice
1 lb. French shallots	1 TB. chopped fresh rosemary
6 cloves garlic, crushed	1 tsp. cracked black pepper
¼ cup olive oil	Lots of sea salt to taste

Boil fingerling potatoes in a large pot of salted water for 10 to 12 minutes or until just tender. Drain, cool under cold water, and pat dry.

Peel shallots and cut in half lengthwise.

Preheat grill to medium-high.

In a large bowl, toss together potatoes, shallots, garlic, olive oil, lemon juice, rosemary, pepper, and salt. Place mixture in a grill basket.

Grill for 10 to 12 minutes or until potatoes are hot and slightly charred.

SERVES 6 TO 8

Tip

French shallots are long oval shallots. If you can't find them, use regular shallots. And if you can't find fingerlings, use mini white or red potatoes.

Cheddar Mashed Potatoes with Grilled Onions

I believe mashed potatoes should be their own food group. Nothing is more comforting than a steaming bowl of mashed potatoes garnished with butter. If you should have leftovers of this recipe, make potato pancakes. Fry them in butter and serve with a poached egg.

2 large red onions, sliced ¼-inch thick
2 TB. olive oil
2 TB. balsamic vinegar
1 TB. Bone Dust BBQ Spice (page 203)
2 lbs. Yukon Gold potatoes, peeled

2 cups shredded aged white cheddar cheese
½ cup whipping cream
¼ cup finely chopped chives
3 TB. butter
Salt and pepper

Preheat grill to high.

In a large bowl, carefully toss together onions, olive oil, vinegar, and Bone Dust BBQ Spice. Place in a grill basket.

Grill for 10 to 12 minutes or until slightly charred and tender. Carefully remove onions from the basket and coarsely chop. Set aside.

In a large pot of salted water, boil potatoes until tender, 15 to 20 minutes. Drain and return to the heat to dry potatoes.

Remove from heat and mash potatoes. Stir in cheddar cheese, cream, chives, butter, and grilled onions. Season to taste with salt and pepper.

SERVES 6

Pamela's Potato and Cauliflower Hash

My lovely Pamela doesn't spend much time in the kitchen, but when she does get cooking, it's always delicious. This is one of her recipes—and my favorite from her repertoire—that is perfect when served with eggs or steak.

⅓ head cauliflower, broken into bite-size pieces

¼ cup vegetable oil

3 cloves garlic, minced

1 large sweet onion, thinly sliced

2 cups cubed cooked Yukon Gold potatoes

1 TB. chopped fresh parsley

Pinch cayenne pepper

Salt and freshly ground black pepper

Blanch cauliflower for 2 to 3 minutes in boiling salted water. Drain and set aside.

Heat oil in a large frying pan over medium-high heat. Sauté garlic and onion, stirring constantly, for 12 to 15 minutes or until onions are caramelized and slightly crisp. (This is the key to this recipe, as sweet onions add a lot of flavor.) With a slotted spoon, transfer mixture to a bowl.

Add a little more oil to your frying pan if necessary and fry potatoes for 12 to 15 minutes, stirring occasionally, until crispy.

Add onions and cauliflower to the pan and stir until mixed. Sauté for 4 to 5 minutes or until all is tender. Add parsley and season to taste with a pinch cayenne, salt, and pepper. Stir thoroughly and serve immediately with fried eggs or grilled steak.

SERVES 4 TO 6

Baked Sweet Potatoes with Maple Orange Butter

 Sweet potatoes are delicious when baked. The skin gets crisp, and the flesh is tender. Drizzled with maple syrup or brown sugar, sweet potatoes make a great accompaniment to ribs and steaks.

8 sweet potatoes	8 TB. Maple Orange Butter (recipe follows)
4 seedless oranges	Salt and pepper to taste

Preheat grill to high.

Cut each potato into ¼-inch slices about three-fourths the way down but not all the way through. You should make at least eight slices per sweet potato.

Thinly slice oranges into rounds. You will need 32 slices (8 slices per orange). Cut each round in half.

Place one square of foil on top of another. Place one sweet potato on the foil. Insert one orange slice in each cut of potato. Crumble 1 tablespoon Maple Orange Butter on top of sweet potato. Season with salt and pepper. Wrap foil tightly around sweet potato.

Repeat with remaining sweet potatoes.

Grill sweet potatoes for 50 to 60 minutes or until they are tender when pierced with a knife.

Carefully unwrap sweet potatoes and serve with extra Maple Orange Butter, if desired.

SERVES 8

Maple Orange Butter

This recipe makes more than you need for the baked sweet potatoes, but it's also great on French toast and pancakes. Freeze for up to 2 months.

½ lb. unsalted butter, softened

¼ cup chopped pecans

¼ cup pure Canadian maple syrup

¼ cup freshly squeezed orange juice

1 TB. chopped fresh thyme

1 tsp. orange zest

½ tsp. coarsely ground black pepper

Salt to taste

In a food processor or mixing bowl, blend butter, pecans, maple syrup, orange juice, thyme, orange zest, pepper, and salt.

Place in a storage container and freeze until needed.

MAKES ABOUT 2 CUPS

Love Potatoes (a.k.a. Super *!&#%*! Potatoes)

Note for the faint of heart: This is the potato dish of romance or heart attack, whichever comes first.

---

24 mini red or white potatoes

2 TB. olive oil

6 cloves garlic, minced

1 large onion, sliced

¼ cup chopped fresh herbs (such as sage, rosemary, and thyme)

2 TB. balsamic vinegar

Salt and pepper to taste

1 cup shredded aged white cheddar cheese

1 cup shredded mozzarella cheese

1 cup shredded Monterey Jack cheese

3 eggs

1½ to 2 cups whipping cream

Place potatoes in a large pot and cover with cold water. Bring to a boil and season with a little salt. Reduce heat to medium and cook potatoes for 15 to 20 minutes or until tender. Drain and let cool.

Preheat oven to 375°F. Spray a 12×9-inch baking dish with nonstick cooking spray.

When potatoes have cooled, press firmly on the top of each one to slightly smash and flatten it. Spread potatoes in the greased baking dish.

In a frying pan over medium-high heat, heat olive oil. Sauté garlic and onion for 5 to 6 minutes, stirring occasionally, until lightly colored and tender. Add herbs, vinegar, salt, and pepper.

Spread onion mixture evenly over potatoes. Combine three cheeses and spread evenly over onions.

In a bowl, whisk together eggs and 1½ cups cream. Season to taste with salt and pepper. Pour over potato-onion-cheese layers. Add additional cream if needed to just cover the layers.

Bake for 40 to 45 minutes or until cheese is melted, golden brown, and bubbling and potatoes are hot. Let stand for 5 minutes.

Serve immediately with The Big Man's Coffee-Crusted Porterhouse steak (page 277), if desired.

SERVES 6

Grilled Onion and Asparagus Risotto

Risotto can be flavored with just about anything you wish. Grilled chicken, shrimp, lobster, corn, and mushrooms make great additions to any risotto.

1 large red onion, sliced into rounds	1 cup Arborio rice
1 lb. asparagus	¼ cup medium-dry white wine
2 TB. balsamic vinegar	4 cups hot chicken stock
4 TB. olive oil (divided use)	1 TB. chopped fresh thyme
Salt and freshly ground black pepper to taste	1 cup shredded aged white cheddar cheese
4 shallots, finely chopped	

Preheat grill to medium-high.

In a large bowl, toss together onion, asparagus, balsamic vinegar, 2 tablespoons olive oil, salt, and pepper. Place in a grill basket.

Grill onions and asparagus for 15 minutes, turning the basket periodically, until they are tender and lightly charred. Carefully remove onions and asparagus from the basket and cool slightly.

Coarsely chop onions. Slice asparagus spears into 1½-inch lengths. Set aside.

To prepare risotto, in a large saucepan heat the remaining 2 tablespoons oil over medium-high heat. Add shallots; cook, stirring, for 30 seconds. Stir in rice; cook for 1 minute, stirring constantly, or until rice is evenly coated with oil.

Stir in white wine and reduce liquid by half. Add ½ cup chicken stock, stirring constantly and waiting until most of the liquid is absorbed before adding more stock. Continue in this manner, adding ½ cup stock at a time, until rice is tender but slightly resistant to the bite, 15 to 20 minutes.

Stir in onions, asparagus, thyme, and cheddar cheese. Season with salt and pepper.

Serve immediately with Apple Cider BBQ Atlantic Salmon (page 388), if desired.

SERVES 4

Rubbin' Is Lovin'

Seasoning Rubs and Pastes

Malabar Pepper Rub

The Malabar coast of India is best known for its black pepper. This rub is a variation of one I discovered on an expedition to Cochin, India. This is a great rub for beef, chicken, and salmon.

¼ cup cracked black peppercorns
¼ cup crushed red chilies
¼ cup coarse kosher salt
2 TB. granulated garlic

2 TB. granulated onion
1 TB. sugar
1 TB. curry powder
1 TB. ground coriander

In a bowl, mix together black peppercorns, crushed red chilies, salt, garlic, onion, sugar, curry powder, and coriander. Store in an airtight container in a cool, dry place away from heat and light.

MAKES ABOUT 1¼ CUPS

Smoked Garlic

Roasted garlic has a natural sweetness that adds wonderful flavor to many dishes, but smoked garlic is something else!

---

8 large heads garlic

Hickory smoking chips, soaked in cold water

Prepare smoker as per manufacturer's instructions to a temperature of 225°F.

Using a sharp knife, cut the top off each head of garlic, exposing cloves.

Place garlic heads cut side down on the top rack of the smoker and close the lid. Smoke garlic for approximately 3 hours, until tender and golden brown.

Remove garlic from smoker and carefully peel the skin from the cloves of garlic.

Gilroy Roasted Garlic Paste

Not all rubs are dry rubs. This paste recipe uses lots of freshly roasted garlic. I remember the first time that I drove through the town of Gilroy, California. Even though my car windows were up, the smell of fresh garlic was so thick in the air that it easily filled the car.

Rub this paste liberally into chicken, lamb, or beef.

---

3 large heads garlic
½ cup (approx.) olive oil
¼ cup grainy mustard
2 TB. chopped fresh parsley

2 TB. chopped fresh rosemary
2 TB. coarsely ground black pepper
1 TB. coarse kosher salt
1 TB. balsamic vinegar

Preheat oven to 325°F.

Separate cloves of garlic and peel them. Place in an ovenproof dish just large enough to hold them. Pour enough olive oil over garlic to cover cloves.

Roast garlic for 30 to 45 minutes or until golden brown and tender. Let cool in oil.

In a food processor, place roasted garlic, ½ cup reserved olive oil, mustard, parsley, rosemary, pepper, salt, and vinegar. Blend until smooth.

Store in a sealed container, refrigerated, for up to 2 weeks.

MAKES ABOUT 2 CUPS

Old Montreal Steak Spice

This has got to be the best rub for steaks. I believe that the saltier the rub, the better the steak will be.

½ cup coarse kosher salt
¼ cup coarsely ground black pepper
¼ cup coarsely ground white pepper
¼ cup mustard seeds
¼ cup cracked coriander seeds

¼ cup granulated garlic
¼ cup granulated onion
¼ cup crushed red chilies
¼ cup dill seed

Combine salt, black pepper, white pepper, mustard seeds, coriander seeds, garlic, onion, crushed chilies, and dill seed.

Store in an airtight container in a cool, dry place away from heat and light.

MAKES 2½ CUPS

Bone Dust BBQ Spice (a.k.a. The Best BBQ Rub)

As you might well know, I love to grill. Well, this is my favorite recipe for a BBQ spice. It is from my *Sticks and Stones* cookbook. It just doesn't get any better than this one.

½ cup paprika
¼ cup chili powder
3 TB. salt
2 TB. ground coriander
2 TB. garlic powder
2 TB. sugar
2 TB. curry powder

2 TB. hot dry mustard
1 TB. black pepper
1 TB. dried basil
1 TB. dried thyme
1 TB. ground cumin
1 TB. cayenne pepper

Mix together paprika, chili powder, salt, coriander, garlic powder, sugar, curry powder, dry mustard, black pepper, basil, thyme, cumin, and cayenne.

Store in an airtight container in a cool, dry place away from heat and light.

MAKES ABOUT 2½ CUPS

Salmon Seasoning

I love salmon. I think growing up with a Newfie dad had something to do with this. Here's a tasty seasoning that blends nicely with the richness of salmon.

¼ cup lemon pepper

¼ cup coarse kosher salt

¼ cup dill seed

¼ cup dried coriander

2 TB. dried dill

1 TB. paprika

1 TB. granulated garlic

1 TB. granulated onion

2 tsp. cayenne pepper

2 tsp. sugar

Combine lemon pepper, salt, dill seed, coriander, dill, paprika, garlic, onion, cayenne, and sugar. Store in an airtight container in a cool, dry place away from heat and light.

MAKES ABOUT 1½ CUPS

Bay Seasoning

Inspired by the countless days I spent crabbing on Chesapeake Bay, here is a classic seasoning for crab boils, shrimp boils, and clam bakes. The most famous of its kind is Old Bay Seasoning, a truly excellent seasoning. I think mine is just a little better, of course, but if you don't have the time to prepare this recipe by all means use Old Bay.

½ cup paprika	¼ cup garlic powder
¼ cup celery salt	¼ cup onion powder
¼ cup coarse kosher salt	¼ cup ground coriander
¼ cup cayenne pepper	¼ cup ground cumin
¼ cup ground black pepper	2 TB. sugar
¼ cup ground white pepper	1 TB. curry powder

Combine paprika, celery salt, salt, cayenne, black pepper, white pepper, garlic powder, onion powder, coriander, cumin, sugar, and curry powder.

Store in an airtight container in a cool, dry place away from heat and light.

MAKES ABOUT 3 CUPS

Hell's Fire Chili Paste

Some folks just like it to be insanely hot. So here it is. Blow your brains out with this rubbing paste. Good luck, and remember to keep lots of water on hand. Also, you might want to use rubber gloves and a mask when preparing this.

---

1 (7 oz.) can smoked chipotle chilies

6 habanero peppers

3 green onions, coarsely chopped

4 cloves garlic

2 limes, juiced

¼ cup chopped fresh cilantro

¼ cup olive oil

1 TB. sugar

2 tsp. salt

In a food processor, combine chipotle chilies, habanero peppers, green onions, garlic, lime juice, cilantro, olive oil, sugar, and salt. Blend until smooth.

Transfer to a small dish. Cover and refrigerate. Keeps for up to 2 weeks.

MAKES ABOUT 1 ½ CUPS

Mocha Coffee Rub

I love the flavor of coffee, and it has a wonderful affinity with beef and lamb.

½ cup mocha-flavored coffee beans
6 cloves garlic, minced
¼ cup chopped fresh rosemary
¼ cup chopped fresh parsley
¼ cup cracked black pepper

¼ cup olive oil
2 TB. molasses
2 TB. balsamic vinegar
Salt to taste

Using the bottom of a heavy frying pan, crush coffee beans.

Stir together crushed coffee beans, garlic, rosemary, parsley, pepper, olive oil, molasses, vinegar, and salt.

Store, refrigerated, in a sealed container. Keeps up to 2 weeks.

MAKES ABOUT 2 CUPS

Tip

I don't recommend using a coffee grinder here because the coffee needs to be coarse, not finely ground.

Herb Mustard Rub

I love to use fresh herbs whenever possible. This combination of fresh herbs and mustard is a great way to enhance poultry and pork.

6 cloves garlic, minced

1 cup chopped fresh herbs (any combination of parsley, sage, rosemary, thyme, tarragon, dill, and savory)

¼ cup Dijon mustard

¼ cup grainy mustard

¼ cup olive oil

2 TB. honey

2 TB. white wine vinegar

1 TB. coarsely ground black pepper

Salt to taste

Combine garlic, herbs, Dijon mustard, grainy mustard, olive oil, honey, vinegar, pepper, and salt. Store, refrigerated, in a sealed container. Keeps up to 2 weeks.

MAKES ABOUT 2 CUPS

Indonesian Cinnamon Rub

Cinnamon adds a natural sweetness to certain foods. It is not just for baking but is an excellent addition to many savory dishes.

This rub can be used on chicken, lamb, and pork.

¼ cup cinnamon	1 TB. ground cloves
2 TB. sugar	1 TB. ground ginger
2 TB. ground cumin	1 TB. garlic powder
2 TB. ground allspice	1 TB. salt

Combine cinnamon, sugar, cumin, allspice, cloves, ginger, garlic powder, and salt.
Store in an airtight container in a cool, dry place away from heat and light.

MAKES ABOUT 1 CUP

Jamaican Jerk Paste

This great recipe has been handed down to my dear friend Bridget from her family in Jamaica. It brings out the zing in any dish. The name "jerk" can only be attributed to the sudden rush your palate feels when eating it.

4 habanero or Scotch bonnet peppers
6 green onions, coarsely chopped
¼ cup water
1 cup fresh cilantro leaves
1 cup fresh parsley leaves
6 cloves garlic
¼ cup olive oil

¼ cup lemon juice
2 TB. ground allspice
2 tsp. salt
1 tsp. ground cloves
1 tsp. ground cumin
1 tsp. black pepper

In a food processor or blender, purée habanero peppers, green onions, and water. Add cilantro, parsley, and garlic; purée until smooth. Add olive oil, lemon juice, allspice, salt, cloves, cumin, and black pepper. Blend until fully incorporated. Store in a sealed container, refrigerated. Keeps up to 2 weeks.

MAKES ABOUT 3 CUPS

Tip

Jerk is a great seasoning for pork and chicken.

Miami Spice Love Paste

Try this sweet and spicy rub on fish, shellfish, chicken, or ribs.

---

6 cloves garlic

2 red finger chili peppers

4 green onions, coarsely chopped

2 TB. orange zest

½ cup orange juice

½ cup fresh cilantro leaves

¼ cup chopped fresh ginger

¼ cup olive oil

¼ cup Grand Marnier

2 tsp. salt

2 tsp. ground fennel

1 tsp. cinnamon

1 tsp. black pepper

In a food processor or blender, combine garlic, chili peppers, green onions, orange zest, orange juice, cilantro, ginger, olive oil, Grand Marnier, salt, fennel, cinnamon, and black pepper. Blend until smooth.

Store, refrigerated, in a sealed container. Keeps up to 2 weeks.

MAKES ABOUT 2 CUPS

Licorice Rub

Toasting spices extracts their natural oils, which brings out more flavor in your recipes. Use this rub on chicken and lamb.

---

4 star anise, broken into pieces
3 (3 inch) cinnamon sticks, broken into small
   pieces
½ cup fennel seeds
¼ cup black peppercorns

1 tsp. whole cloves
1 TB. granulated garlic
1 TB. ground ginger
1 TB. salt

Heat a frying pan over medium heat. Toast star anise, cinnamon sticks, fennel, peppercorns, and whole cloves, stirring, until lightly toasted and fragrant, 3 to 5 minutes.

Using a spice/coffee mill, grind spices into a fine powder. In a bowl, stir together ground spices, garlic, ginger, and salt.

Store in an airtight container in a cool, dry place away from heat and light.

MAKES ABOUT ¾ CUP

Red-Rum Rub

This is a fiery paste ("red-rum" spelled backward is …) that will make you blush.

---

8 red finger chili peppers	¼ cup red paprika
1 small red onion, quartered	¼ cup amber rum
1 red bell pepper, quartered	2 tsp. red cayenne pepper
8 cloves garlic	1 tsp. salt
¼ cup red chili oil	

Preheat oven to 375°F.

In an ovenproof dish, toss together red finger chili peppers, red onion, red bell pepper, garlic, and red chili oil. Roast until all is very lightly charred and tender, 30 to 45 minutes.

In a food processor or blender, purée the mixture until smooth. Add red paprika, rum, red cayenne pepper, and salt. Pulse until incorporated.

Store, refrigerated, in a sealed container. Keeps up to 2 weeks.

MAKES ABOUT 2 CUPS

Hot and Sticky Ribs

Rib Basics

Pork Ribs

Beef Ribs

Buffalo Ribs

Lamb Ribs

Rib Types

Not sure what different types of ribs are available? Read on!

Pork Baby Back Ribs

Baby back ribs are the ultimate rib. Cut from the loin, they are much leaner than spareribs and tend to have a higher meat-to-bone ratio. When prepared properly, these ribs provide the best eating. I recall once organizing the SkyDome Ribfest, a promotion for Loblaws Grocery Stores, during which we cooked a million pounds of baby back ribs.

Whether the ribs are fresh or frozen, look for ribs that have more loin meat attached. A baby back rib should weigh between 1¼ and 2 pounds. Baby back ribs are more expensive than spareribs but are the best quality. As the saying goes, "You get what you pay for."

Pork Spareribs

Spareribs are cut from the side, or underbelly, of the pig. These ribs are quite meaty but are also fattier than baby back ribs. Weighing usually between 2½ and 3½ pounds, these ribs can serve several people. Spareribs are usually sold with the soft bone brisket attached. This cartilage material is tough and fatty and is best trimmed off and used in soup stocks. Ask your butcher to remove the brisket for you.

The term "St. Louis rib" means that the soft bone brisket has been removed, which produces a rib that is more uniform in size and makes for easier cooking and eating. These ribs usually weigh around 2 pounds.

Country-Style Pork Ribs

Country-style pork ribs are extremely meaty. In fact, there are usually just a few small bones attached. These ribs come from the rib end of the pork loin and are loaded with meat. They're priced less than baby back ribs and spareribs. These ribs require a little longer cooking time to ensure tenderness but are well worth the wait.

Pork Back Rib Tail Pieces

I was involved in developing a product for President's Choice called If Pigs Could Fly. This was a frozen appetizer that used a byproduct of the pork baby back rib. When the butcher prepares pork baby back ribs, the small "tail" piece must be removed from the end of the rib. Tail pieces are approximately 6 to 8 inches long and have small flat bones. They are to pork what the wing is to chicken—a great snack food.

Rib tail pieces are not always available and are best ordered through your favorite butcher. Allow at least four to six pieces per person.

Pork Shoulder

A whole pork shoulder consists of the blade bone, shank and foreleg and weighs approximately 15 to 20 pounds. This is a lot of meat, and unless you are feeding a crowd of people and have a lot of time on your hands I do not recommend purchasing a whole shoulder. The whole shoulder is used in BBQ competitions.

You can find at your local butcher or grocery store smaller cuts from the shoulder area. The picnic roast (a.k.a. shoulder roast or Boston butt) is a smaller cut (approximately 5 to 7 pounds) and easier to prepare. The best method for preparation is to slowly smoke the shoulder pieces over low heat. Low and slow makes for succulent and tender.

Beef Ribs

These are enormous ribs that are cut from the loin of beef. They are best ordered from your favorite butcher, since most grocery stores do not carry them. They're usually bought up by the food service industry, which does not leave too many ribs for the retailer. As a chef at the SkyDome, I prepared many prime ribs of beef for our customers. I would often remove the back ribs after the beef was cooked and then grill the ribs and baste them generously with a smoky BBQ sauce. These ribs never made it to the customer, as I would serve them to my staff as a dinner treat.

"Monster Bones" or "Dinosaur Ribs," as they are frequently referred to on menus, are succulent and meaty. Have a lot of napkins on hand because the only true way to eat these is with your hands.

Beef Short Ribs

This inexpensive cut of meat is readily available in grocery stores. It is cut from the belly plate, or the chuck areas, of a steer and is composed of layers of meat, fat and flat rib bones. The fat cap of a short rib should be trimmed before cooking. These ribs are quite chunky and take a fair amount of time to cook.

You may also purchase what are called Maui or Miami ribs, depending where you are from. These ribs are cut approximately ½ inch thick across the short ribs. They have four or five bones in each and can be prepared quickly on the grill once they are marinated.

Lamb Ribs

Lamb ribs are popular in South Africa, Australia, and the South Pacific but are not as well known to North American barbecue aficionados. Lamb ribs are smaller than pork ribs, weighing in at just around a pound. Lamb ribs have a thick fat cap, which should be removed before cooking. There is not a lot of meat on lamb ribs, so allow two racks per person. If you are a lover of lamb, then these ribs will make you really smile.

Cooking Methods

You might be surprised to learn how many ways you can prepare ribs.

Boiling

Some chefs say never to boil ribs. I believe that you can—but make sure that you add some kind of flavoring to the water. Boiling ribs tends to remove the flavor and succulence from the meat, so you need to add something to replace the lost flavor, such as apple cider, pineapple juice, beer, ginger ale, or stock. Boiling is not my favorite method of cooking ribs, but it does tenderize them. I would recommend boiling only pork spareribs and never boiling beef or lamb ribs.

Cooking Time: Cooking liquid temperature 210°F
Allow approximately 30 minutes
per pound
2 to 3 lbs. spareribs 90 minutes
1 to 2 lbs. back ribs 60 minutes

Steaming

My friend Dave Nichol swears by steaming for cooking tender pork ribs. I agree with him. Steaming ribs allows the meat to tenderize without losing its flavor to the water, as in boiling. A large steamer pot will do the job. Flavor the steaming liquid with garlic, onions, and assorted herbs and spices before steaming the ribs. Never steam beef ribs.

Cooking Time: Bring cooking liquid to a boil.
Place steamer insert in pot and
add ribs.
Allow approximately 30 minutes
per pound
2 to 3 lbs. spareribs 90 minutes
1 to 2 lbs. back ribs 60 minutes
1 lb. lamb ribs   45 minutes

Oven Roasting

Oven roasting is a great way to cook ribs. This method suits all types of ribs (pork, beef, and lamb). When preparing ribs for roasting, always rub them with a BBQ seasoning of some flavor. (See Chapter 8 for rubs.) Preheat your oven to 350°F and place seasoned ribs on a wire rack in a roasting pan.

Cooking Time: Preheated 350°F oven.
2 to 3 lbs. spareribs
and beef ribs   75 to 90 minutes
1 to 2 lbs. back rib
and country-style
ribs   60 to 75 minutes
1 lb. lamb ribs   45 to 60 minutes

Grilling

In this method of cooking, ribs are cooked fully on the grill, whereas boiling, steaming, roasting, smoking, and braising all require that you finish the ribs on a hot grill before serving.

Grilling ribs requires low heat, patience, and desire. These three "ingredients" will produce a great-tasting rib. Grilling is best suited for pork back and spareribs. The temperature of your grill should remain at around 325°F. Because cooking on a grill is with dry heat, you need to have some moisture to keep the ribs from drying out. Place a small pan of water in the bottom of the grill among the coals or on top of the grill bars. Marinate your ribs for 4 to 6 hours and then rub them with your favorite BBQ seasoning. Place them on the grill meaty side up, close the lid, and cook the ribs until the meat is tender. Near the end of the cooking, brush the ribs with your favorite BBQ sauce.

Cooking Time: Preheated 325°F grill.

2 to 3 lbs. spareribs and beef ribs	90 minutes
1 to 2 lbs. pork back ribs and country-style ribs	75 minutes
1 lb. lamb ribs	60 minutes

Smoking

Smoking ribs—or real barbecue—is as much an art form as it is a method of cooking. Various styles of smokers are available for backyard use. Whatever kind you use, three basic principles apply. They're the same three principles of grilling ribs as given earlier, but with a few changes. Low heat is a must—around 200 to 225°F. You must have more patience (smoking can take anywhere from 3 to 7 hours, depending on the size and cut of your meat), and your desire will grow. So sit back, relax, crack a cold one, and tend to your ribs.

For best results, use a charcoal smoker. You can smoke on a gas grill, but true lovers of barbecue

smoke only over coals with flavored wood chips. Heat a small amount of charcoal to between 200 and 225°F.

Soak smoking chips in water for at least 1 hour before adding to hot coals. You will need to replenish these chips every so often during the smoking. Try a variety of flavored smoking chips. Hickory and mesquite are the most popular, but cherry, apple, and maple chips offer great flavor as well. When in the South, I like to use pecan wood. It provides a sweet nutty flavor to my smoked ribs.

When the coals are hot, place a dish of hot water in the bottom of the smoker. Place the grill on top of the hot coals.

It is best to marinate your ribs for 4 to 6 hours or overnight and then rub them with your favorite spice rub. Place ribs meaty side up and cover the smoker. Once an hour, check and add additional coals and smoking chips as needed, maintaining the temperature around 200 to 225°F.

Cooking Time: Preheated 200 to 225°F smoker. Soaked smoking chips.

2 to 3 lbs. pork spareribs and beef ribs	3 to 4 hours
6 to 8 lbs. pork picnic or pork butt roasts	5 to 6 hours
1 to 2 lbs. pork back ribs and country-style ribs	3 hours

Braising: My Favorite Cooking Method

I love cooking ribs as much as I love eating ribs. I started out like many, boiling and steaming ribs, but was never satisfied with the results. I then started traveling to different BBQ competitions in search of the best ribs. I learned to love smoked ribs and grilled ribs but knew that the ultimate rib had to be somewhere out there. I then met a rib cooker by the name of Jerry Gibson. Jerry's ribs were incredible. Nirvana was at hand. Jerry told me that braising was the secret to great-tasting ribs. Braising is done in your oven and is a combination of roasting and steaming.

Preheat oven to 325°F. Rub ribs with your favorite BBQ seasoning. Place ribs meat side down overlapping in a roasting pan. Add 1 to 2 cups of liquid (juice, beer, or water) and place 3 to 4 slices of lemon on the back of each rack of ribs. Cover and braise until fully cooked and the bones can be pulled cleanly from the meat.

Cooking Time: Preheated 325°F oven.

2 to 3 lbs. pork spareribs and beef ribs, beef short ribs	2 to 3 hours
1 to 2 lbs. pork back ribs and country-style ribs	2 to 2½ hours
1 lb. lamb ribs	1½ hours

Jalapeño Honey Garlic Baby Back Ribs

That's not a mistake in the recipe—I *mean* 12 cloves of garlic. You can never have enough garlic. These ribs are very sticky. On a sticky scale from 1 to 10, they rate an 11.

---

4 racks pork baby back ribs (each 1 ½ lbs.)
2 TB. Bone Dust BBQ Spice (page 203)
2 lemons, sliced
½ cup lemon juice
1 can ginger ale

JALAPEÑO HONEY GARLIC SAUCE
2 TB. vegetable oil
12 cloves garlic, minced
1 small onion, finely chopped

4 jalapeño peppers, finely chopped
2 cups honey
1 cup chicken stock
½ cup rice vinegar
2 TB. prepared mustard
2 tsp. dry mustard
2 tsp. black mustard seeds
1 tsp. black pepper
½ tsp. cayenne pepper
Salt to taste

Preheat oven to 325°F.

Using a sharp knife, score the membrane on the backside of ribs in a diamond pattern. Rub with Bone Dust BBQ Spice, pressing seasoning into the meat.

Lay ribs meat side down in a roasting pan. Lay 3 to 4 slices lemon on back of each rib. Pour in lemon juice and ginger ale. Cover tightly with lid or foil.

Braise ribs until tender, 2 to 2½ hours. Let cool slightly.

Meanwhile, prepare sauce. Heat oil in a medium saucepan over medium-high heat. Sauté garlic, onion, and jalapeños until tender, 2 to 3 minutes. Add honey, chicken stock, rice vinegar, prepared mustard, dry mustard, and mustard seeds. Bring to a boil, reduce heat to low and simmer for 15 minutes, stirring occasionally. Season with black pepper, cayenne pepper, and salt.

Preheat grill to medium-high.

Grill ribs, basting with sauce, for 6 to 8 minutes per side.

Cut between every third rib and serve.

SERVES 4 TO 6

Guinness-Braised Baby Back Ribs with Sweet Molasses BBQ Sauce

This recipe calls for four cans of Guinness. Two cans are for the ribs, and two cans are for you to drink while preparing this recipe. Guinness rules!

---

4 (1½ lbs.) racks pork baby back ribs
2 TB. Bone Dust BBQ Spice (page 203)
1 large onion, sliced
4 cloves garlic, crushed

4 cans Guinness Irish stout
2 cups gourmet BBQ sauce
½ cup molasses

Preheat oven to 325°F.

Using a sharp knife, score the membrane on the backside of ribs in a diamond pattern. Rub with Bone Dust BBQ Spice, pressing seasoning into meat.

Spread onion and garlic in a roasting pan. Lay ribs on top meat side down. Pour in two cans of Guinness. Cover tightly with lid or foil.

Braise ribs until tender, 2 to 2½ hours. Let cool slightly. Remove ribs from pan and set aside.

Pour Guinness mixture into a large saucepan. Bring to a boil and reduce liquid by half. Stir in BBQ sauce and molasses. Return to a boil, stirring, and remove from heat. Purée sauce until smooth.

Preheat grill to medium-high.

Grill ribs, basting with sauce, for 6 to 8 minutes per side.

Cut between every third rib and serve.

SERVES 4 TO 6

Chili Pineapple Baby Back Ribs

This is a sweet-with-heat glazing sauce. It is great not only on ribs but drizzled over ice cream, too. Try my Smoked Chocolate Crème Fraîche Ice Cream on page 434.

---

4 racks pork baby back ribs (each 1½ lbs.)
6 TB. Indonesian Cinnamon Rub (page 209)
2 onions, sliced
3 cups pineapple juice

CHILI PINEAPPLE BBQ GLAZING SAUCE
2 TB. vegetable oil
4 cloves garlic, minced

½ small onion, finely chopped
1 TB. crushed red chilies
1 (14 oz.) can crushed pineapple
1 cup corn syrup
½ cup water
1 TB. prepared horseradish
Salt

Preheat oven to 325°F.

Using a sharp knife, score the membrane on the backside of ribs in a diamond pattern. Rub with Indonesian Cinnamon Rub, pressing seasoning into meat.

Spread onions in a roasting pan. Lay ribs on top meat side down. Pour pineapple juice over ribs. Cover tightly with lid or foil.

Braise ribs until meat is tender, 2 to 2½ hours. Let cool slightly.

Meanwhile, prepare glazing sauce. Heat oil in a medium saucepan over medium-high heat. Sauté garlic, onion, and crushed chilies until onion is tender, 2 to 3 minutes. Stir in pineapple and its juice, corn syrup, water, and horseradish. Bring to a boil, reduce heat to low, and simmer for 15 minutes, stirring occasionally. Season to taste with salt.

Preheat grill to medium-high.

Grill ribs, basting with glazing sauce, until slightly charred, 6 to 8 minutes per side.

Cut between every third rib and serve.

SERVES 4 TO 6

Baby Back Ribs with Apricot Glazing Sauce

I am—as you can tell—a lover of ribs. They're my favorite food. When cooked until tender and glazed with a rich, flavorful sauce, nothing beats good ribs. This apricot glaze is made easy by using apricot jam. It's sweet with a little heat.

4 racks pork baby back ribs (each 1½ lbs.)
2 TB. Bone Dust BBQ Spice (page 203)
2 oranges, sliced
2 cups orange juice

APRICOT GLAZING SAUCE
2 TB. vegetable oil
4 cloves garlic, minced

1 TB. minced fresh ginger
1 TB. crushed red chilies
2 cups apricot jam
½ cup honey
½ cup water
¼ cup cider vinegar
1 TB. chopped fresh sage
Salt

Preheat oven to 325°F.

Using a sharp knife, score the membrane on the backside of ribs in a diamond pattern. Rub with Bone Dust BBQ Spice, pressing seasoning into meat.

Lay ribs meat side down in a roasting pan. Lay three to four orange slices on back of each rib. Pour in orange juice. Cover tightly with lid or foil.

Braise ribs until tender, 2 to 2½ hours. Let cool slightly.

Meanwhile, prepare glazing sauce. Heat oil in a medium saucepan over medium-high heat. Sauté garlic, ginger, and crushed chilies until tender, 2 minutes. Add apricot jam, honey, water, vinegar and sage, whisking until smooth. Bring to a boil, reduce heat to low and simmer, stirring occasionally, for 15 minutes. Season to taste with salt.

Preheat grill to medium-high.

Grill ribs, basting with glazing sauce, for 6 to 8 minutes per side.

Cut between every third rib and toss with remaining glazing sauce.

SERVES 4 TO 6

Hard Lemonade Steamed Baby Back Ribs with Hard Lemonade BBQ Sauce

My friend Dave Nichol is an inspiration, and I have had the pleasure of cooking for him many times. Dave is very particular about ribs. He believes the best ribs are steamed. I have cooked hundreds of racks of ribs for Dave at many events, and he always insists that we steam them. For Dave, a rib is not good until the super-tender meat easily pulls free from the bone.

4 bottles hard lemonade
4 (1½ lbs.) racks pork baby back ribs
2 TB. Bone Dust BBQ Spice (page 203)

HARD LEMONADE BBQ SAUCE
1 bottle hard lemonade
1 cup honey
1 cup gourmet BBQ sauce
½ cup orange marmalade
2 TB. cider vinegar
Salt and pepper

Pour the hard lemonade into a steamer pot and bring to a boil. Rub ribs with Bone Dust BBQ Spice, pressing seasoning into meat.

Steam ribs on a steamer rack until tender, about 1½ hours.

Meanwhile, prepare sauce. In a medium saucepan, whisk together hard lemonade, honey, BBQ sauce, marmalade, and vinegar. Bring to a boil, reduce heat and simmer for 15 minutes, stirring occasionally. If necessary, thicken with a little cornstarch stirred into water. Remove from heat and season to taste with salt and pepper.

Preheat grill to medium-high.

Grill ribs, basting liberally with sauce, for 8 to 10 minutes per side.

Cut between every third rib and serve.

SERVES 4 TO 6

Cherry Whiskey Smoked Baby Back Ribs

I love to smoke ribs. In fact, I love to smoke just about anything. Low and slow is the key to great smoked ribs, so patience is everything. If you want to cut down the time involved, first steam the ribs until they are tender, then smoke them for 2 hours to allow the smoke flavor to permeate the meat.

4 (1½ lbs.) racks pork baby back ribs
2 cups cherry whisky
2 cups water
½ cup sugar
¼ cup salt
Cherry smoking chips
¼ cup Bone Dust BBQ Spice (page 203)

CHERRY WHISKY GLAZING SAUCE
1 small onion, diced
4 cloves garlic, minced
1 cup gourmet BBQ sauce
½ cup cherry whisky
½ cup honey
¼ cup grape jelly
2 TB. vegetable oil
Cayenne pepper, salt, and black pepper

Using a sharp knife, score the membrane on the backside of ribs in a diamond pattern. Place ribs in a roasting pan. Combine cherry whisky, water, sugar and salt; pour over ribs. Marinate, covered and refrigerated, for at least 4 hours or overnight.

Prepare your smoker according to manufacturer's instructions a temperature of 225°F (see page 219). Soak cherry chips in water while coals are heating.

Remove ribs from marinade (reserving marinade for basting) and rub with Bone Dust BBQ Spice, pressing spices into meat.

Place ribs in smoker and add soaked wood chips to coals. Close lid and smoke ribs, basting every hour with reserved marinade, until ribs are tender and the bones wiggle a little when pulled, 4 to 5 hours. Maintain a constant temperature of 225°F, and replenish coals, water, and wood chips as needed.

Meanwhile, prepare glazing sauce. In a medium saucepan, combine onion, garlic, BBQ sauce, cherry whisky, honey, grape jelly, and oil. Bring to a boil, stirring. Reduce heat and simmer for 15 minutes. Season to taste with a pinch cayenne pepper, salt, and black pepper. Remove from heat.

Preheat grill to medium-high.

Grill ribs, basting liberally with glazing sauce, for 10 to 12 minutes per side.

Cut between every third rib and serve.

SERVES 4 TO 6

Apple Juice Boiled Spareribs with Apple Butter BBQ Sauce

The key to this recipe is lots of apple butter. The BBQ sauce is also great drizzled over baked sweet potatoes.

2 racks pork spareribs (each 2 to 3 lbs.)	**APPLE BUTTER BBQ SAUCE**
8 cups apple juice	1 TB. vegetable oil
2 TB. minced fresh ginger	4 cloves garlic, minced
2 tsp. salt	1 cup apple butter
1 cinnamon stick	1 cup gourmet BBQ sauce
2 bay leaves	½ cup brown sugar
	½ cup apple juice
	1 TB. Worcestershire sauce
	1 TB. chopped fresh thyme
	Salt and pepper to taste

Using a sharp knife, score the membrane on the backside of ribs in a diamond pattern.

In a large pot, bring apple juice, ginger, salt, cinnamon stick, and bay leaves to a boil. Add spareribs, reduce heat to medium-low, cover, and simmer until ribs are tender, about 2 hours. Remove ribs from pot and let cool slightly.

Meanwhile, prepare sauce. Heat oil in a medium saucepan over medium-high heat. Sauté garlic for 1 minute. Stir in apple butter, BBQ sauce, brown sugar, apple juice, and Worcestershire sauce. Bring to a boil, stirring. Reduce heat to medium-low and simmer for 15 minutes. Remove from heat and stir in thyme, salt, and pepper.

Preheat grill to medium-high.

Season ribs with salt and pepper. Grill ribs, basting liberally with sauce, for 8 to 10 minutes per side.

Cut between every third rib and serve.

SERVES 4

Fat Belly BBQ Spareribs

I call these Fat Belly Ribs for two reasons. One, because you should use large, somewhat fatty spareribs. And two, because when you eat them, your belly gets fat. But hey, it's worth every lick!

---

2 (2 to 3 lb.) pork spareribs
¼ cup Bone Dust BBQ Spice (page 203)
8 cloves garlic, minced
2 bottles honey brown lager

FAT BELLY BBQ SAUCE
4 cloves garlic, minced
2 cups smoky BBQ sauce

1 cup ketchup
½ cup brown sugar
½ cup + 1 shot Jack Daniel's Sour Mash Whiskey
¼ cup maple syrup
¼ cup water
1 tsp. ground cumin
1 tsp. cayenne pepper
Salt and freshly ground black pepper to taste

Preheat oven to 325°F.

Using a sharp knife, score the membranes on the backside of the ribs in a diamond patter. Rub with Bone Dust BBQ Spice, pressing seasoning into the meat. Place ribs in a large roasting pan and add garlic and beer. Cover tightly with lid or foil.

Braise ribs until meat is tender, 2 to 2½ hours. Let cool slightly.

Meanwhile, prepare sauce. In a large saucepan, whisk together garlic, BBQ sauce, ketchup, brown sugar, Jack Daniel's, maple syrup, and water. Bring to a boil, reduce heat to low, and simmer for 15 minutes, stirring occasionally. Season with cumin, cayenne black pepper, salt, and pepper. Remove from heat and keep warm.

Preheat grill to medium-high.

Grill ribs, basting liberally with sauce, until slightly charred, 6 to 8 minutes per side.

Cut between every third rib and toss with remaining sauce.

SERVES 4 TO 6

Rum and Raisin Glazed Grilled Spareribs

While in Jamaica, I had a refreshing beverage of Appleton rum and ginger beer served over ice. It was the inspiration for these ribs.

2 (2 to 3 lbs.) racks pork spareribs
½ cup Red-Rum Rub (page 213)
2 cans ginger beer
¼ cup dark rum

RUM AND RAISIN GLAZING SAUCE
2 TB. vegetable oil
1 small onion, finely chopped
1 TB. finely chopped fresh ginger

1 cup water
½ cup golden raisins
½ cup honey
¼ cup brown sugar
¼ cup dark rum
1 TB. chopped fresh thyme
2 tsp. cornstarch, dissolved in 2 TB. water
Salt and cracked black pepper

Using a sharp knife, score the membrane on the backside of ribs in a diamond pattern. Rub with Red-Rum Rub, pressing seasoning into meat. Lay ribs meat side down in a roasting pan and pour in ginger beer and rum to cover. Marinate, covered and refrigerated, at least 4 hours or overnight.

To prepare glazing sauce, heat oil in a medium saucepan over medium-high heat. Sauté onion and ginger until tender, 2 to 3 minutes. Stir in water, raisins, honey, brown sugar, rum, and thyme. Bring to a boil, reduce heat, and simmer for 15 minutes, stirring occasionally. Stir in cornstarch mixture; return to a boil, stirring, until thickened. Remove from heat and season to taste with salt and pepper.

Preheat grill to medium.

Grill ribs, turning every 15 minutes, for 1 hour. Grill for another 30 minutes, basting frequently with sauce.

Cut between every third rib and serve.

SERVES 4

Stuffed Pork Ribs with Curried Fruit Compote

Octoberfest in Kitchener, Ontario, Canada, is always a good time, with plenty of cold beer and lots of good food. Just outside Kitchener is a little restaurant called the Blue Moon, where I first had delicious tender ribs stuffed with a ton of moist bread stuffing. Serve these ribs with a few pints of ice-cold beer. Prost!

---

2 (2 to 3 lbs.) racks pork spareribs
2 TB. Bone Dust BBQ Spice (page 203)
1 lemon, thinly sliced
2 cups apple juice

STUFFING
1 loaf (about 22 slices) enriched white bread
2 cloves garlic, minced
1 onion, diced

2 stalks celery, diced
6 slices bacon, fully cooked and chopped
1 cup diced dried apricots
½ cup golden raisins
1 TB. chopped fresh rosemary
½ cup boiling water
¼ cup melted butter
Salt and pepper
Vegetable oil

Preheat oven to 325°F.

Using a sharp knife, score the membrane on the backside of ribs in a diamond pattern. Rub with Bone Dust BBQ Spice, pressing seasoning into meat. Lay ribs meat side down in a roasting pan. Lay three to four lemon slices on the back of each rib; pour in apple juice. Cover tightly with lid or foil.

Braise ribs until tender, 2 to 2½ hours. Let cool slightly. Reduce oven temperature to 200°F.

While ribs are cooling, prepare stuffing. Cut bread into ½-inch cubes. Spread on a baking sheet and heat in the oven until dry, about 30 minutes.

In a large bowl, combine dried bread, garlic, onion, celery, bacon, apricots, raisins, and rosemary. Add boiling water and melted butter, stirring to fully mix. Season to taste with salt and pepper. The stuffing should hold together but still be moist.

Lay a pork rib, curved side up, on a work surface. Stuff the curved side of rib with all stuffing, pressing it firmly to form a log along the inside of rib. Place other rib, curved side down, on top of stuffing, pressing firmly so it adheres. Tie ribs together with string at 2-inch intervals. Brush ribs with a little vegetable oil.

Preheat grill to medium.

Grill ribs away from direct heat, with the lid closed, until lightly charred and stuffing is hot, 10 to 15 minutes per side. (Using indirect heat will enable you to use your grill more like an oven and grill-roast ribs.) Remove ribs from grill and let stand for 5 minutes.

Cut between every second bone and serve with Curried Fruit Compote (recipe follows).

SERVES 4

Curried Fruit Compote

1 cup diced fresh pineapple	¼ cup plum sauce
½ cup diced dried apricots	¼ cup water
½ cup candied cherries, halved	1 TB. minced fresh ginger
¼ cup candied orange peel	1 TB. curry paste
¼ cup golden raisins	Salt
½ cup corn syrup	

In a medium saucepan, combine pineapple, apricots, cherries, orange peel, raisins, corn syrup, plum sauce, water, ginger, and curry paste. Bring to a boil, stirring. Reduce heat to medium-low and simmer for 15 minutes. Season to taste with salt. Let cool.

MAKES ABOUT 3½ CUPS

Raspberry Chipotle Glazed Spareribs

This sweet and spicy sauce is a perfect match for meaty spareribs. Chipotle chilies in adobo sauce can be found in specialty food stores and in the ethnic section of supermarkets. A chipotle chili is a smoked jalapeño pepper. If you're short on time, use Dan-T's Raspberry Chipotle Sauce instead of making the glaze.

2 (2 to 3 lbs.) racks pork spareribs
3 TB. Bone Dust BBQ Spice (page 203)
3 to 4 cups cranberry juice

RASPBERRY CHIPOTLE GLAZE
1 pint raspberries
1 cup honey

½ cup raspberry jam
½ cup water
¼ cup chipotle chilies in adobo sauce
¼ cup raspberry vinegar
1 TB. chopped fresh ginger
1 TB. chopped fresh mint
Salt and pepper

Using a sharp knife, score the membrane on the backside of ribs in a diamond pattern. Rub with Bone Dust BBQ Spice, pressing seasoning into meat. Lay ribs in a roasting pan and pour in enough cranberry juice to cover. Marinate, covered and refrigerated, at least 4 hours or overnight.

Preheat oven to 350°F.

Discard marinade and place ribs on a rack in the roasting pan. Roast ribs until tender, 75 to 90 minutes.

Meanwhile, prepare glaze. In a small saucepan, combine raspberries, honey, jam, water, chilies, vinegar, ginger, and mint. Bring to a boil, stirring. Reduce heat to low and simmer, stirring occasionally, for 15 minutes. Season to taste with salt and pepper. Purée sauce until smooth. Let cool.

Preheat grill to medium-high.

Grill ribs, basting with lots of glaze, for 8 to 10 minutes per side.

Cut between every third rib and serve.

SERVES 4

Devil's Brewed Roast Chicken with White Trash BBQ Sauce

Root Beer Ribs with Drive-In BBQ Sauce

Grilled Tuna and Vegetable Pan Bagnat

Margarita Wings

Shrimp Parfait with Lucifer Cocktail Sauce

Rocketship 7 Peanut Butter and Jelly Steaks

Cinnamon-Skewered Scallops with Brown Sugar and Peach-Orange Salsa

The Burger Is Better with Butter

Asian-Spiced Country-Style Pork Ribs

Marinating country-style ribs helps tenderize them and boosts their flavor. Patience is everything with this recipe—low and slow, with a few beer chasers.

---

2 (1 to 1½ lbs.) racks country-style pork ribs
¼ cup Bone Dust BBQ Spice (page 203)
4 cloves garlic, minced
1 cup ketchup
1 cup water

½ cup light corn syrup
¼ cup lime juice
¼ cup rice wine vinegar
1 TB. chopped fresh cilantro
1 TB. sambal oelek

Rub ribs with Bone Dust BBQ Spice, pressing seasoning into meat. Place in a roasting pan.

Stir together garlic, ketchup, water, corn syrup, lime juice, vinegar, cilantro, and sambal oelek. Pour over ribs, turning to coat. Marinate, covered and refrigerated, for 6 to 8 hours.

Preheat grill to medium-high.

Remove ribs from marinade (reserving marinade for basting) and grill ribs, turning frequently and basting with reserved marinade, until ribs are cooked and tender and a meat thermometer reads 160°F, 40 to 50 minutes.

Cut into 1-inch-thick slices and serve.

SERVES 6 TO 8

Tip

Sambal oelek is a Thai garlic chili sauce, available in Asian markets.

Grilled Spicy Thai Chili Back Rib Tail Pieces

Hot and spicy to start, and sticky to finish. These are great rib ticklers for the start to a great barbecue.

2 lbs. pork back rib tail pieces	3/4 cup plum sauce
2 TB. Bone Dust BBQ Spice (page 203)	½ cup sweet Thai chili sauce
½ cup coconut milk	¼ cup brown sugar
½ cup water	¼ cup soy sauce
¼ cup lime juice	¼ cup dry sherry
	2 TB. lime juice
SPICY THAI CHILI GLAZE	2 TB. rice wine vinegar
3 green onions, finely chopped	1 TB. chopped fresh cilantro

Rub rib pieces with Bone Dust BBQ Spice, pressing seasoning into meat. In a glass dish large enough to hold rib pieces in one layer, whisk together coconut milk, water, and lime juice. Add rib pieces, turning to coat. Marinate, covered and refrigerated, for at least 6 hours or overnight.

To prepare glaze, in a bowl, whisk together green onions, plum sauce, chili sauce, brown sugar, soy sauce, sherry, lime juice, vinegar, and cilantro.

Preheat grill to medium-high.

Grill rib pieces, basting generously with glaze, for 5 to 6 minutes per side.

Serve immediately.

SERVES 2 TO 4

The Boneless Rib with Mango BBQ Sauce

Sometimes you just want to eat meat and forget about all the bones. This recipe uses the pork loin and produces a tender, succulent boneless rib. Slow braising allows for maximum tenderness and maximum flavor. This one's all meat, baby. No bones about it.

---

1 (3 to 4 lbs. and about 1 foot long) boneless pork loin

½ cup Red-Rum Rub (page 213)

2 lemons, thinly sliced

2 bottles Dave's Island Stinger or hard lemonade

MANGO BBQ SAUCE

1 large ripe mango, peeled and finely chopped

1 jalapeño pepper, seeded and finely chopped

1½ cups gourmet BBQ sauce

½ cup ketchup

½ cup honey

¼ cup orange juice

1 TB. minced fresh ginger

1 TB. lemon juice

Salt to taste

Cut pork loin lengthwise into three equal pieces. The pieces should look similar to a back rib but without bones. Rub "boneless pork rib" with Red-Rum Rub, pressing seasoning into meat. Place pork in a roasting pan. Lay three to four lemon slices on each "rib." Pour Island Stingers over meat. Cover tightly with lid or foil and marinate, refrigerated, for 2 to 4 hours.

Preheat oven to 375°F.

Braise ribs for 1½ hours. Let cool slightly.

Meanwhile, prepare Mango BBQ Sauce. In a medium bowl, whisk together mango, jalapeño, BBQ sauce, ketchup, honey, orange juice, ginger, lemon juice, and salt.

Preheat grill to medium-high.

Grill "ribs," basting liberally with sauce, until lightly charred and hot, 3 to 4 minutes per side.

Cut pork into 1-inch-thick slices to resemble ribs. Transfer to a serving platter and serve immediately with remaining sauce for dipping.

SERVES 8 TO 10

South Carolina Yellow Back Ribs

Yellow BBQ sauce is a South Carolina favorite and is made from prepared mustard. It's tangy, sweet, and a little spicy, with a golden color that delights the eye. Don't use any of those fancy mustards for this recipe. Basic bright yellow prepared mustard is what makes this recipe sing.

---

4 (1½ lbs.) racks baby back ribs

2 TB. Bone Dust BBQ Spice (page 203)

2 oranges, sliced

2 cups orange juice

YELLOW BBQ SAUCE

2 yellow bell peppers, seeded and diced

1 small yellow onion, finely chopped

4 cloves garlic, minced

1 cup prepared mustard

¾ cup cider vinegar

¾ cup orange juice

½ cup honey

1 tsp. turmeric

1 tsp. ground cumin

1 tsp. black pepper

½ tsp. cayenne pepper

Salt to taste

Preheat oven to 325°F.

Using a sharp knife, score the membrane on the backside of ribs in a diamond pattern. Rub with BBQ spice, pressing seasoning into meat. Lay ribs meat side down in a roasting pan. Lay three to four orange slices on the back of each rib. Pour in orange juice. Cover tightly with lid or foil.

Braise ribs for 2 to 2½ hours or until tender. Let cool slightly.

Meanwhile, prepare sauce. In a medium saucepan, combine yellow peppers, onion, garlic, mustard, vinegar, orange juice, honey, turmeric, cumin, black pepper, and cayenne. Bring to a boil, stirring. Reduce heat to medium-low and simmer, stirring occasionally, for 20 to 30 minutes or until reduced by one-third. Season with salt. In a blender, purée mixture until smooth. Let cool.

Preheat grill to medium-high.

Grill ribs for 6 to 8 minutes per side, basting with sauce.

Cut between every third rib and serve.

SERVES 4 TO 6

Pineapple Juice Boiled Spareribs with Sweet-and-Sour Plum Sauce

When you boil your ribs in pineapple juice, you don't need to marinate the meat first. The high acidity of the pineapple juice tenderizes the ribs.

---

2 (2 to 3 lbs.) racks pork spareribs

8 cups pineapple juice

6 cloves garlic

2 tsp. ground cumin

2 tsp. black pepper

1 tsp. cinnamon

SWEET-AND-SOUR PLUM SAUCE

½ cup corn syrup

½ cup plum sauce

½ cup rice wine vinegar

2 TB. ketchup

1 TB. minced fresh ginger

1 TB. soy sauce

Salt and pepper

Using a sharp knife, score the membrane on the backside of ribs in a diamond pattern.

In a large pot bring pineapple juice and garlic to a boil. Add spareribs, reduce heat to medium-low, cover, and simmer for 2 hours or until tender. Remove ribs from pot and cool slightly. Discard braising liquid.

Meanwhile, prepare sauce. In a medium saucepan combine corn syrup, plum sauce, vinegar, ketchup, ginger, and soy sauce. Bring to a boil, stirring. Reduce heat to medium-low and simmer for 15 minutes, stirring occasionally. Season to taste with salt and pepper. Let cool.

Preheat grill to medium-high.

In a small bowl, combine cumin, pepper, and cinnamon. Rub ribs with seasoning mixture. Grill for 8 to 10 minutes per side, basting liberally with sauce.

Cut between every third rib and serve.

SERVES 4

Jalapeño Beer Braised Back Ribs

These ribs are a favorite of my golfing buddy Chris Harper. Chris is a cigar aficionado with a penchant for spicy ribs.

1 large yellow onion, sliced	2 TB. Bone Dust BBQ Spice (page 203)
4 jalapeño peppers, sliced	3 limes, sliced
4 cloves garlic, minced	2 cans beer
4 (1½ lbs.) racks baby back ribs	2 cups gourmet BBQ sauce

Preheat oven to 325°F.

In a bowl, combine onion, jalapeño peppers, and garlic. Spread mixture in a roasting pan.

Using a sharp knife, score the membrane on the backside of ribs in a diamond pattern. Rub with Bone Dust BBQ Spice, pressing seasoning into meat. Lay ribs meat side down on top of onion mixture. Lay three or four lime slices on the back of each rib. Pour in beer. Cover tightly with lid or foil.

Braise ribs for 2 to 2½ hours or until tender. Let cool slightly. Remove ribs from pan and set aside.

Pour onion-beer mixture into a large saucepan and bring to a boil. Reduce liquid by half, stirring occasionally. Add BBQ sauce. Return to boil, then remove from heat. In a blender or food processor, purée sauce until smooth.

Meanwhile, preheat grill to medium-high.

Grill ribs for 6 to 8 minutes per side, basting with sauce.

Cut between every third rib and serve.

SERVES 4 TO 6

Bourbon Smoked St. Louis Spareribs

Sweet bourbon makes a great addition to any BBQ sauce. Ask your butcher to prepare the St. Louis ribs by removing the soft bone brisket.

---

4 (2 to 2½ lbs.) racks St. Louis–style spareribs
2 cups bourbon
2 cups water
½ cup brown sugar
¼ cup salt
Hickory smoking chips
¼ cup Bone Dust BBQ Spice (page 203)

BOURBON BBQ SAUCE
2 cups hickory smoke–flavored BBQ sauce

½ cup bourbon
¼ cup molasses
2 TB. vegetable oil
1 TB. Worcestershire sauce
1 tsp. black pepper
1 tsp. mustard powder
1 small yellow onion, diced
4 cloves garlic, minced
Dash hot sauce
Salt to taste

Using a sharp knife, score the membrane on the backside of ribs in a diamond pattern. Place ribs in a large pan. Stir together bourbon, water, sugar, and salt. Pour over ribs, turning to coat. Marinate, covered and refrigerated, for 4 to 6 hours or overnight.

Prepare smoker as per smoking instructions (page 219). Soak hickory wood chips in water while coals are heating.

Remove ribs from marinade, reserving marinade. Rub ribs with Bone Dust BBQ Spice, pressing seasoning into meat.

Place ribs in smoker and add wood chips to coals. Close the lid and smoke ribs for 4 hours, basting every hour with reserved marinade and replenishing coals and wood chips as needed.

Meanwhile, make sauce. In a medium saucepan, combine BBQ sauce, bourbon, molasses, oil, Worcestershire sauce, pepper, mustard powder, onion, garlic, and hot sauce. Bring to a boil, stirring. Reduce heat and simmer for 15 minutes. Remove from heat. Season with salt.

Preheat grill to medium-high.

Remove ribs from smoker. Grill ribs for 10 to 12 minutes per side, basting liberally with sauce.

Cut between every third rib and serve.

SERVES 4 TO 6

Root Beer Ribs with Drive-In BBQ Sauce

When I was a kid, a Teen Burger and a frosty mug of root beer was an awesome treat. Inspired by that combination, I developed this funky recipe using root beer.

4 (1½ lbs.) racks pork baby back ribs
6 TB. Bone Dust BBQ Spice (page 203)
2 onions, sliced
4 cloves garlic, smashed
4 (375 ml) bottles or cans A&W Root Beer
1 TB. root beer essence or vanilla

DRIVE-IN BBQ SAUCE
1 cup ketchup
½ cup brown sugar
½ cup root beer
2 TB. chopped fresh cilantro
2 TB. water
1 TB. Worcestershire sauce
Salt to taste

Preheat oven to 325°F.

Using a sharp knife, score the membrane on the backside of ribs in a diamond pattern. Season ribs with Bone Dust BBQ Spice, pressing seasoning into meat.

Spread onions and garlic in a roasting pan. Lay ribs meat side down on top of onion mixture.

Stir together root beer and root beer essence; pour over ribs. Cover tightly with lid or foil.

Braise for 2 to 2½ hours or until meat is tender. Let cool slightly.

Meanwhile, make sauce. Whisk together ketchup, brown sugar, root beer, cilantro, water, Worcestershire sauce, and salt.

Preheat grill to medium-high.

Grill ribs for 6 to 8 minutes per side or until lightly charred, basting frequently with sauce.

Cut between every third rib and serve.

SERVES 4 TO 6

Honey Garlic Cinnamon Spareribs

For this recipe, you can never have enough garlic. The more, the better.

---

2 (2 to 3 lbs.) racks pork spareribs
¼ cup Indonesian Cinnamon Rub (page 209)
8 cloves garlic, minced
2 cups water

HONEY GARLIC SAUCE
1 cup honey
½ cup pineapple juice

¼ cup sesame seeds
¼ cup soy sauce
¼ cup rice vinegar
1 tsp. cinnamon
12 cloves garlic, minced
Salt and freshly ground black pepper

Preheat oven to 325°F.

Using a sharp knife, score the membrane on the backside of ribs in a diamond pattern. Season spareribs with Indonesian Cinnamon Rub, pressing spices into meat. Place ribs in a large roasting pan and add garlic and water. Cover tightly with lid or foil.

Braise for 2 to 2½ hours or until meat is tender. Let cool slightly.

Meanwhile, make sauce by mixing together honey, pineapple juice, sesame seeds, soy sauce, vinegar, cinnamon, and garlic. Season to taste with salt and pepper. Bring to a boil. Remove from heat and keep warm.

Preheat grill to medium-high.

Grill ribs for 6 to 8 minutes per side or until lightly charred, basting frequently with sauce.

Cut between every third rib and toss with remaining honey garlic sauce.

SERVES 4 TO 6

Char Siu Country-Style Pork Ribs

Char siu is Chinese sweet roasted pork. This Chinese-style BBQ marinade is traditionally very red in color because of the red food coloring in the sauce. I have included food coloring in the recipe, but you do not have to use it.

---

2 (1 to 1½ lbs.) racks country-style pork ribs
¼ cup Indonesian Cinnamon Rub (page 209)
½ cup brown sugar
½ cup soy sauce
¼ cup hoisin sauce

¼ cup honey
4 cloves garlic, minced
1 to 2 tsp. salt
¼ tsp. red food coloring (optional)

Rub ribs with Indonesian Cinnamon Rub, pressing seasoning into meat. Place in a large roasting pan.

Mix together brown sugar, soy sauce, hoisin sauce, honey, garlic, salt, and food coloring. Pour over ribs, turning to coat. Marinate, covered and refrigerated, for 24 hours.

Preheat grill to medium-high.

Remove ribs from marinade, discarding marinade. Grill for 40 to 50 minutes or until a meat thermometer reads 160°F. Thinly slice and serve.

SERVES 6 TO 8

Barbecued Back Ribs with Maple Bacon BBQ Sauce

Serve these ribs with Cheesy Macaroni Salad (page 73).

---

4 (1½ lbs.) racks pork baby back ribs
2 TB. Bone Dust BBQ Spice (page 203)
2 lemons, sliced
2 cups apple juice

MAPLE BACON BBQ SAUCE
8 slices bacon, diced
6 cloves garlic, minced
1 large onion, diced
1½ cups ketchup

1 cup applesauce
½ cup maple syrup
¼ cup cider vinegar
2 TB. hot sauce
2 TB. Worcestershire sauce
2 tsp. celery salt
1½ tsp. liquid smoke
1 tsp. mustard powder
¼ tsp. cayenne pepper
Salt

Preheat oven to 325°F.

Score the membrane on the backside of ribs in a diamond pattern. Rub with Bone Dust BBQ Spice, pressing season-ing into meat. Lay ribs meat side down in a roasting pan. Lay three or four lemon slices on the back of each rib. Pour in apple juice. Cover tightly with lid or foil. Braise for 2 to 2½ hours or until tender. Let cool slightly.

Meanwhile, prepare sauce. In a medium saucepan over medium heat, fry bacon until it is half-cooked. Drain off all but 3 tablespoons drippings. Add garlic and onions. Fry, stirring, until onions are tender and golden brown. Add ketchup, applesauce, maple syrup, vinegar, hot sauce, Worcestershire sauce, celery salt, liquid smoke, mustard pow-der, and cayenne. Bring to a boil, reduce heat to low, and simmer, stirring occasionally, for 15 minutes. Season with salt to taste. Set aside.

Preheat grill to medium-high.

Remove ribs from pan, discarding braising liquid. Grill ribs for 6 to 8 minutes per side or until lightly charred, bast-ing with sauce.

Cut between every third rib and toss with remaining sauce.

SERVES 4 TO 6

Honey Hoisin–Glazed Grilled Spareribs

These ribs require a generous amount of glazing during the final 30 minutes of grilling. The more baste, the stickier and tastier the ribs will be.

---

2 (2 to 3 lbs.) racks pork spareribs
½ cup Miami Spice Love Paste (page 211)
2 to 4 cans ginger ale

HONEY HOISIN GLAZE
1 cup hoisin sauce
1 cup honey
½ cup orange juice

2 TB. chopped fresh rosemary
2 TB. rice wine vinegar
1 TB. chopped fresh ginger
1 TB. sesame seeds
1 tsp. mustard powder
1 tsp. cracked black pepper
3 green onions, finely chopped
Salt to taste

Using a sharp knife, score the membrane on the backside of ribs in a diamond pattern. Rub with Miami Spice Love Paste, pressing seasoning into meat. Lay ribs in a roasting pan and pour in enough ginger ale to cover. Marinate, covered and refrigerated, for 4 to 6 hours or overnight.

Prepare the glaze. In a medium bowl, combine hoisin sauce, honey, orange juice, rosemary, vinegar, ginger, sesame seeds, mustard powder, black pepper, and green onions. Season with salt and set aside.

Preheat grill to medium.

Remove ribs from roasting pan, discarding liquid. Grill for 90 minutes, turning ribs every 15 minutes. During the last 30 minutes of grilling, baste liberally with honey hoisin glaze.

Cut between every third rib and serve.

SERVES 4

Moroccan Pomegranate–Glazed Back Ribs

 You'll find pomegranate molasses in specialty or Middle Eastern food shops.

4 (1½ lbs.) racks pork baby back ribs
2 TB. Bone Dust BBQ Spice (page 203)
2 oranges, sliced
2 cups orange juice

POMEGRANATE GLAZE
2 TB. olive oil
1 TB. chopped fresh ginger
4 cloves garlic, minced
1 cup pomegranate molasses
½ cup honey

¼ cup lemon juice
1 TB. chopped fresh cilantro
1 TB. chopped fresh parsley
1 TB. chopped fresh mint
3 green onions, finely chopped
1 TB. sesame seeds
1 tsp. ground cumin
1 tsp. black pepper
¼ tsp. nutmeg
Salt to taste

Preheat oven to 325°F.

Using a sharp knife, score the membrane on the backside of ribs in a diamond pattern. Rub with Bone Dust BBQ Spice, pressing seasoning into meat. Lay ribs meat side down in a roasting pan. Lay three or four orange slices on back of each rib. Pour in orange juice. Cover tightly with lid or foil.

Braise for 2 to 2½ hours or until tender. Let cool slightly.

Meanwhile, prepare pomegranate glaze. In a medium saucepan over medium heat, heat oil. Sauté ginger and garlic, stirring, for 2 to 3 minutes or until tender. Add pomegranate molasses, honey, lemon juice, cilantro, parsley, mint, and green onions. Bring to a boil, stirring occasionally. Reduce heat and simmer, stirring, for 10 minutes. Remove from heat and stir in sesame seeds, cumin, pepper, nutmeg, and salt.

Preheat grill to medium.

Remove ribs from roasting pan, discarding liquid. Grill for 10 to 12 minutes per side, basting with glaze.

Cut between every third rib and serve.

SERVES 4 TO 6

Mahogany Glazed Back Rib Tail Pieces (a.k.a. If Pigs Could Fly)

This classic Chinese glaze makes ribs rich in color and flavor. Mildly spiced, these appetizer rib pieces will draw crowds to the table.

---

6 cups pineapple juice
2 lbs. pork back rib tail pieces
2 TB. Licorice Rub (page 212)

MAHOGANY GLAZE
¾ cup plum sauce
½ cup hoisin sauce

¼ cup soy sauce
¼ cup dry sherry
¼ cup rice wine vinegar
¼ cup brown sugar
8 cloves garlic, minced
1 TB. minced fresh ginger
3 green onions, finely chopped

Pour pineapple juice into a steamer pot and bring to a boil. Rub the back rib tail pieces with Licorice Rub and place in top portion of steamer. Steam ribs for 45 to 60 minutes or until tender.

Meanwhile, prepare glaze. In a bowl, whisk together plum sauce, hoisin sauce, soy sauce, sherry, vinegar, brown sugar, garlic, ginger, and green onions. Set aside.

Preheat grill to medium-high.

Grill rib pieces for 5 to 6 minutes per side, basting generously with glaze.

Serve immediately.

SERVES 2 TO 4

Tandoori Back Ribs

If you want to save a little time, buy a commercial tandoori paste, readily available in specialty food shops or in the ethnic section of grocery stores.

TANDOORI MARINADE
2 cups plain yogurt
1 TB. lemon juice
2 tsp. salt
¼ cup paprika
2 TB. ground cumin
1 TB. cayenne pepper
1 TB. ground coriander
1 TB. ground cardamom

1 TB. cinnamon
1 TB. black pepper
1 tsp. ground cloves
¼ cup clarified butter
1 TB. minced fresh ginger
6 cloves garlic, minced

4 (1½ lbs.) racks pork baby back ribs

In a large bowl, blend yogurt, lemon juice, and salt. Set aside.

In a small bowl, combine paprika, cumin, cayenne, coriander, cardamom, cinnamon, black pepper, and cloves.

In a frying pan, heat clarified butter over medium heat until hot but not smoking. Add ginger and garlic; sauté, stirring, for 1 to 2 minutes or until tender. Add spice blend and fry, stirring, for 30 seconds to 1 minute, being careful not to burn spices. Transfer spices to yogurt and whisk until fully incorporated.

Using a sharp knife, score the membrane on the backside of ribs in a diamond pattern. Lay ribs in a large dish. Pour tandoori marinade over ribs, turning to coat. Marinate, covered and refrigerated, for 4 to 6 hours or overnight.

Preheat oven to 350°F.

Remove ribs from marinade, reserving marinade. Place ribs on a rack in a roasting pan. Roast ribs for 1 to 1¼ hours or until tender.

Preheat grill to medium-high.

Grill ribs for 8 to 10 minutes per side, basting with tandoori marinade.

Cut between every third rib and serve.

SERVES 4

The Boneless Rib (a.k.a. Beer-Marinated Boneless Pork Rib with Beer BBQ Sauce)

Ribs are delicious but are mostly bone. This boneless rib is a pork loin cut into three lengthwise, slowly braised, then grilled. All meat and all tender—no bones about it.

1 (3 to 4 lbs. and about 1 foot long) boneless
    pork loin
½ cup Bone Dust BBQ Spice (page 203)
2 lemons, thinly sliced
2 bottles beer

BEER BBQ SAUCE
1½ cups hickory smoke–flavored BBQ sauce
1 cup beer
½ cup brown sugar
½ cup ketchup
1 TB. lemon juice
2 tsp. Bone Dust BBQ Spice (page 203)
Salt to taste

Cut pork loin lengthwise into three equal pieces. The pieces should look similar to a back rib but without bones. Rub pork with Bone Dust BBQ Spice, pushing spices into meat. Place pork in a roasting pan. Lay three or four lemon slices on each "rib." Pour beer over pork. Marinate, covered and refrigerated, for 2 to 4 hours.

Preheat oven to 375°F.

Cover ribs tightly with lid or foil. Braise for 1½ hours or until tender. Let cool in beer.

While ribs are cooling make sauce. Whisk together BBQ sauce, beer, brown sugar, ketchup, lemon juice, Bone Dust BBQ Spice, and salt.

Preheat grill to medium-high.

Remove pork from marinade, discarding marinade. Grill "ribs" for 3 to 4 minutes per side or until lightly charred, basting liberally with sauce.

Slice pork into 1-inch-thick slices to resemble ribs. Transfer to a serving platter and serve with remaining sauce for dipping.

SERVES 8

BBQ Beef Short Ribs

Braising these ribs slowly makes them fall-off-the-bone tender.

4 lbs. beef short ribs, cut into 6-inch lengths	1 cup chili sauce
½ cup Old Montreal Steak Spice (page 202)	¼ cup honey
¼ cup vegetable oil	3 TB. sambal chili paste
4 cloves garlic, chopped	2 TB. Worcestershire sauce
1 can beer	1 TB. chopped fresh cilantro
1 cup BBQ sauce	1 large onion, sliced

Preheat oven to 325°F.

In a large bowl, toss beef ribs with Old Montreal Steak Spice and vegetable oil.

In another bowl whisk together garlic, beer, BBQ sauce, chili sauce, honey, sambal, Worcestershire sauce, and cilantro. Stir in onion and set aside.

In a frying pan over medium-high heat, sear ribs for 2 to 3 minutes per side or until lightly charred. Transfer ribs to a roasting pan. Pour sauce over ribs and stir to coat evenly. Cover with lid or foil. Braise for 1½ to 2 hours or until meat is tender and can be easily separated from the bone.

Transfer ribs to a platter, reserving pan liquids, and let cool for 15 to 20 minutes.

Meanwhile, preheat grill to medium-high.

Grill ribs for 5 to 6 minutes per side or until lightly charred and tender, basting with pan liquids.

SERVES 6 TO 8

Refrigerator Short Ribs

I first cooked these ribs with my dad in our hometown of Paris, Ontario. We were on our own for a few weeks, and Dad brought home some beef short ribs. After a little research on how to prepare them, we dug around in the fridge for some ingredients and came up with this recipe.

1 cup all-purpose flour	2 stalks celery, diced
1 tsp. salt	1 green bell pepper, thinly sliced
1 tsp. black pepper	1 cup prepared yellow mustard
1 tsp. mustard powder	½ cup corn syrup
½ tsp. cayenne pepper	½ cup malt vinegar
4 lbs. beef short ribs	¼ cup chopped fresh parsley
¼ cup vegetable oil	1½ cups water
2 large Spanish onions, sliced	Salt
8 cloves garlic, minced	

Preheat oven to 325°F.

In a bowl, blend flour, salt, pepper, mustard powder, and cayenne. Roll short ribs in seasoned flour, shaking off any excess flour.

In a large frying pan over medium-high heat, heat oil. Fry ribs until golden brown on all sides, about 3 minutes per side. Transfer ribs to a roasting pan.

In a bowl, combine onions, garlic, celery, and green pepper. Spread mixture over ribs. In the same bowl stir together the prepared mustard, corn syrup, vinegar, parsley, and water. Season to taste with salt. Pour over ribs. Cover tightly with lid or foil. Braise for 1½ to 2 hours or until tender.

Transfer ribs to a platter, reserving mustard-onion mixture, and let cool for 15 to 20 minutes.

Meanwhile, preheat grill to medium-high.

Grill ribs for 5 to 6 minutes per side or until lightly charred and tender, basting with pan liquids. Serve with remaining mustard-onion mixture.

SERVES 6 TO 8

Maui Beef Ribs

Cut from the ends of a beef rib roast and the plate, these short ribs are made up of flat rib bones with layers of meat and fat. Ask your butcher to prepare the short ribs Maui, or Miami, style. These ribs will be about ½ inch thick and 1½ inches wide and have five rib bones. Marinate for at least 6 hours, then grill quickly over high heat.

¼ cup vegetable oil

¼ cup brown sugar

¼ cup dry sherry

¼ cup balsamic vinegar

2 TB. chopped fresh ginger

2 TB. molasses

1 TB. sesame oil

6 cloves garlic, minced

2 shallots, diced

4 green onions, finely chopped

1 stalk lemon grass, pale green part only, smashed and finely chopped

2 tsp. cracked black pepper

1 tsp. salt

4 lbs. (about 15 to 20 pieces) beef short ribs, cut across the bones ½ inch thick

---

In a glass dish large enough to hold ribs, combine vegetable oil, sugar, sherry, vinegar, ginger, molasses, sesame oil, garlic, shallots, green onions, lemon grass, pepper, and salt.

Add ribs, turning to coat. Marinate, covered and refrigerated, for 4 to 6 hours or overnight.

Preheat grill to high.

Remove ribs from marinade, reserving marinade. Grill for 2 to 3 minutes per side, basting liberally with reserved marinade.

SERVES 4 TO 6

Drumheller Beef Ribs

Drumheller, in the Badlands of Alberta, is the home of "dinosaur graveyards"—an archaeological site that has uncovered dinosaur bones from millions of years ago. My "dinosaur bones" recipe calls for prime rib of beef. Allow a half rack of ribs per person. These delicious ribs are slowly smoked over hickory wood chips and basted with a smoky onion BBQ sauce.

---

2 (5 lb.) racks prime rib of beef back ribs
¼ cup Bone Dust BBQ Spice (page 203)
Hickory smoking chips

SMOKY ONION BBQ SAUCE
3 TB. vegetable oil
2 onions, sliced

8 cloves garlic, chopped
2 cups hickory smoke–flavored BBQ sauce
¼ cup brown sugar
¼ cup dark rum
1 TB. chopped fresh rosemary
1 tsp. liquid smoke
Salt and pepper to taste

Tip

Ask your butcher to cut the racks of beef ribs in half lengthwise (across the bones) to give you narrow racks of ribs similar to pork spareribs.

Rub racks with Bone Dust BBQ Spice, pressing seasoning into meat. Cover and marinate at room temperature for 30 minutes.

To prepare sauce, heat oil in a large saucepan. Sauté onions and garlic, stirring, until caramelized. Add BBQ sauce, sugar, rum, rosemary, and liquid smoke. Bring to a boil; reduce heat and simmer for 15 minutes, stirring occasionally. Season with salt and pepper and set aside.

Prepare smoker as per smoking instructions (page 219). Soak hickory wood chips in water while coals are heating.

Add wood chips to coals and place ribs in smoker. Close the lid and smoke ribs for 3 to 4 hours, basting every hour with sauce and replenishing coals and wood chips as needed.

Remove ribs from smoker and glaze with extra sauce.

Serve immediately with lots of wet cloths and napkins.

SERVES 4

Smoked Garlic BBQ Beef Short Ribs

Beef short ribs need a good, long braise to tenderize them. But the wait is worth it. Letting the braised ribs cool slightly before you grill them allows the meat to "settle." These ribs are absolutely succulent.

---

4 lbs. beef short ribs, cut into 6-inch lengths
½ cup Red-Rum Rub (page 213)
12 cloves smoked garlic (page 200) or
   roasted garlic (page 201), mashed
1 cup honey
1 cup gourmet BBQ sauce
½ cup dark rum

½ cup ketchup
½ cup water
2 TB. Dijon mustard
1 TB. chopped fresh thyme
1 TB. Worcestershire sauce
Salt and pepper to taste
½ cup vegetable oil

Preheat oven to 325°F.

Rub ribs with Red-Rum Rub, pressing seasoning into meat.

In a bowl, whish together smoked garlic, honey, BBQ sauce, rum, ketchup, water, mustard, thyme, Worcestershire sauce, salt, and pepper. Pour into a roasting pan.

In a frying pan over high heat, heat vegetable oil. Sear ribs until lightly charred, 2 to 3 minutes per side. Transfer ribs to the roasting pan, turning to coat with sauce. Cover tightly with lid or foil.

Braise ribs until meat is tender and can be easily separated from the bone, 1½ to 2 hours.

Transfer ribs to a platter (reserving pan liquid) and let cool slightly.

Preheat grill to medium-high.

Grill ribs, basting with pan liquid, until lightly charred and tender, 5 to 6 minutes per side.

SERVES 6 TO 8

Spicy Korean Beef Short Ribs

My version of these tasty ribs—known as bulgogi—is easy to prepare. This is a perfect recipe to start any backyard barbecue.

4 green onions, finely chopped	2 TB. sambal oelek (Thai garlic chili sauce)
6 cloves garlic, minced	1 TB. chopped fresh cilantro
¼ cup brown sugar	1 TB. sesame oil
¼ cup vegetable oil	2 tsp. toasted sesame seeds
¼ cup soy sauce	2 tsp. cracked black pepper
¼ cup rice vinegar	4 lbs. (about 15 to 20 pieces) beef short ribs, cut across
¼ cup dry sherry	the bones ½ inch thick
2 TB. chopped fresh ginger	

In a glass dish large enough to hold ribs in one layer, whisk together green onions, garlic, brown sugar, vegetable oil, soy sauce, rice vinegar, sherry, ginger, sambal oelek, cilantro, sesame oil, sesame seeds, and pepper. Add ribs, turning to coat. Marinate, covered and refrigerated, at least 4 hours or overnight.

Preheat grill to medium-high.

Remove ribs from marinade. Pour marinade into a small saucepan. Bring to a boil, reduce heat and simmer for 5 minutes. Remove from heat.

Grill ribs, basting liberally with heated marinade, 2 to 3 minutes per side.

SERVES 4 TO 6

Big Bones Beef Ribs with Jack's Devilishly Good BBQ Sauce

Two-fisted eating is a requirement when tackling the monster beef rib. You know you have done a good job of eating when your hands, arms, chest, and face are covered with sticky sauce.

---

2 (5 lb.) racks prime rib of beef back ribs
¼ cup Old Montreal Steak Spice (page 202)

JACK'S DEVILISHLY GOOD BBQ SAUCE
2 TB. vegetable oil
1 small onion, diced
4 cloves garlic, chopped
2 cups hickory smoke–flavored BBQ sauce

1 cup steak sauce
½ cup maple syrup
¼ cup Jack Daniel's Sour Mash Whiskey
2 TB. malt vinegar
1 TB. chopped fresh thyme
1 TB. cracked black pepper
Salt to taste

Rub racks with Old MontrealSteak Spice, pressing seasoning into meat. Marinate, covered at room temperature, for 30 minutes.

To prepare sauce, heat oil in a medium saucepan over medium-high heat. Sauté onion and garlic until tender. Stir in BBQ sauce, steak sauce, maple syrup, Jack Daniel's, vinegar, thyme, pepper, and salt. Bring to a boil, reduce heat to low, and simmer for 15 minutes, stirring occasionally.

Preheat grill to medium-high.

Grill ribs until seared, 4 to 5 minutes per side. Move ribs to the upper rack of the grill, close the lid, and grill-roast ribs, basting occasionally with sauce, until tender, 30 to 45 minutes.

Remove ribs from grill and glaze with extra sauce. Serve immediately with lots of wet naps and napkins.

SERVES 6 TO 8

Tip

Ask your butcher to cut the racks in half lengthwise across the bones to give you a narrow rack of ribs, similar to pork spareribs.

Five Doors North Buffalo Ribs with Amaretto BBQ Sauce

Buffalo ribs are not the easiest thing to find, so you might have to order them from your butcher. They are similar to beef ribs but they have a stronger, gamier flavor. Make sure you cook them until they're very tender. They're a bit expensive, and you do not want to spend good money only to have tough, undercooked ribs.

Five Doors North is a Toronto restaurant owned by Chef Vito Rizzuto. He prepared these for me one night but would not divulge his recipe. This is what I came up with.

2 (3 to 4 lb.) racks buffalo ribs
¼ cup Bone Dust BBQ Spice (page 203)
2 bottles beer

AMARETTO BBQ SAUCE
2 cups hickory smoke–flavored BBQ sauce
½ cup brown sugar
¼ cup steak sauce
¼ cup ketchup
¼ cup amaretto
Salt and pepper

Rub ribs with Bone Dust BBQ Spice, pressing seasoning into meat. Place ribs in a roasting pan and marinate at room temperature for 30 minutes.

Preheat oven to 375°F.

Pour beer over ribs. Cover tightly with lid or foil.

Braise ribs until very tender, about 1½ hours. Let cool slightly.

Meanwhile, prepare sauce by whisking together BBQ sauce, brown sugar, steak sauce, ketchup, and amaretto. Season to taste with salt and pepper.

Preheat grill to medium-high.

Grill ribs, basting liberally with sauce, for 8 to 10 minutes per side.

Slice between every bone and serve immediately.

SERVES 8

Honey Mustard Grilled Lamb Ribs

Lamb ribs are a Greek party favorite, and they're one of my favorite foods. If you've never had them, make a point of getting some and munching away. You might have to order these from your butcher.

---

8 racks lamb ribs
¼ cup Herb Mustard Rub (page 208)
1 large onion, sliced
12 cloves garlic, minced
2 lemons, thinly sliced
1 TB. chopped fresh rosemary
1 to 2 cups white wine

HONEY MUSTARD GLAZING SAUCE
2 green onions, finely chopped
1 cup honey
½ cup prepared mustard
2 TB. old-fashioned grainy mustard
2 TB. lemon juice
1 TB. chopped fresh parsley
Salt and pepper to taste

Preheat oven to 325°F.

Using a sharp knife, score ribs on both sides in a diamond pattern. Rub with Herb Mustard Rub, pressing seasoning into meat.

Place onion, garlic, lemon slices, rosemary, and wine in a roasting pan. Arrange ribs on top. Cover tightly with lid or foil.

Braise ribs until tender, about 1½ hours. Let cool slightly.

To prepare glazing sauce, whisk together green onions, honey, prepared mustard, grainy mustard, lemon juice, parsley, salt, and pepper.

Preheat grill to medium-high.

Grill ribs, basting with glazing sauce, for 4 to 5 minutes per side.

Cut between every second bone and serve with grilled potatoes.

SERVES 4

Grilled Lamb Ribs with Sweet Jalapeño BBQ Glaze

Lamb ribs are tender and delicious. You will not always find them in grocery stores, so special-order them through your specialty meat shop or butcher.

---

8 (8 to 10 oz. trimmed) racks lamb ribs
¼ cup Licorice Rub (page 212)
1 large onion, sliced
2 TB. chopped garlic
2 lemons, thinly sliced
2 cups water

SWEET JALAPEÑO BBQ GLAZE
1 cup jalapeño jelly
3 TB. cider vinegar
2 TB. lemon juice
1 TB. chopped fresh cilantro
Black pepper to taste

Preheat oven to 325°F.

With a sharp knife, score lamb ribs on both sides in a diamond pattern. Season ribs with Licorice Rub, pressing spices into meat.

Place onion, garlic, lemon slices, and water in a large roasting pan. Arrange ribs on top of onion mixture. Cover tightly with lid or foil. Bake for 1½ hours or until tender. Let cool.

Meanwhile, make glaze. In a small saucepan, stir together jalapeño jelly, vinegar, and lemon juice. Bring to a boil and whisk until smooth. Remove from heat and stir in cilantro and pepper. Let cool.

Preheat grill to medium-high.

Grill ribs, basting with glaze, for 4 to 5 minutes per side.

Cut between every second bone and serve with grilled potatoes, if desired.

SERVES 4

Thai Marinated Lamb Ribs with Spicy Peanut Sauce

This is my friend Chef Wendy Baskerville's recipe for grilled lamb ribs with a spicy peanut sauce. Wendy prepared these tasty ribs for me when she owned Babette's Feast Catering in Toronto.

½ cup coconut milk

1 stalk lemon grass, pale green part only, smashed and chopped

3 limes, juiced

2 small spicy Thai green chilies

1 TB. chopped fresh ginger

6 cloves garlic, minced

2 TB. brown sugar

2 TB. vegetable oil

1 tsp. cracked black pepper

8 (8 to 10 oz. trimmed) racks lamb ribs

SPICY PEANUT SAUCE

2 TB. vegetable oil

2 shallots, diced

2 cloves garlic, minced

1 TB. minced fresh ginger

1 cup crunchy peanut butter

1 cup coconut milk

½ cup dry sherry

1 lime, zested and juiced

¼ cup rice wine vinegar

1 TB. sambal chili paste

1 TB. chopped fresh cilantro

In a glass dish large enough to hold lamb, stir together well coconut milk, lemon grass, lime juice, chilies, ginger, garlic, sugar, oil, and pepper.

With a sharp knife, score lamb ribs on both sides in a diamond pattern. Add ribs to marinade, turning to coat. Marinate, covered and refrigerated, for 4 to 6 hours.

Meanwhile, make sauce. Heat vegetable oil in a medium saucepan over medium heat. Sauté shallots, garlic, and ginger, stirring, until tender. Add peanut butter, coconut milk, and sherry, stirring until smooth. Add lime zest and juice, vinegar, sambal, and cilantro. Bring to a low boil, stirring to prevent sticking, and simmer for 5 to 10 minutes, stirring occasionally. Let cool.

Preheat grill to medium.

Remove ribs from marinade, reserving marinade. Grill for 20 to 30 minutes per side or until tender, basting with marinade.

Meanwhile, reheat peanut sauce.

Remove ribs from grill. Cut between every second rib and serve with warmed peanut sauce for dipping.

SERVES 4

Tip

Lamb ribs can be hard to find, so you may need to order them from your butcher. Cook the ribs over medium to medium-low heat; you want to cook them slowly to allow all the flavors to permeate the meat and to keep the meat from burning and drying out.

Lip-Smacking Tenderloins

Veal

Pork

Lamb and Game

Steak Cuts

So many choices …

Tenderloin

Of all the steak cuts, the tenderloin is the most tender. The tenderloin comes from the short loin of beef; it lies between the rib and the sirloin and never really does anything but lie there and be tender. The tenderloin may be cooked whole or cut into wonderfully tender steaks. Be careful not to overcook this cut. It does not have a lot of fat, so it tends to dry out and become tough the more it cooks.

Striploin

The striploin steak is one of the most popular cuts of beef. It comes from the top loin muscle in the short loin of beef. It is best grilled to medium-rare and is often served with a peppercorn sauce. This steak is known by many names, the most popular being the New York strip steak and Kansas City steak. A bone-in striploin steak is known as a shell steak.

Rib-Eye Steak

This steak is cut from between the rib and chuck section. The bone-in rib steak is also known as the cowboy steak. The rib steak is an extremely tender cut of beef. This steak is heavily marbled with fat, giving it maximum flavor. It is best to grill this steak to medium-rare, which allows the internal fat to melt and bring out the natural juices and flavor.

T-Bone Steak

This steak is named after the shape of its bone, a large T that separates the striploin from the small tenderloin. Cut from the center of the short loin, this is a large steak, often best shared, but if you're truly hungry it is a real meal for one. I like to serve this steak with lots of sautéed onions and mushrooms and topped with crumbled blue cheese.

Porterhouse Steak

A porterhouse steak is cut from the large end of the short loin and also has the same T-shaped bone as the T-bone. It has a larger tenderloin portion and is truly a meal for two—it's sometimes called the king of steaks. It is often cut into 2-inch-thick portions weighing approximately 36 ounces. Rub this steak with garlic, black pepper, and fresh rosemary and grill it over medium-high heat.

Sirloin Steak

Cut from the area between the short loin and round, the sirloin has three main muscles. Cut into steaks, they are quite flavorful but require marinating to make them a little more tender. A teriyaki marinade is the most popular marinade used on sirloin steaks.

Flank Steak

The flank steak comes from the lower hind region of beef. It is a tougher cut of steak that requires marinating to make it tender. As it does not have a lot of internal fat, be careful not to overcook it. Marinated in an Asian marinade, this steak will have great flavor. It is best sliced thinly when served and is a great steak for a salad or steak sandwich.

Hanger Steak

The hanger steak hangs between the rib cage and loin cage. Hanger steaks have a little stronger flavor than regular steaks and need to be very fresh. Ask your butcher for this tender cut of beef, which isn't usually found in grocery stores. Marinate it with stronger-flavored herbs and spices and lots of garlic. It is best cooked rare to medium and sliced thinly.

Cooking Steak

How do you like your steak cooked?

Blue Rare   A blue rare steak is quickly charred on the outside and barely cooked on the inside. For best results, bring the steak to room temperature before cooking.

Rare   A rare steak has a cool red center.

Medium-rare   A medium-rare steak has a warm red center.

Medium   A medium steak has a pink center and the juices are clear.

Medium-well   A medium-well steak has a hot pink center, and the juices are clear.

Well-done   A well-done steak is gray throughout without any trace of pink and the juices are clear.

Super well-done   This steak is weighted with a brick until heavily charred on the outside and without any trace of pink and no juices inside.

How to Test for Doneness for Your Perfect Steak

The best way to test for doneness on a steak is to use a meat thermometer.

Blue rare	130°F
Rare	130 to 140°F
Medium-rare	140 to 145°F
Medium	145 to 150°F
Medium-well	150 to 160°F
Well-done	160 to 170°F
Super well-done	170°F plus

The next best method to test for doneness is the Hand Touch Method. Shake one hand loose so that it is completely relaxed. With your other hand, touch the soft fleshy part of your relaxed hand at the base of your thumb. This soft texture is similar to the texture of a blue rare to rare steak.

Now touch your thumb and forefinger together and again touch the base of your thumb. This texture is similar to a medium-rare steak.

Next, touch your thumb to your middle finger. This firmer texture is similar to the texture of a medium steak.

Next, touch your thumb to your fourth finger. The semi-firm texture at the base of your thumb is similar to a medium-well steak.

Last, touch your thumb to your pinky finger. The very firm texture at the base of your thumb is similar to a well-done steak.

This method of testing for a steak is relatively easy and you will never find yourself looking for a thermometer while grilling.

One last note: Never cut the meat to test for doneness. Cutting the steak lets all the natural juices escape, leaving you with a dry and tasteless piece of meat.

Bacon-Wrapped Fillet with Lobster and Cheddar Topping

I love surf and turf, especially when the surf is lobster. You can use thawed frozen lobster or crab-meat, but be sure to squeeze out the excess moisture first.

6 to 12 slices thick-cut bacon
6 (about 8 oz.) beef tenderloin fillets
2 TB. Old Montreal Steak Spice (page 202)

LOBSTER AND CHEDDAR TOPPING
1½ cups cooked lobster meat
1½ cups shredded aged white cheddar cheese

1 cup cream cheese, softened
1 egg white
¼ cup fresh bread crumbs
1 TB. chopped fresh parsley
1 TB. lemon juice
Pinch cayenne pepper
Salt and pepper to taste

Fry bacon until slightly cooked and still flexible, 2 to 3 minutes per side. Drain on paper towels.

Rub fillets all over with Old Montreal Steak Spice, pressing seasoning into meat. Wrap each fillet with 1 slice bacon. (Use a half slice extra if bacon does not quite make it all the way around.) Seal with a toothpick and set aside to marinate for 30 minutes.

Meanwhile, prepare topping. In a bowl, combine lobster meat, cheddar cheese, cream cheese, egg white, bread crumbs, parsley, lemon juice, cayenne pepper, salt, and pepper.

Preheat grill to medium-high.

Grill fillets for 4 to 5 minutes per side for medium-rare and until bacon is crispy. During the last 2 minutes of cooking, evenly spread 2 tablespoons topping on each steak. Close the lid until topping is heated through.

Remove fillets from grill. Remove toothpicks, and serve with extra topping.

SERVES 6

Grilled Beef Tenderloin with Smoked Chocolate Cream Sauce

 The combination of smoke and sweet is a perfect match for grilled beef tenderloin. When I smoke white chocolate, I like to use a flavored hardwood, such as cherry, apple, pecan, or almond.

---

4 (6 oz. and 1½ inches thick) beef tenderloin fillets
¼ cup Old Montreal Steak Spice (page 202)

SMOKED CHOCOLATE CREAM SAUCE
2 TB. butter
2 cloves garlic, minced

1 shallot, finely chopped
1 small jalapeño pepper, seeded and finely chopped
1 cup heavy cream
1 cup smoked chocolate (page 431), coarsely chopped
½ cup chocolate liqueur
1 tsp. chopped fresh thyme
Salt and pepper to taste

Preheat grill to medium-high.

Rub fillets all over with Old Montreal Steak Spice, pressing seasoning into meat. Set aside.

To prepare sauce, melt butter in a small saucepan over medium-high heat. Sauté garlic, shallot, and jalapeño until tender, 1 to 2 minutes. Stir in ¼ cup cream; bring to a boil. Reduce heat to low. Stirring constantly, add smoked chocolate a little at a time, alternating with remaining cream.

Gently simmer until thickened, about 5 minutes. Whisk in chocolate liqueur, thyme, salt, and pepper. Remove from heat and keep warm.

Grill fillets for 4 to 5 minutes per side for medium-rare.

Remove fillets from grill and thinly slice across the grain. Serve drizzled with sauce.

SERVES 4

Rum-Soaked Jerk Strip Steak with Jerk Butter

I cooked these babies while filming my television show *King of the Q*. There we were on the beach grilling thick steaks that were spicy hot and full of flavor. I cooked USDA Prime Aged steaks that were heavily marbled and oh so tender.

---

4 (8 to 10 oz., 1-inch-thick) New York
    striploin steaks
¼ cup + 2 TB. Jamaican Jerk Paste (page 210)

½ cup dark rum
½ cup butter, softened

Season steaks with 2 tablespoons Jamaican Jerk Paste, pressing seasoning into meat. Place steaks in a glass dish large enough to hold them in one layer. Pour over rum, turning steaks to coat. Marinate, covered and refrigerated, for 4 hours.

Preheat grill to medium-high.

In a bowl, stir together butter and remaining ¼ cup Jamaican Jerk Paste.

Grill steaks, basting with a little jerk butter, for 4 to 5 minutes per side for medium-rare.

Serve immediately with an extra dollop jerk butter.

SERVES 4

Smoked New York Strip Steak

Low and slow makes these steaks sing with smoke and flavor.

6 (16 oz., 2-inch-thick) New York striploin
  steaks
¼ cup Bone Dust BBQ Spice (page 203)
Hickory smoking chunks

SMOKED STEAK GLAZING SAUCE
3 cloves garlic, minced
½ cup hickory smoke–flavored BBQ sauce
¼ cup Glayva Scotch liqueur
¼ cup ketchup
2 TB. brown sugar
2 TB. malt vinegar
1 TB. chopped fresh rosemary
Salt and pepper to taste

Rub steaks with Bone Dust BBQ Spice, pressing seasoning into meat. Set aside.

Prepare glazing sauce. In a medium saucepan, whisk together garlic, BBQ sauce, Glayva, ketchup, brown sugar, vinegar, rosemary, salt, and pepper. Set aside.

Prepare your smoker according to manufacturer's instructions to a temperature of 225°F (see page 219). Add soaked hickory smoking chunks.

Place steaks on smoking rack and close the lid. Smoke steaks for 2½ to 3 hours for medium-rare, replenishing smoking chips, coals, and water as required.

About 15 minutes before steaks are done, heat glazing sauce over medium heat, stirring occasionally, until hot, 10 to 15 minutes.

Serve steaks immediately topped with glazing sauce.

SERVES 6

Cabernet-Marinated New York Strip Steak with Caesar Compound Butter

I like my Caesar dressing loaded with garlic, anchovies, and Parmesan cheese. Here I turn the ingredients of a Caesar dressing into a compound butter. A slice of steak lathered with Caesar butter is delicious. Try this butter for garlic bread, too!

---

4 (12 oz.) New York striploin steaks
2 cups cabernet
2 to 3 TB. Old Montreal Steak Spice (page 202)

CAESAR COMPOUND BUTTER
½ lb. butter, softened
½ cup grated Parmesan cheese

2 TB. lemon juice
1 TB. capers, coarsely chopped
2 tsp. chopped fresh parsley
1 tsp. cracked black pepper
4 anchovy fillets, coarsely chopped
4 cloves garlic, minced
Salt to taste

Place steaks in a glass dish large enough to hold them in one layer. Pour in cabernet, turning to coat. Marinate, covered and refrigerated, for 2 hours.

Prepare Caesar Compound Butter. In a bowl, combine butter, Parmesan cheese, lemon juice, capers, parsley, black pepper, anchovies, garlic, and salt.

Preheat grill to medium-high.

Remove steaks from marinade and season with Old Montreal Steak Spice, pressing seasoning into meat. Grill steaks for 4 to 5 minutes per side for medium.

Thinly slice steaks across the grain and serve topped with a dollop or two Caesar Compound Butter.

SERVES 4

Grilled New York Strip Steak with Smoked Oysters and Bacon BBQ Sauce

While on a trip to Halifax, I was served smoked oysters with my steak. What an unexpected treat! In my version, the bacon BBQ sauce balances out the flavors.

4 slices smoked bacon, diced
4 cloves garlic, minced
1 can oysters, drained
½ cup gourmet BBQ sauce
¼ cup chopped fresh parsley

2 TB. butter
Salt and pepper to taste
4 (12 oz.) New York striploin steaks
2 TB. Old Montreal Steak Spice (page 202)

Tip

Fresh smoked oysters take approximately 1 hour to smoke at 150°F.

Preheat grill to medium-high.

In a medium frying pan, cook bacon over medium heat, stirring frequently, until lightly crisp, 5 to 6 minutes. Drain off all but 1 tablespoon fat. Add garlic and cook, stirring, for 1 minute. Stir in smoked oysters and BBQ sauce; bring to a low boil. Add parsley, butter, salt, and pepper, whisking until butter is melted. Remove from heat and keep warm.

Season steaks with Old Montreal Steak Spice, pressing seasoning into meat.

Grill steaks for 3 to 4 minutes per side for medium-rare or to desired doneness. Remove steaks from grill and let rest for 5 minutes.

Serve steaks topped with warm sauce.

SERVES 4

The Stuffed Cowboy Steak

This big steak with lots of stuffing is a cowboy treat. This meal is for sharing. Have a couple friends over to help you out with this biggie.

---

2 (24 oz., 2- to 3-inch-thick) bone-in rib steaks
½ cup Old Montreal Steak Spice (page 202)

COWBOY STUFFING
4 TB. butter
4 cloves garlic, minced
2 green onions, finely chopped
1 red onion, diced
1 green bell pepper, diced
½ cup corn kernels

1 (7 oz.) can chipotle chilies in adobo sauce, puréed (divided use)
¼ cup boiling water
1 TB. chopped fresh cilantro
2 cups cornbread stuffing mix
1 cup diced Monterey Jack cheese
Salt and pepper to taste

HOT BUTTER BASTE
⅓ cup melted butter
¼ cup lemon juice

Using a sharp knife, make an incision 1 inch long in the side of each steak. Carefully cut a large pocket inside each steak, being careful to not cut all the way through the steak. Rub steaks with Old Montreal Steak Spice, rubbing seasoning into meat. Set aside.

To prepare stuffing: In a large saucepan, melt butter over medium-high heat. Sauté the garlic, green onions, red onion, green pepper, and corn until tender, 3 to 5 minutes. Stir in one-quarter of the puréed chipotle chilies, boiling water, and cilantro. Remove from heat. Stir in stuffing mix. Let mixture stand for 10 minutes. Stir in cheese and season with salt and pepper.

Stuff each steak with 1 to 1½ cups stuffing, pressing it firmly into the pocket. Secure with a toothpick, if necessary.

Preheat the grill to medium-high.

To prepare Hot Butter Baste, in a small saucepan, melt butter. Stir in remaining chipotle purée and lemon juice. Bring to a boil and remove from heat.

Grill steaks, basting with Hot Butter Baste, for 8 to 10 minutes per side for medium-rare and until stuffing is hot.

Serve immediately.

SERVES 2 TO 4

Italian Diablo Rib Steak

I like to use the long and curly Italian green hot chilies. Their heat is sweet and is accentuated by grilling or roasting.

---

4 (12 oz., 1½-inch-thick) boneless rib steaks
¼ cup Gilroy Roasted Garlic Paste (page 201)
¼ cup balsamic vinegar
¼ cup olive oil
1 TB. cracked black pepper
Grated Parmesan cheese

DIABLO TOMATO SAUCE
3 Italian green hot chilies or jalapeño peppers
1 large red bell pepper
2 TB. olive oil

4 cloves garlic, minced
1 small onion, finely chopped
1 lb. ripe plum tomatoes, seeded and coarsely chopped
   (or 1 [19 oz.] can whole plum tomatoes, drained and chopped)
3 TB. tomato paste
½ cup chicken stock
1 bay leaf
1 tsp. salt
1 TB. chopped fresh oregano or basil
Pepper

Rub steaks with Gilroy Roasted Garlic Paste, pressing seasoning into meat. In a glass dish large enough to hold steaks in one layer, whisk together vinegar, oil, and black pepper. Add steaks, turning to coat. Marinate, covered and refrigerated, for 4 hours.

Preheat grill to medium-high.

To prepare sauce, grill-roast hot chilies and red pepper, with the lid closed, until charred and tender. Place in a bowl and cover with plastic wrap. Let stand 5 minutes. Peel, seed, and chop chilies and red pepper.

In a medium saucepan, heat oil over medium heat. Cook garlic and onion, stirring, until tender, 3 to 4 minutes. Stir in grilled chilies and red pepper, tomatoes, tomato paste, stock, bay leaf, and salt. Bring to a low boil, reduce heat, and simmer, stirring occasionally, for 30 to 40 minutes. The sauce should be thick and a little spicy. Discard bay leaf. Stir in oregano and season to taste with salt and pepper. Remove from heat and keep warm.

Preheat grill to medium-high.

Grill steaks for 4 to 5 minutes per side for medium-rare.

Thinly slice steaks across the grain and serve topped with sauce and grated Parmesan cheese.

SERVES 4

Thai Sirloin Steak Wraps

This is a fun recipe for the whole family to prepare. Lay out all the ingredients and let everyone make their own wrap.

6 (6 oz.) sirloin steaks	**MARINADE**
2 TB. Indonesian Cinnamon Rub (page 209)	4 green onions, finely chopped
1 small red onion, thinly sliced	½ cup hoisin sauce
1 carrot, cut into julienne strips	½ cup soy sauce
1 red bell pepper, thinly sliced	¼ cup vegetable oil
2 green onions, thinly sliced	¼ cup honey
2 cups bean sprouts	¼ cup rice vinegar
1 cup Thai basil leaves	2 TB. sambal oelek (Thai garlic chili sauce)
Salt	1 TB. cracked black pepper
12 round Thai rice paper wrappers	1 TB. sesame oil
12 green lettuce leaves	2 tsp. toasted sesame seeds

Rub steaks with Indonesian Cinnamon Rub, pressing seasoning into meat.

Prepare marinade. In a bowl, whisk together chopped green onion, hoisin sauce, soy sauce, vegetable oil, honey, rice vinegar, sambal oelek, black pepper, sesame oil, and sesame seeds. Set aside one-quarter of marinade.

Pour remaining marinade over steaks, turning to coat, and marinate, covered and refrigerated, for 2 to 4 hours.

Preheat grill to medium-high.

In a bowl, combine red onion, carrot, red pepper, green onions, bean sprouts, and basil leaves. Add reserved marinade and toss well. Season to taste with salt.

Remove steaks from marinade (reserving marinade). Grill steaks for 2 to 3 minutes per side for medium-rare. Remove steaks from grill and let rest for 5 minutes. Thinly slice each steak across the grain.

Working with one rice paper wrapper at a time, soak wrapper in a bowl of warm water until flexible, about 1 minute; drain and pat dry on a tea towel. Place a lettuce leaf on the wrapper, trimming to fit if necessary. Place half a sliced steak down the center of the leaf. Top with ½ cup vegetable mixture and roll up wrap into a cone shape. Repeat to make five more wraps.

SERVES 6

Hot and Spicy Beef Sirloin Kebabs

This is a spicy dish. The Sriacha chili sauce is the key to making this recipe zing. You can find Sriacha in Asian food stores. It's usually sold in a squeeze bottle.

4 lbs. beef sirloin	¼ cup Sriacha chili sauce
4 cloves garlic, chopped	¼ cup rice wine vinegar
1 cup ketchup	2 TB. chopped fresh cilantro
½ cup honey	Salt and pepper

Cut beef into 2-inch cubes.

In a bowl, whisk together garlic, ketchup, honey, chili sauce, rice vinegar, and cilantro. Season to taste with salt and pepper. Set aside half marinade.

Add beef to marinade, turning to coat, and marinate, covered and refrigerated, for 4 to 6 hours.

Meanwhile, soak eight (10- to 12-inch) bamboo skewers in hot water for 30 minutes (or use metal skewers).

Preheat grill to medium-high.

Skewer five or six beef pieces onto each skewer. Grill skewers, basting frequently with reserved marinade, for 4 to 5 minutes per side for medium.

Serve with grilled vegetable kebabs.

SERVES 8

The Big Man's Coffee-Crusted Porterhouse with Roquefort Butter

I dedicate this steak to me. I am a big man, and this is my steak.

4 (36 oz.) porterhouse steaks	Olive oil
½ cup Mocha Coffee Rub (page 207)	Roquefort Butter (recipe follows)

Rub each steak with Mocha Coffee Rub, pressing seasoning into meat. Brush steaks with olive oil and place in a glass dish. Marinate, covered and refrigerated, for 2 to 4 hours.

Preheat grill to high.

Grill steaks for 10 to 12 minutes per side for medium.

Remove from the grill and let rest for 3 minutes.

Serve steaks topped with Roquefort Butter.

SERVES 4

Roquefort Butter

½ cup unsalted butter, softened	2 tsp. lemon juice
½ cup crumbled Roquefort cheese	½ tsp. Bone Dust BBQ Spice (page 203)
2 tsp. chopped fresh rosemary	Salt to taste

In a food processor or mixing bowl, thoroughly blend butter, Roquefort cheese, rosemary, lemon juice, Bone Dust BBQ Spice, and salt.

Transfer to a storage container and freeze until needed.

MAKES ABOUT 1 CUP

The Big Man's Porterhouse Steak with Dijon Cream Sauce

I dedicate this steak to me. I am still the big man, and this is my steak for 2003. Have lots of crusty bread on hand to sop up the Dijon Cream Sauce (which is also awesome with steamed fresh mussels).

4 (36 oz.) Porterhouse steaks
½ cup Malabar Pepper Rub (page 200)
Olive oil

DIJON CREAM SAUCE
2 TB. butter
2 shallots, finely chopped
4 cloves garlic, minced

1 TB. chopped fresh thyme or rosemary
2 tsp. mustard seeds
½ cup dry white wine
1½ cups heavy cream
¼ cup Dijon mustard
1 (125 g) log creamy goat cheese
Salt and freshly ground black pepper

Rub each steak with Malabar Pepper Rub, pressing seasoning into meat. Brush each steak with olive oil and place in a glass dish. Marinate, covered and refrigerated, for 2 to 4 hours.

Preheat grill to medium-high.

Grill steaks for 12 to 15 minutes per side for medium. Remove steaks from grill and let rest for 5 minutes.

While steaks are grilling, prepare sauce. Melt butter in a medium saucepan over medium heat. Sauté shallots and garlic until tender, about 2 minutes. Stir in thyme and mustard seeds; sauté for 1 minute. Add wine. Bring to a boil and reduce liquid by half. Add cream, mustard, and goat cheese, whisking until cheese is incorporated. Bring to a boil, reduce heat to low and simmer until sauce thickens, 5 to 10 minutes. If sauce gets too thick, add a little wine to thin it down. Season to taste with salt and pepper.

Serve steaks drizzled with sauce.

SERVES 4 TO 8

Grilled T-Bone Steak with Stilton and Port Sauce

Three of my favorite things on one plate: a thick T-bone where the tenderloin melts in your mouth and the striploin has a thick fatty cap; Stilton; and a rich port sauce. Adjust the amount of Stilton to suit your taste—though I like lots.

---

4 (20 oz., 1½-inch-thick) T-bone steaks
¼ cup Old Montreal Steak Spice (page 202)
4 TB. cold butter
2 shallots, finely chopped
2 cloves garlic, minced
1 tsp. chopped fresh thyme

1 bay leaf
2 cups port
1 cup beef or veal stock
Salt and pepper
1 to 2 cups crumbled Stilton cheese

Rub steaks with Old Montreal Steak Spice, pressing seasoning into meat. Cover and marinate at room temperature for 2 hours.

To prepare sauce, melt 1 tablespoon butter in a medium saucepan over medium-high heat. Sauté shallots and garlic for 1 minute or until tender and transparent. Stir in thyme, bay leaf, and port. Bring to a boil and reduce liquid by half. Strain port and discard solids.

Return port to the saucepan and return to a boil. Stir in stock. Reduce heat to low and simmer until sauce has thickened, 10 to 15 minutes. Remove from heat and season to taste with salt and pepper. Whisk in the remaining 3 tablespoons butter, 1 tablespoon at a time, until fully incorporated. Keep sauce warm.

Preheat grill to medium-high.

Grill steaks for 6 to 8 minutes per side for medium-rare, basting with melted butter during the final few minutes of grilling. Remove from grill and let steaks rest for 5 minutes.

Serve steaks topped with crumbled Stilton and drizzled with sauce.

SERVES 4

Steakhouse London Broil

This quick and easy recipe requires top-quality flank steak. Don't skimp here—buy the best, USDA Prime. The better the quality of flank steak, the less marinating time is required.

---

1 (2 to 3 lb.) flank steak
3 TB. Old Montreal Steak Spice (page 202)
½ cup vegetable oil
¼ cup red wine
¼ cup Dijon mustard
2 TB. red wine vinegar
1 TB. chopped fresh rosemary

STEAKHOUSE STEAK SAUCE
½ cup store-bought steak sauce
¼ cup ketchup
¼ cup red wine
2 TB. brown sugar

Trim flank steak of excess fat and membrane. Using a sharp knife, score both sides of the flank steak in a diamond pattern, cutting about ¼ inch deep.

Rub steak with Old Montreal Steak Spice, pressing seasoning into meat. In a glass dish large enough to hold steak, whisk together vegetable oil, wine, mustard, vinegar, and rosemary. Add steak, turning to coat. Cover and marinate at room temperature for 2 hours.

To prepare sauce, in a bowl, whisk together steak sauce, ketchup, wine, and sugar.

Preheat grill to high.

Grill steak, basting with sauce, until charred but still rare, 5 to 6 minutes per side. Slice steaks very thinly diagonally across the grain.

Serve with grilled Portobello mushrooms and red onions.

SERVES 4 TO 6

Grilled Flank Steak Pinwheels

This fun recipe requires a little bit of work, but the result is well worth it. As a bonus, it uses an inexpensive cut of meat.

1 (2 to 3 lb.) flank steak	**STUFFING**	2 TB. vegetable oil
6 cloves garlic, minced	1 lb. lean ground beef	4 cloves garlic, minced
¼ cup balsamic vinegar	1 TB. Dijon mustard	1 small onion, diced
¼ cup vegetable oil, plus extra for brushing	2 tsp. Worcestershire sauce	2 cups sliced assorted mushrooms
	1 tsp. ground cumin	½ cup sliced green olives
2 TB. chopped fresh herbs	1 tsp. chili powder	1 TB. chopped fresh thyme
2 TB. cracked black pepper	1 tsp. garlic powder	Salt and pepper to taste

With a sharp knife, cut down the center of the flank steak, making a deep incision almost but not quite all the way through. Open steak so it lies flat and place between two sheets of plastic wrap. Lightly pound flank steak with the smooth side of a meat mallet until ½ inch thick and about 12 × 18 inches.

In a glass dish large enough to hold steak, whisk together garlic, vinegar, oil, herbs, and pepper. Marinate, covered and refrigerated, for 4 to 6 hours.

Meanwhile, prepare stuffing. In a large bowl, combine ground beef, mustard, Worcestershire sauce, cumin, chili powder, and garlic powder.

Heat vegetable oil in a large frying pan over medium-high heat. Sauté garlic, onion, and mushrooms until just tender. Let cool slightly. Add to ground meat mixture along with olives, thyme, salt, and pepper. Stir well.

Remove flank steak from marinade (reserving marinade). Spread stuffing evenly over steak, pressing it firmly onto meat. Starting at the wide end, roll steak into a log. Tie with string at 2-inch intervals. Cover and refrigerate for 30 minutes.

Meanwhile, preheat grill to medium-high.

Cut flank roll into 1½-inch pinwheel slices. Brush each pinwheel with oil and season with salt and pepper. Grill pinwheels for 4 to 5 minutes per side, basting with reserved marinade.

Serve immediately.

SERVES 6

Grilled Shell Steak with Country Cream Gravy and Virginia Ham

Back in 1993, Pamela and I were camping in Cape Hatteras, North Carolina. We had a great day, playing in the surf and having not a care in the world—except what we should eat that evening. We were tired of watching our neighbors dine on bologna and we were out of beer. So we made a trek up the coast to buy more beer and look for a place to eat. I can't remember the name of the joint we ate at, but the grilled shell steak was awesome. Here's my version.

4 (16 oz.) New York shell steaks, bone-in or boneless
¼ cup Malabar Pepper Rub (page 200)
¼ cup melted butter
8 (2 oz.) thin slices cured Virginia ham

COUNTRY CREAM GRAVY
2 TB. butter
2 TB. all-purpose flour
2 cups milk
½ cup heavy cream
1 TB. chopped fresh sage
2 tsp. Worcestershire sauce
Pinch cayenne pepper
Salt and freshly ground black pepper to taste

Rub steaks with Malabar Pepper Rub, pressing seasoning into meat. Set aside.

Prepare gravy by melting butter over medium heat in a medium saucepan. Stir in flour and cook, stirring, for about 1 minute, being careful not to burn it. Whisking constantly, add milk a little at a time until smooth. Bring to boil, stirring. Reduce heat to low and simmer, stirring occasionally, for 15 minutes. Stir in cream and cook until gravy is thick, 5 to 10 more minutes. Stir in sage, Worcestershire sauce, cayenne, salt, and black pepper. Remove from heat and keep warm.

Preheat grill to medium-high.

Grill steaks, brushing with melted butter, for 8 to 10 minutes per side for medium.

Top each steak with two slices Virginia ham and ladle gravy over each steak.

SERVES 4

Round Steak Roll-Ups

The eye of roast or steak is an inexpensive cut of meat. It has very little internal fat; therefore, it is quite lean and tends to be a little tough. For best cooking results, use medium-high to high heat and grill steak quickly.

2 lbs. eye of round roast
¼ cup Old Montreal Steak Spice (page 202)
4 TB. butter
4 cloves garlic, minced
1 small onion, finely chopped
½ cup chopped oil-packed sun-dried tomatoes
2 TB. capers, coarsely chopped

¼ cup grated Parmesan cheese
¼ cup fresh bread crumbs
1 TB. fresh basil
Salt and pepper to taste
12 slices bacon
12 hamburger buns
Roasted Garlic Mayo (recipe follows)

Cut roast into ½-inch-thick slices (you should have at least 12 slices). Places steaks between two sheets of plastic wrap and gently pound with flat side of a meat mallet until meat is thin. Rub each steak with Old Montreal Steak Spice. Set aside.

Melt butter in a saucepan over medium heat. Cook garlic, onion, sun-dried tomatoes, and capers until heated through, 3 to 4 minutes. Remove from heat and let cool slightly. Stir in Parmesan, bread crumbs, basil, salt, and pepper. Stuffing should be a little moist. If necessary, add a little melted butter or olive oil.

Spread stuffing evenly over each steak. Roll up steaks from the wide end and wrap each with a slice of bacon. Secure with a toothpick if necessary.

Grill roll-ups, turning frequently, until bacon is crisp and stuffing is heated through, 5 to 8 minutes.

Remove toothpicks and serve on hamburger buns, drizzled with Roasted Garlic Mayo.

SERVES 6 TO 8

Continued ...

Roasted Garlic Mayo

4 cloves roasted garlic (page 201), mashed
1 cup mayonnaise

1 TB. lemon juice
Salt and pepper to taste

Whisk together garlic, mayonnaise, and lemon juice. Season to taste with salt and pepper.

MAKES ABOUT 1 CUP

Cedar-Planked Garlic Beef Tenderloin Roast with Smoked Garlic and Sun-Dried Tomato Cream Sauce

GQ magazine called me a crazy Canuck. It's true!

---

1 (4 lb.) beef tenderloin
1 cup Gilroy Roasted Garlic Paste
  (page 201)
¼ cup pink peppercorns, cracked

**SMOKED GARLIC AND SUN-DRIED
TOMATO CREAM SAUCE**
2 TB. butter
2 shallots, finely chopped
12 cloves smoked garlic (page 200)
½ cup chopped oil-packed sun-dried tomatoes
½ cup white wine

2 cups heavy cream
½ cup grated Parmesan cheese
2 green onions, thinly sliced
Salt and pepper
Special equipment: 2 untreated cedar planks
  (at least 10×8×⅝ inch), soaked in
  water overnight

Rub tenderloin with Gilroy Roasted Garlic Paste, pressing seasoning into meat. Press peppercorns evenly over meat. Transfer to a glass dish and marinate, covered and refrigerated, for 4 to 6 hours.

Preheat grill to high.

Place soaked planks on the grill, one on top of the other, and close the lid. Let planks heat for 2 to 3 minutes or until they start to crackle and smoke.

Carefully open the lid and place tenderloin on the planks. Close the lid and roast tenderloin for 10 minutes. Reduce heat to medium and roast for 30 to 40 minutes for medium-rare. A meat thermometer should read 135°F. Carefully open the lid (avoiding the billowing smoke) and remove beef from the grill; let rest for 10 minutes.

While meat is roasting, prepare sauce. Melt butter in a medium saucepan over medium heat. Sauté shallots and smoked garlic until tender, about 1 minute. Stir in tomatoes and wine. Bring to a boil and reduce wine by one-quarter. Stir in cream and Parmesan. Return sauce to a boil, reduce heat to low, and simmer until sauce is thick, about 10 minutes. Remove from heat and stir in green onions, salt, and pepper.

Cut tenderloin into 1-inch-thick slices and serve with sauce.

SERVES 8

Tip

Use roasted garlic if you don't have a smoker.

Dad's Wheelbarrow Steak

As a kid, I never wanted to have any of my friends over for a BBQ. This was not because of the food served (that was always outstanding), but because my dad had the most embarrassing barbecue in town. After our real charcoal grill rusted out and the legs fell off and that last juicy steak hit the dirt, my dad decided that he'd be thrifty and use his wheelbarrow. Well, life was never the same. So this recipe is dedicated to my dad, whose unorthodox grill still cooked a mean steak.

1 (4 lb., 3-inch-thick) sirloin steak
¼ cup Malabar Pepper Rub (page 200)
8 cloves garlic, minced
1 cup dry red wine
¼ cup vegetable oil

¼ cup ketchup
2 TB. chopped fresh herbs (such as parsley, sage, and rosemary)
1 TB. Worcestershire sauce
Salt to taste

Tip

When buying a large steak, choose one that is a uniform thickness. I like a relatively thick steak, about 3 to 4 inches. Buy a top-quality cut of sirloin, meaning AAA Canadian Beef or USDA Prime or Certified Black Angus. The better the quality of beef, the tastier your steak will be.

Rub steak with Malabar Pepper Rub, pressing seasoning into meat.

In a glass dish large enough to hold steak, whisk together garlic, wine, vegetable oil, ketchup, herbs, Worcestershire sauce, and salt. Add steak, turning once to coat. Marinate, covered and refrigerated, for 6 hours or overnight.

Preheat wheelbarrow to high.

Remove steak from marinade, reserving marinade. Grill steak for 10 to 12 minutes per side for medium, basting with marinade. Remove from the grill and let rest for 10 minutes.

Thinly slice steak across the grain and serve with prepared horseradish and steak sauce.

SERVES 4 TO 6

Classic Bacon-Wrapped Fillet with Sauce Béarnaise

The reason a lot of people wrap a fillet in bacon is because the bacon fat adds the bulk of flavor to the fillet. The bacon also helps retain the steak's moisture, keeping it tender.

6 to 12 slices thick bacon	**SAUCE BÉARNAISE**	1 TB. dry sherry
6 (8 oz.) beef tenderloin fillets	¼ cup cider vinegar	1 cup + 2 TB. clarified butter
2 TB. Old Montreal Steak Spice (page 202)	2 sprigs fresh tarragon	1 TB. chopped fresh tarragon
	1 small shallot, diced	1 TB. Dijon mustard
	2 TB. water	1 tsp. lemon juice
	4 black peppercorns	Dash hot sauce
	4 egg yolks	Dash Worcestershire sauce
	2 TB. dry white wine	Salt and pepper to taste

Fry bacon for 2 to 3 minutes per side or until slightly done. (You do not want to fry the bacon crisp or you will not be able to wrap it around fillets.) Remove from pan and pat dry with paper towels to remove excess fat. Set aside.

Rub fillets all over with Old Montreal Steak Spice, pressing seasoning into meat.

Wrap each fillet with 1 slice bacon. Use a half slice extra if bacon does not quite make it all the way around. Secure with a toothpick and set aside to marinate at room temperature for 30 minutes.

Meanwhile, make sauce. In a small saucepan bring vinegar, tarragon, shallot, water, and peppercorns to a boil. Reduce heat and simmer for 3 to 4 minutes or until liquid has reduced by half. Remove from heat and strain. Discard solids and let liquid cool.

In a medium bowl whisk egg yolks, white wine, sherry, and cooled vinegar mixture. Place over a pot of simmering water and whisk constantly until the mixture is thick enough to form a ribbon when drizzled from the whisk. Be careful not to turn this into scrambled eggs. Remove from heat.

Tip

I like to precook my bacon to prevent too much grill flare-up.

Continued ...

Whisking constantly, slowly add clarified butter a little at a time until all butter has been absorbed. Season with chopped tarragon, mustard, lemon juice, hot sauce, Worcestershire sauce, salt, and pepper. Remove from heat and keep warm over hot water.

Preheat grill to medium-high.

Grill beef for 4 to 5 minutes per side for medium and until bacon is crispy.

Remove toothpicks and serve fillets drizzled with sauce Béarnaise.

SERVES 6

Oscar's Steak Oscar

Classic steak Oscar is beef tenderloin topped with crabmeat, asparagus, and Hollandaise sauce. It is a delicious recipe, but I think my friend Oscar's version is a little more hip and definitely has more flavor.

1 lb. asparagus	1 lb. Dungeness crabmeat, picked over
4 (8 oz.) New York striploin steaks	2 TB. Dijon mustard
2 TB. Old Montreal Steak Spice (page 202)	2 TB. whipping cream
½ cup brandy	2 tsp. chopped fresh dill
¼ cup olive oil	2 green onions, finely chopped
4 cloves garlic, minced	Cayenne pepper, black pepper, and salt
¼ cup butter	1 (125 g) wheel Brie, cut into 12 wedges
½ cup chopped shallots	

Blanch asparagus in boiling water until tender-crisp. Cool under cold running water; drain. Cut into 1-inch pieces. Set aside.

Season steaks with Old Montreal Steak Spice, pressing seasoning into meat. In a glass dish large enough to hold steaks, whisk together brandy, olive oil, and garlic. Add steaks, turning to coat. Marinate, covered and refrigerated, for 1 to 2 hours.

Preheat grill to medium-high.

Melt butter in a large frying pan over medium-high heat. Sauté shallots for 2 to 3 minutes or until transparent and tender. Add asparagus; sauté for another 2 to 3 minutes. Add crabmeat, mustard, whipping cream, dill, and green onions. Bring to a boil. Remove from heat and season to taste with cayenne, black pepper, and salt. Let cool slightly.

Remove steaks from marinade, reserving marinade. Grill for 3 to 4 minutes per side for medium-rare, basting with marinade.

Divide crab mixture into 4 equal portions and spread 1 portion evenly on top of each steak. Top each steak with 3 slices Brie. Close the lid and cook for 1 to 2 minutes or until cheese starts to melt.

Serve immediately.

SERVES 4

Red-Rum Cowboy Steak

I remember my first cowboy steak. It was at Chef Mark Miller's Red Sage Restaurant in Washington, D.C., and it was truly amazing, weighing in at around 24 ounces. Seasoned nicely with a BBQ rub and served with a mountain of crispy fried onions, Mark's steak is the benchmark for all other cowboy steaks.

---

2 (24 oz., 2- to 3-inch-thick) bone-in rib
   steaks
½ cup Red-Rum Rub (page 213)

RUM BUTTER SAUCE
6 TB. cold butter (4 TB. cut into pieces)
4 cloves garlic, minced
½ cup dark rum
¼ cup BBQ sauce
Salt to taste

Rub steaks with Red-Rum Rub. Marinate, covered and refrigerated, for 2 hours.

Preheat grill to medium-high.

Meanwhile, prepare sauce. Melt 2 tablespoons butter in a small saucepan over medium-high heat. Add garlic; sauté for 2 to 3 minutes. Add rum. Bring to a boil and reduce liquid by half. Stir in BBQ sauce. Bring to a boil and remove from heat. Gradually whisk in remaining butter until fully incorporated. Season with salt. Set aside.

Grill steaks for 8 to 12 minutes per side for medium-rare.

Slice each steak and serve drizzled with sauce. You might have to fight over the bones.

SERVES 4

Spicy Marinated Sirloin Steak with Seafood Cream Sauce

I first did this recipe on the set of *Cottage Country* with a 4-pound sirloin steak. The crew went crazy for the spicy tender grilled steak garnished with a rich shrimp cream sauce. This recipe, using 8-ounce individual sirloin steaks, is a little more user-friendly.

½ cup orange juice

¼ cup soy sauce

¼ cup olive oil

2 TB. Hell's Fire Chili Paste (page 206)

4 cloves garlic, chopped

6 (8 oz.) sirloin steaks

Seafood Cream Sauce (recipe follows)

In a glass dish large enough to hold steaks, whisk together orange juice, soy sauce, and olive oil.

In a small bowl, mix together Hell's Fire Chili Paste and garlic. Wearing rubber gloves (as this mix might burn your hands), rub steaks all over with paste, pressing seasoning into meat. Place steaks in orange juice mixture, turning to coat. Marinate, covered and refrigerated, for 4 to 6 hours.

Preheat grill to high.

Remove steaks from marinade and discard marinade. Grill steaks for 4 to 5 minutes per side for medium-rare. Remove from the grill and let rest a few minutes before serving.

Thinly slice each steak and top with Seafood Cream Sauce.

SERVES 6

Continued ...

Seafood Cream Sauce

3 TB. butter

4 shallots, finely chopped

2 cloves garlic, minced

3 TB. all-purpose flour

1 TB. Bone Dust BBQ Spice (page 203)

3 cups chicken or fish stock

1 cup whipping cream

1 cup cooked baby shrimp

1 cup crabmeat, picked over

1 cup bay scallops

2 TB. brandy

1 TB. chopped fresh parsley

Dash hot sauce

3 green onions, minced

Salt and pepper to taste

In a medium saucepan over medium heat, melt butter. Cook shallots and garlic for 1 minute or until tender and translucent. Add flour; cook, stirring, for 1 minute, being careful not to burn flour. Stir in Bone Dust BBQ Spice.

Add chicken stock a little at a time, whisking constantly to prevent lumps. Bring to a rolling boil, reduce heat and simmer for 30 minutes, stirring occasionally.

Stir in cream and return to a boil.

Stir in shrimp, crab, scallops, brandy, parsley, hot sauce, green onions, salt, and pepper.

Serve immediately.

MAKES ABOUT 6 CUPS

Rocketship 7 Peanut Butter and Jelly Steak

As a kid I used to spend some mornings watching Commander Tom on *Rocketship 7*, a kids' show out of Buffalo. It was pure silliness, and this recipe is a tribute to the show.

---

4 (12 oz.) New York striploin steaks
2 to 3 TB. Old Montreal Steak Spice (page 202)
Cranberry Sauce (recipe follows)

PEPPERCORN PEANUT SAUCE
1 TB. olive oil
1 large shallot, finely chopped
¼ cup sweet rice wine
⅓ cup whipping cream
¼ cup smooth peanut butter
2 tsp. cracked black pepper
Salt to taste

Season steaks with Old Montreal Steak Spice, pressing seasoning into meat. Marinate, covered and refrigerated, for 1 hour.

To prepare sauce, heat oil over medium-high heat in a medium saucepan. Add shallots; sauté for 2 to 3 minutes or until tender. Add sweet rice wine. Bring to a boil and reduce liquid by half. Reduce heat to medium. Whisk in cream and peanut butter until smooth. Stir in black pepper and salt. (If sauce becomes too thick, just add a little water to thin it down.) Set aside and keep warm.

Preheat grill to high.

Grill steaks for 4 to 5 minutes per side for medium.

Thinly slice steaks across the grain and drizzle with Peppercorn Peanut Sauce. Serve garnished with 1 tablespoon Cranberry Sauce.

SERVES 4

Continued ...

Cranberry Sauce

1½ cups cranberries (thawed if frozen), picked over

⅓ cup sugar

¼ cup water

¼ cup orange juice

Wash and drain cranberries. Put berries, sugar, water, and orange juice in a large saucepan. Slowly bring to a boil, stirring occasionally. Cover and cook, stirring occasionally, for 10 minutes or until cranberries burst. Skim and cool.

MAKES ABOUT 1 CUP

GQ Magazine's Cedar-Planked Beef Tenderloin Stuffed with Blue Cheese

Beef and blue cheese are often found on the same table—think hefty steak with a forerunner of salad with blue cheese dressing. In this recipe, I've gone one better by partnering these two full-flavored items in one spectacular dish. So good even *GQ* wanted it!

---

6 (6 oz.) well-aged beef tenderloin fillets
6 TB. blue cheese
2 tsp. fresh lemon juice
Salt and freshly ground black pepper to taste
6 (8-inch long) sprigs fresh rosemary
6 cloves garlic, minced
2 TB. chopped fresh rosemary

2 TB. grainy mustard
2 TB. olive oil
1 TB. coarsely ground black pepper
1 TB. balsamic vinegar
Special equipment: 1 untreated cedar plank (10×8×⅝ inch),
    soaked in water overnight

Using a sharp knife, make an incision 1-inch long in the side of each fillet. Using your finger, make a pocket inside fillet. In a bowl, combine blue cheese, lemon juice, salt, and pepper. Mash together until well incorporated. Divide into six equal portions. Stuff into each fillet, pushing stuffing well into the center. Wrap a sprig of rosemary around each stuffed fillet. Secure with a toothpick.

In a glass dish, whisk together garlic, chopped rosemary, mustard, oil, black pepper, and vinegar. Place fillets in marinade, turning to coat completely. Marinate, covered and refrigerated, for 4 to 6 hours.

Preheat grill to high.

Place soaked cedar plank on the grill and close the lid. Bake the plank for 3 to 4 minutes or until it starts to crackle and smoke. Place fillets on the plank, evenly spaced. Close the lid and bake for 12 to 15 minutes for medium. Carefully open the lid (avoiding the billowing smoke) and remove fillets from the grill.

Serve immediately.

SERVES 6

Grilled New York Strip Steak with Garlic Butter Escargots

I got this idea for steak and escargots from Chef Robert Clark of C Restaurant in Vancouver. His version is as delightful as mine. If you are ever in Vancouver, be sure to eat at C. Robert's signature dish there is octopus bacon-wrapped scallops, a heavenly dish.

---

4 (12 oz.) New York striploin steaks
2 TB. Old Montreal Steak Spice (page 202)
6 TB. butter (4 TB. cut in pieces)
8 cloves garlic, minced
2 shallots, diced

1 (125 g) can escargots, drained
¼ cup cognac
2 TB. chopped fresh parsley
Pinch nutmeg
Salt and pepper

Tip

If your grill has a side burner, you can prepare the escargots while the steaks are grilling. If not, prepare them before you grill the steaks and keep the escargots warm.

Preheat grill to medium-high.

Season steaks with Old Montreal Steak Spice, pressing seasoning into meat.

Grill steaks for 3 to 4 minutes per side for medium-rare.

Meanwhile (or ahead of time), melt 2 tablespoons butter in a medium saucepan. Sauté garlic and shallots for 2 to 3 minutes or until translucent and tender. Add escargots; sauté for 3 to 4 minutes more until snails are hot. Add cognac and carefully flambé to remove alcohol. When the flames have died down, stir in remaining butter, parsley and nutmeg. Remove from heat and season to taste with salt and pepper.

Serve steaks topped with garlic butter escargots.

SERVES 4

Roasted Red Pepper and Brie-Crusted Beef Tenderloin

I prepared this dish for the guests of Patrick Racing while at the CART Race in Chicago. I grilled 450 individual steaks for race day. Your recipe is for six, a little easier to prepare and just as delicious.

---

6 (8 oz.) beef tenderloin fillets

2 TB. Old Montreal Steak Spice (page 202)

2 red bell peppers

2 TB. olive oil

1 small yellow onion, sliced

4 cloves garlic, minced

1 TB. chopped fresh thyme

2 TB. balsamic vinegar

2 green onions, chopped

1 (125 g) wheel Brie, diced

Salt and pepper to taste

Preheat grill to medium-high.

Season fillets with Old Montreal Steak Spice, pressing seasoning into meat. Marinate, covered and refrigerated, for 2 hours.

Roast peppers on the grill, turning periodically, until peppers are charred and blistering. Place peppers in a plastic bag and seal tightly. (The heat from peppers will produce steam that makes the skin easier to peel.) After 10 minutes, peel and seed peppers. Let cool.

Heat oil in a frying pan over medium-high heat. Sauté onion and garlic, stirring occasionally, for 5 to 10 minutes or until tender and slightly browned. Add thyme and vinegar, stirring to scrape up any brown bits. Transfer to a bowl and let cool.

Preheat grill to medium-high.

Thinly slice or dice roasted red peppers. Add to onion and garlic. Add green onions, Brie, salt, and pepper. Stir well. Shape into six ½-inch-thick patties about the same diameter as fillets.

Grill fillets for 3 to 4 minutes on one side. Turn steaks and top each with a pepper/Brie patty. Close the lid and cook for 3 to 4 more minutes for medium-rare.

Serve immediately.

SERVES 6

Teriyaki Steak

I like to add a little sambal chili paste to my teriyaki marinade to give it a little kick.

---

6 (6 oz.) sirloin steaks
2 TB. Indonesian Cinnamon Rub (page 209)

TERIYAKI MARINADE
½ cup dry sherry
½ cup soy sauce
⅓ cup brown sugar
¼ cup minced fresh ginger

¼ cup rice wine vinegar
¼ cup vegetable oil
1 TB. chopped fresh cilantro
1 TB. sesame oil
2 tsp. sambal chili paste
1 tsp. black pepper
4 green onions, finely chopped
4 cloves garlic, minced

Season the steaks with Indonesian Cinnamon Rub, pressing seasoning into meat. Place in a glass dish large enough to hold steaks.

In a bowl, combine sherry, soy sauce, sugar, ginger, rice wine vinegar, vegetable oil, cilantro, sesame oil, sambal, pepper, green onions, and garlic. Whisk until sugar has dissolved. Reserve ½ cup Teriyaki Marinade for basting. Pour remaining marinade over steaks, turning to coat. Marinate, covered and refrigerated, for 4 hours.

Preheat grill to medium-high.

Remove steaks from marinade, discarding marinade. Grill steaks for 3 to 4 minutes per side for medium-rare, basting liberally with reserved Teriyaki Marinade.

Thinly slice each steak across the grain and serve.

SERVES 6

Grilled T-Bone Steak with Chimichurri Sauce

Chimichurri is an Argentinean sauce made with parsley, chilies, and vinegar. It is full of flavor and is an excellent sauce for this big steak. Chimichurri also makes a great marinade.

4 (20 oz., 1½-inch-thick) T-bone steaks
¼ cup Bone Dust BBQ Spice (page 203)
¼ cup melted butter

CHIMICHURRI SAUCE
1 bunch flat-leaf parsley
6 green onions, cut into 2-inch lengths
12 cloves garlic

2 jalapeño peppers, halved lengthwise
½ cup olive oil
¼ cup fresh oregano leaves
¼ cup red wine vinegar
1 TB. cracked black pepper
1 tsp. ground cumin
Salt

Rub steaks with Bone Dust BBQ Spice, pressing seasoning into meat. Marinate, covered and refrigerated, for 2 hours.

To make sauce: In a food processor, combine parsley, green onions, garlic, jalapeño peppers, olive oil, oregano, vinegar, pepper, and cumin. Pulse until coarsely blended. Season to taste with salt. Set aside.

Preheat grill to medium-high.

Grill steaks for 5 to 6 minutes per side for medium-rare, basting with melted butter during the final few minutes of grilling. Remove from grill and let steaks rest for 3 minutes.

Serve each steak drizzled with Chimichurri Sauce.

SERVES 4

Melanie's Steak Tartare

My dear friend and *Cottage Country* chef Melanie Dunkelman created this wonderful recipe for steak tartare.

---

1 lb. beef tenderloin, fully trimmed

1 large shallot, finely diced

½ jalapeño pepper, seeded and finely chopped

2 egg yolks

2 TB. chopped flat-leaf parsley

1 TB. chopped capers

1 TB. Dijon mustard

1 TB. ketchup

1 TB. olive oil

2 tsp. Worcestershire sauce

Salt and freshly ground black pepper to taste

Dash hot sauce if you like it spicier (optional)

A squeeze of lemon juice to increase acidity (optional)

Tip

When preparing this recipe, make sure your beef is very cold, because you do not want to serve warm steak tartare. Cold meat is also easier to chop. I prefer to use a chef's knife to chop the beef rather than a food processor, because the meat has a better texture and looks more classical.

Using a sharp chef's knife, finely chop beef tenderloin. Place in a large bowl.

Add shallot, jalapeño pepper, egg yolks, parsley, capers, mustard, ketchup, olive oil, Worcestershire sauce, salt, and pepper. Mix well with a wooden spoon. Adjust seasoning with hot sauce or lemon juice, if desired.

Divide steak tartare among four plates. Serve with toasted thin slices of baguette and fries, if desired.

SERVES 4

Raise a Little Hell Steak

A tribute to one of my all-time favorite Canadian bar bands, Trooper. Fast, furious, and fiery. This goes great with an ice-cold beer.

---

1 (2 lb.) trimmed flank steak
½ cup Hell's Fire Chili Paste (page 206)

¼ cup bourbon
¼ cup olive oil

Using a sharp knife, score both sides of flank steak in a diamond pattern making cuts ¼-inch deep. Rub steak with Hell's Fire Chili Paste, pressing paste into meat.

In a glass dish large enough to hold steak, whisk together bourbon and olive oil. Add steak, turning to coat. Marinate, covered and refrigerated, for 4 hours.

Preheat grill to medium-high.

Grill steak for 3 to 4 minutes for medium-rare. Remove from grill and let meat rest for 3 minutes.

Thinly slice steak across the grain and serve with Grilled New Potato and Cheddar Salad (page 57), if desired.

SERVES 6

BBQ Beef Brisket

Smoked beef brisket is a Texas favorite, but it takes a long time to prepare over a low and slow grill. My version is a little quicker and provides tender, full-flavored results.

1 (5 lb.) beef brisket, trimmed	2 cups chili sauce
¼ cup Bone Dust BBQ Spice (page 203)	2 cups BBQ sauce
6 cloves garlic, minced	2 cans ginger ale
1 large Spanish onion, sliced	2 bay leaves
3 jalapeño peppers, sliced	Salt and pepper to taste

Preheat oven to 350°F.

Season beef brisket with the Bone Dust BBQ Spice, pressing seasoning into meat. Set aside.

In a large roasting pan toss together garlic, onion, and jalapeño peppers. Lay brisket on top of onion mixture.

In a bowl, whisk together chili sauce, BBQ sauce, and ginger ale. Pour over brisket, making sure brisket is covered. (Make up more sauce if necessary.) Add bay leaves. Cover tightly with lid or foil and cook for 2 to 2½ hours or until meat is tender when pierced with a fork. Let cool slightly.

Preheat grill to medium-high.

Transfer brisket to a plate. Discard bay leaves. Transfer onion mixture to a saucepan and bring to a boil. Using a hand blender, purée sauce. Adjust seasoning with salt and pepper.

Grill brisket for 15 to 20 minutes per side or until tender, basting liberally with sauce.

Thinly slice brisket and serve with extra sauce and Memphis-Style Creamy Coleslaw (page 71), if desired.

SERVES 8

BBQ-Baked Cast-Iron-Pan Meatloaf

Meatloaf is not just for the oven anymore. Cooking meatloaf on a grill adds a wonderful smokiness to the meat. This recipe makes a hearty meatloaf.

1 lb. ground chuck or sirloin	1 TB. chopped garlic
1 lb. regular ground pork	1 TB. chopped fresh herbs
¾ cup fresh bread crumbs	1 TB. Bone Dust BBQ Spice (page 203)
¾ cup BBQ sauce	1 tsp. salt
2 eggs, lightly beaten	1½ cups shredded aged cheddar cheese
1 onion, diced	

Preheat grill to high. Lightly grease a 10-inch cast-iron frying pan.

In a large bowl, thoroughly combine ground chuck, ground pork, bread crumbs, BBQ sauce, eggs, onion, garlic, herbs, Bone Dust BBQ Spice, and salt. Turn meatloaf mixture into the pan, pressing down firmly.

Place pan in grill, close the lid, and bake for 35 to 50 minutes or until a meat thermometer reads 160°F. Top with cheese and cook another 10 minutes or until cheese melts.

Serve with BBQ Gravy (recipe follows) and Cheddar Mashed Potatoes with Grilled Onions (page 192), if desired.

SERVES 8

Tip

Slice any leftovers 1 inch thick, grill them over low heat, basting with your favorite BBQ sauce, and serve on a fresh roll.

Continued ...

BBQ Gravy

¼ cup butter

2 onions, diced

1 tsp. chopped garlic

¼ cup all-purpose flour

1½ cups beef stock

1 cup BBQ sauce

Salt and pepper to taste

In a medium saucepan, melt butter over medium heat. Sauté onions and garlic for 2 to 3 minutes or until tender and transparent.

Add flour and cook, stirring constantly, for 4 to 5 minutes, being careful not to burn flour.

Add beef stock ½ cup at a time, stirring constantly, until smooth and thickened.

Stir in BBQ sauce, salt, and pepper.

Reduce heat to low and simmer for 15 minutes, stirring occasionally. Strain and adjust seasoning.

MAKES 3 CUPS

Grilled Garlic Hanger Steak

Hanger steak is a relatively new steak on restaurant menus. It hangs between the rib cage and loin cage. Hanger steaks have a little stronger flavor than regular steaks and need to be very fresh. Ask your butcher for this tender and delicious piece of meat, because you will not find it in grocery stores.

---

1 (1 lb.) hanger steak, trimmed ·   **Salt and pepper to taste**
2 TB. Gilroy Roasted Garlic Paste (page 201)

Rub hanger steak all over with Gilroy Roasted Garlic Paste. Marinate, covered and refrigerated, for 1 hour.

Preheat grill to high.

Season steak with salt and pepper. Grill for 5 to 6 minutes per side for medium-rare. Remove from grill and let rest for 3 or 4 minutes.

Thinly slice across the grain and serve with Dijon mustard and horseradish.

SERVES 2

Roll in the Hay Wrapped Steak #2 with Gentleman's Relish

Wrapping a steak in hay is one of my favorite ways to prepare a steak. Version #1 of this recipe appeared in my *Sticks and Stones Cookbook.* This is my second version.

---

4 handfuls hay
1 bunch rosemary, partially dried
1 bunch oregano, partially dried
1 bunch thyme, partially dried

1 (750 ml) bottle inexpensive red wine
4 (8 oz.) rib-eye steaks
½ cup Herb Mustard Rub (page 208)
¼ cup olive oil

In a large bucket, soak hay, rosemary, oregano, and thyme in three-quarters of the wine for at least 30 minutes.

Rub steaks with Herb Mustard Rub, pressing seasoning firmly into meat. In a glass dish large enough to hold steaks, whisk together remaining wine and olive oil. Add steaks, turning to coat. Marinate, covered and refrigerated, for 1 hour.

Preheat grill to high.

Remove a handful of hay from wine and shake off excess liquid. On a work surface, spread hay evenly to approximately double the length of one steak. Place one steak at the bottom end of the hay. Carefully roll up steak in hay. Repeat with the remaining steaks.

Place wrapped steaks on the grill and close the lid. After 7 or 8 minutes, carefully open the lid. Be careful—when you open the lid, the hay will be fed with oxygen and burn much faster. The hay will burn off and sear the meat. Turn steaks and grill for another 3 to 4 minutes for medium-rare.

Serve each steak with a dollop of Gentleman's Relish (recipe follows).

SERVES 4

Gentleman's Relish

This is my version of the classic Harrods recipe.

½ cup chopped shallots
½ cup chopped green olives
¼ cup coarsely chopped capers
¼ cup coarsely chopped gherkins
¼ cup olive oil
2 TB. grainy mustard
2 TB. lemon juice

1 TB. chopped fresh parsley
1 TB. chopped fresh thyme
6 anchovy fillets, finely chopped
2 cloves garlic, chopped
1 tsp. cracked black pepper
Salt to taste

In a bowl, combine shallots, olives, capers, gherkins, olive oil, mustard, lemon juice, parsley, thyme, anchovies, garlic, pepper, and salt (be careful adding salt, because capers and anchovies are quite salty).

Cover and refrigerate for 2 hours before using. Will keep for up to 2 weeks.

MAKES ABOUT 2 CUPS

Roberto Moreno's Lime Veal Chop

I was CART race car driver Roberto Moreno's chef for the 2000 race season, and one of his favorite dishes to eat after a race is a grilled veal chop marinated in fresh lime juice. A simple and delicious meal.

---

5 limes	¼ cup olive oil
2 TB. chopped fresh rosemary	4 (16 oz.) bone-in veal rack chops
2 TB. Dijon mustard	Salt to taste
4 cloves garlic, minced	

Cut a lime into eight slices; set aside. Zest one lime and juice three.

In a glass dish large enough to hold chops, whisk together lime zest and juice, rosemary, mustard, garlic, and olive oil. Add chops, turning to coat. Marinate, covered and refrigerated, for 4 to 6 hours.

Preheat grill to medium-high.

Remove chops from marinade, reserving marinade. Season chops with salt. Grill for 6 to 8 minutes per side for medium-rare, basting with marinade.

Meanwhile, grill lime slices until tender and lightly charred.

Serve each veal chop garnished with two grilled lime slices.

SERVES 4

Veal Tenderloin with Roasted Garlic, Gorgonzola, and Mushrooms

Three of my all-time favorite foods served with succulent veal tenderloin. Who could ask for more?

---

2 heads garlic

2 TB. olive oil

Salt and freshly ground black pepper

4 (6 oz., 1½-inch-thick) veal tenderloin fillets

¼ cup Gilroy Roasted Garlic Paste (page 201)

2 TB. butter

4 shallots, diced

1 cup sliced brown mushrooms

1 cup sliced shiitake mushrooms

1 cup quartered chanterelle mushrooms

2 TB. balsamic vinegar

1 TB. chopped fresh thyme

¼ cup veal stock

1 cup crumbled Gorgonzola cheese

Preheat oven to 325°F.

Peel papery outer skins from garlic. Cut the top third off each head, exposing cloves. Drizzle each with olive oil and season to taste with salt and pepper. Wrap in foil. Roast garlic for 45 to 60 minutes or until tender and golden brown. Open foil package and let garlic cool slightly. Squeeze roasted garlic into a small bowl and set aside.

Meanwhile, rub fillets with Gilroy Roasted Garlic Paste, pressing paste into meat. Marinate, covered and refrigerated, for 30 minutes.

Preheat grill to medium-high.

Melt butter in a frying pan over medium-high heat. Sauté shallots for 2 minutes or until tender and translucent. Add all mushrooms; sauté for 8 to 10 minutes, stirring, until tender. Stir in vinegar, thyme, and roasted garlic. Add veal stock, bring to a boil, and reduce liquid by half. Season to taste with salt and pepper and remove from heat. Set aside and keep warm.

Grill veal for 3 to 4 minutes per side for medium-rare.

Toss mushroom mixture with Gorgonzola cheese and serve over each grilled tenderloin.

SERVES 4

Grilled Veal Chops with Mushroom Fricassee and Buffalo Mozzarella

I prepared this dish for CART race car driver Roberto Moreno when he was in Toronto for the 2001 Molson Indy. Roberto's comment? It was the best veal he'd ever had.

---

2 lemons, juiced
4 cloves garlic, minced
¼ cup olive oil
2 TB. chopped fresh rosemary
2 TB. Dijon mustard
Cracked black pepper
4 (16 oz.) bone-in veal rack chops

MUSHROOM FRICASSEE
¼ cup olive oil
4 shallots, finely chopped
4 cloves garlic, minced
2 cups sliced oyster mushrooms
1 cup sliced shiitake mushrooms
1 cup sliced brown mushrooms

1 cup sliced exotic mushrooms (chanterelles, morels, porcini, or puffballs)
¼ cup port
¼ to ½ cup veal stock
2 large balls buffalo mozzarella cheese, each cut into 4 slices

---

In a glass dish large enough to hold chops in one layer, whisk together lemon juice, garlic, oil, rosemary, and mustard. Season to taste with lots of pepper. Add chops, turning to coat. Marinate, covered and refrigerated, for 4 to 6 hours.

To prepare Mushroom Fricassee, heat oil in a large saucepan over medium-high heat. Sauté shallots, garlic, and all mushrooms until tender, 8 to 10 minutes.

Add port and cook, stirring, for 1 minute. Stir in stock. Bring to a boil, reduce heat to low, and simmer, stirring occasionally, for 10 minutes. Remove from heat and keep warm.

Preheat grill to medium-high.

Remove chops from marinade (reserving marinade). Grill chops, basting with marinade, for 6 to 8 minutes per side for medium-rare. When chops are just done, move them to the side of the grill. Top each chop with one-fourth the mushroom fricassee and one or two slices buffalo mozzarella. Close the lid and heat until cheese is melted and bubbling. Serve immediately.

SERVES 4

Grilled Veal Liver with BBQ Sauced Bacon and Onions and Grilled Apples

When I worked at Rhodes restaurant in Toronto, one of the house specialties was grilled veal liver with bacon and onions, cooked however you liked it.

---

8 slices thick-cut bacon, cut crosswise into ¼-inch-thick strips

1 large Spanish onion, sliced

4 cloves garlic, minced

1½ cups gourmet BBQ sauce

¼ cup apple butter

2 TB. apple cider vinegar

1 TB. chopped fresh sage

Salt and pepper to taste

4 Granny Smith apples

2 TB. lemon juice

8 (3 to 4 oz., ½-inch-thick) slices veal liver

Vegetable oil

Cook bacon in a medium saucepan over medium-high heat, stirring, until crisp, 5 to 8 minutes. Using a slotted spoon, remove bacon from the pot and set aside. Drain off all except 2 tablespoons bacon fat. Sauté onions and garlic until onions are tender and golden brown, 8 to 10 minutes. Stir in BBQ sauce, apple butter, vinegar, and sage. Bring to a boil, reduce heat, and simmer for 5 minutes. Stir in bacon, salt, and pepper. Remove from heat and keep warm.

Preheat grill to medium-high. Season the grill rack well (liver tends to stick).

Core apples and cut into ½-inch-thick rounds. Place apples in a bowl and add lemon juice and enough water to cover. (This will prevent apples from turning brown.)

Rub liver with vegetable oil and sprinkle both sides with salt and pepper to taste.

Grill apple slices until lightly charred, 3 to 5 minutes per side. Season to taste with salt and pepper. Move apples to upper rack to keep warm.

Grill liver for 1 to 2 minutes per side for medium-rare. Be careful—and patient—when turning liver, as it tends to stick to the grill.

Serve liver topped with bacon and onions and two slices grilled apple.

SERVES 4

Grilled Veal Tenderloin with Horseradish Gremolata

Gremolata is a traditional garnish for veal dishes. It combines parsley, lemon zest, and garlic with olive oil or melted butter. It is a tart accompaniment for succulent veal.

4 (8 oz., 1½-inch-thick) veal tenderloin fillets
¼ cup Old Montreal Steak Spice (page 202)
Olive oil

HORSERADISH GREMOLATA
¼ cup olive oil
6 cloves garlic, minced

2 lemons, zested and juiced
1 cup chopped fresh parsley
½ cup freshly grated horseradish
¼ cup grated Parmesan cheese
1 TB. chopped fresh oregano
1 tsp. cracked black pepper
Salt to taste

Season veal with Old Montreal Steak Spice, pressing seasoning into meat. Brush with olive oil and set aside.

To make gremolata, in a small saucepan, heat olive oil over medium heat. Cook garlic until tender, 1 to 2 minutes. Remove from heat and let cool slightly. Stir in lemon zest and juice, parsley, horseradish, Parmesan cheese, oregano, pepper, and salt.

Preheat grill to medium-high.

Grill veal for 3 to 4 minutes per side for medium-rare.

Serve each steak topped with 2 tablespoons gremolata.

SERVES 4

Sticky Love Chops

This sticky, delicious sauce is modeled after Chinese orange sauce. You'll find dried orange peel in Asian food stores. Try this sauce on chicken, too.

6 (6 oz., 1-inch-thick) pork loin chops	4 (1-inch) pieces dried orange peel
2 TB. Miami Spice Love Paste (page 211)	4 dried whole small Asian red chilies
¼ cup brown sugar	3 cloves garlic, minced
2 TB. water	1 TB. finely chopped fresh ginger
½ cup freshly squeezed orange juice	Salt and pepper
2 TB. soy sauce	2 tsp. cornstarch, dissolved in 2 TB. water
3 TB. butter (divided use)	

Rub pork chops with Miami Spice Love Paste, pressing seasoning into meat. Marinate, covered and refrigerated, for 2 hours.

Meanwhile, prepare orange sauce. Heat brown sugar and water in a small heavy saucepan over medium heat, stirring occasionally with a wooden spoon, until caramel is thick and a light golden brown. Immediately remove from heat. Whisking constantly, add orange juice and soy sauce in a steady stream. Whisk in 2 tablespoons butter. Bring to a boil and simmer for 5 minutes. Remove from heat.

In another small saucepan, melt remaining 1 tablespoon butter over medium-high heat. Sauté orange peel, chilies, garlic, and ginger until tender, 1 to 2 minutes. Pour in orange sauce. Bring to a boil, reduce heat to low, and simmer for 10 minutes, stirring occasionally. Season to taste with salt and pepper.

Stir in cornstarch mixture. Return to a boil, reduce heat to low, and simmer, stirring, until sauce is thick, 2 to 3 minutes. Remove glaze from heat.

Preheat grill to medium-high.

Grill chops for 5 minutes. Turn them, brush with glaze, and grill until just cooked through and juices run clear, another 5 to 6 minutes.

Serve chops with remaining glaze.

SERVES 6

Southwest Pork Chops with Charred Corn and Poblano Crust

Ask your butcher to prepare these thick-cut frenched pork loin chops for you. Be careful not to over-cook them, or they'll be dry and tough.

---

4 (16 oz., 2-inch-thick) frenched pork loin chops

¼ cup + 2 tsp. Bone Dust BBQ Spice (page 203)

6 cloves garlic, chopped

1 can beer

¼ cup vegetable oil

¼ cup Dijon mustard

2 TB. chopped fresh cilantro

1 TB. crushed red chilies

2 ears corn, husked

1 small red onion

1 small white onion

2 poblano peppers

8 slices thick-cut bacon, cut crosswise into ¼-inch-thick strips

2 TB. honey

¼ cup gourmet BBQ sauce

1 TB. hot sauce

1 tsp. Worcestershire sauce

4 slices pepper Jack cheese

Rub pork chops with ¼ cup Bone Dust BBQ Spice, pressing seasoning into meat. In a glass dish large enough to hold chops in one layer, whisk together garlic, beer, oil, mustard, cilantro, and crushed chilies. Add chops, turning to coat evenly. Marinate, covered and refrigerated, for 4 to 6 hours.

Preheat grill to medium-high.

Grill corn, red onion, and white onion until lightly charred, 5 to 10 minutes. Set aside. Roast poblano peppers, with the lid closed, until charred, 10 to 15 minutes. Peel, seed, and thinly slice poblano peppers. Thinly slice onions. Cut kernels from corn. Combine corn, onions, and peppers in a bowl.

Fry bacon until crisp. Reduce heat to low and add grilled vegetables, honey, BBQ sauce, hot sauce, Worcestershire sauce, and remaining 2 teaspoons Bone Dust BBQ Spice. Mix thoroughly and cook until heated through. Remove from heat and let topping cool.

Preheat grill to medium-high.

Grill chops for 4 to 5 minutes per side. Move chops to the top rack of the grill and close the lid. Cook chops with indirect heat until just cooked through and juices run clear, 10 to 15 minutes.

Spread ¼ cup topping on each chop and top with 1 slice cheese. Close the lid and cook until cheese has melted. Serve immediately.

SERVES 4

Grilled Ham Steak with Pineapple Sauce

You can find ham steaks in most grocery stores. I look for large steaks that have a center leg bone still intact—usually a sign that the ham has not been processed too much. One steak is usually good for two to four people, but this recipe is pretty delicious, so I suggest that one steak feeds two.

1 (14 oz.) can crushed pineapple, drained
1 cup pineapple juice
½ cup orange marmalade
¼ cup sugar

2 tsp. dry mustard
12 maraschino cherries, quartered
2 (1-inch-thick) large smoked ham steaks

In a medium saucepan, combine crushed pineapple, pineapple juice, marmalade, sugar, and mustard. Bring to a boil, reduce heat, and simmer, stirring occasionally, until thickened, about 15 minutes. Remove from heat and stir in cherries. Keep sauce warm.

Preheat grill to medium-high.

Cut the edges of ham steak at 2-inch intervals to prevent steaks from curling up on the grill. Grill steaks until lightly charred, 4 to 5 minutes per side.

Cut steaks into 2 or 4 pieces. Serve with sauce.

SERVES 2 TO 4

Grilled Butterflied Pork Tenderloin with Wasabi Teriyaki Glazing Sauce

This is a fast and easy recipe and one of my favorite pork recipes. It's all in the sauce. If you're lucky enough to have any leftovers, thinly slice them for a sandwich.

2 (¾ to 1 lb.) pork tenderloins
½ cup Bone Dust BBQ Spice (page 203)

WASABI TERIYAKI GLAZING SAUCE
2 TB. vegetable oil
1 tsp. sesame oil
4 cloves garlic, minced
1 TB. finely chopped fresh ginger

½ cup brown sugar
¼ cup rice vinegar
¼ cup mirin (sweet rice wine) or medium-dry sherry
¼ cup soy sauce
¼ cup water
1 TB. prepared horseradish
1 tsp. wasabi powder
Salt and pepper to taste

To prepare glazing sauce, in a medium saucepan over medium-high heat, heat vegetable oil and sesame oil. Sauté garlic and ginger until transparent and tender, 3 to 4 minutes. Stir in brown sugar, rice vinegar, mirin, soy sauce, and water. Bring to a boil, reduce heat, and simmer, stirring occasionally, for 15 minutes. Remove from heat and whisk in horseradish, wasabi powder, salt, and pepper. Let cool.

Trim pork tenderloins of any excess fat and sinew. To butterfly pork, with a sharp knife, cut along the length of tenderloins, making a deep incision about three-fourths the way through. Open up tenderloins so they lie flat and place between two plastic wrap sheets. Lightly pound tenderloins with the smooth side of a meat mallet until they are 1 inch thick.

Rub tenderloins with Bone Dust BBQ Spice, pressing seasoning into meat. Place tenderloins in a glass dish and pour three-quarters of the glazing sauce over pork. (Reserve remaining sauce for glazing.) Marinate, covered and refrigerated, for 2 hours.

Preheat grill to medium-high.

Grill tenderloins, basting liberally with reserved glazing sauce, for 4 to 5 minutes per side for medium. Let tenderloins rest for 5 minutes.

Thinly slice tenderloins and serve glazed with remaining sauce.

SERVES 6

Jerk Rotisserie of Pork Loin with Maple Jerk BBQ Sauce

While filming *King of the Q* in Jamaica, I had the pleasure of preparing this dish for our first episode. This is an easy way to prepare tender succulent pork.

1 (4 to 5 lb., 12- to 18-inch-long) boneless
    pork loin
2 bottles beer
1 cup Jamaican Jerk Paste (page 210)
½ cup sugar
¼ cup salt

MAPLE JERK BBQ SAUCE
2½ cups gourmet BBQ sauce
½ cup maple syrup
¼ cup Jamaican Jerk Paste (page 210)
½ bottle beer

Place pork loin in a deep roasting pan or large resealable plastic bag.

Whisk together beer, Jamaican Jerk Paste, sugar, and salt. Pour over pork loin and marinate, covered and refrigerated, for 24 hours.

To prepare sauce, whisk together BBQ sauce, maple syrup, Jamaican Jerk Paste, and beer.

Preheat grill to high.

Discard marinade and skewer pork with the rotisserie rod. Secure loin with the rotisserie spikes. Place pork on the rotisserie, season with salt, and close the lid. Sear meat for 15 minutes.

Reduce heat to medium-low and cook, basting frequently with sauce, until a meat thermometer reads 150°F (for medium), 1 to 1½ hours.

Remove pork from the rotisserie and carefully remove the rotisserie rod. Let meat rest for 10 minutes.

Give pork a final baste and cut into 1-inch-thick slices. Serve with remaining sauce.

SERVES 8

Redneck Riviera Smoked Boston Butt with Jack Daniel's BBQ Sauce

Chef Bill Hahne is the president of the Research Chefs Association in North America and is an avid meat smoker. As he says, he lives along the Redneck Riviera, a stretch of beach along the coast of Mississippi and the Gulf of Mexico. Bill has converted his beer fridge into a smoker on his front porch. (Personally, Bill, I would have gotten another fridge for the beer.)

The key to a successful smoked pork shoulder is the low and slow method of smoking. Bill adds a little twist that will ensure tender, mouth-watering pulled pork every time. Once the shoulder is cooked, he places it in the refrigerator, loosely covered, for 24 hours. Then he puts the pork in a large pot, covers it with a blend of water and Jack Daniel's, and simmers it for 2 hours. The meat literally shreds off the bone, pig-pickin' style!

---

1 (7 to 9 lb.) bone-in Boston butt pork shoulder roast
1 cup Bone Dust BBQ Spice (page 203)
Mesquite or hickory smoking chunks, soaked in water for at least 30 minutes

2 cups Jack Daniel's Sour Mash Whiskey (divided use)
3 cups hickory smoke–flavored BBQ sauce
½ cup malt vinegar
¼ cup brown sugar
Salt and pepper

Tip

By the way, Boston butt is the smoker's term for pork shoulder.

Rub pork with Bone Dust BBQ Spice, pressing seasoning into meat.

Prepare your smoker according to manufacturer's instructions to a temperature of 225°F, using about 12 charcoal coals (see page 219). Place pork shoulder on the top rack of the smoker and close the lid. Add soaked wood chunks to the charcoal for the first 2 hours of cooking. (I like to put the chips directly on the hot coals.)

Smoke pork for 6 to 8 hours, until a meat thermometer inserted in the thickest part of the meat nearest the bone reads 180°F and when you pull on the blade bone it pulls clean from the meat. Adjust the air vents to maintain a temperature of 225°F and replenish coals and water as needed. If the meat looks dry, spray it with a little water or Jack Daniel's.

Transfer pork to a bowl and loosely cover with plastic wrap. Refrigerate for at least 24 hours or up to a week.

Put pork in a large pot. Add 1 cup Jack Daniel's and enough water to cover. Bring to a boil, reduce heat to low, and simmer for 2 hours.

Meanwhile, prepare sauce. Whisk together remaining 1 cup Jack Daniel's, BBQ sauce, vinegar, and brown sugar.

Remove pork from the pot and let rest for 10 minutes. Using a fork or your hands, shred meat from the bone into small strips. Place meat in a large bowl and add sauce a little at a time, mixing thoroughly. Season to taste with salt and pepper. Some folks like their pulled pork dry, and others like it saucy.

Serve pulled pork piled high on fresh buns.

SERVES 10 TO 12

Sour Mash Whiskey Grilled Pork Tenderloin

Lynchburg, Tennessee, is the home of Jack Daniel's Sour Mash Whiskey. For a refreshing summer-time drink, add 6 ounces lemonade to 2 whiskey shots and serve with a sprig of mint.

---

3 (¾ to 1 lb.) pork tenderloins, trimmed
½ cup Licorice Rub (page 212)

SOUR MASH WHISKEY GLAZING SAUCE
2 TB. butter
4 cloves garlic, minced
1 small onion, finely diced
1 TB. chopped fresh sage

2 cups brown sugar
¼ cup Jack Daniel's Sour Mash Whiskey
¼ cup beef stock
¼ cup water
2 TB. red wine vinegar
2 TB. Worcestershire sauce
1 TB. hot sauce
Salt and pepper

Rub tenderloins with Licorice Rub, pressing seasoning into meat. Marinate, covered and refrigerated, for 4 hours.

In a medium saucepan, melt butter over medium-high heat. Sauté garlic and onion for 3 to 4 minutes, stirring, until translucent and tender. Add sage; cook, stirring, for 2 more minutes. Stir in sugar, whiskey, stock, water, vinegar, Worcestershire sauce, and hot sauce. Bring to a boil, reduce heat, and simmer for 15 minutes, stirring occasionally. Season to taste with salt and pepper. Set aside.

Preheat grill to medium-high.

Grill tenderloins for 6 to 8 minutes per side for medium, basting liberally with whiskey sauce.

Remove tenderloins from grill and let rest for 5 minutes. Thinly slice and serve glazed with remaining sauce.

SERVES 6

Apple Cider Pork Butt Steaks

My friend Olaf loves pork shoulder butt steaks. He says it's the best part of the pig and provides the most flavor when marinated in apple cider and grilled. Serve these steaks with grilled apple slices and Ruby Red Cabbage Slaw (page 70).

1 cup apple cider	8 cloves garlic, chopped
½ cup honey	1 onion, sliced
¼ cup soy sauce	3 green onions, sliced
1 TB. cracked black pepper	6 (8 oz., 1½-inch-thick) pork shoulder butt steaks
1 TB. chopped fresh cilantro	Salt to taste

In a glass dish large enough to hold the steaks, stir together cider, honey, soy sauce, pepper, cilantro, garlic, onion slices, and green onions. Add steaks, turning to coat. Marinate, covered and refrigerated, for 4 to 6 hours.

Preheat grill to medium-high.

Remove pork steaks from marinade and season with salt. Transfer marinade to a saucepan. Bring to a boil and reduce liquid by one-third. Using a hand blender, purée cider sauce until smooth.

Grill steaks for 5 to 6 minutes per side, basting liberally with cider sauce. Serve steaks drizzled with extra cider sauce.

SERVES 6

Beer Brine–Marinated Rotisserie of Pork Loin with Grilled Pineapple BBQ Sauce

Use a dark ale or strong lager to marinate the pork. It adds a nice nutty flavor.

1 (4 lb., 12- to 18-inch-long) boneless pork loin
½ cup Indonesian Cinnamon Rub (page 209)
4 bottles dark beer
1 cup water

½ cup brown sugar
¼ cup salt
6 cups Grilled Pineapple BBQ Sauce (recipe follows)
Special equipment: grill rotisserie rod

Rub pork loin with Indonesian Cinnamon Rub, pressing spices into meat.

In a deep roasting pan or large plastic bag, whisk together beer, water, brown sugar, and salt. Add pork loin, turning to coat. Marinate, covered and refrigerated, for 24 hours.

Preheat grill to high.

Remove pork from marinade, discarding marinade. Skewer pork with the rotisserie rod. Secure with the rotisserie spikes.

Place pork on the grill. Season with salt, close the lid, and sear pork for 15 minutes.

Reduce heat to medium-low and cook, basting frequently with Grilled Pineapple BBQ Sauce, for 1 to 1½ hours or until a meat thermometer reads 150°F for medium.

Remove pork from the rotisserie. Carefully remove rotisserie rod. Let meat rest for 10 minutes. Give a final baste and cut into 1-inch-thick slices.

Serve with extra pineapple sauce.

SERVES 8

Grilled Pineapple BBQ Sauce

1 pineapple, peeled and sliced into ½-inch-
  thick rounds
4 TB. vegetable oil (divided use)
Salt and pepper to taste
1 small onion, diced

3 cloves garlic, minced
3 cups hickory smoke–flavored BBQ sauce
½ cup brown sugar
½ cup bourbon
¼ cup Dijon mustard

Preheat grill to medium-high.

Rub 2 tablespoons vegetable oil all over pineapple slices and season slices with salt and pepper.

Grill pineapple for 3 to 4 minutes per side or until golden brown, tender, and lightly charred. Let cool. Cut pineapple into ¼-inch cubes.

In a large saucepan, heat remaining 2 tablespoons oil. Add onion and garlic; sauté for 3 to 4 minutes or until tender. Add BBQ sauce, brown sugar, bourbon, and mustard. Bring slowly to a boil, stirring.

Stir in pineapple. Adjust seasoning.

MAKES ABOUT 6 CUPS

Southern BBQ Pulled Pork

True Southern BBQ is slow-roasted and smoked for hours over moderately hot coals. It takes some time, but the result is mouthwatering and absolutely fantastic. A charcoal grill will give you the best flavor, but you can also use a gas grill. Keep the temperature at medium-low and place your soaked wood chips in a metal smoking tray on the grill beside the meat.

1 lemon, sliced	Mesquite, hickory, or cherry wood smoking chips, soaked in water for 30 minutes (optional)
1 large onion, sliced	
8 cloves garlic, minced	
2 TB. mustard seeds	**CAROLINA VINEGAR BBQ SAUCE**
2 TB. dried marjoram	¾ cup cider vinegar
2 TB. salt	¼ cup brown sugar
3 cans Sprite	1 cup ketchup
1 cup water	1 TB. Worcestershire sauce
1 (4 to 5 lb.) pork shoulder roast	1 tsp. hot sauce
¼ cup Bone Dust BBQ Spice (page 203)	Salt to taste

Tip

Pulled, by the way, means shredded.

In a large pot, combine lemon, onion, garlic, mustard seeds, marjoram, salt, Sprite, and water. Add pork shoulder, turning to coat. Marinate, covered and refrigerated, for 24 to 48 hours.

Remove pork shoulder from the marinade, discarding marinade. Rub with Bone Dust BBQ Spice, pressing seasoning into meat.

Prepare a charcoal grill for indirect cooking. Pile 3 to 4 pounds charcoal on one side of the grill and set alight. Close the lid, leaving the vents at the bottom and top open. When the coals are gray and hot, place a foil pan of water on the grill over the hot coals. (This will add moisture to the dry heat of charcoal.) If desired, add soaked wood chips to the coals for the first 2 hours of cooking.

Place pork shoulder on the grill opposite the hot coals. Close the lid and heat to 200 to 225°F. Adjust the vents at the base of the grill to maintain this temperature.

Cook pork for 5 to 6 hours or until a meat thermometer inserted into the thickest part of the meat reads 180°F and when you pull on the blade bone it pulls clean from the meat. Open the lid only to replenish the water and coals. If the meat looks dry, drizzle it with a little extra Sprite.

Remove shoulder from the grill, cover with foil, and let rest for 15 minutes.

Meanwhile, make sauce. In a bowl, whisk together vinegar, sugar, ketchup, Worcestershire sauce, hot sauce, and salt.

Remove crackling skin from pork and thinly slice. Pull meat by hand or with a fork.

Place meat in a large bowl and add sauce a little at a time, mixing thoroughly. Some people like their pulled pork dry and others like it saucy.

Serve piled high on fresh buns alongside Ruby Red Cabbage Slaw (page 70), if desired.

SERVES 8

Luau Stuffed Leg of Lamb

Treat the macadamia nuts like gold; they're expensive and delicious. If you want, substitute pecans.

---

2 red chilies, finely chopped
6 cloves garlic, minced
4 green onions, finely chopped
2 cups diced fresh pineapple
½ cup chopped macadamia nuts
½ cup fresh bread crumbs
2 TB. curry paste
1 TB. finely chopped fresh ginger
1 TB. chopped fresh parsley

½ cup pineapple juice
¼ cup melted butter
1 (4 to 5 lb.) boneless leg of lamb, butterflied
¼ cup Bone Dust BBQ Spice (page 203)

HONEY MUSTARD BASTE
½ cup butter
½ cup honey
½ cup pineapple juice

To prepare the baste, in a small saucepan, melt butter over medium heat. Whisk in honey and pineapple juice until fully incorporated. Set aside.

In a bowl, combine chilies, garlic, green onions, pineapple, macadamia nuts, bread crumbs, curry paste, ginger, and parsley. Add pineapple juice and melted butter a little at a time, stirring to incorporate. Stuffing should be a little moist.

Open up butterflied lamb leg and rub with Bone Dust BBQ Spice, pressing seasoning into meat. Spread stuffing evenly over the inside of the lamb leg.

Starting from the wide end, roll up leg. Tie securely with string.

Preheat grill to high.

Insert the rotisserie rod and place lamb on the grill. Sear lamb for 8 to 10 minutes. Reduce heat to medium and continue to roast, brushing occasionally with baste, until a meat thermometer reads 140 to 145°F (for medium), 60 to 70 minutes. Remove lamb from grill and let rest for 5 minutes.

Thinly slice and serve.

SERVES 8

Lamb Loin Chops with Pecan Goat Cheese

I first made this recipe on the set of *King of the Q,* and since then it has become a barbecue favorite at my home. Tender lamb chops don't need to marinate. Just season, grill, baste, and consume.

12 (2-inch-thick) lamb loin chops
¼ cup Old Montreal Steak Spice (page 202)
8 cloves garlic, minced
½ cup steak sauce
¼ cup ketchup
¼ cup honey

1 TB. chopped fresh rosemary
1 TB. Worcestershire sauce
Salt and pepper
½ cup coarsely crushed smoked pecans
½ cup creamy goat cheese
¼ cup butter, softened

Rub chops with Old Montreal Steak Spice, pressing seasoning into meat.

In a bowl, whisk together garlic, steak sauce, ketchup, honey, rosemary, and Worcestershire sauce. Season to taste with salt and pepper.

In another bowl, combine pecans, goat cheese, and butter.

Preheat grill to medium-high.

Grill chops, basting liberally with the sauce, for 6 to 8 minutes per side for medium-rare.

Serve chops topped with a dollop pecan goat cheese.

SERVES 4

Hot and Spicy Grilled Rack of Lamb

I like to use large racks of lamb from the United States or Australia. I find that these racks tend to have a little more meat as well as a nice amount of marbling and external fat, which add great flavor to a very simple grilling dish.

2 (1½ lb.) frenched lamb racks
¼ cup Licorice Rub (page 212)
2 TB. vegetable oil
2 cloves garlic, minced
4 jalapeño peppers, seeded and thinly sliced
3 red finger chili peppers, thinly sliced

½ cup stem ginger or orange marmalade
¼ cup apple juice
1 TB. chopped fresh cilantro
1 lime, juiced
Salt and pepper

Rub lamb racks with Licorice Rub, pressing seasoning into meat. Cover and marinate at room temperature for 1 hour.

Heat oil in a medium saucepan over medium heat. Sauté garlic, jalapeño, and chili peppers until tender, 2 to 3 minutes. Stir in marmalade and apple juice. Bring to a low boil, reduce heat to low, and simmer for 10 minutes, stirring occasionally. Stir in cilantro and lime juice. Season to taste with salt and pepper. Remove sauce from heat and set aside.

Preheat grill to medium-high.

Sear lamb for 2 to 3 minutes per side. Move lamb to the top rack for indirect cooking. Reduce heat to medium and close the lid. Grill-roast, basting occasionally with sauce, for 12 to 15 minutes for medium-rare. Remove lamb from grill and let rest for 5 minutes.

Slice between every rib bone and serve with reheated remaining sauce.

SERVES 4

Grilled Lamb Leg Steaks with Tropical Salsa

The lamb leg steak is an inexpensive cut of meat. If requires a few hours of marinating to tenderize, but once grilled, it is delicious.

6 (8 oz., 1½-inch-thick) lamb leg steaks
¼ cup Miami Spice Love Paste (page 211)
½ cup pineapple juice
¼ cup dark rum
¼ cup olive oil

TROPICAL SALSA
1 cup diced fresh pineapple
1 papaya, peeled, seeded, and diced

1 mango, peeled and diced
1 red bell pepper, diced
1 red onion, diced
1 jalapeño pepper, seeded and finely chopped
1 green onion, finely chopped
1 TB. chopped fresh thyme
1 lime, juiced
Pinch cayenne pepper
Salt and pepper to taste

Rub lamb steaks with Miami Spice Love Paste, pressing seasoning into meat. In a glass dish large enough to hold lamb in one layer, whisk together pineapple juice, rum, and oil. Add lamb, turning to coat. Marinate, covered and refrigerated, for 4 hours.

Prepare salsa by combining pineapple, papaya, mango, red pepper, red onion, jalapeño, green onion, thyme, lime juice, cayenne, salt, and pepper.

Preheat grill to medium-high.

Grill lamb for 6 to 8 minutes per side for medium.

Serve each steak topped with salsa.

SERVES 6

Sweet-and-Spicy Lamb Kebabs

Serve these grilled kebabs with grilled pita bread brushed with garlic and olive oil, and with grilled vegetable kebabs or salad.

1 cup ketchup	1 TB. crushed chilies
½ cup steak sauce	1 TB. coarsely ground black pepper
½ cup honey	1 tsp. hot sauce
¼ cup malt vinegar	6 cloves garlic, chopped
2 TB. chopped fresh rosemary	Salt to taste
2 TB. olive oil	1 (3 lb.) boneless leg of lamb

In a large bowl, combine ketchup, steak sauce, honey, vinegar, rosemary, oil, crushed chilies, pepper, hot sauce, garlic, and salt. Set aside half the mixture for basting.

Cut lamb into 1½-inch cubes. Add lamb to bowl, turning to coat. Marinate, covered and refrigerated, for 4 to 6 hours.

Preheat grill to medium-high. Soak eight bamboo skewers in warm water for 30 minutes. (Or use metal skewers.) Skewer five or six lamb pieces onto each skewer. Discard marinade.

Grill lamb skewers for 3 to 4 minutes per side for medium, basting frequently with reserved marinade.

SERVES 6 TO 8

Grilled Indian-Spiced Butterflied Leg of Lamb with Refreshing Raita

Inspired by the southwest flavors of India, this is a recipe for delicate lamb marinated with garam masala and served with a refreshing yogurt sauce. If you don't find garam masala in the spice section of your supermarket, look in the ethnic section of grocery stores and in Indian food shops.

---

1 (4 to 5 lb.) boneless leg of lamb, butterflied
¼ cup + 1 tsp. garam masala
10 cloves garlic, minced
1 cup plain yogurt
½ cup orange juice
2 TB. olive oil
1 TB. chopped fresh ginger

1 TB. chopped fresh mint
2 red chilies, finely chopped
4 green onions, chopped
½ cup clarified butter

RAITA
1½ cups plain yogurt
2 TB. lime juice

1 TB. chopped fresh mint
2 plum tomatoes, seeded and chopped
1 clove garlic, minced
½ small red onion, diced
½ seedless cucumber, peeled and diced
Salt to taste

Rub lamb with ¼ cup garam masala, pressing spices into meat.

In a glass dish large enough to hold the lamb, whisk together two-thirds the garlic, yogurt, orange juice, oil, ginger, mint, chilies and green onions. Add lamb, turning to coat. Marinate, covered and refrigerated, for 4 to 6 hours.

To prepare raita, in a bowl, combine yogurt, lime juice, mint, tomatoes, garlic, onion, cucumber, and salt. Cover and refrigerate for 1 hour to allow flavors to develop.

Preheat grill to medium-high.

In a small bowl, combine clarified butter, remaining garlic, and remaining 1 teaspoon garam masala for basting lamb.

Remove lamb from marinade, scraping off the excess marinade. Discard marinade. Season lamb with salt.

Sear lamb for 5 to 6 minutes per side, brushing with garlic butter mixture. Reduce heat to medium-low, close the lid, and grill lamb, turning once and brushing liberally with garlic butter, for 20 to 30 minutes or until a meat thermometer inserted into the thickest part of the meat reads 140 to 145°F for medium-rare.

Remove lamb from grill and let rest for 5 minutes.

Thinly slice and serve with raita.

SERVES 8

Grilled Lamb Chops with Cumin Raisin Marmalade Sauce

I like to have my butcher cut my lamb chops at least 2 inches thick. This not only gives me more meat to enjoy but also lessens the chance of overcooking this tender meat.

---

12 (2-inch-thick) lamb chops
¼ cup Gilroy Roasted Garlic Paste (page 201)
¼ cup malt vinegar
¼ cup orange juice
¼ cup olive oil
2 TB. grainy mustard

CUMIN RAISIN MARMALADE SAUCE
2 TB. butter
1 TB. chopped fresh ginger
1 tsp. ground cumin
¼ cup Grand Marnier
1 cup orange marmalade
½ cup orange juice
½ cup golden raisins
1 TB. chopped fresh mint
Salt and pepper to taste

Rub lamb chops with Gilroy Roasted Garlic Paste, pressing seasoning into meat.

In a shallow dish, whisk together vinegar, orange juice, olive oil, and mustard. Add lamb chops, turning to coat. Marinate, covered and refrigerated, for 4 hours.

To prepare marmalade sauce, melt butter in a medium saucepan over medium heat. Sauté ginger for 2 to 3 minutes or until tender. Add cumin; sauté for 1 minute, stirring.

Deglaze pan with Grand Marnier, stirring well. Add marmalade and orange juice, stirring until smooth. Bring mixture to a boil, reduce heat, and simmer for 15 minutes.

Stir in raisins, mint, salt, and pepper. Remove from heat and keep warm.

Preheat grill to medium-high.

Remove chops from marinade, reserving marinade. Grill chops for 6 to 8 minutes per side for medium-rare, basting with marinade.

Serve three chops per person drizzled liberally with raisin marmalade sauce.

SERVES 4

Grilled Lamb Leg Steaks with Goat Cheese and Green Olive Tapenade

Ask your butcher to prepare these delicious, inexpensive steaks. They can be bone-in or boneless. Have them cut at least 1½ inches thick.

12 cloves garlic, minced
½ cup dry sherry
¼ cup sherry vinegar
¼ cup olive oil
2 TB. chopped fresh rosemary
2 TB. Dijon mustard
2 tsp. coarsely ground black pepper
6 (8 oz., 1½-inch-thick) lamb leg steaks

GREEN OLIVE TAPENADE

1 cup pitted green olives
¼ cup capers
3 TB. chopped fresh parsley
1 TB. chopped fresh thyme
1 TB. anchovy paste
1 TB. lemon juice
4 cloves garlic, chopped
¼ cup balsamic vinegar
¼ cup olive oil
Salt and pepper to taste
1 cup crumbled goat cheese, softened

In a glass dish large enough to hold steaks, whisk together garlic, sherry, vinegar, oil, rosemary, mustard, and pepper. Add lamb steaks, turning to coat. Marinate, covered and refrigerated, 4 to 6 hours.

Make tapenade. In a food processor, pulse olives, capers, parsley, thyme, anchovy paste, lemon juice, and garlic until coarsely chopped. Add vinegar and oil; pulse until incorporated. Season with salt and pepper. Transfer to a bowl and blend in goat cheese. Adjust seasoning. Refrigerate until needed.

Continued ...

Preheat grill to medium-high.

Remove lamb steaks from marinade, reserving marinade. Grill for 5 to 6 minutes per side for medium-rare, basting with marinade.

Serve each steak topped with a large dollop tapenade.

SERVES 6

Grilled Venison Rack with Blueberry Compote

In 1997, five chef friends and I had the pleasure of teaching for a few days at the Chef John Folse Culinary Institute in Thibodaux, Louisiana. We prepared a Canadian-themed six-course dinner for the alumni and invited guests. We flew in Canadian Red Deer venison, which I prepared on an enormous smoker/grill.

2 racks frenched venison (4 bones each)
¼ cup Malabar Pepper Rub (page 200)
¼ cup maple syrup
¼ cup grainy mustard
¼ cup Canadian whisky
¼ cup olive oil
2 TB. dried savory
6 cloves garlic, minced
Salt to taste

BLUEBERRY COMPOTE
2 cups fresh or frozen blueberries
½ cup sugar
½ cup water
¼ cup Canadian whisky
½ tsp. vanilla

Season venison racks with Malabar Pepper Rub, pressing seasoning into meat.

In a glass dish large enough to hold racks, whisk together maple syrup, mustard, whisky, oil, savory, garlic, and salt. Add racks, turning to coat. Marinate, covered and refrigerated, for 4 to 6 hours.

Preheat grill to medium-high.

To make compote, in a medium saucepan, combine blueberries, sugar, water, whisky, and vanilla. Bring to a boil, reduce heat, and simmer, stirring occasionally, for 20 to 30 minutes or until berries burst and sauce is thickened. Set aside and keep warm.

Remove venison racks from marinade, reserving marinade. Grill racks for 7 to 8 minutes per side for medium-rare, basting with marinade. Remove racks from grill and let rest for 5 minutes.

Meanwhile, reheat blueberry compote if necessary.

Cut each rack into four thick chops and spoon blueberry compote over each chop.

SERVES 8

Grilled Buffalo Steaks with Apricot Cognac Sauce

 Buffalo meat is a little more full flavored than beef. Rare to medium-rare is the best way to serve tender and moist buffalo. If you overcook buffalo, it will be dry and tough.

6 (6 to 8 oz.) buffalo striploin steaks
2 TB. Bone Dust BBQ Spice (page 203)
1 cup port wine
½ cup olive oil
2 TB. Dijon mustard
1 TB. chopped fresh rosemary
1 tsp. cracked black pepper
8 juniper berries
4 cloves garlic, minced

APRICOT COGNAC SAUCE
2 TB. butter
3 shallots, diced
6 dried apricots, chopped
¼ cup white wine vinegar
1 cup chicken stock
¼ cup apricot jam
½ cup cognac
Salt and pepper

Season steaks with Bone Dust BBQ Spice, pressing seasoning into meat.

In a glass dish large enough to hold steaks, whisk together port, olive oil, mustard, rosemary, pepper, juniper berries, and garlic. Add buffalo steaks, turning to coat. Marinate, covered and refrigerated, for 4 hours.

Meanwhile, prepare sauce. In a small saucepan over medium-high heat, melt butter. Sauté shallots, stirring, for 2 minutes or until translucent and tender. Add apricots; sauté for 1 minute more. Add vinegar; bring to a boil and reduce liquid by half. Add chicken stock and apricot jam. Return to a boil, reduce heat, and simmer for 10 minutes.

Remove from heat. Using a hand blender, blend sauce until smooth. Return to heat, stir in cognac, and bring to a boil. Season to taste with salt and pepper. Remove from heat and keep warm.

Preheat grill to medium-high.

Remove buffalo steaks from marinade, discarding marinade. Grill for 2 to 3 minutes per side for medium-rare.

Serve steaks topped with apricot cognac sauce.

SERVES 6

Grilled Venison Rack Chops with Smoked Chocolate and Poblano Chili Sauce

Yes, you read this correctly—smoked chocolate with venison. Trust me, the rich flavor of the venison blends magnificently with the buttery smoked chocolate.

2 frenched venison racks (each with 8 ribs)
¼ cup Bone Dust BBQ Spice (page 203)
2 TB. butter
2 cloves garlic, minced
1 shallot, finely chopped
2 poblano peppers, roasted, peeled, seeded, and cut into 1-inch strips

1 cup heavy cream
¼ cup cognac
1 cup smoked bittersweet chocolate (page 431), coarsely chopped
1 TB. chopped fresh savory
Salt and pepper to taste

Rub venison with Bone Dust BBQ Spice, pressing seasoning into meat.

Melt butter in a small saucepan over medium-high heat. Sauté garlic and shallot until tender, 1 to 2 minutes. Add poblano peppers, cream, and cognac. Bring to a boil and reduce heat. Stirring constantly, add chocolate a little at a time until melted. Simmer gently until thick, about 5 minutes. Stir in savory, salt, and pepper. Remove sauce from heat and keep warm.

Preheat grill to medium-high.

Grill racks for 7 to 10 minutes per side for medium-rare. Remove racks from grill and let rest for 5 minutes.

Cut each rack into four thick chops and spoon chocolate sauce over each chop.

SERVES 8

Hot Buttered Breasts and Thighs

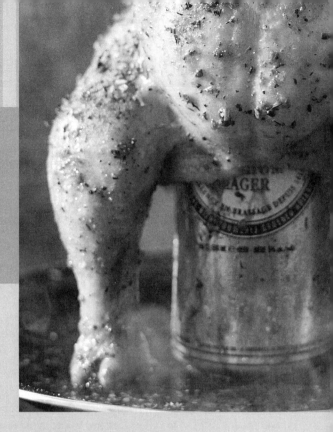

Cornish Hen

Quail

Duck

Smoked Maple Bourbon Glazed Chicken Halves

Grill-roasted half chickens are a sticky feast when the glaze is made with bourbon and maple syrup—a combination that is hard not to drink.

2 (3 to 4 lb.) chickens	**¼ cup brown sugar**
½ cup Hell's Fire Chili Paste (page 206)	**¼ cup bourbon**
Mesquite smoking chips or chunks	**¼ cup orange juice**
½ cup maple syrup	**Salt and pepper to taste**

Using a pair of poultry or kitchen shears, cut along each side of the backbone. Using a sharp knife, cut through the breast bone to separate chickens into two halves. Rub with Hell's Fire Chili Paste, pressing seasoning into skin and meat.

Prepare your smoker according to manufacturer's instructions to a temperature of 225°F (see page 219). Add soaked mesquite smoking chips.

Place chicken skin side up on smoking rack and close the lid. Smoke chickens until fully cooked (a meat thermometer will read 180°F), 4 to 6 hours, replenishing smoking chips, coals, and water as required.

Meanwhile, prepare glaze. In a large bowl, whisk together maple syrup, brown sugar, bourbon, orange juice, salt, and pepper.

Preheat grill to medium.

Place chickens on grill bone side down. Close the lid and grill-roast, basting with the glaze, until skin is crisp and chicken is hot, 5 to 10 minutes.

Serve with remaining glaze.

SERVES 4

Grilled Boneless Half Chicken with Raspberry Compound Butter

To make your life a little easier, ask your butcher to debone and halve the chickens for you, leaving the skin intact. The question of whether to have white meat or dark meat is never an issue with this dish—you get both! You get the breasts and thighs and those oh-so-delicious legs to nibble on—and no bones. Pure chicken decadence.

---

2 chickens, boned and halved
½ cup Herb Mustard Rub (page 208)
1 cup thawed frozen raspberries, juices reserved
½ cup honey
¼ cup vegetable oil
½ cup raspberry wine vinegar

RASPBERRY COMPOUND BUTTER
½ lb. butter, softened
2 TB. cracked black pepper
1 TB. Chambord raspberry liqueur
Thyme
½ pint fresh raspberries
Salt

Rub chickens with Herb Mustard Rub, pressing seasoning into meat and skin. Place chicken halves in a glass dish large enough to hold them in one layer.

In a small bowl, whisk together frozen raspberries and juice, honey, oil, and vinegar. Pour half the marinade over chickens, turning to coat evenly. Marinate, covered and refrigerated, for 4 to 6 hours. Reserve remaining marinade for basting.

Meanwhile, prepare compound butter. In a food processor, blend together butter, pepper, Chambord, and thyme until smooth. Add fresh raspberries; pulse until incorporated. Season to taste with a little salt. Transfer butter to a container and refrigerate until needed. Butter will keep, refrigerated, for up to 2 weeks.

Preheat grill to medium-high.

Grill chickens, skin side down, for 5 minutes. Turn over and baste skin liberally with reserved marinade. Grill for 6 to 8 minutes until fully cooked. Turn over again and baste meat side.

Serve chicken halves with a dollop compound butter.

SERVES 4

Grilled Boneless Half-Chicken with Sweet-and-Sour BBQ Sauce

Years ago, when I was a chef at Perry's Restaurant in Toronto, I served this dish as a special every Thursday evening. There was one customer who would come in religiously every week and have two orders to himself.

4 boneless skin-on half-chickens
2 TB. Bone Dust BBQ Spice (page 203)

SWEET-AND-SOUR BBQ SAUCE
1 cup honey
½ cup ketchup
¼ cup lemon juice

2 TB. chopped fresh rosemary
2 TB. olive oil
1 tsp. Worcestershire sauce
4 cloves garlic, minced
Hot sauce to taste
Salt and pepper to taste

Tip

Ask your butcher to debone the half-chickens, leaving the skin intact.

Season chicken with Bone Dust BBQ spice. Marinate, covered and refrigerated, for 4 to 6 hours.

To prepare sauce, in a small saucepan whisk together honey, ketchup, lemon juice, rosemary, olive oil, Worcestershire sauce, garlic, and hot sauce. Over medium heat, stirring occasionally, bring sauce to a boil. Reduce heat to low and simmer for 10 minutes, stirring occasionally. Season with salt and pepper. Let cool.

Preheat grill to medium-high.

Grill chicken skin side down for 6 to 8 minutes. Turn and baste skin liberally with sauce. Grill for another 6 to 8 minutes. Turn again and baste the meat side. Remove chicken from the grill.

Serve with the remaining sauce.

SERVES 4

Grilled Chicken and Vegetable Lasagna

I have never been a fan of lasagna. Its not that lasagna is not good, but I am just not a fan of tomato sauce and cheese. My Pamela has requested me to make lasagna on many occasions, and I have not obliged until now. I made this version of the classic on a grill and with a cream sauce instead. It is rich and decadent and has a ton of cheese. Enjoy!

---

4 (6 oz.) boneless, skinless chicken breasts

2 TB. Bone Dust BBQ Spice (page 203)

¼ cup + 2 TB. vegetable oil

4 Portobello mushroom caps

2 zucchini, cut in half lengthwise

2 red bell peppers, halved lengthwise

1 eggplant, sliced lengthwise ¼ inch thick

1 fennel bulb, halved lengthwise

1 large Spanish onion, sliced into ½-inch-thick rounds

¼ cup balsamic vinegar

Salt and pepper to taste

3 cloves garlic, minced

2 TB. chopped fresh herbs

4 cups shredded mozzarella cheese

2 cups shredded Friulano or provolone cheese

¼ cup dry bread crumbs

6 (8×10-inch) sheets fresh pasta

PARMESAN CREAM SAUCE

4 TB. butter

2 cloves garlic, minced

5 TB. all-purpose flour

4 cups chicken stock

1 cup grated Parmesan cheese

1 cup heavy cream

1 tsp. Worcestershire sauce

Salt and pepper to taste

2 cups ricotta cheese

Preheat grill to medium-high.

Rub chicken with Bone Dust BBQ Spice, pressing seasoning into meat and skin. Rub with 2 tablespoons oil.

In a large bowl, combine mushroom caps, zucchini, red peppers, eggplant, fennel, onion, remaining ¼ cup oil, vinegar, salt, and pepper. Toss well.

Grill chicken until fully cooked, 5 to 6 minutes per side. Let cool.

Continued ...

Grill vegetables, turning occasionally, until just cooked and slightly charred, 15 to 20 minutes. Let cool.

To prepare cream sauce, melt butter in a medium saucepan over medium-high heat. Sauté garlic until tender, about 2 minutes. Add flour, stirring constantly until fully mixed, being careful not to burn. Whisking constantly, add stock a little at a time until fully incorporated. Bring to boil, reduce heat to low, and simmer, stirring occasionally, until fairly thick, about 20 minutes. Whisk in Parmesan, cream, Worcestershire sauce, salt, and pepper. Let cool. When sauce has cooled, whisk in ricotta cheese.

Preheat oven to 375°F. Spray a 10×8×3-inch lasagna pan with nonstick cooking spray.

Cut chicken and vegetables into ½-inch-thick slices and toss with garlic and herbs.

Combine mozzarella and Friulano cheeses.

Sprinkle lasagna pan with bread crumbs. Spread ½ cup cream sauce evenly in the pan. Lay two pasta sheets over sauce. Spread half the chicken mixture evenly over pasta. Spread 1 cup sauce over chicken mixture. Top with 2 cups cheese. Lay two more pasta sheets over cheese. Top with remaining chicken mixture, 1 cup sauce, and 2 cups cheese. Finish with two more pasta sheets, remaining sauce, and remaining cheese.

Bake, uncovered, until the corners are bubbling and the top is golden brown, about 1½ hours.

Let rest for 10 minutes before serving.

SERVES 8

Grilled Chicken Breasts Stuffed with Peaches, Brie, and Shrimp

For this recipe, it is easiest if you buy hotel-style chicken breasts suprêmes. These are large, skin-on boneless chicken breasts (about 6 to 8 ounces each) with the wing drumstick attached. Ask your butcher to prepare these breasts for you.

8 (6 to 8 oz.) chicken suprêmes
¼ cup Bone Dust BBQ Spice (page 203)
1 (125 g) wheel Brie or Camembert, cubed
¼ cup cream cheese, softened
2 peaches, peeled and diced
1 shallot, diced

2 green onions, finely chopped
1 TB. chopped fresh thyme
1 TB. apple cider vinegar
Salt and pepper to taste
8 large shrimp, peeled, deveined, and cooked

Cut tenderloins from breasts. Place tenderloins between two sheets of plastic wrap and gently flatten with the smooth side of a meat mallet. Set aside.

Using a sharp knife, cut an incision down the center of the breast about ½ inch deep. With the tip of the knife, make an angled cut on each side of the initial cut into but not all the way through the breast. With your fingers, push the meat aside to make a large pocket. Season chicken inside and out with Bone Dust BBQ Spice.

In a food processor, blend Brie and cream cheese. Transfer mixture to a bowl and stir in the peaches, shallot, green onions, thyme, vinegar, salt, and pepper.

Divide Brie stuffing into eight equal portions. Place a portion of stuffing in the palm of your hand. Press one shrimp into stuffing. Mold stuffing around shrimp to encase it. Place stuffing in a chicken pocket and press firmly to slightly flatten.

Place a tenderloin over stuffing and tuck the edges into the pocket. Press the edges firmly together to make a tight seal. Repeat with remaining breasts.

Preheat grill to medium-high.

Grill chickens, starting skin side down, until fully cooked, 6 to 8 minutes per side.

Serve immediately.

SERVES 8

Chinese Lemon Grilled Chicken Breasts

You know your favorite Chinese restaurant that serves that tangy lemon chicken? Well, I think I've captured that wonderful flavor for you. Lots of fresh lemon juice adds zing in this recipe.

6 boneless, skinless chicken breasts	¼ cup sugar
2 TB. Indonesian Cinnamon Rub (page 209)	¼ cup pineapple juice
3 lemons, zested and juiced (divided use)	1 TB. rice vinegar
3 cloves garlic, minced	2 tsp. crushed red chilies
1 TB. finely chopped fresh ginger	2 tsp. cornstarch, dissolved in 2 TB. water
1 TB. vegetable oil	2 green onions, finely chopped
2 tsp. sesame oil	Salt and pepper

Rub chicken with Indonesian Cinnamon Rub, pressing seasoning into meat.

In a glass dish large enough to hold chicken in one layer, whisk together ¼ cup lemon juice, garlic, ginger, vegetable oil, and sesame oil. Add chicken, turning to coat. Marinate, covered and refrigerated, for 4 to 6 hours.

In a medium saucepan, combine remaining lemon juice, lemon zest, sugar, pineapple juice, vinegar, and crushed chilies. Bring to a low boil. Stir in cornstarch mixture. Reduce heat and simmer, stirring, until thickened. Remove from heat and stir in green onions. Season sauce to taste with salt and pepper.

Preheat grill to medium-high.

Grill chicken, basting with sauce, until golden brown and fully cooked, 5 to 6 minutes per side.

Serve immediately with remaining warmed sauce.

SERVES 6

Hot Buttered Love Chicken Thighs with Honey Butter

The best cut of chicken for me is the underrated thigh. Not only is the thigh inexpensive, but it also has more flavor and succulence than any other part of the chicken. Slowly grill-roast these thighs, basting them lusciously with honey butter glazing sauce.

---

12 chicken thighs

¼ cup Indonesian Cinnamon Rub (page 209)

½ lb. + 1 TB. cold butter (½ lb. cubed)

8 cloves garlic, minced

1 TB. finely chopped fresh ginger

½ cup honey

¼ cup lemon juice

1 TB. chopped fresh sage

1 TB. curry paste

Salt and pepper

Rub chicken with Indonesian Cinnamon Rub, pressing seasoning into meat and skin. Set aside.

To prepare glazing sauce, melt 1 tablespoon butter in a medium saucepan over medium heat. Sauté garlic and ginger until tender, 2 to 3 minutes. Add honey, lemon juice, sage, and curry paste, stirring until fully incorporated. Slowly bring to a boil and remove from heat. Whisk in cubed butter a little at a time until fully incorporated. Season to taste with salt and pepper.

Preheat grill to medium-high.

Sear chicken for 2 to 3 minutes per side and move to a cooler part of the grill. Close the lid and grill-roast thighs, basting every 10 minutes with lots of glazing sauce, until fully cooked, 20 to 30 minutes. Move chicken directly over heat source and grill for 1 to 2 minutes more to crisp the skin.

Baste once again and serve.

SERVES 6

BBQ Chicken Steaks

What is a chicken steak? Simply put, it's a butterflied boneless chicken thigh. You can leave the skin on for added flavor or remove it for a leaner recipe.

---

12 boneless chicken thighs
¼ cup Bone Dust BBQ Spice (page 203)
4 cloves garlic, minced
1 small onion, finely chopped
¾ cup gourmet BBQ sauce
¼ cup corn syrup

¼ cup ketchup
¼ cup steak sauce
1 TB. chopped fresh rosemary
1 TB. Worcestershire sauce
1 TB. cracked black pepper

Soak 24 (6- to 8-inch) bamboo skewers in warm water for 1 hour. (Or use metal skewers.)

Rub chicken with Bone Dust BBQ Spice, pressing seasoning into meat. Skewer each thigh with two skewers in an X pattern. (This will keep chicken flat during grilling.)

In a medium saucepan over medium heat, combine garlic, onion, BBQ sauce, corn syrup, ketchup, steak sauce, rosemary, Worcestershire sauce, and pepper. Slowly bring to a boil, stirring occasionally. Simmer for 10 minutes. Remove sauce from heat.

Preheat grill to medium-high.

Grill chicken, basting with sauce, until fully cooked and slightly charred, 5 to 6 minutes per side.

SERVES 6

Killer Thai Drumsticks

BEEROMETER 1-2

These are great for a backyard BBQ or picnic. Eat them hot or cold, but just eat them.

12 chicken drumsticks
¼ cup Bone Dust BBQ Spice (page 203)
4 cloves garlic, minced
2 green onions, minced
3 limes, juiced

½ cup sweet Thai chili sauce
1 TB. chopped fresh cilantro
½ cup melted butter
Salt and pepper

Preheat grill to medium-high.

Rub chicken with Bone Dust BBQ Spice, pressing seasoning into skin.

In a bowl, whisk together garlic, green onions, lime juice, chili sauce, and cilantro. Whisk in melted butter until fully incorporated. Season sauce to taste with salt and pepper.

Place chicken in a grill basket. Grill chicken, basting liberally with sauce, until fully cooked, 8 to 10 minutes per side.

Carefully remove chicken from grill basket and toss in remaining sauce.

Serve immediately or cool thoroughly and place in an airtight container for a picnic.

SERVES 6

Tip

Look for sweet Thai chili sauce in Asian grocery stores.

Bacon-Wrapped BBQ Drumsticks

Bacon should be its own food group. It just makes things taste better. And wrapped around these drumsticks, it also makes everything taste better.

---

12 chicken drumsticks or thighs
¼ cup Bone Dust BBQ Spice (page 203)
12 slices bacon
Whole cloves
4 cloves garlic, minced
1½ cups ketchup

½ cup maple syrup
2 TB. lemon juice
1 TB. chopped fresh thyme
1 TB. Worcestershire sauce
Salt and pepper

Rub chicken pieces with Bone Dust BBQ Spice, pressing seasoning into meat and skin. Roll one bacon slice around each piece of chicken and fasten with a toothpick. Stick one or two whole cloves into each piece of chicken.

In a bowl, whisk together garlic, ketchup, maple syrup, lemon juice, thyme, and Worcestershire sauce. Season sauce to taste with salt and pepper.

Preheat grill to medium.

Place chicken in a grill basket. Grill chicken, basting liberally with sauce, until fully cooked and bacon is crisp, 10 to 12 minutes per side. (If bacon causes a flare-up, move chicken to the cooler side of grill and cook indirectly.)

Carefully remove chicken from grill basket and toss in remaining sauce.

Serve immediately or cool thoroughly and place in an airtight container for a picnic.

SERVES 6

Citrus Chicken Breasts with Papaya Salsa

BEEROMETER 1

The juices of lemon, lime, and orange make a terrific marinade.

6 (6 oz.) boneless skinless chicken breasts
2 TB. Indonesian Cinnamon Rub (page 209)
1 lemon, juiced
1 orange, juiced
2 limes, juiced
3 cloves garlic, minced
1 jalapeño pepper, finely chopped
1 TB. chopped fresh ginger
1 TB. chopped fresh cilantro
Salt to taste

PAPAYA SALSA
1 ripe papaya, peeled, seeded and diced
1 small red onion, diced
1 red bell pepper, diced
2 green onions, finely chopped
1 jalapeño pepper, finely chopped
2 TB. lime juice
1 TB. chopped fresh cilantro
1 TB. olive oil
2 tsp. chopped fresh mint
Salt and freshly ground black pepper to taste

Rub chicken with Indonesian Cinnamon Rub, pressing seasoning into meat.

In a glass dish, whisk together lemon juice, orange juice, lime juice, garlic, jalapeño pepper, ginger, and cilantro. Add chicken breasts, turning to coat. Marinate, covered and refrigerated, for 4 to 6 hours.

Meanwhile, prepare papaya salsa. In a bowl, combine papaya, red onion, red pepper, green onions, jalapeño pepper, lime juice, cilantro, oil, mint, salt, and pepper.

Preheat grill to medium-high.

Remove chicken breasts from marinade, discarding marinade, and season with salt. Grill for 5 to 6 minutes per side or until golden brown and fully cooked.

Top each chicken breast with a spoonful of papaya salsa and serve.

SERVES 6

Tip

If you can't find ripe papaya, use cantaloupe, mango, or watermelon.

Grilled Chicken Breasts Stuffed with Goat Cheese and Prosciutto

Rich goat cheese blended with Italian prosciutto makes a delicious stuffing for chicken. My friend Rosa's mother first made a version of this chicken for me to try. I've since modified it for the grill. Rosa, it's fantastic!

8 (6 oz.) boneless skin-on chicken breasts	½ cup finely chopped dried apricots
¼ cup Bone Dust BBQ Spice (page 203)	1 TB. chopped fresh oregano
Salt and pepper to taste	1 TB. balsamic vinegar
1 cup julienned prosciutto	1 tsp. coarsely ground black pepper
1 cup ricotta cheese	2 green onions, finely chopped
½ cup crumbled goat cheese	Salt to taste

Preheat grill to medium-high.

Lay chicken breasts skin side down. Remove chicken tenderloins. Lightly pound tenderloins flat. Set aside.

Using a sharp knife, cut a pocket about 1-inch deep from the top of the breast to the bottom. Using your fingers, carefully push the meat aside to make a large pocket. Season chicken inside and out with Bone Dust BBQ Spice, salt, and pepper.

In a large bowl, mix together prosciutto, ricotta, goat cheese, apricots, oregano, vinegar, pepper, and green onions. Season to taste with salt.

Divide stuffing into eight equal portions and shape each portion into a firmly packed oval.

Place one stuffing portion into each chicken cavity. Place a flattened tenderloin over the cavity, and tuck tenderloin into the opening, firmly pressing the edges to make a tight seal.

Grill chicken skin side down for 6 to 8 minutes, then turn and grill for another 6 to 8 minutes or until chicken is fully cooked and stuffing is hot.

SERVES 8

Tandoori Chicken Legs

Tandoori refers to Indian dishes that have been marinated in yogurt and spices and then roasted in a clay oven called a tandoor. In Toronto, my favorite Indian BBQ restaurant is Dhaba. Chef Preetay makes wonderful tandoori dishes of chicken, seafood, and lamb. I like to first pan-roast the spices to bring out their natural aromatic flavors, which will intensify any dish.

TANDOORI MARINADE
2 cups plain yogurt
1 TB. lemon juice
2 tsp. salt
¼ cup paprika
2 TB. ground cumin
1 TB. cayenne pepper
1 TB. ground coriander
1 TB. ground cardamom

1 TB. cinnamon
1 TB. black pepper
1 tsp. ground cloves
¼ cup clarified butter
1 TB. minced fresh ginger
6 cloves garlic, minced

12 chicken legs

In a large bowl, blend yogurt, lemon juice, and salt. Set aside.

In a small bowl, combine paprika, cumin, cayenne, coriander, cardamom, cinnamon, black pepper, and cloves.

In a frying pan, heat clarified butter over medium heat until hot but not smoking. Add ginger and garlic; sauté, stirring, for 1 to 2 minutes until tender. Add spice blend and fry, stiffing, for 30 seconds to 1 minute, being careful not to burn spices. Transfer spices to yogurt and whisk until fully incorporated.

Using a sharp knife, make ¼-inch-deep slashes in chicken at ½-inch intervals.

Add chicken to tandoori marinade and toss to coat. Marinate, covered and refrigerated, for 24 hours.

Preheat grill to medium.

Remove chicken from marinade, scraping off excess marinade. Grill chicken for 10 to 15 minutes per side or until meat is fully cooked.

SERVES 6

Honey Mustard Chicken Thighs

Chicken thighs are already the tastiest part of the bird. Add this sauce, and you'll have an instant BBQ favorite.

8 cloves garlic, minced
¼ cup honey
¼ cup prepared mustard
2 TB. soy sauce
2 TB. lemon juice

1 TB. finely chopped fresh ginger
1 TB. chopped fresh cilantro
2 tsp. lemon pepper
12 chicken thighs

In a medium bowl, combine garlic, honey, mustard, soy sauce, lemon juice, ginger, cilantro, and lemon pepper.

Place chicken thighs in a glass dish and pour half the honey mustard mixture over chicken, turning to coat. Marinate, covered and refrigerated, for 4 hours. Reserve remaining sauce for basting.

Preheat grill to medium-high.

Remove thighs from marinade, discarding marinade, and grill for 6 to 8 minutes per side, basting liberally during the final 5 minutes of grilling with reserved honey mustard sauce.

Serve immediately with Singapore Noodle Salad (page 69), if desired.

SERVES 6

Orange Teriyaki Chicken Thighs

Big flavors from the grill are made easy with flavorful chicken thighs and a sweet teriyaki sauce.

12 boneless chicken thighs
1 TB. Bone Dust BBQ Spice (page 203)

ORANGE TERIYAKI MARINADE
4 green onions, finely chopped
4 cloves garlic, minced
½ cup orange juice
½ cup soy sauce

⅓ cup corn syrup
¼ cup minced fresh ginger
¼ cup vegetable oil
¼ cup rice wine vinegar
1 TB. chopped fresh cilantro
1 TB. sesame oil
2 tsp. sesame seeds
1 tsp. coarsely ground black pepper

Soak 24 (6-inch) bamboo skewers in warm water for 1 hour.

Rub chicken with Bone Dust BBQ Spice, pressing seasoning into meat. Skewer each thigh with two skewers. (This will help keep chicken flat on the grill.) Place thighs in a glass dish.

In a bowl, whisk together green onions, garlic, orange juice, soy sauce, corn syrup, ginger, vegetable oil, vinegar, cilantro, sesame oil, sesame seeds, and black pepper. Pour half the mixture over chicken, turning to coat. Marinate, covered and refrigerated, for 4 to 6 hours. Reserve remaining marinade for basting.

Preheat grill to medium-high.

Remove chicken thighs from marinade, discarding marinade, and grill for 4 to 5 minutes per side or until fully cooked and slightly charred, basting frequently with reserved marinade.

SERVES 6

Tip

For a little zing add some freshly grated horseradish!

Maple Garlic Chicken Drumsticks

Grilled chicken drumsticks are a perfect accompaniment to any summer picnic. These can be served hot or prepared ahead and served cold.

4 cloves garlic, minced
2 green onions, minced
1 jalapeño pepper, finely chopped
¼ cup Dijon mustard
¼ cup maple syrup

1 tsp. sesame seeds
1 tsp. sesame oil
12 chicken drumsticks
Salt and freshly ground black pepper to taste

Tip

If you do not have maple syrup, substitute corn syrup or honey.

Preheat grill to medium-high.

In a large bowl, whisk together garlic, green onions, jalapeño pepper, mustard, maple syrup, sesame seeds, and sesame oil.

Season chicken with salt and pepper. Place chicken in a grill basket.

Grill chicken for 8 to 10 minutes per side or until fully cooked, basting liberally with maple mixture.

Carefully remove chicken from grill basket and toss in remaining maple mixture.

Serve immediately or cool thoroughly and place in an airtight container for a picnic.

SERVES 6

Devil's Brewed Roast Chicken with White Trash BBQ Sauce (a.k.a. Beer Can Chicken, Beer Butt Chicken, and Drunken Chicken)

This fun and tasty recipe is a version of classic Texas Drunken Chicken. I first learned of this wonderful way of cooking chicken while on a visit to the Kansas City BBQ Competition. It makes a moist and tender chicken with a crispy outside.

While at the Grand Prix of Houston I prepared this recipe for the pit crew. I grill-roasted 32 drunken chickens at once on our massive grill. It was a sight to behold—and what an aroma!

2 (3 to 4 lb.) chickens
½ cup Bone Dust BBQ Spice (page 203)
2 (375-ml) cans lager or ale
¼ cup butter

¼ cup hot sauce
2 TB. lemon juice
Special equipment: 4 foil pie plates

Preheat grill to medium-high.

Wash chickens inside and out with cold water and pat dry with paper towels. Rub chickens inside and out with Bone Dust BBQ Spice, pushing rub firmly onto the birds so it adheres.

Open beer cans. Take a sip out of each beer for good luck. Just a sip, now—not the whole can.

Put one pie plate inside another. Place one beer can on the doubled-up pie plates. Place one chicken over a beer can so the beer can is in the cavity of the bird and the bird is standing upright. Repeat for other chicken.

To prepare basting sauce: In a small saucepan over medium heat, melt butter. Stir in hot sauce and lemon juice. Heat, stirring, until mixed.

Continued . . .

Place chickens on their pie plates on the grill. Close the lid and roast the chickens for 50 to 60 minutes or until fully cooked and golden brown, basting liberally with sauce. (To check for doneness insert a meat thermometer into the thigh. It should read 160°F.)

Serve with White Trash BBQ Sauce (recipe follows) and the juices that have collected in the pie plates.

SERVES 4 TO 6

White Trash BBQ Sauce

1 cup ranch-style dressing	1 TB. chopped fresh thyme
1 cup mayonnaise	1 TB. cracked black pepper
$\frac{1}{2}$ cup whipping cream	1 TB. Worcestershire sauce
$\frac{1}{2}$ cup milk	2 tsp. hot sauce
2 TB. lemon juice	1 tsp. salt
1 TB. chopped fresh parsley	3 cloves garlic, minced

In a medium saucepan, combine all the ingredients. Over medium heat, bring the mixture to a boil, stirring constantly. Adjust seasoning. Keep warm over low heat.

MAKES ABOUT 3$\frac{1}{2}$ CUPS

BBQ Jerk Turkey with Grilled Banana BBQ Sauce

On a recent trip to Jamaica, I had the pleasure of eating jerk turkey with grilled bananas. In my version of this island dish, I make a sauce with the grilled bananas.

2 boneless skin-on turkey breasts (2 lbs. total)
¼ cup Jamaican Jerk Paste (page 210)
2 TB. lime juice
2 TB. vegetable oil

GRILLED BANANA BBQ SAUCE
4 bananas, unpeeled
2 TB. vegetable oil

1 onion, diced
1 cup gourmet BBQ sauce
1 cup chicken stock
½ cup orange juice
1 TB. Jamaican Jerk Paste (page 210)
1 TB. brown sugar
1 TB. cider vinegar

Wash and pat dry turkey breasts. Mix together jerk paste, lime juice, and oil. Carefully push jerk marinade under the skin and rub into turkey meat and over the skin. Place in a glass dish and marinate, covered and refrigerated, for 4 to 6 hours.

Preheat grill to high.

To make sauce, grill unpeeled bananas until charred and tender. Peel bananas.

In a medium saucepan over medium heat, heat oil. Sauté the onion for 3 minutes or until tender. Add bananas, BBQ sauce, chicken stock, orange juice, jerk paste, brown sugar, and vinegar. Bring to a boil, reduce heat, and simmer for 10 minutes, stirring occasionally.

In a blender or food processor, purée sauce until smooth. Strain and cool.

Preheat grill to medium-high.

Grill turkey breasts skin side down for 10 to 12 minutes. Turn and grill for another 10 to 12 minutes, basting liberally with banana sauce. Turkey is done when a meat thermometer reads 160°F.

Thinly slice turkey breasts and serve with remaining sauce.

SERVES 8 TO 12

Pineapple-Brined Smoked Turkey with Bourbon BBQ Sauce

There are no rules that say you can only eat turkey at Thanksgiving, Christmas, or Easter. Roasting a turkey the traditional way with a savory stuffing is outstanding, but when it comes to summertime, I like to smoke a turkey and baste it with a bourbon BBQ sauce.

1 bunch savory, chopped
10 cloves garlic, smashed
10 juniper berries
4 bay leaves
8 cups pineapple juice
2 cups sugar
1 cup salt
1 (10 to 12 lb.) turkey

¼ cup vegetable oil
¼ cup Bone Dust BBQ Spice (page 203)
Hickory smoking chips soaked in water for 1 hour

BOURBON BBQ SAUCE
2 cups gourmet BBQ sauce
1 cup pineapple juice
½ cup bourbon

In a large pot, combine savory, garlic, juniper berries, bay leaves, pineapple juice, sugar, and salt. Bring to a boil, stirring occasionally. Remove from heat and cool completely.

Place turkey in a bucket or other container large enough to hold it. Pour pineapple brine over turkey. Marinate, covered and refrigerated, for 24 hours.

Preheat grill to medium.

To make sauce, combine BBQ sauce, pineapple juice, and bourbon.

Remove turkey from brine, discarding brine, and pat dry with paper towels. Rub turkey all over with vegetable oil and then Bone Dust BBQ Spice. Place turkey in a large foil roasting pan. Tuck the legs and wings in close to the body.

Place turkey on the grill, add smoking chips to coals or smoking box, close the lid and cook for 30 to 40 minutes per pound or until fully cooked, basting every 30 minutes with Bourbon BBQ Sauce and replenishing smoking chips as needed. (If the skin or wing tips should start to get black, cover turkey with pieces of foil.) Turkey is cooked when a meat thermometer inserted in the thickest part of the thigh reads 180°F.

Let turkey rest for 15 minutes before carving.

SERVES 6 TO 10

Asian Grilled Turkey Steaks

Ask your butcher to prepare turkey steaks cut from the breast. Each steak should be at least 1-inch thick and weigh about 6 ounces.

4 green onions, thinly sliced

3 cloves garlic, chopped

¼ cup soy sauce

¼ cup dry sherry

2 TB. maple syrup

1 TB. chopped fresh ginger

1 TB. chopped fresh cilantro

1 TB. sesame oil

1 tsp. sesame seeds

1 tsp. crushed chilies

Salt and freshly ground black pepper to taste

6 (6 oz.) turkey steaks

½ cup hoisin sauce

In a glass dish large enough to hold turkey steaks, whisk together green onions, garlic, soy sauce, sherry, maple syrup, ginger, cilantro, sesame oil, sesame seeds, crushed chilies, salt, and pepper. Add turkey, turning to coat. Marinate, covered and refrigerated, for 4 hours.

Preheat grill to medium-high.

Remove turkey steaks from marinade, discarding marinade, and grill for 4 to 5 minutes per side, basting liberally with hoisin sauce.

SERVES 6

Rotisserie Turkey Breasts with Oyster Cornbread Stuffing

If you ask your butcher to get you small turkey suprêmes (boneless, skin-on breasts), this recipe won't take as long. If you want, you can also use large chicken breasts. You'll need a grill rotisserie basket for this recipe.

4 (12 to 16 oz.) turkey breasts
¼ cup Bone Dust BBQ Spice (page 203)
2 TB. butter
1 dozen fresh oysters, shucked and liquor reserved

4 slices thick-cut bacon, diced
1 small onion, diced
1 stalk celery, diced
4 cloves garlic, minced
2 to 3 cups dry cornbread cubes

¼ cup melted butter
¼ bottle honey brown lager
1 TB. chopped fresh sage
Salt and pepper
Your favorite spicy BBQ sauce

Cut tenderloins from breasts. Place tenderloins between two sheets of plastic wrap and gently flatten with the smooth side of a meat mallet. Set aside.

Using a sharp knife, cut an incision down the center of the breast about ½ inch deep. With the tip of the knife, make an angled cut on each side of the initial cut into but not all the way through the breast. With your fingers, push the meat aside to make a large pocket. Season turkey inside and out with Bone Dust BBQ Spice.

In large saucepan, melt butter over medium heat. Lightly fry oysters until they are just firm. Using a slotted spoon, transfer oysters to paper towels to drain.

Add bacon to the pan and fry until crisp. Drain off all but 2 tablespoons fat. Add onion, celery, and garlic; sauté for 4 to 5 minutes. Add reserved oyster liquor, cornbread, melted butter, beer, and sage. Stuffing should be moist but not too wet, and just a little sticky. Season to taste with salt and pepper. Let cool. Fold in oysters.

Divide stuffing into four equal portions. Place stuffing in each turkey pocket, pressing firmly to tightly pack the cavity. Place a tenderloin over stuffing and tuck the edges into the pocket. Firmly press the edges together to make a tight seal. Repeat with remaining breasts.

Set up grill rotisserie according to manufacturer's instructions. Preheat grill to high (400°F).

Place turkey breasts in a grill rotisserie basket and secure mesh lid. Insert grill rod through basket. Grill turkey, basting lightly with BBQ sauce, until fully cooked (a meat thermometer will read 180°F), 25 to 30 minutes.

Cut breasts in half and serve immediately.

SERVES 8

Grilled Turkey Steaks with Apple Cream Sauce

Turkey steaks are cut from a boneless, skinless breast. Have your butcher cut these steaks 1 to 1½ inches thick

---

8 (6 oz., 1-inch-thick) turkey steaks
¼ cup Herb Mustard Rub (page 208)
1 cup ranch dressing
2 TB. cracked black peppercorns
2 TB. vegetable oil

APPLE CREAM SAUCE
2 TB. butter

1 small yellow onion, sliced
2 green apples, thinly sliced
¼ cup golden raisins
2 TB. apple brandy
½ cup heavy cream
¼ cup honey
¼ cup ranch dressing
Salt and pepper

Rub turkey with Herb Mustard Rub, pressing seasoning into meat. In a glass dish large enough to hold turkey in one layer, whisk together ranch dressing, peppercorns, and oil. Add turkey, turning to coat. Marinate, covered and refrigerated, for 4 hours.

To prepare sauce, melt butter in a medium saucepan over medium-high heat. Sauté onion until tender, 2 to 3 minutes. Stir in apples and raisins; sauté for 4 to 5 minutes, stirring gently.

Add apple brandy, scraping up any brown bits. Stir in cream, honey, and ranch dressing. Bring to a low boil, reduce heat, and simmer until sauce is thickened, 4 to 5 minutes. Season to taste with salt and pepper. Remove from heat and keep warm.

Preheat grill to medium-high.

Grill turkey until fully cooked, 4 to 5 minutes per side.

Serve immediately with sauce.

SERVES 8

Grand Marnier Cornish Hens

When preparing this recipe, I always like to have a little extra Grand Marnier by the grill—for guzzling purposes.

---

4 Cornish game hens
2 oranges, thinly sliced
1 onion, thinly sliced
¼ cup olive oil
2 TB. chopped fresh tarragon
1 TB. chopped fresh ginger

1 TB. mustard seeds
1 TB. cracked black pepper
½ cup Grand Marnier (divided use)
¼ cup melted butter
Salt to taste

Using poultry shears, split each Cornish hen down the middle on each side of the backbone to remove the backbone. Using a sharp knife, carefully debone the breast and legs.

In a glass dish large enough to hold hens, combine oranges, onion, olive oil, tarragon, ginger, mustard seeds, pepper, and ¼ cup Grand Marnier. Add hens, turning to coat. Marinate, covered and refrigerated, for 4 to 6 hours.

Preheat grill to medium-high.

Mix together remaining ¼ cup Grand Marnier and melted butter.

Remove hens from marinade, discarding marinade, and season with salt. Grill hens skin side down for 5 to 6 minutes, basting with Grand Marnier butter. Turn and grill, basting, for another 5 to 6 minutes or until fully cooked, crisp and delicious.

SERVES 4

Grilled Butterflied Cornish Hens with Hard Lemonade Glazing Sauce

On a hot summer's day, nothing is more refreshing to drink than one of those hard lemonade coolers. And here's a recipe where you can eat it, too.

---

4 Cornish game hens	1 onion, thinly sliced	2 cans hard lemonade (divided use)
¼ cup Herb Mustard Rub (page 208)	¼ cup olive oil	¼ cup honey
2 lemons, thinly sliced	2 TB. chopped fresh sage	2 TB. cold butter
8 cloves garlic, minced	1 TB. cracked black pepper	Salt to taste

---

Soak 8 (7- to 10-inch) bamboo skewers in water for 15 minutes. (Or use metal skewers.)

Rinse and pat dry game hens. Using a pair of poultry or kitchen shears, cut along each side of the backbone. Using a sharp knife, carefully remove the rib cage, breast bone, and leg bones. Rub hens with Herb Mustard Rub, pressing seasoning into skin and meat.

Place hens skin side up and bring the legs up snugly to the body. Skewer each hen in an X pattern, starting by inserting a skewer through one leg and through the opposite breast, exiting near the wing. Repeat on the other side.

In a bowl, combine lemon slices, garlic, onion, olive oil, sage, pepper, and 1½ cans hard lemonade. Pour half the marinade into a glass dish large enough to hold hens. Place hens on top and cover with remaining marinade. Marinate, covered and refrigerated, for 2 hours.

Meanwhile, in a small saucepan over medium heat, whisk together remaining ½ can hard lemonade (that is, if you haven't drunk it yet) and honey. When hot, whisk in the butter until fully incorporated. Remove glazing sauce from heat.

Preheat grill to medium-high.

Remove hens from marinade and season with salt. Grill hens, starting with skin side down and basting with glazing sauce, until fully cooked and crisp, 6 to 8 minutes per side.

Serve immediately.

SERVES 4

Tip

If you don't want to do it yourself, have your butcher remove the thigh bones, back bone, and rib cage from the Cornish hens.

Butterflied Quail with Raspberry Syrup

Ask your butcher to butterfly and remove the backbone of the quail. Quails are small. One is fine as an appetizer but allow two or three per person for a main course.

RASPBERRY SYRUP
½ pint raspberries
½ cup brown sugar
½ cup maple syrup
½ cup water
¼ cup Chambord or other raspberry liqueur

¼ cup olive oil
¼ cup raspberry vinegar
1 TB. chopped fresh tarragon
12 quails, butterflied
Salt and pepper to taste

To make syrup, in a small saucepan combine raspberries, brown sugar, maple syrup, water, and Chambord. Bring to a boil, stirring, reduce heat to low, and simmer for 10 minutes. Purée mixture in a blender. Strain through a fine sieve to remove seeds. Set aside.

In a large bowl, whisk together olive oil, raspberry vinegar, and tarragon. Add quails, turning to coat. Marinate, refrigerated, for 1 to 2 hours.

Preheat grill to medium-high.

Remove quails from marinade, discarding marinade, and season with salt and pepper. Grill quails for 2 to 3 minutes per side, basting with the raspberry syrup.

Serve immediately with remaining raspberry syrup.

SERVES 6

Southern Comfort BBQ Quail

Southern Comfort is a liqueur made with bourbon and peaches. Another great thing to do with Southern Comfort is use it as a baste for your favorite belle or beau.

12 butterflied boneless quail

¼ cup Bone Dust BBQ Spice (page 203)

Olive oil

¾ cup gourmet BBQ sauce

¼ cup Southern Comfort

¼ cup maple syrup

1 TB. cracked black pepper

1 TB. chopped fresh lemon thyme

2 TB. butter

Pinch cayenne pepper

Salt to taste

Soak 24 (7-inch) bamboo skewers in water for 15 minutes. (Or use metal skewers.)

Rub quail with Bone Dust BBQ Spice, pressing seasoning into flesh.

Place quail skin side up and bring the legs up snugly to the body. Skewer each quail in an X pattern, starting by inserting a skewer through one leg, under the leg bone and through the opposite breast, exiting near the wing. Repeat on the other side. Brush each quail with a little olive oil and set aside.

In a small saucepan over medium-high heat, whisk together BBQ sauce, Southern Comfort, maple syrup, pepper, and thyme. Bring to a low boil, stirring constantly. Remove from heat and whisk in butter, cayenne, and salt. Keep the sauce warm.

Preheat grill to medium-high. Grill quail skin side down for 2 to 3 minutes. Turn and continue to cook, basting with the sauce, for another 2 to 3 minutes.

Serve immediately.

SERVES 6

Tip

Ask your butcher to butterfly and remove the backbone and rib cage of the quail.

Grilled Duck Breasts with Vanilla Rhubarb Chutney

Duck is best served rare or medium-rare. Be careful not to overcook it, or it will be tough.

4 (8 to 12 oz.) boneless duck breasts
2 TB. Malabar Pepper Rub (page 200)

VANILLA RHUBARB CHUTNEY
2 TB. olive oil
1 small red onion, diced
1 TB. chopped fresh ginger

3 stalks rhubarb
1 vanilla bean, split lengthwise
¼ cup sugar
¼ cup honey
¼ cup cider vinegar
Pinch ground mace
Pinch ground allspice
¼ cup Stoli brand vanilla-infused vodka

Using a sharp knife, score the skin side of the duck breasts in a diamond pattern, slicing about ¼-inch deep into the fat. Season duck breasts with Malabar Pepper Rub, pressing seasoning meat. Set aside.

Preheat grill to medium-high.

To prepare chutney, in a medium frying pan, heat oil over medium-high heat until hot but not smoking. Add onion and ginger; sauté for 2 to 3 minutes, stirring occasionally, until tender. Add rhubarb and cook, stirring, until rhubarb is a bit browned.

Add vanilla bean, sugar, honey, vinegar, mace, and allspice. Bring to a boil, stirring. Reduce heat to low and simmer for 10 minutes, stirring occasionally. Add vodka and cook, stirring occasionally, for 5 more minutes. Set aside.

Grill duck breasts skin side down for 4 to 6 minutes or until the skin is golden brown and crisp. (Be careful of flare-ups from the dripping duck fat. If flare-ups occur, reduce grill heat and move duck breasts so they are not directly over the flames.) Turn duck breasts and grill for another 5 to 8 minutes for medium-rare. Duck breasts should be golden brown and firm to the touch.

Thinly slice each breast and serve with Vanilla Rhubarb Chutney.

SERVES 4 TO 6

Grilled Duck Breasts with Balsamic Fig Glazing Sauce

 Duck breasts are high in fat and tend to flare up on the grill. Sear them quickly on the skin side and then continue to cook them indirectly to reduce flare-ups. I recommend keeping the lid open and staying by the grill for the entire cooking time.

4 (8 to 12 oz.) boneless duck breasts
¼ cup Malabar Pepper Rub (page 200)
¼ cup balsamic vinegar
½ cup apple juice
2 TB. vegetable oil
1 TB. chopped fresh thyme

BALSAMIC FIG GLAZING SAUCE
6 dried figs, coarsely chopped
¼ cup amaretto
1 cup balsamic vinegar
2 TB. olive oil
4 cloves garlic, minced
2 large shallots, finely chopped

½ cup honey
¼ cup water
1 TB. chopped fresh thyme
1 vanilla bean, split
Pinch nutmeg
½ cup pecan halves, toasted and coarsely
    chopped

Using a sharp knife, score the skin side of the duck breasts in a diamond pattern, slicing about ¼ inch deep into the fat. Season duck with Malabar Pepper Rub, pressing seasoning into meat.

In a glass dish large enough to hold the duck in one layer, whisk together ¼ cup balsamic vinegar, apple juice, vegetable oil, and thyme. Add duck, turning to coat. Marinate, covered and refrigerated, for 4 hours.

Meanwhile, in a small bowl, soak figs in amaretto for 1 hour.

In a small, heavy saucepan, bring balsamic vinegar to a boil; reduce by half. Remove from heat.

Heat olive oil in a medium saucepan over medium-high heat. Sauté garlic and shallots until tender, 2 to 3 minutes. Add reduced balsamic vinegar, figs and amaretto, honey, water, thyme, vanilla bean, and nutmeg. Bring to a boil, reduce heat to low, and simmer for 15 minutes, stirring occasionally. Remove glazing sauce from heat; discard vanilla bean. Using a hand blender, purée sauce until smooth.

Preheat the grill to medium-high.

Grill duck, skin side down, until the skin is golden brown and crisp, 4 to 6 minutes. (If flare-ups occur, reduce grill heat and move duck so it is not directly over the flames.) Turn duck and grill, basting with glazing sauce, for 5 to 8 minutes for medium-rare. Duck should be golden brown and firm to the touch.

Remove duck from the grill and thinly slice each breast across the grain. Serve topped with pecans and remaining glaze.

SERVES 4 TO 6

Smoked Peking Duck

BEEROMETER 3-4

Patience is the key to smoking—along with a few beers. Enjoy a few cold brews while tending to your duck.

1 (4 to 5 lb.) duck
3 TB. Indonesian Cinnamon Rub (page 209)
2 star anise
1 cinnamon stick
1 orange, peeled and sliced crosswise
Cherry smoking chips or chunks
Chinese crêpes
Thinly sliced green onions

PEKING SAUCE
1 TB. vegetable oil
2 tsp. sesame oil
4 cloves garlic, minced
1 TB. finely chopped fresh ginger
1 tsp. crushed red chilies
2 oranges, juiced

1 cup plum sauce
½ cup hoisin sauce
¼ cup brown sugar
¼ cup mirin (sweet rice wine)
3 TB. soy sauce
2 TB. rice vinegar
Salt and pepper

Tip

You'll find Chinese crêpes in the freezer section of Asian grocery stores.

Rinse duck inside and out and pat dry. Rub duck all over with Indonesian Cinnamon Rub, pressing seasoning into meat and skin. Place star anise, cinnamon stick, and orange slices inside duck.

Prepare your smoker according to manufacturer's instructions to a temperature of 225°F (see page 219). Add soaked cherry smoking chips.

Place duck on smoking rack and close the lid. Smoke duck until fully cooked (a meat thermometer will read 180°F), 4 to 6 hours. Replenish smoking chips, coals, and water as required.

Meanwhile, prepare sauce. Heat vegetable oil and sesame oil in a medium saucepan over medium-high heat. Sauté garlic, ginger, and crushed chilies until garlic is tender, 2 to 3 minutes. Add orange juice, plum sauce, hoisin, brown sugar, mirin, soy sauce, and rice vinegar; bring to a boil, stirring. Remove from heat and season to taste with salt and pepper. Set aside.

Preheat grill to medium-low.

Cut smoked duck in half. Place duck on grill bone side down and close the lid. Grill-roast until the skin is crisp and duck is hot, 5 to 10 minutes.

Cut duck into four portions and serve with warmed sauce, Chinese crêpes, and green onions.

SERVES 4

Grilled Foie Gras with Peach and Cumin Chutney

In 1997, I spent a few weeks cooking in Tel Aviv. Israel is a beautiful country with a dynamic culture and a flare for creating some amazing food, including a lot of foie gras! This delicious liver is a grilled specialty in the Hatikva neighborhood of Tel Aviv. My friend Beto Escalada took me to a local taverna called the White Goose, where we dined on cubed and skewered foie gras seasoned well with salt. I was in heaven and close to the holy land. Here is my grilled foie gras.

1¼ lb. piece duck foie gras	1 cup cider vinegar	1 tsp. salt
Salt and pepper	¾ cup brown sugar	Pinch cayenne pepper
4 peaches, peeled and sliced	½ cup golden raisins	¼ cup pomegranate molasses
1 small onion, diced	¼ cup chopped candied ginger	¼ cup cranberry or pomegranate juice
1 red bell pepper, diced	1 tsp. ground cumin	2 TB. granulated sugar

Carefully cut away any surface imperfections and visible tendons on foie gras. Cut foie gras into slices ½-inch thick and weighing about 3 ounces each. You need at least 8 slices. Place on a parchment-lined tray and refrigerate until needed.

Prepare chutney. In a large saucepan, combine peaches, onion, red pepper, vinegar, brown sugar, raisins, ginger, cumin, salt, and cayenne pepper. Bring to a boil, stirring occasionally; reduce heat and simmer, stirring, until thick, 15 to 20 minutes. Remove from heat and keep warm.

Prepare glaze by combining pomegranate molasses, juice, and granulated sugar in a small saucepan. Bring to a boil, stirring, and simmer until thick, about 5 minutes. Set aside.

Preheat grill to high.

With a sharp knife, score both sides of foie gras in a diamond pattern ¼ inch deep. Season with salt and pepper.

Place foie gras in a grill topper and grill for 1 to 1½ minutes per side. Be careful of flare-ups; foie gras is full of delicious fat. Be prepared with a spray bottle of water to douse flames.

To serve, place 2 slices of foie gras on each plate. Garnish with chutney and drizzle with glaze. Serve with mixed baby greens.

Tip

Look for pomegranate molasses in specialty or Middle Eastern grocery stores.

SERVES 4

Wet 'n' Wild Seafood

Hot Smoked Halibut

Smoked halibut is also great in soups and chowders. And I like to fold it into creamy mashed potatoes.

---

2 (12 oz., 1½-inch-thick) halibut fillets
2 TB. Bone Dust BBQ Spice (page 203)
¼ cup apple cider vinegar
¼ cup apple juice
2 TB. sugar

2 TB. vegetable oil
¼ cup melted butter
¼ cup gourmet BBQ sauce
1 TB. apple butter
Hickory smoking chips

Rub halibut with Bone Dust BBQ Spice, pressing seasoning into flesh. In a glass dish large enough to hold halibut in one layer, whisk together vinegar, apple juice, sugar, and oil. Add halibut, turning to coat. Marinate for 30 minutes.

Meanwhile, in a small bowl, whisk together melted butter, BBQ sauce, and apple butter.

Prepare your smoker according to manufacturer's instructions to a temperature of 225°F (see page 219). Add hickory smoking chips.

Place halibut on the top smoking rack. Baste with apple butter baste and close the lid. Smoke halibut for 1½ to 2½ hours, replenishing smoking chips, coals, and water as required. Halibut is cooked when it easily flakes with a fork.

Carefully transfer halibut to a serving platter and cut each fillet in half.

Serve immediately with tartar sauce and grilled bread.

SERVES 4

Grilled Monster Halibut Steak with Pernod Mustard Mop and Pernod Butter

Be patient when grilling this big steak, and do not turn it too often. A "mop" is a thin BBQ sauce that is basted liberally on food.

---

1 (1½ to 2 lb., 1½-inch-thick) monster
   halibut steak
3 TB. Old Montreal Steak Spice (page 202)
Olive oil, for brushing

PERNOD MUSTARD MOP
2 shallots, finely chopped
¼ cup melted butter
¼ cup corn syrup
¼ cup Dijon mustard
¼ cup grainy mustard
¼ cup Pernod

2 TB. white wine vinegar
1 TB. chopped fresh tarragon
1 TB. cracked black pepper
1 tsp. dry mustard
Salt to taste

PERNOD BUTTER
¼ lb. butter, softened
2 TB. Pernod
1 TB. chopped fresh thyme
1 tsp. cracked black pepper
Pinch salt

Rub Old Montreal Steak Spice into halibut flesh. Brush with olive oil. Set aside.

To prepare Pernod Mustard Mop, in a bowl, whisk together shallots, melted butter, corn syrup, Dijon mustard, grainy mustard, Pernod, vinegar, tarragon, pepper, dry mustard, and salt. Set aside.

To prepare Pernod Butter, in a small bowl, combine butter, Pernod, thyme, pepper, and salt. Cover and refrigerate until needed.

Preheat grill to medium-high.

Place halibut on a well-oiled grill topper. Grill, basting frequently with the mustard mop, until the center bone of the halibut can be pulled cleanly from the flesh, 12 to 15 minutes per side (8 to 10 minutes per inch of thickness). Remove halibut from the grill and cut into four portions. Serve topped with a dollop Pernod butter.

SERVES 4

Banana Leaf-Wrapped Mahi Mahi with Tropical Fruits

While in Jamaica filming *King of the Q,* I had the opportunity to do a little deep-sea fishing. I caught a 25-pound, 44-inch-long mahi mahi. It was delicious, so fresh and full of flavor. Mahi mahi is a firm-fleshed fish, which makes it great for the grill. If you can't find mahi mahi, use grouper, halibut, sea bass, or red snapper.

---

6 (6 oz., 1-inch-thick) skinless mahi mahi fillets

3 TB. Bone Dust BBQ Spice (page 203)

1 seedless orange, peeled and segmented

1 small red onion, diced

1 red bell pepper, diced

1 cup diced fresh mango

1 cup diced fresh pineapple

1 TB. chopped fresh parsley

1 TB. finely chopped fresh ginger

1 TB. curry paste

Salt and pepper to taste

2 large banana leaves

6 TB. cold butter

Tip

You can find banana leaves in Asian and West Indian markets.

Season mahi mahi with Bone Dust BBQ Spice, pressing seasoning into flesh.

In a bowl, combine orange segments, onion, red pepper, mango, pineapple, parsley, ginger, curry paste, salt, and pepper.

Cut banana leaves into six 12-inch squares. Place 1 spoonful fruit mixture in the middle of each square. Place 1 fillet on fruit; top each with 1 tablespoon butter and another spoonful fruit mixture. Fold up the bottom of the leaf, fold in the sides and fold down the top; press firmly to seal the packages. Tie each with string.

Preheat grill to medium-high.

Grill bundles, turning once, for 6 to 8 minutes per side.

Let rest for 3 minutes.

Carefully unwrap bundles and serve immediately.

SERVES 6

Smoked Marlin Steak with Bacon Aïoli

 Heavenly is all I can say!

---

2 (8 to 10 oz., 1½-inch-thick) marlin steaks
¼ cup Old Montreal Steak Spice (page 202)
1 TB. crushed red chilies
¼ cup olive oil
Cherry or apple smoking chips

BACON AÏOLI
2 slices bacon, diced and fried crisp

1 clove garlic, minced
½ cup mayonnaise
¼ cup sour cream
2 TB. lemon juice
1 TB. chopped fresh dill
Dash hot sauce
Salt and pepper to taste

Rub marlin with Old Montreal Steak Spice and crushed chilies, pressing seasoning into flesh. Brush with olive oil and set aside.

To prepare aïoli, in a bowl, combine bacon, garlic, mayonnaise, sour cream, lemon juice, dill, hot sauce, salt, and pepper.

Prepare your smoker according to manufacturer's instructions to a temperature of 175°F (see page 219). Add soaked cherry smoking chips.

Place marlin on top rack of smoker and close the lid. Smoke for 45 to 60 minutes for medium doneness, replenishing smoking chips, coals, and water as required.

Thinly slice marlin and serve hot or cooled with bacon aïoli.

SERVES 2 TO 4

Stuffed Monkfish Tails

Monkfish is a firm, meaty fish that is great for the grill. It is rich in flavor and is often called the poor man's lobster. This recipe requires a little extra work, but the results are incredible.

2 (1 lb.) monkfish tails
¼ cup Herb Mustard Rub (page 208)
3 TB. butter
4 cloves garlic, minced
1 small onion, diced
1 small fennel bulb, diced

1 TB. chopped fresh thyme
3 cups stale bread cubes
2 TB. lemon juice
Salt and pepper to taste
4 (¼-inch-thick) bacon slices
3 TB. Dijon mustard

Using a sharp knife, remove any skin from monkfish. Cut carefully down one side of the backbone between the bone and flesh. Repeat on other side, removing backbone and cutting each tail into two fillets. Rub monkfish with Herb Mustard Rub, pressing seasoning into the flesh. Cover and marinate for 20 minutes.

Meanwhile, prepare stuffing. Melt butter in a medium saucepan over medium-high heat. Sauté garlic, onion, fennel, and thyme until vegetables are tender. Add bread cubes and lemon juice, stirring until fully mixed. If the stuffing is too dry, add a little white wine. Remove from heat, season with salt and pepper, and let cool slightly.

In a frying pan, cook bacon until crisp. Drain on paper towels. Brush bacon with Dijon mustard.

Lay two fillets on a work surface with the thicker end close to you. Place a slice of bacon on each fillet. If the bacon is too long, trim a little off. Press half the stuffing firmly along the length of each fillet. Top with remaining bacon. Lay the remaning fillets on top with the thicker end away from you so the "sandwich" is an even thickness. Tie the stuffed fillets together with string at 1-inch intervals.

Preheat the grill to medium-high.

Grill monkfish, turning occasionally, until evenly cooked, 15 to 20 minutes.

Slice monkfish into 1½-inch-thick medallions and serve immediately with a squeeze of lemon.

SERVES 4

Grilled Pickerel in Foil

Getting tired of grilled fish? Well, here's a change. Wrap delicate fillets of pickerel, sole, turbot, or catfish in foil with some flavorings and steam your fish on the grill. It cooks evenly and is always a great surprise when opened.

---

4 (6 oz.) pickerel fillets
3 TB. Bay Seasoning (page 205)
½ seedless cucumber
4 cloves garlic, minced
1 large sweet onion, sliced
¼ cup mayonnaise

¼ cup sour cream
2 TB. lemon juice
1 TB. lemon pepper
1 TB. chopped fresh dill
Salt

Trim pickerel so each fillet is no more than 6 inches long. Rub fish with Bay Seasoning, pressing seasoning into flesh. Set aside.

Peel cucumber, cut in half lengthwise and thinly slice. In a bowl, combine cucumber, garlic, onion, mayonnaise, sour cream, lemon juice, lemon pepper, and dill. Season to taste with salt.

Cut four foil sheets 12 × 24 inches and fold each piece in half to make a 12-inch square. Place one fillet on one side of each piece of foil, leaving a good-size margin at the edge. Top each fillet with cucumber mixture. Fold over the foil and crimp the edges to seal well.

Preheat grill to medium-high.

Grill pouches for 8 to 10 minutes per side.

Transfer pouches to plates and carefully open at the table.

SERVES 4

Grilled Salmon with Blackberry Ginger Compote

I first made this salmon dish for Gord Ash, the former manager of the Toronto Blue Jays. I poached the salmon in duck fat for a few minutes and then finished it on the grill. Gord and his guests loved it. I even think they licked their plates. What a party, but that's a whole other story.

6 (6 oz.) Atlantic salmon fillets	2 tsp. toasted sesame seeds
3 TB. Indonesian Cinnamon Rub (page 209)	Salt and pepper to taste
3 green onions, finely chopped	
1 lime, juiced	**BLACKBERRY GINGER COMPOTE**
¼ cup olive oil	2 cups fresh blackberries
¼ cup honey	½ cup sugar
¼ cup white wine	½ cup water
2 TB. minced fresh ginger	¼ cup amaretto
1 TB. chopped fresh mint	1 tsp. minced fresh ginger

Rub salmon with Indonesian Cinnamon Rub, pressing seasoning into flesh. In a glass dish large enough to hold salmon in one layer, whisk together green onions, lime juice, olive oil, honey, wine, ginger, mint, sesame seeds, salt, and pepper. Add salmon, turning to coat. Cover and marinate for 30 minutes.

Meanwhile, prepare compote. In a medium saucepan, combine blackberries, sugar, water, amaretto, and ginger. Bring to a boil, stirring occasionally. Reduce heat and simmer, stirring occasionally, until berries burst and sauce is thickened, 10 to 15 minutes. Remove from heat and keep warm.

Preheat grill to medium-high.

Remove salmon from marinade (reserving marinade for basting). Grill salmon, basting with marinade, until just cooked through, 5 to 8 minutes per side.

Serve immediately with compote.

SERVES 6

Cedar-Planked Salmon with Crab and Scallop Crust

Planking is probably my signature method. I have written a book on the subject *(Sticks and Stones: The Art of Grilling on Plank, Vine and Stone)*, and I am always looking for different ways to plank that oh-so-famous salmon. This recipe was prepared for my show *King of the Q,* and let me tell you, getting fresh salmon in Jamaica was a difficult chore!

---

6 (10 to 12 oz.) skinless Atlantic salmon fillets
¼ cup Bay Seasoning (page 205)

CRAB AND SCALLOP CRUST
1 bunch green onions, chopped
1 large red onion, finely chopped
3 cloves garlic, minced
1½ cups cooked crab or lobster meat

1 cup shredded mozzarella cheese
¼ cup BBQ sauce
1 TB. Bay Seasoning (page 205)
1 TB. chopped fresh dill
12 large sea scallops
Special equipment: 1 untreated red cedar plank (at least 12×10×1 inch), soaked in water at least 4 hours or overnight

---

Preheat grill to high.

Rub salmon all over with Bay Seasoning, pressing seasoning into flesh. Place salmon on the plank.

In a bowl, combine green onions, red onion, garlic, crabmeat, mozzarella, BBQ sauce, Bay Seasoning, and dill. Top salmon with this mixture, pressing it gently to make it adhere.

Using a sharp knife, slice each scallop into four or five rounds. Lay six to eight scallop slices evenly over crusted salmon.

Place the plank on the grill and close the lid. Grill until salmon is just cooked through and scallops are golden, 12 to 15 minutes. Periodically check the plank; if it is burning, spray it with water and move it to a cooler part of the grill.

Serve salmon smoking on plank.

SERVES 6

Grilled Salmon with Fennel Hash and Crisp Pancetta

My chef buddy Olaf first prepared this awesome recipe for me at his restaurant On the Curve. Thanks, Olaf—you are the master.

6 (8 oz.) skinless Atlantic salmon fillets
¼ cup Salmon Seasoning (page 204)
¼ cup balsamic vinegar
2 TB. chopped fresh dill
2 TB. grainy Dijon mustard
2 TB. olive oil
1 TB. coarsely ground black pepper

12 slices pancetta
Lemon wedges, for garnish

FENNEL HASH
2 TB. olive oil
1 small onion, diced
4 cloves garlic, minced

1 small fennel bulb, diced
6 large green olives, sliced
¼ cup capers
2 TB. balsamic vinegar
1 TB. chopped fresh dill
Salt and pepper
2 TB. butter

Tip

If your grill doesn't have a side burner, make the hash ahead of time and keep it warm.

Rub salmon with Salmon Seasoning, pressing seasoning into flesh.

In a glass dish large enough to hold salmon in one layer, whisk together vinegar, dill, mustard, oil, and pepper. Add salmon, turning to coat. Marinate for 30 minutes, basting occasionally with marinade.

Preheat grill to medium-high.

Grill salmon until just cooked through, 4 to 5 minutes per side.

While salmon is cooking (or ahead of time), prepare fennel hash. Heat oil in a large frying pan on the side burner. Sauté onion, garlic, and fennel until just tender, 4 to 5 minutes. Stir in olives, capers, vinegar, dill, salt, and pepper. Remove from heat and stir in butter until melted. Keep warm.

When salmon is just cooked, move it to a warm area of the grill away from direct heat. Grill pancetta until crisp. Pat with paper towels to remove excess fat.

Serve salmon topped with fennel hash and pancetta. Garnish with lemon wedges.

SERVES 6

Nelson's Blood Smoked Salmon

In Newfoundland, salmon was often dipped in a dark rum before it was smoked. In my dad's village, this rum was called Nelson's Blood, a dark syrupy rum with lots of flavor.

---

1 (4 to 6 lb.) side Atlantic salmon, boneless and skin on	½ cup salt
	½ cup sugar
2 TB. Bone Dust BBQ Spice (page 203)	½ cup dark rum, plus extra for brushing
2 cups chopped fresh dill	Maple smoking chips or chunks

Place salmon skin side down on a cookie sheet with sides at least ½ inch high. Rub salmon with Bone Dust BBQ Spice, pressing seasoning into flesh. Sprinkle evenly with dill.

Stir together salt and sugar. Sprinkle evenly over salmon and pat firmly. Pour rum over salmon. Cover with plastic wrap. Place a 2- to 3-pound weight on top of salmon and refrigerate for 24 hours.

Prepare your smoker according to manufacturer's instructions to a temperature of 175°F (see page 219).

Rinse salmon under cold water and pat dry with paper towels. Place salmon on top rack and brush with a little rum. Add soaked smoking chips and close the lid. Smoke salmon until just cooked and still moist, 2½ to 3½ hours, replenishing smoking chips, coals, and water as required.

Remove salmon from smoker and let cool completely. Thinly slice and serve with cream cheese and bagels or any way you wish.

SERVES 12

Bacon-Wrapped Sea Bass Kebabs with a Grand Pineapple Syrup

Sea bass is a wonderfully delicate fish. I do not recommend undercooking this fish, as that tends to toughen it. I prefer to cook it just through, so it is tender and succulent. The bacon adds flavor, and the fat and helps keep the fish moist.

2 lbs. skinless sea bass fillets (each 2 inches thick)

1 TB. Bay Seasoning (page 205)

16 slices bacon, partially cooked and still flexible

GRAND PINEAPPLE SYRUP

2 green onions, finely chopped

1 small Scotch bonnet pepper, seeded and finely chopped

4 cloves garlic, chopped

½ cup corn syrup

¼ cup Grand Marnier

¼ cup pineapple juice

2 TB. olive oil

1 TB. minced fresh ginger

1 TB. chopped fresh cilantro

Salt and pepper to taste

Soak 8 (10-inch) bamboo skewers in warm water for 30 minutes. (Or use metal skewers.)

Cut sea bass into 2-inch chunks (you should have at least 16 chunks). Rub sea bass with Bay Seasoning.

Wrap one bacon slice around each chunk and push two bamboo skewers through bacon side, putting four chunks on each kebab.

To prepare syrup, in a small bowl, whisk together green onions, Scotch bonnet pepper, garlic, corn syrup, Grand Marnier, pineapple juice, olive oil, ginger, cilantro, salt, and pepper.

Preheat grill to medium-high.

Grill kebabs, basting with pineapple syrup and turning carefully, until fish is just cooked through, 15 to 20 minutes.

Serve immediately with Tropical Coleslaw (page 39).

SERVES 4

Grilled Shark with Tangerine Vinaigrette

If you're not a fan of shark, try this recipe with tuna, marlin, or swordfish. Some people say shark is a soup fish, but I disagree. When prepared properly, shark is tender, meaty, and full of flavor.

---

4 (6 oz., 1-inch-thick) shark steaks
2 TB. Bay Seasoning (page 205)
1 cup buttermilk
2 cloves garlic, minced
2 green onions, minced
¼ cup tangerine juice
¼ cup white wine vinegar

2 TB. honey
1 TB. chopped fresh thyme
1 TB. crushed red chilies
¼ cup vegetable oil
Salt and pepper
Olive oil for brushing
2 oranges, peeled and segmented

Rub shark with Bay Seasoning, pressing seasoning into the flesh. Place shark in a glass dish and pour buttermilk over, turning shark to coat. Marinate, covered and refrigerated, for 30 to 45 minutes.

Meanwhile, prepare vinaigrette. In a bowl, whisk together garlic, green onions, tangerine juice, vinegar, honey, thyme, and crushed chilies. While whisking, pour in oil in a slow, steady stream, whisking until emulsified. Season to taste with salt and pepper.

Preheat grill to medium-high.

Remove shark from marinade and brush with a little oil. Grill shark, basting with vinaigrette, until fork-tender, 5 to 8 minutes per side. Do not overcook shark.

Serve immediately drizzled with extra vinaigrette and topped with orange segments.

SERVES 4

Planked Crab-Stuffed Rainbow Trout

Planked trout is wonderful. I first planked trout for my television show *Cottage Country*. The trout was stuffed with lemon and sage. It was delicious, but this version, as Emeril would say, is "kicking it up a notch."

---

4 (10 to 12 oz.) rainbow trout, scales, bones, and fins removed, head and tail intact
Salt and pepper
2 TB. butter
2 shallots, finely chopped
1 clove garlic, minced
2 green onions, finely chopped
1 leek, cleaned, cut in half lengthwise and thinly sliced

1½ cups fresh lump crabmeat
½ cup mayonnaise
¼ cup fresh bread crumbs
2 TB. chopped fresh dill
2 TB. lemon juice
Special equipment: 2 untreated cedar planks (at least 10×8×1 inch), soaked in water for 4 to 6 hours

---

Rinse trout inside and out and pat dry with paper towels. Using a sharp knife, make 3 incisions ½ an inch deep and 2 inches apart on each side of the trout. Season trout inside and out with salt and pepper.

Melt butter in a medium frying pan over medium-high heat. Sauté shallots, garlic, green onions, and leek until tender, 3 to 4 minutes. Let cool slightly. In a bowl, combine leek mixture, crabmeat, mayonnaise, bread crumbs, dill, and lemon juice. Season to taste with salt and freshly ground black pepper. Mix thoroughly.

Spoon stuffing into trout cavities. Secure with toothpicks.

Preheat grill to high.

Place soaked planks on the grill and close the lid. Let the planks heat for 3 to 4 minutes or until they start to crackle and smoke.

Carefully open the lid and place two trouts on each plank. Close the lid and bake trout until fish is firm to the touch and easily flakes with a fork, 15 to 20 minutes. Periodically check the planks; if they are burning, spray with water and move them to a cooler part of the grill.

Serve trout immediately.

SERVES 4

Grilled Atlantic Salmon Fillets with Grapefruit Maple Mustard Glaze

Fresh grapefruit is a wonderful way to spark up any grilled seafood. Cut a grapefruit in half and squeeze the juice over the salmon just before serving to add a burst of flavor.

MARINADE AND GLAZE
1 cup ruby red grapefruit juice
½ cup pure Canadian maple syrup
2 TB. chopped fresh dill
2 TB. whole-grain Dijon mustard

2 TB. olive oil
1 TB. coarsely ground black pepper
8 (6 oz.) Atlantic salmon fillets, skinned
¼ cup Salmon Seasoning (page 204)
1½ grapefruits

In a small bowl, whisk together grapefruit juice, maple syrup, dill, mustard, olive oil, and pepper.

Season salmon with Salmon Seasoning, pressing seasoning into flesh. Place salmon evenly in a shallow dish large enough to hold it in one layer. Pour half the marinade over salmon, turning to coat. Marinate for 30 minutes, turning occasionally.

Place remaining marinade in a small saucepan and warm it over medium heat.

Slice grapefruit into ½-inch-thick slices. Set aside.

Preheat grill to medium-high.

Remove salmon from marinade, reserving marinade. On a lightly seasoned grill, grill the salmon for 3 to 4 minutes per side or until just cooked, basting with marinade you used to marinate salmon.

While salmon is grilling, brush grapefruit slices with a little oil and grill for 2 to 3 minutes per side.

When salmon is cooked, squeeze the ½ grapefruit over fish.

Serve with grilled grapefruit slices and heated marinade.

SERVES 8

Apple Cider BBQ Atlantic Salmon

Salmon is my favorite fish. It is not only full of flavor, but it's also very good for you—it's loaded with a healthy fat called the omega-3 fatty acid.

APPLE CIDER BBQ SAUCE
2 TB. olive oil
3 cloves garlic, minced
3 shallots, finely chopped
1 cup apple cider
1 cup gourmet BBQ sauce
1 TB. chopped fresh herbs
   (thyme, rosemary, sage)

1 TB. fresh lemon juice
1 tsp. coarsely ground black pepper
Salt

6 (6 oz.) Atlantic salmon fillets, skinned
1 to 2 TB. Salmon Seasoning (page 204)

In a medium saucepan, heat olive oil over medium-high heat. Sauté garlic and shallots for 2 to 3 minutes or until tender.

Add apple cider; bring to a boil and reduce liquid by half. Add BBQ sauce, herbs, lemon juice, and black pepper. Return to a boil, reduce heat to low, and simmer for 10 minutes. Season to taste with salt. Let cool slightly.

Preheat grill to medium-high.

Season salmon with the Salmon Seasoning, pressing seasoning into flesh.

Grill salmon for 4 to 5 minutes per side, basting liberally with cider sauce.

Serve salmon with an extra drizzling of sauce.

SERVES 6

Tandoori Planked Salmon

The flavor of tandoori seasoning and cedar work well together in this India-meets-the-Pacific-Northwest dish.

6 (6 oz.) Atlantic salmon fillets
Tandoori Marinade (page 247)

Special equipment: 1 untreated cedar plank (at least 10×8×1 inch), soaked in water overnight

Place salmon in a large glass dish and pour Tandoori Marinade over it, turning to coat. Marinate, covered and refrigerated, for 2 hours.

Preheat grill to high.

Place soaked plank on the grill and close the lid. Let the plank heat for 3 to 4 minutes or until it starts to crackle and smoke.

Remove salmon from marinade, scraping off excess marinade. Discard marinade.

Carefully open the lid and place salmon on the plank. Close the lid and bake salmon for 12 to 15 minutes or until it flakes easily with a fork. Periodically check the plank; if it is burning, spray it with water and reduce heat to medium.

Carefully remove the plank from the grill and serve salmon immediately.

SERVES 6

Cedar-Planked Salmon with Citrus BBQ Sauce

Planking is one of the easiest ways to prepare seafood on the grill. It brings full flavor to salmon and other seafood without too much fuss.

CITRUS BBQ SAUCE
1 small red onion, diced
2 cloves garlic, minced
3 green onions, chopped
1½ cups BBQ sauce
½ cup orange marmalade
¼ cup chopped fresh dill

2 TB. orange juice
1 TB. coarsely ground black pepper
Salt to taste
6 (6 oz.) Atlantic salmon fillets
Special equipment: 1 untreated cedar plank (at least 10×8×1 inch), soaked in water overnight

Preheat grill to high.

In a bowl, combine onion, garlic, green onions, BBQ sauce, marmalade, dill, orange juice, black pepper, and salt. Heavily crust the top of each salmon fillet with the mixture, pressing down gently.

Place soaked plank on the grill and close the lid. Let the plank heat for 3 to 4 minutes or until it starts to crackle and smoke.

Carefully open the lid and place salmon on the plank. Close the lid and bake salmon for 12 to 15 minutes or until it flakes easily with a fork. Periodically check the plank; if it is burning, spray it with water and reduce heat to medium.

Carefully remove the plank from the grill and serve salmon immediately.

SERVES 6

Cedar-Planked Haddock Stuffed with Crab, Shrimp, and Cheddar Cheese

Planking is such an easy way to prepare seafood. You can almost stick it on the grill and forget it.

---

6 (6 oz.) skinless haddock fillets
Salt and freshly ground black pepper to taste
1 cup crabmeat
1 cup baby shrimp, roughly chopped
1 cup shredded cheddar cheese
½ cup dry bread crumbs

¼ cup melted butter
1 TB. chopped fresh dill
1 TB. lemon juice
2 shallots, finely chopped
3 green onions, finely chopped
1 clove garlic, finely chopped

Preheat grill to high.

With a sharp knife, cut an incision lengthwise in the top of each fillet, cutting about three-quarters the way through the fish. Using your fingers, open the incision to make a large pocket. Season fillets with salt and pepper.

In a bowl, combine crabmeat, shrimp, cheddar cheese, bread crumbs, melted butter, dill, lemon juice, shallots, green onions, and garlic. Season to taste with salt and freshly ground black pepper, and mix thoroughly.

Divide stuffing into six equal portions. Pack stuffing into each pocket. It doesn't matter if some stuffing is on top of the fish.

Place soaked plank on the grill and close the lid. Let the plank heat for 3 to 4 minutes or until it starts to crackle and smoke.

Carefully open the lid and place stuffed fillets on the plank. Close the lid and bake haddock for 12 to 15 minutes or until it flakes easily with a fork. Periodically check the plank; if it is burning, spray it with water and reduce heat to medium.

Carefully remove the plank from the grill and serve haddock with Creamed Spinach (page 187), if desired.

SERVES 6

Grilled Stuffed Arctic Char with Apricot Glaze

This recipe takes a bit of time to prepare, but it is easy to grill and dazzling on the plate.

---

2 leeks, trimmed, leaves separated and
    washed (16 leaves needed)
¼ cup butter
1 sweet onion, thinly sliced
4 cloves garlic, chopped
2 TB. chopped fresh sage
½ cup diced dried apricots
1 TB. lemon juice

Salt and pepper to taste
4 (1 lb.) Arctic char or 8 fillets with skin

APRICOT GLAZE
½ cup apricot jam
¼ cup butter
¼ cup tangerine juice
1 tsp. cracked black pepper

In a pot of boiling water, blanch leek leaves for 1 minute or until tender and bright. Cool in ice water. Drain on paper towels.

In a medium frying pan over medium-high heat, melt butter. Sauté onion, garlic, and sage for 3 minutes or until tender. Remove from heat and stir in dried apricots, lemon juice, salt, and pepper. Set aside.

If using whole fish, rinse fish with cold water inside and out. Pat dry with paper towels. Fillet fish, removing the head, backbone, and rib cage. Season fish with salt and pepper.

Lay three or four leek leaves on a work surface with the root ends facing you. Place one fillet skin side down crosswise across the leeks. Top evenly with one-quarter the onion mixture. Lay a second fillet skin side up on the onion stuffing. Roll up fish in leeks to make a tight wrap. Repeat with other fish. Wrap tightly in plastic and refrigerate for 1 hour to allow fish and leeks to set.

Preheat grill to medium-high.

To make glaze: In a small saucepan, combine apricot jam, butter, tangerine juice, and pepper. Heat, stirring, until melted and blended.

Unwrap fish from plastic and grill for 8 to 10 minutes per side, basting liberally with glaze. Use a large spatula to turn fish.

Slice fish into four to six rounds and serve with a drizzling of apricot glaze.

SERVES 8

Grilled Sea Bass Fillets

Some chefs might like to serve sea bass rare to medium-rare, but I find it tastes better when just cooked through. It is then flaky and tender with lots of flavor.

1 TB. olive oil	¼ cup steak sauce
1 red onion, diced	2 TB. lemon juice
4 cloves garlic, chopped	Salt and pepper to taste
2 TB. chopped fresh thyme	6 (6 oz.) sea bass fillets
2 green onions, finely chopped	1 TB. Bay Seasoning (page 205)
½ cup gourmet BBQ sauce	

In a medium saucepan, heat olive oil over medium-high heat. Sauté onion and garlic for 2 to 3 minutes or until tender. Add thyme and green onions; cook, stirring, for 1 minute. Add BBQ sauce, steak sauce, and lemon juice. Bring to a boil, reduce heat to medium-low, and simmer for 15 minutes, stirring occasionally. Season with salt and pepper. Pour into a glass dish large enough to hold fish and let cool.

Season fillets with Bay Seasoning, pressing seasoning into flesh. Add to marinade, turning to coat. Cover and let marinate at room temperature for 1 hour.

Preheat grill to medium-high.

Remove fillets from marinade, reserving marinade. Sear sea bass fillets for 1 to 2 minutes per side. Reduce heat to medium, close grill lid, and grill roast for 5 to 8 minutes per side until the flesh is tender and flaky.

SERVES 6

Grilled Halibut T-Bone Steaks with Grapefruit Avocado Butter Sauce

The T-bone steak of the sea is just as flavorful as a steak.

1 cup grapefruit juice

¼ cup olive oil

2 TB. chopped fresh tarragon

1 TB. cracked black pepper

1 tsp. mustard powder

2 shallots, finely chopped

2 green onions, finely chopped

1 jalapeño pepper, finely chopped

Sea salt to taste

6 (8 oz.) halibut T-bone steaks

½ grapefruit

In a glass dish large enough to hold fish, whisk together grapefruit juice, olive oil, tarragon, black pepper, mustard powder, shallots, green onions, jalapeño, and salt. Add halibut, turning to coat. Cover and marinate at room temperature for 1 hour.

Preheat grill to medium-high.

Remove halibut from marinade, reserving marinade for basting. Grill for 6 to 8 minutes per side or until the center bone of halibut can be pulled cleanly from meat, basting frequently with marinade.

When halibut is cooked, squeeze grapefruit juice over fish.

Serve with Grapefruit Avocado Butter Sauce (recipe follows).

SERVES 6

Grapefruit Avocado Butter Sauce

6 TB. cold butter (4 TB. cut in pieces)

4 shallots, chopped

2 cloves garlic, chopped

½ cup grapefruit juice

¼ cup Riesling white wine

1 grapefruit, peeled and segmented

1 avocado, diced

1 TB. chopped fresh parsley

Salt and pepper

In a small saucepan over medium-high heat, melt 2 tablespoons butter. Sauté shallots and garlic for 2 minutes or until tender. Add grapefruit juice and wine. Bring to a boil and reduce liquid by half.

Reduce heat to low and whisk in remaining butter until smooth.

Gently stir in grapefruit, avocado, and parsley. Season to taste with salt and pepper.

MAKES ABOUT 1 CUP

Tuna Pepper Steak

Tuna steaks are one of the easiest seafoods to grill. Their firm texture allows for easy preparation. The less you cook firm-fleshed fish like tuna, swordfish, and marlin, the tastier it will be.

6 (6 oz., 1½-inch-thick) tuna steaks
¼ cup Malabar Pepper Rub (page 200)
¼ cup olive oil
½ cup oyster sauce

¼ cup rice wine vinegar
¼ cup honey
2 green onions, finely chopped

Preheat grill to high.

Rub tuna steaks with Malabar Pepper Rub, pressing seasoning into fish. Brush steaks with olive oil.

In a bowl, stir together oyster sauce, vinegar, honey, and green onions.

Grill tuna steaks for 2 minutes per side for rare, basting with oyster sauce glaze.

Slice tuna steaks and serve with Sesame Shrimp and Snap Pea Salad (page 66), if desired.

SERVES 6

Sugarcane-Skewered Swordfish with Lemon Honey Glaze

The natural sweetness of sugarcane blends well with the firm texture of swordfish. This is an easy recipe that can be prepared in minutes. Look for sugarcane in grocery stores or specialty markets.

---

1 (8 inch) stick fresh sugarcane, peeled and quartered
4 (8 oz., 1½-inch-thick) center-cut swordfish steaks
1 TB. Bay Seasoning (page 205)

¼ cup olive oil
¼ cup lemon juice
¼ cup honey
1 TB. chopped fresh cilantro
Salt and pepper to taste

Preheat grill to medium-high.

Using a sharp knife, cut a point on one end of each sugarcane skewer. Insert one sugarcane skewer into the side of each swordfish steak.

Season swordfish with Bay Seasoning and then brush with olive oil. Set aside.

In a small bowl, whisk together lemon juice, honey, cilantro, salt, and pepper.

Grill swordfish for 4 to 5 minutes per side for medium, brushing liberally with lemon honey glaze.

SERVES 4

Cinnamon-Skewered Scallops with Brown Sugar Butter and Peach-Orange Salsa

The idea for this recipe came from my chef friend Niall Hill. Niall is working his culinary charms in Ireland and has a flare for great-tasting food. I call him the sexy chef, for his food is full of passion. Marrying scallops and cinnamon sticks might seem odd, but the two go perfectly well together.

BROWN SUGAR BUTTER
½ cup butter, softened
3 TB. sultana raisins
2 TB. brown sugar
2 TB. orange juice
½ tsp. chopped fresh thyme

PEACH-ORANGE SALSA
2 oranges
4 peaches, peeled and thinly sliced
1 red bell pepper, diced
1 jalapeño pepper, seeded and finely chopped
1 shallot, finely chopped
¼ cup orange blossom honey
2 TB. Grand Marnier
2 TB. olive oil

2 tsp. chopped fresh cilantro
Salt and freshly ground black pepper to taste
6 (at least 5-inch) cinnamon sticks
24 jumbo sea scallops
⅓ cup orange juice
⅓ cup olive oil
2 TB. Indonesian Cinnamon Rub (page 209)
1 TB. rice vinegar
Salt to taste

Tip

Soaking the cinnamon sticks not only prevents burning but extracts more cinnamon flavor.

Soak cinnamon sticks for at least 1 hour.

To prepare brown sugar butter, in a small bowl, combine butter, raisins, brown sugar, orange juice, and thyme. Mix until well blended. Cover and refrigerate.

To prepare peach-orange salsa, grate 1 teaspoon zest from an orange. Set aside. Peel and segment oranges, removing membranes. In a large bowl, combine orange zest and segments, peaches, red pepper, jalapeño, shallot, honey, Grand Marnier, olive oil, cilantro, salt, and black pepper. Cover and refrigerate.

Skewer four scallops onto each cinnamon stick. Place in one layer in a glass dish.

In a small bowl, stir together orange juice, olive oil, Indonesian Cinnamon Rub, rice vinegar, and salt. Pour over scallop skewers, turning to coat. Marinate, covered and refrigerated, for 30 minutes.

Preheat grill to medium-high. (If you wish, use a grill screen to prevent the skewers from falling through the grill.)

Remove scallops from marinade, reserving marinade, and grill for 2 to 4 minutes per side or until scallops are just cooked through, basting with marinade.

Serve each skewer with 1 tablespoon brown sugar butter and one-sixth of the orange salsa.

SERVES 6

Tip

Try skewering lamb, chicken, beef, or turkey with cinnamon sticks for a boost of flavor.

Grilled Crab-Stuffed Jumbo Shrimp with Papaya Sauce

For this recipe you will need extra-large jumbo shrimp, which are a lot easier to stuff than small shrimp.

---

1 cup fresh crabmeat, drained
⅓ cup firm ricotta cheese
2 TB. lemon juice
1 TB. chopped fresh cilantro
2 tsp. Bay Seasoning (page 205)
1 egg, lightly beaten
3 shallots, finely diced

2 green onions, finely chopped
2 cloves garlic, chopped
Salt and pepper to taste
8 extra-large jumbo shrimp (3 to 5 per lb.), tail on, peeled and deveined
1½ cups cornflake crumbs

In a large bowl, mix together thoroughly crabmeat, ricotta cheese, lemon juice, cilantro, Bay Seasoning, egg, shallots, green onions, garlic, salt, and pepper. Cover and refrigerate.

Preheat grill to high.

Using a sharp knife, cut along the back of each shrimp almost all the way through to butterfly the shrimp. Gently spread the meat apart to make a cavity. Season shrimp with salt and pepper.

Fill each shrimp with 2 to 3 tablespoons crab stuffing, pressing firmly. Sprinkle stuffed shrimp with cornflake crumbs and press gently so they adhere.

Grill shrimp for 3 to 5 minutes. Carefully move shrimp to the cool side of the grill for indirect cooking and cook shrimp for 4 to 5 more minutes or until they are firm but not tough and stuffing is hot.

Serve with Papaya Sauce (recipe follows).

SERVES 4

Papaya Sauce

1 ripe papaya, peeled and seeded	1 TB. sugar
1 large orange, juiced	1 tsp. hot sauce (optional)
½ cup grapeseed oil	Salt and pepper to taste

In a food processor or blender, purée papaya and orange juice until very smooth.

While still puréeing, slowly add oil until fully incorporated.

Add sugar, hot sauce, salt, and pepper. Pulse to blend.

Transfer to a bowl, cover, and refrigerate until needed.

MAKES ABOUT 2 CUPS

Hot and Spicy Grilled Shrimp

The shrimp-loving heat-seekers among you will go for this recipe big time! To increase the heat even more, add a finely chopped jalapeño or Scotch bonnet pepper.

2 lbs. jumbo shrimp (12 to 15 per lb.), peeled
   and deveined
2 TB. Bay Seasoning (page 205)
1 cup ketchup
2 TB. brown sugar
2 TB. chopped fresh cilantro
2 TB. hot sauce

2 TB. Worcestershire Sauce
4 green onions, finely chopped
4 cloves garlic, finely chopped
1 lemon, juiced
Salt and pepper to taste
Lime wedges, for garnish

Soak six (8- to 10-inch) bamboo skewers in warm water for 1 hour. (Or use metal skewers.)

In a large bowl, toss shrimp with Bay Seasoning, making sure to coat all shrimp.

Thread five or six shrimp onto each skewer and place in a glass dish large enough to hold the skewers in one layer.

In a bowl, stir together ketchup, brown sugar, cilantro, hot sauce, Worcestershire sauce, green onions, garlic, lemon juice, salt, and pepper. Pour half of this mixture over shrimp and marinate for at least 15 minutes. Reserve remaining sauce for basting.

Preheat grill to medium-high.

On a well-seasoned grill, grill shrimp for 2 to 3 minutes per side or until opaque and just cooked through, basting with reserved marinade.

Serve immediately with lime wedges.

SERVES 6

Grilled Oysters with Mango BBQ Sauce

I prepared this recipe for the Taste of CART Chef Competition at the Mid Ohio Race in August 2000. This was one of the recipes that helped me win the competition.

18 fresh oysters	1 TB. chopped fresh ginger
1 mango, peeled, seeded, and diced	1 TB. lime juice
3 cloves garlic, minced	Dash hot sauce
1 cup gourmet BBQ sauce	Salt and pepper
2 TB. chopped fresh cilantro	9 slices bacon
2 TB. vegetable oil	2 cups shredded Monterey Jack cheese

To shuck the oysters, grip each oyster flat side up in a folded kitchen towel. Find a small opening between the shells near the hinge and pry open with an oyster knife. Carefully remove top shell and discard or use for decoration. Holding oyster over a bowl to catch the liquor, loosen oyster from the shell by running the oyster knife underneath the body. Carefully remove oyster from the shell and drain on paper towels. Set aside shell bottoms.

In a medium saucepan, combine oyster liquor, mango, garlic, BBQ sauce, cilantro, oil, ginger, lime juice, and hot sauce. Bring to a boil, reduce heat, and simmer, stirring occasionally, for 10 minutes. In a blender or food processor, purée until smooth. Season to taste with salt and pepper. Set sauce aside.

Preheat grill to medium-high.

Fry bacon until it is just cooked but not crisp. Drain on paper towels and cut each slice in half.

Wrap each oyster with one half-slice bacon and place in a reserved oyster shell. Top each oyster with 1 tablespoon mango BBQ sauce and sprinkle each with Monterey Jack cheese.

Place the oyster shells on the grill and close the lid. Grill for 10 minutes.

SERVES 6

Grilled Garlic Beer Butter Lobster Tails

For this recipe, I like to use big, meaty Caribbean lobster tails. On a recent trip to Antigua, I prepared this recipe on the beach one evening for my love, Pamela, and me. Succulent lobster tails basted with garlic butter and beer … couldn't ask for much more.

4 (8 oz.) frozen Caribbean lobster tails	2 TB. lemon juice
4 tsp. Bay Seasoning (page 205)	1 TB. chopped fresh dill
1 cup beer	8 cloves garlic, minced
½ cup butter	Salt and pepper to taste

Partially thaw lobster tails. Using a sharp knife, cut down the center of each tail—into the meat but not all the way through. Spread tail open to butterfly it. Season each tail with Bay Seasoning.

Place a sheet of foil on the grill and heat to medium-high.

In a small saucepan, combine beer, butter, lemon juice, dill, garlic, and salt and pepper to taste. Slowly heat, stirring, until butter is melted and sauce is hot.

Brush lobster tails with garlic beer butter sauce and place meat side down on the foil. Grill for 6 to 7 minutes, basting with sauce, until meat is opaque and just cooked. Do not overcook tails, or they will be tough.

Serve lobster with remaining sauce for dipping.

SERVES 2 TO 4 WITH LOTS OF CHAMPAGNEA

Spicy Grilled Shrimp Tostada Napoleons with Avocado Tomatillo Salsa

A tostada is a fried tortilla, available in specialty or South American grocery stores. It is often topped with refried beans and shredded beef, chicken, or pork. I made this dish one Saturday afternoon for my friend Melanie. We used habanero and green peppers from her garden and tomatillos and green onions from mine. For an added bonus in this recipe, add some fresh lump crabmeat to each layer.

2 lbs. jumbo shrimp, peeled and deveined
2 TB. Bay Seasoning (page 205)
9 (6 inch) corn tostadas
2 cups shredded Monterey Jack cheese
Lime wedges and cilantro leaves, for garnish

LIME GLAZE
6 cloves garlic, minced
2 limes, juiced
½ cup light corn syrup
¼ cup olive oil
1 TB. chopped fresh cilantro
1 TB. chopped fresh parsley
Salt and pepper

AVOCADO TOMATILLO SAUCE
1 ear corn
1 small red onion, halved lengthwise
3 green onions, finely chopped
6 tomatillos, chopped
2 ripe avocados, chopped
1 ripe mango, peeled and diced
1 small habanero pepper, seeded and finely chopped
1 green bell pepper, diced
1 lime, juiced
2 TB. olive oil
2 TB. apple cider vinegar
1 TB. chopped fresh cilantro

Soak four (8- to 10-inch) wooden skewers in warm water for one hour. (Or use metal skewers.)

In a large bowl, toss shrimp with Bay Seasoning, making sure to coat shrimp well. Thread shrimp equally onto each skewer. Set aside.

Continued...

To prepare glaze, in a bowl, whisk together garlic, lime juice, corn syrup, oil, cilantro, and parsley. Season to taste with salt and pepper. Set aside.

To prepare salsa, preheat grill to medium-high. Grill corn and red onion until lightly charred and tender, 8 to 10 minutes. Let cool. Cut kernels of corn from the cob. Dice onion.

In a bowl, combine corn, red onion, green onion, tomatillo, avocado, mango, habanero pepper, green pepper, lime juice, oil, vinegar, and cilantro. Mix thoroughly. Salsa should be like a chunky paste. Season to taste with salt and pepper. Set aside.

Preheat grill to medium-high. On a well-seasoned rack, grill shrimp, basting with lime glaze, until opaque and just cooked, 2 to 3 minutes per side.

Remove shrimp from skewers and cut each shrimp in half lengthwise. Toss shrimp with a little lime glaze and season with salt and pepper.

Spread 2 tablespoons salsa evenly over a tostada. Top with 8 to 10 shrimp halves; sprinkle with ⅓ cup cheese. Place another tostada on top of cheese and repeat avocado, shrimp, and cheese layers. Top with a final tostada. Repeat with remaining tostadas to make two more napoleans.

Cut each napolean in half and serve immediately garnished with lime wedges and cilantro leaves.

SERVES 6

Butterflied Shrimp Four Ways

Here are four easy bastes for grilled butterflied shrimp. They're also great with salmon, scallops, and any other of your favorite grilled dishes.

---

12 colossal shrimp (8 to 9 per lb.)	**Salt and pepper**

Peel shrimp, leaving the tails intact.

Using a sharp knife, cut lengthwise down the back of the shrimp about three-quarters the way through. Rinse under cold water to remove the vein. Pat dry with paper towels. Run your fingers along the cut, pressing firmly to slightly flatten and butterfly shrimp. Season to taste with salt and pepper.

Preheat grill to high.

Grill shrimp, basting with one of the four following basting sauces, until opaque and just cooked through, 3 to 4 minutes per side.

SERVES 4

Super Garlic Butter Baste

½ lb. butter	1 TB. Bone Dust BBQ Spice (page 203)
12 cloves garlic, minced	1 TB. sugar
2 lemons, zested and juiced	1 TB. cracked black pepper
¼ cup chopped fresh chives	Salt to taste
¼ cup white wine	

In a small saucepan, melt butter over medium heat. Stir in garlic, lemon juice and zest, chives, wine, Bone Dust BBQ Spice, sugar, pepper, and salt. Slowly heat, stirring occasionally, for 5 to 10 minutes. Remove from heat and keep warm.

MAKES ABOUT 2 CUPS

Continued ...

Tandoori Baste

Look for tandoori paste in specialty food stores and East Indian markets.

¼ lb. butter
6 cloves garlic, minced
¼ cup tandoori paste
¼ cup lime juice

¼ cup honey
1 TB. minced fresh ginger
½ cup yogurt

In a small saucepan, melt butter over medium heat. Whisk in garlic, tandoori paste, lime juice, honey, and ginger. Slowly heat, whisking occasionally, for 5 to 10 minutes. Remove from heat and whisk in the yogurt. Let cool.

MAKES ABOUT 2 CUPS

Smoky BBQ Baste

---

2 cloves garlic, minced
3 small shallots, diced
1½ cups gourmet BBQ sauce
¼ cup steak sauce
2 TB. Bone Dust BBQ Spice (page 203)
2 TB. brown sugar

2 TB. Jack Daniel's Sour Mash Whiskey
2 TB. malt vinegar
1 TB. chopped fresh sage
Dash liquid smoke seasoning
Salt and pepper

In a small saucepan over medium heat, whisk together garlic, shallots, BBQ sauce, steak sauce, Bone Dust BBQ Spice, sugar, whiskey, vinegar, sage, and liquid smoke. Season to taste with salt and pepper. Bring to a low boil, stirring occasionally. Remove from heat and keep warm.

MAKES ABOUT 2 CUPS

Orange Jalapeño Baste

½ lb. butter

3 jalapeño peppers, seeded and finely diced

½ cup orange juice

½ cup honey

1 TB. finely chopped fresh ginger

1 TB. cracked black pepper

1 TB. chopped fresh cilantro

Salt to taste

In a small saucepan, melt butter over medium heat. Whisk in jalapeños, orange juice, honey, ginger, black pepper, and cilantro. Heat, whisking occasionally, for 10 minutes. Season with salt to taste. Remove from heat and keep warm.

MAKES ABOUT 2 CUPS

Sugarcane-Skewered Appleton Rum Jumbo Shrimp

After a day of filming in southern Jamaica, the crew and I stopped off at the Appleton Distillery, where we found rows of sugarcane along with casks of rum. This recipe is inspired by that day.

2 (12-inch-long) pieces fresh sugarcane

12 super-jumbo shrimp (5 to 10 per lb.), peeled and deveined

3 TB. Bone Dust BBQ Spice (page 203)

4 green onions, chopped

1 cup Appleton rum

¼ cup olive oil

¼ cup orange juice

1 TB. chopped fresh cilantro

Salt and pepper to taste

RUM GLAZE

½ cup brown sugar

½ cup Appleton rum

¼ cup orange juice

2 tsp. cornstarch, dissolved in 1 TB. water

2 TB. cold butter

Peel sugarcane and cut each piece lengthwise into six skewers. With a sharp knife, cut a point on one end of each skewer.

Thread one shrimp onto each skewer. Season shrimp with Bone Dust BBQ Spice.

In a glass dish large enough to hold the 12 skewers, whisk together green onions, rum, oil, orange juice, cilantro, salt, and pepper. Add skewers, turning to coat shrimp. Cover and marinate for 20 to 30 minutes.

Prepare glaze by heating the sugar, rum, and orange juice in a small saucepan over medium heat. Stir in cornstarch mixture. Bring to a low boil, stirring, and remove from heat. Whisk in cold butter until fully incorporated. Season to taste with salt and pepper.

Preheat grill to medium-high.

Grill shrimp, basting liberally with the glaze, until just cooked through, opaque, and firm to the touch, 3 to 4 minutes per side.

SERVES 4 TO 6

Grilled Oysters Rockefeller

One of my chefs on the set of *King of the Q,* Mike McColl, worked for a while at Rodney's Oyster House in Toronto. One day Mike prepared these tasty treats for me.

1 lb. fresh spinach	Dash hot sauce
2 TB. butter	Pinch nutmeg
4 cloves garlic, minced	Salt and pepper
3 small shallots, diced	1½ cups fresh lump crabmeat
1 cup heavy cream	18 oysters
¼ cup grated Parmesan cheese	2 cups shredded Swiss cheese
1 TB. chopped fresh tarragon	Lemon juice, for drizzling

Blanch spinach briefly in a pot of boiling water. Refresh under cold running water. Drain well and cool. With your hands, squeeze out moisture. Chop spinach.

Melt butter in a medium frying pan over medium-high heat. Sauté garlic and shallots until tender, 2 to 3 minutes. Stir in cream. Bring to a boil and reduce cream by half. Whisk in Parmesan cheese, tarragon, hot sauce, nutmeg, salt, and pepper. Remove from heat. Stir in spinach and crabmeat.

To shuck oysters, grip each oyster flat side up in a folded kitchen towel. Working over a bowl to catch liquor, find a small opening between the shells near the hinge and pry open with an oyster knife. Carefully remove the top shell (discard it or use for decoration). Loosen oyster from the shell by running the oyster knife underneath the body. Gently remove oyster from the shell and place it on paper towels to drain. Set aside the bottom shells. Add oyster liquor to spinach sauce.

Place an oyster in each bottom shell. Top each oyster with 1 heaping tablespoon sauce. Sprinkle with Swiss cheese.

Preheat grill to medium-high.

Place oyster shells on a grill topper and place on grill. Close the lid and grill until cheese is melted and bubbling, 10 to 12 minutes.

Transfer oysters to a serving platter, drizzle with a little lemon juice, and serve.

SERVES 6

Grilled Calamari with Balsamic Butter Sauce

Soaking calamari in buttermilk before grilling tenderizes the squid.

---

12 medium fresh or thawed frozen whole
    squid
1 cup buttermilk
2 TB. Malabar Pepper Rub (page 200)
4 cloves garlic, minced
¼ cup olive oil
¼ cup balsamic vinegar
2 TB. chopped fresh basil

BALSAMIC BUTTER SAUCE
5 TB. butter (divided use)
4 cloves garlic, minced
4 shallots, diced
2 TB. capers, drained
½ cup balsamic vinegar
Salt and pepper

Pull the mantle (body) from the tentacles. Remove and discard the hard transparent pen (backbone) and other inner matter from the body of the squid. Rinse under cold water and peel off the outer membrane.

Cut the eye section away from the tentacles and remove the hard bone (beak) from the center of the tentacles. Rinse under cold water and pat dry.

Using a sharp knife, score the body of the squid every ½ inch, cutting about two-thirds the way into the flesh. Place body and tentacles in a glass dish and cover with buttermilk, turning to coat. Marinate, covered and refrigerated, for 4 hours.

Discard buttermilk and pat dry with paper towels. Season squid inside and out with Malabar Pepper Rub. In the glass dish, whisk together garlic, oil, vinegar, and basil. Add squid, turning to coat. Marinate for 20 minutes.

Meanwhile, prepare sauce. Melt 2 tablespoons butter in a small saucepan over medium-high heat. Sauté garlic, shallots, and capers until tender, 2 to 3 minutes. Stir in vinegar. Bring to a boil and reduce vinegar by half. Remove from heat and whisk in remaining 3 tablespoons butter, 1 tablespoon at a time, whisking until incorporated. Season to taste with salt and pepper. Set aside and keep warm.

Preheat grill to medium-high.

Drain squid well. Grill squid until just cooked through, 3 to 4 minutes per side.

Transfer calamari to a platter and pour over balsamic butter sauce.

SERVES 6

Grilled Jumbo Frogs' Legs

While vacationing on Marco Island in Florida, I grilled up some tender tootsies of jumbo Florida frogs' legs. That was the first time I'd ever grilled frogs' legs. It was a fun experience, and hey, they do taste like chicken!

---

12 pairs fresh or thawed frozen frogs' legs
¼ cup Bay Seasoning (page 205)
¼ cup + 2 TB. chili-flavored soy sauce
¼ cup vegetable oil
2 green onions, minced
4 cloves garlic, minced

¾ cup oyster sauce
¼ cup rice vinegar
2 TB. sake or rice wine
1 TB. sesame seeds
2 tsp. cracked black peppercorns
2 tsp. sesame oil

Rub frogs' legs with Bay Seasoning, pressing seasoning into meat. Place legs in a glass dish. Whisk together ¼ cup chili-flavored soy sauce and oil. Pour over legs. Cover and marinate for 30 to 45 minutes.

Meanwhile, prepare sauce. In a bowl, whisk together remaining 2 tablespoons chili-flavored soy sauce, green onions, garlic, oyster sauce, vinegar, sake, sesame seeds, pepper, and sesame oil.

Preheat grill to medium-high.

Grill frogs' legs, basting with sauce, until meat is firm and opaque, 3 to 5 minutes per side.

Serve immediately.

SERVES 4

Lovely Libations and Delicious Desserts

Island Pink Lemonade Rum Punch

While in Jamaica, I had this refreshing rum punch at a beach bar. It's a great way to wash down some spicy jerk pork.

---

1 (12 oz.) can frozen concentrated pink
    lemonade
24 oz. water
1 can ginger ale

1 cup dark rum
8 sprigs mint
2 lemons, thinly sliced
1 pint raspberries

Place the concentrated pink lemonade in a large pitcher. Add 2 lemonade cans of water, ginger ale, rum, mint, and lemon slices. Stir to blend.

Add the raspberries and fill with ice.

Serve immediately.

SERVES 8

Tequila Honey Orange Cooler

I first made this delicious drink with a wonderful product called Honeydew, a frozen concentrated orange drink with honey. It's a real summertime treat. If you can find Honeydew, use it in place of the orange juice. Don't leave out the honey, though. This drink still needs it.

1 cup crushed ice	2 maraschino cherries
1 cup orange juice	1 tsp. cherry syrup
¼ cup gold tequila	2 sprigs mint
2 TB. honey	2 TB. Grand Marnier

Place the crushed ice in a cocktail shaker. Add the orange juice, tequila, and honey. Shake it up big time, baby.

Place 1 cherry, ½ tsp. of cherry syrup, and 1 sprig of mint in each of 2 martini glasses.

Strain tequila mix into glasses. Top each with 1 TB. of Grand Marnier and serve.

SERVES 2

Sour Cherry Bourbon Coolers

When fresh sour cherries are in season, make this cooler. It is best if you let the cherries soak in the bourbon for two or three days to allow for the fullest flavor.

---

24 pitted sour cherries
1½ cups bourbon
2 cups black cherry juice

2 cans cola
8 sprigs fresh mint

Place the sour cherries in a large jar. Pour the bourbon over the cherries. Seal the jar and refrigerate for 2 or 3 days. Fill 8 large glasses with ice. Place 3 soaked cherries in each glass. Equally divide the bourbon among the glasses. Pour ¼ cup black cherry juice into each glass.

Top with cola and garnish with fresh mint.

SERVES 8

Maple Carrot Iced Tea

Carrots have a natural sweetness that is ideal for this summertime drink. You can also replace the carrots with fresh peeled beets. The results are delicious—and the color is outstanding.

4 cups water	2 oranges, juiced
½ cup maple syrup	1 lemon, juiced
6 large carrots, peeled and shredded	6 black peppercorns
1 green apple, peeled and sliced	4 sprigs thyme

In a large saucepan bring the water and maple syrup to a boil. Add the carrots, apple, orange juice, lemon juice and peppercorns. Return to a boil. Remove from the heat and let steep for 30 minutes.

Strain, discarding the solids, and chill.

Serve over ice with a sprig of fresh thyme.

SERVES 4

Aloha Frozen Pineapple Margarita

Try this twist on the old lime favorite. Use a good tequila; I like golden tequila. By the way, it takes a lot of muscle to squeeze a pineapple. I recommend a juicer.

---

16 ice cubes

1 cup pineapple juice

4 oz. tequila

2 oz. peach schnapps

1 oz. coconut-flavored rum

Fresh pineapple wedges, for garnish

Coat the rims of two cocktail glasses with sugar and chill them.

In a blender, combine the ice, pineapple juice, tequila, schnapps, and rum. Blend until the ice is crushed.

Pour into the glasses and garnish with a wedge of pineapple.

SERVES 2

Amanoka Rum Punch

For the juice blend, use your choice of orange, guava, mango, passion fruit, and pineapple.

---

1 cup sugar

2 cups water

4 cups fruit juice blend

3 cups dark rum

1 cup fresh lime juice

Plenty of ice

Pineapple wedges and orange slices, for garnish

In a medium saucepan, heat the sugar and water, stirring, until the sugar dissolves and the mixture is clear. Bring to a boil and remove from heat. Let cool completely.

In a pitcher, combine the sugar syrup, fruit juices, rum, and lime juice. Stir well.

Fill 4 highball glasses with ice cubes. Pour in the punch. Garnish with pineapple wedges and orange slices.

SERVES 4

Almond Tequila Sunrise

The more tequila, the better. Tequila is a good thing!

8 ice cubes

4 oz. orange juice

4 oz. tequila

2 oz. amaretto

Drizzle grenadine

6 fresh raspberries

Place four ice cubes in each of two old-fashioned glasses.

In a cocktail shaker, combine orange juice, tequila, and amaretto. Shake well.

Pour over ice. Drizzle a little grenadine into the drinks and garnish with raspberries.

SERVES 2

Calico Float

The Calico Kitchen was a hamburger joint on the outskirts of my hometown, Paris, Ontario. I remember they had a pretty tasty burger. But what I remember most was cherry Coke floats that we would add a little cherry whisky to.

2 large scoops good vanilla ice cream
4 oz. cherry whisky
2 cans Cherry Coke

1 cup heavy cream
2 maraschino cherries, for garnish

Put 1 scoop ice cream in each of two milkshake glasses. Pour 2 ounces cherry whisky into each glass and top with cherry Coke. Top each with a ½ cup cream and garnish with cherries.

Serve with parfait spoons and straws.

SERVES 2

Chocolate Banana Rum Milkshakes (a.k.a. Dirty Banana)

Milkshakes are a fantastic drink, rich, thick, and icy cold. A really good milkshake should be made with the richest ice cream. A really good milkshake should be so thick that it makes your eyes bulge. And a really good milkshake should be so cold that your brain freezes.

My favorite drink in Jamaica was the Dirty Banana. Some people make this with ice, but I much prefer it made with chocolate ice cream.

1 ripe banana	1 to 2 cups milk
4 scoops chocolate ice cream	Chocolate syrup, for drizzling
4 oz. rum	1 cup whipped cream
2 oz. rum cream liqueur or Irish cream liqueur	2 maraschino cherries, for garnish

Put banana, ice cream, rum, and rum cream liqueur in a blender. Blend briefly. Pour in milk a little at a time, pulsing until smooth and desired consistency.

Pour into 2 milkshake glasses. Drizzle with a little chocolate syrup. Top each with ½ cup whipped cream and a maraschino cherry.

Serve with straws.

SERVES 2

Iced Coffee Frappé

It seems that every day there is a new coffeehouse opening up someplace on some corner in some town, and they all seem to serve the same stuff. Café au lait, cappuccino, latte, espresso, half decaf, unsweetened, short, tall, grande, venti, blah, blah, blah. It is all so boring. So liven up your morning cup of joe with this decadent and loaded frappé. And if it's still not good enough for you, replace the ice with ice cream.

12 to 16 ice cubes	3 oz. coffee liqueur
½ cup heavy cream	1 oz. amaretto
¼ cup condensed milk	1 cup cold coffee
4 oz. vodka	¼ cup chocolate shavings, for garnish

In a blender, combine the ice, cream, condensed milk, vodka, coffee liqueur, and amaretto. Blend until smooth. Divide the coffee among 4 milkshake glasses. Pour in equal amounts frappé. Garnish with chocolate shavings and serve with straws.

SERVES 4

Grilled Bacon-Wrapped Bananas with Bourbon Honey Sauce

I know it sounds weird, but try it. The sweet and salt combination really works.

Try these with baby bananas wrapped in half a slice of bacon. Serve with smoked chocolate ice cream (page 434). It may seem a little nutty, but it really works, baby.

4 to 8 slices bacon	**Pepper**
4 ripe but firm bananas	

Partially cook the bacon until most of the fat has been rendered but bacon is still flexible. Drain on paper towels and let cool.

Peel the bananas. Wrap each banana with 1 or 2 slices bacon, starting at one end and coiling around the banana. Secure with toothpicks. Season with pepper.

Prepare Bourbon Honey Sauce (recipe follows).

Preheat grill to medium.

Grill bananas, turning occasionally, until the bacon is crisp and the bananas are lightly charred and heated through, 5 to 8 minutes. During the last few minutes, baste with Bourbon Honey Sauce.

Serve with ice cream and drizzled with sauce.

SERVES 4

Bourbon Honey Sauce

½ cup honey	2 TB. water
½ cup light corn syrup	1 sprig fresh thyme
2 oz. bourbon	Pinch cracked black pepper

In a small saucepan, combine the honey, corn syrup, bourbon, water, thyme, and pepper. Bring to a boil, stirring occasionally. Reduce heat to low and simmer for 5 minutes. Remove from heat and let cool slightly.

MAKES ABOUT 1 ¼ CUPS

Grilled Fruit Kebabs with Butter Rum Sauce

Use firm-fleshed fruit for grilling. I tend to stay away from berries on the grill, although jumbo strawberries can be grilled without too much difficulty. Fruit does not take a long time on the grill; you really just need to warm the fruit, which brings out more of its natural sweetness.

½ **pineapple**
1 small cantaloupe, peeled and seeded
4 ripe but firm kiwifruit, peeled
2 peaches

½ **cup Grand Marnier**
Cracked black pepper to taste
1 pint fresh raspberries
Vanilla ice cream

Soak eight (10-inch) bamboo skewers in warm water for 15 minutes. (Or use metal skewers.)

Cut pineapple and cantaloupe into 1- to 2-inch chunks (at least 16 pieces from each). Put in a large bowl. Cut each kiwifruit into 4 wedges; add to bowl. Cut each peach into 8 wedges; add to bowl.

Pour Grand Marnier over and season with pepper. Gently toss. Marinate for 20 minutes.

Thread equal amounts of fruit onto skewers.

Prepare Butter Rum Sauce (recipe follows).

Preheat grill to medium-high.

Grill kebabs, turning carefully, until lightly charred and heated through, 2 to 3 minutes per side. Brush each kebab with Butter Rum Sauce during the last minute of cooking.

Serve with ice cream and extra sauce.

SERVES 4 TO 8

Butter Rum Sauce

¾ cup brown sugar	2 oz. spiced rum
¾ cup heavy cream	Pinch nutmeg
¼ lb. butter	½ cup golden raisins

In a medium saucepan over medium heat, bring brown sugar, cream, butter, rum, and nutmeg to a boil, stirring constantly. Reduce heat to low, stir in raisins and simmer for 5 minutes.

Remove from heat and let cool for 5 minutes before using.

MAKES ABOUT 2 CUPS

Coconut Fruit Salad

It is truly satisfying to be able to extract the meat from a fresh coconut. I learned a few new tricks on how to open coconuts from my friends in Jamaica. But to learn these tricks, you will have to watch my show *King of the Q.*

For a stunning presentation, cut dried coconuts in half and remove the meat, using the shell as your bowl.

---

2 ripe coconuts

1 ripe mango, peeled and cut into 1-inch chunks

1 ripe papaya, peeled, seeded and cut into 1-inch chunks

1 cup sliced strawberries

¼ cup honey

¼ cup orange juice

2 oz. coconut rum

1 oz. amaretto

1 cup raspberries

1 cup blueberries

1 star fruit, cut crosswise into 8 slices

Fresh mint sprigs, for garnish

Crack the coconut shell by hitting it firmly with a hammer. It may take a few whacks but the shell should eventually crack. Break open shell and drain off any coconut water, saving it for salad. Carefully remove meat from shell and cut meat into small pieces. You will need about 2 cups coconut chunks.

In a bowl, combine coconut chunks, reserved coconut water, mango, papaya, strawberries, honey, orange juice, coconut rum, and amaretto; gently mix. Fold in raspberries and blueberries.

Spoon salad into bowls or coconut shells. Garnish with slices of star fruit and sprigs of fresh mint. Serve immediately.

SERVES 4 TO 6

Smoked Chocolate

Smoking chocolate is not a normal everyday-cooking thing to do. You need a lot of patience and a little bit of luck (you don't want the chocolate to melt). You will be cold-smoking the chocolate; it is necessary to maintain a low temperature, no higher than 135°F. You can use many types of smoking chips to add flavor to your chocolate; I like to use cracked whole pecans in the shell for a distinctive sweet, nutty flavor.

---

2 lbs. milk, dark, or white chocolate bars (at least 1 inch thick)

24 pecans in the shell, cracked lightly and soaked in water for 30 minutes

---

Remove the top rack of your smoker and wrap it in foil. Place chocolate on the wrapped rack.

Prepare your smoker according to manufacturer's instructions to a temperature of 135°F, using 12 to 15 charcoal briquettes. Fill the water tray with ice and a few cups cold water. (This will help keep the temperature low and the smoke cool.) Note that when you initially place the hot coals in the smoker the temperature may go over 400 degrees. If this happens, remove lid and allow the charcoal to cool.

Place the rack with chocolate in the highest position of the smoker and as far away from the heat source as possible. Close the lid. Add 4 or 5 pecans to the hot coals.

Smoke chocolate until it is soft but not starting to melt, 35 to 45 minutes. Watch it carefully. Add more pecans and water periodically, being careful to maintain the temperature. If it gets too hot, remove the cover to allow the heat to escape. Do not worry about losing the smoke, because it does not take much smoke to add flavor to chocolate.

Remove chocolate from grill and let cool completely. Store in plastic bags.

Peanut Butter Cupcakes with Smoked Chocolate Butter Frosting

Serve these babies with a scoop of ice cream or a cold glass of milk (or beer).

---

2 cups all-purpose flour
3 tsp. baking powder
½ tsp. salt
¾ cup heavy cream
1 tsp. vanilla
1½ cups brown sugar

½ cup crunchy peanut butter
⅓ cup butter
2 large eggs, beaten
½ cup raspberry jam
Smoked Chocolate Butter Frosting (recipe follows)

Preheat oven to 350°F. Line 2 muffin tins with paper liners.

Sift together flour, baking powder, and salt; set aside. Combine cream and vanilla; set aside.

In a large bowl, cream sugar, peanut butter, and butter until light and fluffy. Beat in eggs. Alternately beat in flour mixture and cream mixture.

Spoon batter into muffin tins. Swirl 1 teaspoon raspberry jam into each cupcake.

Bake both tins on the middle rack of the oven until a toothpick inserted in the center comes out clean, 20 to 25 minutes. Transfer cupcakes to a cooling rack and let cool completely.

Spread frosting evenly and thickly over cupcakes.

MAKES ABOUT 24 CUPCAKES

Smoked Chocolate Butter Frosting

4 TB. butter, at room temperature	3 oz. smoked chocolate (page 431)
2 cups icing sugar (divided use)	6 TB. heavy cream
⅛ tsp. salt	1 tsp. vanilla

In a medium bowl, cream butter until soft. Stir in 1½ cups icing sugar and salt.

Melt chocolate in a double boiler set over barely simmering water. Add cream and stir until well blended.

Alternately stir chocolate and remaining icing sugar into frosting. Stir in vanilla. If batter is too thick, stir in a little heavy cream.

MAKES ENOUGH FROSTING FOR 2 DOZEN CUPCAKES

Smoked Chocolate Crème Fraîche Ice Cream

In all my years as a chef and all my years of eating tubs of ice cream I have never come across Smoked Chocolate Ice Cream. This is a fun recipe and delicious, too. Carefully smoke your chocolate and then prepare this decadent ice cream recipe.

3 cups heavy cream	12 large egg yolks
2 cups half-and-half cream	1 cup crème fraîche or sour cream
2 vanilla beans, split lengthwise	¼ cup lemon juice
1½ cups sugar	12 oz. smoked chocolate pieces (page 431)

In a heavy saucepan, combine heavy cream and half-and-half. Scrape out vanilla bean seeds and add these, and bean, to the pot. Slowly bring mixture to a boil. Remove from heat and let cool slightly.

In a large bowl, whisk together sugar and egg yolks until thick and smooth. Whisking constantly, slowly pour heated cream into egg mixture.

Return custard to saucepan and cook over medium heat, stirring constantly with a wooden spoon, until custard thickens and leaves a trail when a finger is drawn across the spoon, 8 to 10 minutes. Be careful not to boil custard. Strain through a fine mesh strainer and keep warm.

Whisk crème fraîche and lemon juice into warm custard until smooth.

Melt chocolate in the top of a double boiler set over barely simmering water. Whisk warm chocolate into warm custard until fully incorporated. Let cool, then chill.

Prepare ice cream in an ice cream machine according to manufacturer's instructions. Transfer to a plastic container and freeze until needed.

MAKES ABOUT 2 QUARTS

Grilled Pineapple with Molasses Rum Glaze

Grilling pineapple brings out its natural sugars. Grilled pineapple makes a great dessert but it's also wonderful when used in BBQ sauces and salsas.

---

1 ripe pineapple	1 tsp. cracked black pepper
½ cup molasses	½ tsp. ground mace
¼ cup dark rum	Coconut ice cream
¼ cup orange juice	

Using a sharp knife, cut top and bottom off pineapple. Stand pineapple upright and, slicing from top to bottom, remove skin. Cut out any sharp "eyes." Cut pineapple in half lengthwise. Set aside.

Preheat grill to medium-high.

In a small saucepan bring molasses, rum, orange juice, pepper, and mace to a boil. Reduce heat and simmer, stirring, for 5 minutes.

Grill pineapple cut side down for 10 minutes, basting with molasses mixture. Reduce heat to medium-low, close the lid and grill for another 10 to 15 minutes or until golden brown, hot and tender.

Use tongs and a spatula to carefully transfer pineapple to a cutting board. Slice each half crosswise into 12 slices. Serve 3 or 4 slices pineapple with coconut ice cream.

SERVES 8

Lydia's BBQ Baked Banana Boats

My friend Lydia made this ooey gooey delight for me at the cottage one summer. This is her favorite summertime recipe. Thanks, Lydia, for all the summer days at Wasaga Beach.

---

4 bananas, unpeeled
¼ cup semisweet chocolate chips
¼ cup butterscotch chips

¼ cup chopped pecans
1 cup mini marshmallows
Vanilla ice cream

Preheat grill to high.

Using a sharp knife, make 2 incisions about 1 inch apart along the inside curve of the banana and remove and discard the strip of peel. Gently pull open the remaining peel but do not remove it.

Cut banana (not the peel) into 1-inch-thick rounds, leaving fruit in the peel.

Mix together chocolate chips, butterscotch chips, and pecans. Push mixture between banana slices. Top with mini marshmallows. Wrap each stuffed banana in heavy-duty foil.

Place banana boats on the grill and close the lid. Bake for 8 minutes or until bananas are tender and chocolate and butterscotch chips and marshmallows have melted.

Carefully open the foil. Serve with vanilla ice cream.

SERVES 4

Grilled Lemon Pound Cake with Stewed Summer Berry Pot

Create some great grilled flavors with this lemony pound cake. Lightly grilled pound cake is the perfect match for stewed summer berries.

3 cups all-purpose flour	6 medium eggs
½ tsp. baking powder	1 cup milk
1 cup + 3 TB. butter, softened	1½ tsp. vanilla
½ cup shortening	1 tsp. lemon zest
3 cups sugar	2 TB. lemon juice

Preheat oven to 325°F. Grease and flour an 8- or 10-inch tube pan.

Sift together flour and baking powder.

In a mixing bowl, cream butter, shortening, and sugar until smooth. Add eggs and beat well.

Add flour, alternating with milk. Stir in vanilla, lemon zest, and lemon juice.

Turn batter into tube pan. Bake for 1½ hours or until a tester comes out clean. Let cool on a rack.

Preheat grill to medium.

Run a knife around the edge of the pan, invert and remove pound cake. Slice cake into 1- to 2-inch-thick slices. Lightly butter both sides.

Grill for 1 to 2 minutes per side or until lightly golden and toasted.

Serve with Stewed Summer Berry Pot (recipe follows) and 1 spoonful vanilla or coconut ice cream.

SERVES 8

Continued ...

Stewed Summer Berry Pot

My friend Olaf finds that this is a great way to use up leftover summer berries. Waste not, want not! This is also terrific on ice cream.

1 pint raspberries	2 cups cranberry juice
½ pint red currants	½ cup sugar
½ pint blueberries	1 cinnamon stick
1½ cups pitted sour cherries	1 orange, juice and zest
1½ cups sliced strawberries	1½ TB. quick-cooking tapioca
2 cups dry red wine	

In a mixing bowl, gently toss together raspberries, red currants, blueberries, sour cherries, and strawberries. Transfer 2 cups berries to a food processor and purée.

In a large saucepan mix berry purée with red wine, cranberry juice, sugar, cinnamon stick, orange juice, and orange zest. Bring to a boil, stirring. Reduce heat and simmer, stirring occasionally, for 15 minutes. Stir in tapioca and return to a boil, stirring until thick.

Strain berry mixture through a fine sieve set over a bowl, reserving liquid. Pour hot liquid over fresh berries and gently fold together.

MAKES 8 CUPS

Grilled Peaches with Bourbon Honey

 Fresh sweet peaches are meant for the grill. Lightly warmed and charred, then drizzled with bourbon-infused honey, they're a real summer treat.

6 ripe peaches
2 TB. grapeseed oil
¼ tsp. nutmeg
Cracked black pepper to taste

¼ cup honey
¼ cup bourbon
Vanilla ice cream

Preheat grill to medium-high.

Slice peaches in half and remove pit. Brush peach halves with grapeseed oil. Season with nutmeg and black pepper. Set aside.

In a small saucepan over low heat, warm honey and bourbon, stirring until blended.

Grill peach halves cut side down for 3 to 4 minutes or until lightly charred and warm. Turn, baste with bourbon honey mixture and grill for 5 more minutes or until fully cooked and tender.

Serve peach halves with 1 scoop vanilla ice cream and drizzled with remaining bourbon honey.

SERVES 6

Rhubarb and Bourbon Fool

Be foolish. Make a fool and have a tasty, easy dessert.

---

1 lb. fresh rhubarb, cut in 1-inch pieces

¼ cup water

½ cup (approx.) sugar

¼ cup bourbon

Pinch cinnamon

2 cups whipping cream

½ cup chocolate chips

Cracked black pepper to taste

In a medium saucepan over medium-high heat simmer rhubarb and water, covered and stirring occasionally, for 10 to 15 minutes or until rhubarb is tender.

Stir in sugar to taste. Simmer for 10 more minutes.

Remove from heat and stir in bourbon and cinnamon. Let cool completely, then chill.

When rhubarb is cold, in a large bowl, whip cream to stiff peaks. Gently fold rhubarb and chocolate chips into whipped cream, being careful not to overmix.

Spoon fool into 6 chilled serving glasses and garnish with black pepper.

SERVES 6

Dark Chocolate Orange Bread Pudding with Whisky Orange Compote

I first prepared this dessert for the U.S. ambassador to Canada with then Ambassador Chef Corey Haskins. The richness of buttery croissants and chocolate is truly decadent!

---

16 day-old croissants (or 1 baguette),
   cut into 1-inch pieces
2 cups milk
2 cups orange juice
2 cups granulated sugar
2 TB. vanilla
1 tsp. cinnamon
1 tsp. nutmeg
3 eggs
1½ cups coarsely chopped bitter or
   semisweet chocolate

½ cup coarsely chopped pecans
2 TB. brown sugar

WHISKY ORANGE COMPOTE
3 cups orange juice
½ cup sugar
½ cup Canadian whisky
2 tsp. cornstarch
2 TB. cold water
2 oranges, peeled and segmented

Preheat oven to 350°F. Grease a 13×9×2-inch baking pan.

Place croissant pieces in a large bowl. Pour milk and orange juice over croissants. Let stand 20 minutes or until liquid is absorbed. Spread croissant pieces evenly in baking dish.

In a medium bowl whisk sugar, vanilla, cinnamon, nutmeg, and eggs together until thick. Stir in chocolate and pecans.

Pour over croissant pieces. Sprinkle with brown sugar.

Bake for 50 to 60 minutes or until just set and a knife comes out clean. Let pudding stand for 10 minutes before serving.

While bread pudding is baking, make orange compote. In a medium saucepan over medium-high heat, bring orange juice, sugar, and whisky to a boil, stirring. Reduce heat to medium and simmer for 5 minutes.

Stir cornstarch into 2 tablespoons cold water until smooth. Stir into juice mixture and simmer, stirring, for 5 minutes or until thick. Stir in orange segments; simmer for 5 more minutes.

Serve compote warm with chocolate orange bread pudding.

SERVES 8 TO 10

Cast-Iron-Baked Strawberry Apple Crisp

BEEROMETER 3-4

Using your grill as an oven keeps you from heating up your kitchen on those warm summer days.

4 cups sliced strawberries	½ cup all-purpose flour
3 cups peeled, cored and thinly sliced apples	½ tsp. cinnamon
½ cup sugar	½ tsp. ground mace
¼ cup amaretto	½ cup butter
¾ cup rolled oats	½ cup chopped pecans
¾ cup brown sugar	

Preheat grill to medium. Butter an 8- to 10-inch cast-iron frying pan.

In a large bowl, toss together strawberries, apples, sugar, and amaretto. Pour fruit mixture into the cast-iron pan.

Wipe out the bowl and in it combine oats, brown sugar, flour, cinnamon, and mace. Cut in butter until mixture resembles coarse crumbs. Stir in pecans. Sprinkle topping over fruit.

Place crumble on the grill and close the lid. Bake for 50 to 60 minutes or until fruit is soft and topping is crisp and golden brown. Let stand for 15 minutes.

Serve with ice cream.

SERVES 8

Index